WHO?

THE BONE SHRINE CRIMES, BOOK TWO

SCOTT MACFARLANE

NichéEc
Imprints

THE BONE SHRINE CRIMES
Book Two:
WHO?
Biff McCoy serves as a college intern with the State Patrol in a heart-felt quest to unearth her best friend's killer. Her pesky, expressive personality attracts both peril and insight. An inherited homicide and drug investigation that has been blatantly corrupted is on the verge of becoming shelved and cold. When the prospect of discovering any fresh clues grows dire, Biff doesn't know what to believe, even doubting whether her new and first lover can be trusted to help her with solving this daunting case.

WARNING: The actual Bone Shrine site near Moses Lake, Washington was permanently closed to the public following the first edition publication of *The Bone Shrine* novel.

THE PUBLISHER

NichéEco Imprints
P.O. Box 381
Clear Lake, WA 98235

https://www.nicheeco.com

WHO? The Bone Shrine Crimes, Book Two

First Edition Paperback and eBook, copyright ©2025 by **SCOTT MacFARLANE**

NichéEco Imprints, Publisher

Cover Art & Design, ©2025

BRENDA MATTSON

Editor

CATE PERRY

Library of Congress Control Numbers

(PRINT editions ISBN: 978-1-7368570-4-5)

(for e-BOOK ISBN: 978-1-7368570-3-8)

❀ Created with Vellum

DEDICATION

for BRENDA,

my wonderful wife

EPIGRAPH

"To understand the world, listen to the owl's silent flight."

--unknown

CONTENTS

CHAPTER 1

THE BUST

"Up from the muck," said my boss. I wrote down the date--Friday, the 13th, April 2001. Washington State Patrol Special Operations Captain Duke Condran plopped a dry, corrugated box down next to me on the only open spot at my worktable. Inside, I noticed a smaller wooden box covered with mud and grit. "An old angler dropped this off. Reeled it in this morning," he added.

My stomach sank. The fisherman might as well have exhumed my dead friend's cremation urn, not that any ashes existed. Her killer hadn't been found and her body was still in the morgue as evidence. "Pulled out of the Bone Shrine pond?" I asked in a whisper, but knowing the answer. I held back tears since the Moses Lake field office was full of a dozen state patrol S.W.A.T. members with all eyes on my boss, the box, and me. The team sat scattered around the room waiting for Captain Condran's order to launch the day's planned bust.

At the turn of the year he appropriated the back end of the open field office and set up *Investigation Central* for solving the Bone Shrine murder and the heroin deal gone sideways. The space included a wide, fold-up worktable for me, his desk, a locking file cabinet, and two freestanding bulletin boards to help us solve the case. Condran patted me on the shoulder and asked if I knew who this wooden box belonged to.

Of course, I knew. "It's from Gunnar Larsson's Buddhist shrine," I said. "His mom said we could take it from his doublewide, the place I'm renting. We used it for Mary's memorial, the one we held at the same pond where––" I often talked in spurts, but couldn't finish this sentence. Bit my lower lip instead.

After a deep breath, I tapped the corner of the incense box. "Gunnar left this behind when he bolted for Sweden on the day after the murder."

I didn't get how the captain was connecting Gunnar's box to any Bone Shrine crimes. What did Mary practicing Nichiren Buddhism, the way Gunnar and I did, have anything to do with solving *her* murder?

Condran tapped the worktable, impatiently. "I can't spend time on this today, Biff, not with the bust. However, the incense box might help show us what role Gunnar Larsson actually had in the Bone Shrine crimes."

"How so, Boss?" I asked.

"Check it out," he said, tapping the corner. I knew he was convinced that Mary's murder was far more likely committed by the seller of the heroin that night, not the expected buyer. The disappearance of the China White right before the deal went down gave the sellers motive to kill Mary. She'd been at the Bone Shrine pond, site of the drug deal, and had given birth just before some wicked, deranged, greed-mongering, drug sludger had gotten away with murdering her, my dear friend.

"The buyer's investment would have still been unspent and whole," the captain would say to me. "There was no motive for them to kill anyone."

Seemed logical. They wouldn't have paid for what they never received. When reconstructing the events on the night in question, the boss insisted it would have appeared to the seller that Mary must have known where her boyfriend, Joe Gardner, had hidden a quarter-million dollar stash of the seller's China White heroin before it could be sold. And, today, we wouldn't be planning to bust the local *Tramposo* gang if Captain Condran wasn't convinced that these drug dealers were the actual sellers. I looked hard at the mucky box, still confused at how this item would help us.

Condran tapped again, directing me to look inside a round opening on the front side of the muddy box. A gold medallion left a hole where it had gone missing. Another medallion was still intact and featured a sacred crane on extended wings lifting in flight. Both coins had been inset in the face of the box when we submerged it at the very spot where Mary had gone under. Into the opening behind the missing medallion, at one end of a monofilament leader, a single fishhook curled around a hidden shaft.

"So what if some geriatric fisherman just happened to hook the thing this way?" I whispered to the captain. "What does this have to do with Mary's murder last August? We didn't submerge this incense box until our December memorial for her."

During the December memorial, one hundred days after her drowning, Rochelle and Kuma and me agreed that my friend was stuck in the *in-between* like a hungry ghost. Mary needed to be sure her newborn was safe, as well as her boyfriend.

The only sign I got from this fished-up box was nothing I could explain to law enforcement officers like the captain. My best friend—even with her baby and boyfriend now safe—still hadn't let go. I touched the muck on the edge of the box and shuddered. Mary lingered in the *in between* to help me avenge her death. Shivers coiled down my vertebrae. The captain had been warning me that Mary's murder case was tenuous and on the verge of going cold.

Condran opened the wooden box lid and lifted out the metal tray designed for holding bits of burning incense. He motioned for me to examine the open box to see what the fishhook was attached to. "That angler pointed this out to me."

I leaned forward on my hard office chair and, from the inside, saw what was inset there.

"Is that a skeleton key?" I asked.

"No. It's too flat," Condran insisted.

"A lockbox key?" I asked. "There's a number—'1897'—stamped on one end."

"Exactly. The fisherman said he knew about that girl drowning in the pond last summer. When he found the key, he thought it might be related somehow."

To look more closely, I stood up from the worktable and bent completely over the box. With customary grace, my ample backside bumped into our large bulletin board, the one with criss-crossing yarns of different colors linking persons-of-interest in our case. Reacting to my clumsiness, Condran managed to catch the large board before it crashed down to the linoleum floor.

Applause from the idle S.W.A.T. team filled the open room. "Nice catch, Captain!"

With all eyes on my mishap, I sat down quickly. Condran reached around and patted the cork side of the board. "Until today's bust nets us some real progress," he said, "all we've had so far is a web of double-crossing yarns."

Once in a while, the captain sported an odd sense of humor. As for me, I was still embarrassed by my clumsiness and looked down at my Birkenstocks, nothing to help my embarrassment, just a new pair of hippie sandals Mom bought for me before I started this internship. I envisioned Mary rolling her eyes if she'd ever caught sight of my dated and clunky fashion statement. I'd half-expected her to insist I also wear my hair parted down the middle with extensions to my waist so I could recreate *her* own college look from 1970.

The captain made sure the bulletin board was stable before reaching inside his desk behind the worktable. Two months ago, I started assisting Condran with our case paperwork. We'd both followed through with our informal agreement made on the day Joe's trial ended. I'd enrolled in the local, Big Bend Community College and its criminal justice program rather than going to Lewis & Clark, a much more prestigious college in Portland. As the Washington State Patrol's Special Operations Director, the captain had pulled some strings to make me his intern--a temporary personal assistant--for the time he was uprooted to Moses Lake to solve this investigation. I guess he really did like the way I handled myself to help foil the kidnapping and smuggling attempts of Linh Riggleman, the once that helped clear Joe of his felony charges.

The boss set a stack of index cards and a Columbia Basin area phone book on the worktable beside me. "We need to know what Gunnar is hiding in his lockbox," he said. "Starting Monday, I want you to go out with a clear, full-sized photograph of this key. Talk to managers at every bank, credit union and savings-and-loan in

Wanapum County. Use the stamped number––1897––to find a wall of lockboxes possessing a match. Or simply see if any of them have the master lockbox key to accompany this one."

"Gladly," I said. The captain knew how much shuffling papers in our makeshift office was making me a bit *loco*. So what if I'd whined a bit too much about doing actual sleuthing for our case? Condran indulged my youthful assertiveness, but then kept creating new tasks that anchored me to this field office chair.

"While we're out conducting our search today, I'd like you to get the lockbox prospect list prepared."

The man definitely underestimated me.

"Oh, and please wear these today since you're not in the field office and will be a supporting participant of our State Patrol operation."

Before I could respond to either my assignment or what I could see was a uniform of some sort, the captain pivoted. I turned around to look.

"You made it!" said the Captain when a short, thin man with a matching narrow nose, thick, black-rimmed glasses and bristled, gray hair approached, his gait brisk.

"Bit of a traffic snarl through Snoqualmie Pass," he said with a nasally voice that also helped me recognize him from Joe's trial. Dr. Henry Schloss had testified in November about what little evidence survived the August crimes. Even now, we weren't any farther along than we'd been during the attempted kidnapping of baby Grace in December. Mainly, the Wanapum County chief investigator, Roger Riggleman, had mucked up, quite intentionally, most of the Bone Shrine crime scene.

One of the Special Weapons and Tactics team leaders walked up and leaned in. He spoke quietly. "Captain, surveillance has eyes on the target vehicle. The black Hummer is stirring up dust and heading towards the *Tramposo* compound."

Condran didn't hesitate. "Listen up," he said and stood furrowing his thick brows. He then, for effect he removed his wire-rimmed glasses, and spoke with a booming voice to everyone assembled in the large room. "Don't veer from our staging plan. And, once we're amassed north of George, remember to wait for my order to mobilize before encircling the compound."

Half-past-two and the room full of bulletproofed cops vibrated like a hive of black hornets taking flight.

I excused myself and went into our modest two-stall ladies room to change. My intern's wardrobe that my mom helped me assemble, was decidedly un-cop-like. The frills on my tan, cotton blouse were especially out of place for going on an actual bust.

I unfastened five, fat wooden buttons the size of silver dollars. They kept my blouse together from sternum to solar plexus. Two more buttons secured the stylish, wide breast pocket flaps. Mom had insisted on buying me matching tan office slacks that fit great once I hemmed up the cuffs to match my short legs. My nice, stocky curves––how Mom described them––seemed to be softening with all the sitting I was doing at college classes and in the field office these last three-and-a-half months.

The Birks sported comfy soles, but were so Sixties. For today at least, I'd be able to exchange them for the basic black, lace-up shoes in the uniform bag that Condran had given me. After undressing, I hung my civilian clothes on hooks along the ladies room wall.

The Docker cargo pants fit surprisingly well, as did my oxford-style, button-up work-shirt. I most loved the embroidering above the pocket on the right side:

Elizabeth M.
WSP–Special Ops Intern

It was the first official work uniform I'd ever had, and I suspected the use of my given name had something to do with not helping any perps identify me too easily. Only my mother ever called me *Elizabeth,* though, and mostly if she was mad at whatever trouble I'd unearthed.

Standing in front of the mirror above the sink, I pulled my blonde hair back in a ponytail. The image staring back ay me reinforced how glad I was to be moving on from the tribute hairdo memorializing Mary Quinn. Several of Mary's girlfriends in The Dalles had adopted her Goth-black dye job. The last thing I put on was a one-layer, forest-green, zip-up jacket with *Washington State Patrol* spelled out on one side.

I hustled out the front door. The captain had me and Dr. Schloss follow his team from the field office. Condran had been disappointed when he couldn't secure a state patrol helicopter for surveillance, or one of the W.S.P.'s own K-9 dogs. The small parking lot at the field office was full of Washington State Patrol vehicles, all being quickly occupied for the bust. Condran perked up when––on cue it seemed––Sergeant Jack Pack approached in his Wanapum Sheriff SUV with *K-9 Unit* stenciled on the rear quarter panels. "And at least now we have a dog," the captain told Dr. Schloss.

The captain motioned for the sergeant to come over so Dr. Schloss could show off W.S.P.'s brand new forensic van. "It's a rolling lab, and well-stocked inside," Schloss said in his high, but proud voice. The fancy van was definitely chock-a-block full. Schloss showed us by setting in place a stow-away tabletop and two fold-up chairs in the open back floor of the van's cargo area. "It serves as a mobile work station," he said.

We listened to Condran in the driver's seat when he radioed the two S.W.A.T. team lieutenants. In each group were four patrol SUV's, half of them bulletproofed. He directed them to head out towards the *Tramposo* compound located thirty miles west. From what I recalled of our planning efforts, one team would converge from the east and the other from the south on separate dirt access roads.

I watched Sergeant Pack, his handlebar mustache jiggling, directing his shepherd from the van to an empty lot across the street so the dog could pee. "Since Jack Pack works for the Wanapum County Sheriff, aren't you a bit leery inviting him to our bust?" I asked.

"Contract work. We'll need his dog's nose," said the captain, sounding impatient to get going. "Besides, Pack is one of the few Wanapum cops that I do trust.

"Escher's definitely Joe's hero dog," I said.

"Helped young Mr. Gardner beat his fabricated murder and heroin rap," Schloss added.

"Dr. Schloss was also quite helpful for the trial," Condran said, probably to let the scientist know, once again, how much his trek east of the Cascades to assist us today was appreciated.

"Just so you know, Captain, my key forensic colleague at the D.E.A. has made some inroads with U.S. Customs," Schloss said. "Since the drug-related activity looks to be interstate, if not international in scope, we've been authorized one week of federally supervised lab analysis of the gold Krugerrands."

The news gave me a tinge of optimism knowing that these were the ones confiscated in the baby stroller during the infant's kidnapping in December.

"Why the delay?" I asked.

"U.S. Customs had all the evidence they needed with these coins being taken directly from Mrs. Riggleman in the act of smuggling," Condran responded to me. "They don't need fingerprints to prove their federal smuggling charge."

"They've been reluctant to jeopardize their compelling set of evidence by releasing the coins to the Washington State Patrol lab for further analysis," Schloss added. "If these coins are related in any way to the Bone Shrine heroin deal, then we want to know if any prints can be found on them belonging to the *Tramposos* or the like."

"Is that so any *Tramposo* prints on the baby buggy coins would link them to the Rigglemans somehow?" I asked, just as K-9 Sergeant Pack returned with his dog.

"Possibly," said Schloss looking away from the Dutch Shepherd and back at me.

"The forensic process allows the evidence to dictate the conclusions, so we'll see what any of the prints we find actually reveal. I hope to have a report for Captain Condran by next week," he added.

"So Captain, is it true that your investigation is on the verge of being relegated to a cold case?" Pack asked.

"Your opponent in the Sheriff's race probably wishes that were true," Condran told the county's K-9 sergeant.

"I wouldn't be sticking my neck out here by running for Wanapum Sheriff if I knew the state patrol was about to abandon this case," said Pack. "Makes it look like Sheriff Usk's department ain't tainted."

Schloss leaned over to shake Sergeant Pack's hand. "Thanks again for your help during the Gardner trial investigation. If the incumbent wins, it will be a sad day indeed in Wanapum County," the scientist said before handing Pack a business card. "If you ever find yourself out of work, then call me. I'm well enough placed with the State Patrol that I'm confident we could find you alternative K-9 related employment."

Condran patted Schloss on the shoulder. "That's very true," he said to Pack.

"Thank you for that," Pack said to both men before telling his dog to sit at his heel. Escher was a bit small for a Shepherd, maybe two feet at the shoulders. The dog's brindled, white-and-black coat was like that Dutch artist's crazy-tight drawings, all geometric and trippy where white geese flew one way and, in the space between the birds, a flock of black geese were flying the other direction. From Joe's trial when Escher had found traces of matching China White in Roger Riggleman's department-issued camera case. I wondered if the Shepherd could detect odors as well as the Dutch artist could draw.

The captain placed all the fingers of one hand on his forehead and, with his thumb, tapped the edge of his glasses in that distracted, Columbo, TV-detective kind of way. Then, willfully, he dropped his arm and commanded the team of black-clad, bullet-proof vested S.W.A.T. officers to depart in their line of SUV's.

"You'll no doubt want me to hold back until the search site is fully secured," said Schloss.

"If you could drive to George, Washington in about forty-five minutes, then we should have some dawn light. The *Tramposo* compound will be visible to the north across the farm fields," Condran said.

The boss slurped another dose of caffeine from his well-stained Thermos. "Biff, why don't you go back inside and grab those index cards and phone book." Condran tapped the nifty table top in the back of the van. "Use this as your workstation until we're finished with our search and Dr. Schloss needs your help."

"Yes, sir," I said.

The captain turned and spoke to Sergeant Pack. "If you don't mind, Jack, I'll ride with you. Brief you on today's search."

"Of course," said the sergeant.

Once Pack and Condran drove off, Dr. Schloss had a few phone calls to make. It took me a whopping half-hour to complete my list of banks to target, so I spent the rest of the time studying the names on our cork board covered with yarn and thumbtacks. What we really needed was someone, actually anyone in the know, who would be willing to talk.

"Wear this," Dr. Schloss said, more like an order than a request. The bulletproof vest with W.S.P. on the back fit over my Washington State jacket more snugly than his did, but he was skinny for a cop and I wasn't exactly slender.

"Why the bulletproofing?" I asked. "Didn't know we were going anywhere near the line-of-fire."

"The captain will call us once the *Tramposo* compound is secured, but I always err on the side of caution."

Obedience wasn't my strongest trait, but I zipped up the vest and climbed into the passenger seat. The set-up inside the van smelled vinyl-new with its lab-related items packaged and unopened. Before getting on I-90 westbound, Schloss turned the van slowly.

"This is the Chevron minimart where Deputy Sheriff Zach Riggleman, Roger's son, gave Joe a ride back to the Bone Shrine pond on that ugly night of Mary's murder," I reminded him. "Kind of weird that the Washington State Patrol Field Office is so close to this spot."

"I didn't realize that," he said and turned onto the onramp before looking quickly my way. "Aren't you from Oregon, like the young victim?" he asked while accelerating.

"Yep. The Dalles."

"What brought you back up to Moses Lake?" he answered.

"I enrolled in the local community college. Big Bend has a criminal justice program that allows me to intern on this case."

"Good choice, if you want to be a detective," he replied while checking his mirror to merge. "I remember how well Captain Condran took charge of efforts leading to the arrest of Roger Riggleman on those felony tampering charges."

"'Tampering' sounds too soft," I couldn't help saying. "The chief investigator obliterated the crime scene."

Schloss didn't disagree and nodded very slowly.

"I just want us to find Mary's killer," I added. "Too bad my mother calls this internship my unhealthy obsession."

"Healthy or unhealthy, this case warrants solving," he said in a matter-of-fact tone.

Small signs along the barbed wire freeway fencing announced

corn, sugar beets, potatoes and the like, but the April fields were still fallow. "Captain Condran also harbors an obsession with solving the Bone Shrine crimes," I said. "And, I mean it's more than just offering inroads into the drug-rings connected with her death."

"Starting with how the underground operation benefited from the suspicious activities of local officials, like Roger Riggleman," he said. "Our Washington State Patrol was stonewalled during its investigation there. Didn't yield much at all for our case."

We quieted and continued westbound on the flat, straight section of I-90. The thirty miles to the roadside village of George gave me time to sort out my thoughts. This morning, my criminal justice instructor informed her two dozen students that our final paper was due in two weeks. She wanted a case study highlighting a singular core challenge for the criminal justice process. I knew that the Bone Shrine crimes offered numerous possibilities for my paper, but my mind didn't know where to begin. We weren't even done wading deep in a marsh of unfinished work.

Dr. Schloss pulled into the George, Washington truck stop at Martha Inn and parked in a spot across I-90 that faced north towards the *Tramposo* compound. The van was directly beneath the diner's neon road-sign.

"F-Van. Radio check, please," came the voice of Captain Condran.

It was about time, I thought. He had told us that the 'F' was short for 'forensic.' Schloss answered the captain's call with, "10-4. This is F-Van, parked as directed."

"Stand by where you are," the boss directed.

I rifled inside the glove compartment and found a pair of binoculars and did my best to focus them on a farmstead oasis, one of many dotting the irrigated Columbia River Basin. Like the others, it was shade-protected from the relentless eastern Washington sun by looming rows of poplars and pines. Here, the farmstead and trees gave cover for the *Tramposo* gang's drug compound. The boss was convinced that this was where the gang hid the inner workings of its drug enterprise, including stashes of contraband and the processing operation for supplying the local druggies. He knew this gang controlled the local turf in the Columbia Basin, but he also suspected that the *Tramposos* were closely tied to a major Mexican cartel that was using this local gang to bribe key officials wherever they gained a foothold in the state.

I handed the binoculars to Dr. Schloss and recalled how two of the *Tramposos* had tried to beat Joe senseless during his first day in jail, the morning after Mary drowned. Then, three months later, on the night before Joe secured his release in court, a young Wanapum County Jail inmate died from snorting too much pure China White heroin given to him by a newly incarcerated who'd smuggled it in the jail. The lab-work by Schloss determined that the China White from the Bone Shrine matched the heroin used in the gang-related overdose, but not that the *Tramposos* were directly connected. The captain was convinced otherwise. Due to the fight with Joe the morning after Mary drowned, and a *Tramposo* being busted selling China White in Moses Lake, he was sure the gang were perpetrators in the Bone Shrine crimes.

I hopped out of the van. Schloss still focused through the binoculars. On this chill, April afternoon, I'd expected to see a cloud of dust rising into the air, but there was none. The only thing I could hear was the intermittent passing of semi's and smaller vehicles on the interstate. When they weren't passing east or west, I'd like to say I tolerated an annoying electric buzz from the neon sign above the van. "I feel like I'm about to be zapped while standing here," I said instead, and pointed above my head.

Dr. Schloss stood outside and stretched his legs, too. "Hadn't noticed until you brought it to my attention."

The day grew as quiet as it was still.

He handed back the binoculars. I bent down from my waist, listened, and then looked hard towards the *Tramposo* compound. Still no hint of an active bust.

The sun glared and after two more 18-wheelers disappeared towards Moses Lake, the eerie buzzing resumed overhead. Against a backdrop of no freeway noise, I jumped and grabbed the side mirror when a boom startled us.

"Sounded like a thirty-ought-six," said Schloss, tapping his heart.

"More like a canon," I replied looking towards the *Tramposo* compound.

Crisp bangs filled the air.

Rapid fire bursts.

Different weapons.

"A gunfight," said Dr. Schloss. He motioned me back inside the van.

Breathe, I told myself.

An all-out firefight.

I watched through binoculars.

The gunfire stopped. Silence blanketed us, except for the neon sign.

"What timing! Mother nature calls," said Schloss. "This won't take no for an answer."

He hurried off with a fresh plume of dust lifting above the compound. I wondered if the captain was sending some of his S.W.A.T. team back south towards the freeway?

I locked my doors, especially with Schloss gone. I rolled down my window. Just a crack to listen for more gun shots. Nothing erupted from the compound. The plume of dust edged its way towards I-90 and stopped. The vehicle wheels probably found pavement.

"F-Van," came the captain's voice over the radio. "Stay where you are, but take cover inside the vehicle."

Before I could answer, a jet-black Hummer rolled into the Martha Inn parking lot and pulled up close to me. Its passenger window rolled open with a four-inch gap. No time to roll up my own window that had nowhere near the shiny dark tinting of their Hummer. My forensic van had no tinting at all. They saw me too clearly, especially through the open gap. My body went catatonic. I expected to find myself shot during a 'drive-by' by pissed-off *Tramposos.*

In the narrow opening of the Hummer's front passenger window, a man took off his sunglasses. Dark eyes beneath black brows bore a hole through me. My body froze and the black, dusty Hummer spun out.

In the side mirror, Dr. Schloss was exiting the café. Once the Hummer racing away, he got to a knee, but had trouble pulling his service pistol from its holster hidden beneath his bulletproof vest. Schloss didn't have a chance to fire off a single shot before the *Tramposo* getaway vehicle disappeared down a George side street.

I sat stunned, but watched Schloss holster his gun when hurrying back to the forensic van. He hopped back into the driver's seat and uncoiled the cord to the radio microphone. He nearly yelled into the receiver. "A black Hummer, Captain. Yes. She's unharmed. Here she is."

"I'll live," I said and described the brief encounter. "I'm only a bit shook up. I'm more worried about your team. Is everyone okay?" "

The captain, without answering, directed us to wait out of sight, in the rear of the forensic van. "Don't leave that spot until I arrive."

~

CHAPTER 2

COLD MESSAGE

Condran and Sergeant Pack got out of the Wanapum Sheriff K-9 unit. Condran hustled to where Schloss and I waited inside the Forensic van beneath the Martha Inn sign.

"So, you're okay?" the captain asked us.

We both nodded. I got out and watched Pack lead his dog from the rear of the K-9 SUV.

"He wants to make sure the blood on Escher's coat is not from Escher," Condran told me. Red stain intruded on the brindled white patterns of the Dutch Shepherd's coat. Sergeant Pack gave a thumb's up to Captain Condran.

Pack then came over with Escher on leash to hand me a brochure. "Since I suspect I may be in hot water at work, I figure I might as well ask for your vote, young lady."

Large block letters stated, *JACK PACK for SHERIFF--The Change We Need.* I scanned his list of qualifications, all law enforcement related, nothing political. The man was far braver than I would ever be. Pack was taking on his own boss, Sheriff Colton Usk, for the top law enforcement post in Wanapum County. *The Change We Need.* Was it a veiled slam at the corruption within the department where he worked?

"Only one problem. I'm still registered to vote in Oregon," I told the K-9 sheriff, "but I'll hand them out to my criminal justice class-mates." At this Jack gave me a short stack of brochures and thanked me. I scratched Escher's ears when Schloss told Condran that, since there was no incriminating evidence to process, then he'd be heading back over the Cascades. Condran nodded and thanked him for helping out before motioning for me to get in the backseat of the K-9 unit in front of Escher.

When the three of us drove the opposite way back to Moses Lake, the captain brought me up to speed on the bust. His words came out in bursts.

Escher had sniffed out the lead *Tramposo*.

A half-dozen Pit Bull terriers ran towards them alongside a barrel-chested Rottweiler.

Away from the old farmhouse, the gang leader hid in a small outbuilding.

The S.W.A.T. team smoke-bombed the place.

Coughing and pissed, the thick *Tramposo* ran from the building.

A shiny, black Hummer raced up.

"That's when Escher jumped the man," said Pack. "My dog latched onto one arm to keep the *Tramposo* from running. That's when I spotted the Rottweiler crouching down, about to lunge for Escher's throat."

Condran glanced over at me with a sadness I'd never seen from him. "I never shot at a dog before, let alone killed one."

"Don't forget how you saved Escher's life with that bullet," Pack told Condran and glanced at me seated right behind the captain. "He fired the moment the Rottweiler made its move towards my Shep-herd. That's also when Escher released his bite on the Tramposo to jump away." Pack turned back before fixing his eyes on the road again. "That's also when the lead *Tramposo* rolled away and jumped inside an opened, rear door of the gang's Hummer. The bullet proof rig raced off through a hidden hole in the perimeter of the compound's fence."

"The hole that my troopers failed to secure," said Condran, sounding disappointed with his day.

"Forget getting down on yourself, Captain," said Pack. "You and I both know the *Tramposos* were tipped off."

"And I bet I know from where," I said. "We really do need to get you elected sheriff," I added, reaching up to pat him on the shoulder.

We drove in silence the rest of the way to the field office parking lot. Pack let us out and said he couldn't stick around. Condran thanked him politely for his help and watched the K-9 cop depart with Escher. Scattered clouds filled the crisp-cold April night that was darkening into a deep purple.

"Won't see you until next week," I told the captain when only the two of us stood in the lot. "On Sunday I'm driving down to my parents for Easter dinner in The Dalles," I told him.

"Easter. That's right. I almost forgot," he said.

"Which makes today both Friday, the 13th, and Good Friday, the day they hung Jesus up on the cross," I said.

"I always wondered what was 'good' about getting crucified," Condran said, looking up at the darker horizon of night. "I'll be catching holy hell for this bust. And, except for that Rottweiler, I'm amazed no one was killed. Pack was right. They were tipped off. The gang thoroughly scrubbed their place of any contraband. Every crawl space, nook, and even the closets of the compound were spotless."

"No drug haul, no gangbanger arrests, not even any rolling paper. It really isn't looking good for our case, is it Boss?" I asked, the low tone of my voice matching my own bummed-out mood.

"Nope. Not good at all."

When I told Condran that I needed to change back into my regular clothes, he unlocked the field office door. Once my big buttoned blouse and the matching slacks covered my body, I slipped the Birks on, too, before placing my new uniform inside the bag the captain had issued me. I found a cubby-hole where I could store it in the ladies room.

When the captain let me out the front door, I wished him a good weekend and could see him watching me cross the parking lot before I climbed into my Loyale. His protectiveness felt strangely good. The streetlamp shimmered over the lime-green of my car.

～

My mind stayed foggy as I steered the compact Subaru towards the freeway onramp beside the same old Chevron minimart and *taqueria* that Joe had walked to so he could fill up his empty gas can.

Our bust had been a thorough bust.

I breathed in deep, worried about Escher, worried about the case, worried about going back to a cold, empty doublewide. Then, just before turning towards the I-90 onramp, I jerked sideways, but managed to hit the brakes. A gun barrel rammed my skull into the driver's side window with a thud. The silencer on the pistol jammed into my temple.

"Drive! No! Not the freeway," came the deep Hispanic voice. "Go that way." He pointed towards the freeway frontage road on the south side of I-90. I eased forward, not fast, not slow, but on the verge of freaking out.

The stout man had been tucked into a tight ball under a dark blanket of mine that I kept on the back seat. I cried out, but my throat only gasped strangely. My startled, furious eyes did the screaming for me.

In the rearview mirror, I caught a glimpse of this thick man's dark, wide eyes––definitely the ones I'd just seen staring me down outside Martha Inn. The rest of his face was covered with a black, stretch-nylon mask. His gun barrel continued pressing hard into my temple.

"Watch the road!" His words came at me stern and hard.

I squeezed the steering wheel until my knuckles hurt, and mostly to keep my hands from shaking. Along scabland made eerie from moonlight, I eased down the I-90 frontage road.

"Please don't hurt me," I begged.

"*¡Quieté!*" the stocky man told me, this time harsher.

I drove steadily away from Moses Lake. If it hadn't been for that barrel pressed hard against my temple, I might have slammed on the brakes and jumped from my car. I looked into the solid black night. Where would I run to? We were too far from anywhere for such a stupid, escape attempt miles from town. Not a single car passed us on the frontage road.

"Turn there!" he yelled and pointed away from the freeway frontage towards a gravel path.

I gasped again but did what he said. I knew all too well where we were. I set the parking brake near the new heavy gate leading into the Potholes Wildlife Refuge, my heart pounding even more. I heard the rear driver-side door open and I was told to open my door, too. "Step slow," came the command. I didn't look, but sensed a pistol still trained at the back of my head.

I pulled the door latch carefully and pushed it open with my shoulder.

"*Ahora!*"

I did as he directed and stepped out to where his pistol barrel was pointed beside the gate. When I turned to face him, he pulled off his mask. I winced. Why had he shown his face to me? Did he want me to be able to identify him in a jail lineup. Was I this man's dead-girl walking and would never be able to point him out to another soul.

"Stupid cop dog," he said and lifted the short-sleeved arm of his loose, black, button-up shirt. He grimaced and lightly touched the Ace Bandage wrapped around his bicep. In the Loyale headlights, the head *Tramposo* looked down at his bite wound. I was also able to see, high on his cheek, a small tattoo of a howling coyote.

I closed my eyes, even though I knew none of this stuff happening to me was going to vanish.

"Off with those. Off!" He spoke with authority but I froze and shivered. When I looked, his eyes were burning black. "Are you deaf? The shoes!"

"No!" I yelled after his warning bullet hit near the stout steel gate where I still stood shivering. I yanked off my Birkenstocks and tossed them gently towards his feet.

With his good right arm, the *Tramposo* frisbee-ed each sandal into the dark where the bitterbrush grew. Good riddance, I thought, but why, with a gun still aimed my way, was shoe fashion a fleeting thought?

"The pants, too," he yelled and motioned for me to take them off.

I took my time lowering them to the ground and carefully draping them over the top of the wide gate. His glare, tone, and posture grew impatient.

"Are you deaf, *chica*? Those silk panties, too."

I tried to swallow but my throat and tongue were too dry. He shot a second warning bullet closer to my ankle. I jumped back from the flying sand, even though his silencer barely made a sound. What was the bastard planning? I shuddered and shimmied my undies over my full hips and let them fall to my bare feet. Stepping free, at least the big buttoned blouse I wore was long enough to cover me down to my mid-thighs. But how long before he had me strip naked?

I crossed my arms under my chest realizing how vulnerable I was with this stupid prudish pose. Still, I didn't unfold the arms, otherwise he'd see me shaking even more.

Stepping close and holding the barrel of his gun, he used the butt of the grip to thump the wide, brown, wooden button holding a breast pocket-flap in place. I felt a jolt of fear from impact up into my throat. "I like those big brown buttons. Do your nipples look like them?"

I tightened my crossed arms higher to cover the pockets, but didn't answer. "You can show me soon enough," he added before pointing his gun down the path beyond the new entry gate.

With bare feet on the sand, I turned and walked in front of him. Was he planning to rape me before drowning me? Even Mary wasn't raped first. The tears started flowing. "Please don't," my voice pleaded.

The faster I walked, the faster he went. When I slowed, he pushed the barrel of his pistol into my spine and growled: "Why you stopping?"

I trembled.

I knew this dirt bike trailhead that led off through the scablands, the path that Nils Larsson had shown me. He'd let me ride Gunnar's repaired Husqvarna now that his son was in Sweden. Father and son knew all the trails surrounding Moses Lake.

In the near dark, I could make out the same pond where Mary's face had been shoved beneath the scummy water. My head spun.

"Ouch," I yelled when a sticker impaled me between two toes. I hopped on one foot and refused to bend over for him. Somehow, I kept my balance and plucked out the sticker. The stinging stopped.

The sand on the path forced my feet to trudge. The crude road flattened. I could see marshy reeds ahead, but only barely. Had it been this dark when they found newborn Grace floating in this same pond? I looked hard to see where any of the dirt bike trails intersected into this drivable path, but couldn't make out any variation in the arid landscape. How could I trick this creep? I was weaker, unarmed, and the barefoot one. My short legs weren't all that fast. We walked several feet farther to the stone landing used by fishermen, the spot where Mary's memorial had been held.

"Turn your ass around!"

When I did as told, the man was waving his handgun like an index finger. I stood as tall as my legs would allow. My eyes widened and I froze in place like a stiff department store mannequin.

"You don't answer me before. Do you like how those buttons look like nipples?"

I resisted the urge to puke. My knees trembled. Why didn't he just shoot me?

"Unbutton your shirt!"

Very slowly, I did as directed, but with trembling fingers, I only managed the top one.

With the barrel of his handgun still trained on my head, he knelt down and without looking at the pond, he cupped scummy water in his free palm. Underhanded, he flung cold drops all over my face and blouse. "Faster. Or do you want to drown in this pond?"

My jaw dropped wide and my shoulders started to heave. I all but ripped the second button from the blouse and tried to stop the fabric from flapping open to reveal any more than necessary.

"¡*Por favor!*" I cried in the way that I wished wasn't so meek.

He pointed his gun at my face again. "You know what *por favor* means?" he asked and scowled, then waited for my answer.

"It means 'please' since I'm asking you to not hurt me." I just about fainted when, through his silencer, he fired a third bullet two feet from my ankle.

"No! *Por Favor* means 'for the favor.'"

"What do you want from me?" I asked, folding my arms at my breasts again.

"Drop your hands!" Once again, he stepped closer and rapped the end of his pistol barrel on the wooden button that held down a pocket flap.

My eyes clogged with tears. One look at this bastard and I could tell that, unlike Mary and Joe, the first man I had would be a rapist. I lifted my chin and stared as best I could at his hardened eyes.

"Look at you. Did I make you strip naked?"

I shrugged. Not yet, I thought.

"Answer me. Did I make you strip off your clothes?" he yelled.

"No." I didn't hesitate this time. "Please don't do this to me."

"Do what?" The way he waved his pistol at my face made me more nervous than the bullets he fired off near my feet. "Did I tell you to climb in the pond?"

"No," I said, hoping that maybe he wouldn't.

"Then guess what, sexy little *chica*? This is your lucky day."

"Lucky?" I asked, not believing my ears. The bust was botched, and this piece of work had just abducted me.

The stocky Latin man growled his words. "You tell your Captain that it's time for him to back off. And, that means call off his dogs." He paused and looked me up and down. "Starting now. If he don't back down, then he gets him one big ass, big time, cartel drug war––*muy grandé*––with body parts of dead troopers floating in every corner of this state."

I didn't really know what his gang was capable of doing, but shuddering, I nodded.

"You tell your *jefe* that the *Tramposos* don't rape, don't drown no women. Tell me. Did I hurt you?"

I managed to shake my head.

"Did I strip you naked?"

I whispered, "No."

"Are you drowned and dead?"

I shook my head again.

"You tell *El Capitán* to cease-fire with *Los Tramposos* until he finds his real killer." His eyes glared harshly, darkly.

The weird thing was what my gut instinct told me. This thug was on the up-and-up.

He stepped closer and, in another quick motion with the pistol, tapped the other breast pocket button with his pistol. I stood totally still. Had he just changed his mind about harming me?

In the cold night air, my barely clothed body shook hard. The man's eyes glared like shiny coal about to be lit on fire. He pointed his pistol at the surface of the pond and fired. A big Great Horned owl hooted and lifted up from the brush to fly close overhead, making the *Tramposo* look skyward where the stars silhouetted the bird. "That owl saw who done it that night to your *amiga*," he said and then looked down at me. "*El Gringo Loco* weren't no *Tramposo.*"

El Gringo Loco? What was he saying? I didn't dare ask.

He pressed his gun barrel hard enough into my breast to make me wince. "Ten minutes. You wait here. Now tell me exactly what you planning to tell *El Capitán.*"

"I'll tell him to back off."

"What else you tell him?"

"That you decided not to rape and drown me."

"Decided?" he yelled and winced again at the dog bite on his arm. "I never was going to rape your ass. I was never going to drown you! *Tramposos* don't treat women like whores."

"You brought me here and did all this just to tell me it was a crazy white guy, *Gringo Loco,* who killed Mary Quinn?" I asked rapid-fire, but still afraid of what he might do next. "You don't want to know what I think of you, but guess what, *señor?* Right now, my boss needs to find *El Gringo Loco* more than he's going to want to take down your *Tramposo* game. So, yes, I'll tell him to back off." I don't know why I decided to fight his fire with fire, except I knew he thought I was useful to him now.

Careful, I told myself. I was still his pawn, the messenger who needed to know how pissed off the *Tramposos* were at being targeted with the bust. Half-dressed and shivering, I needed to show him that I understood, so I kept up my fast-talk. "It's totally effed up, but I see why your ugly threats to harm me were warning shots, along with those bullets you fired in the sand, too close to my toes. There's just something, though. Something. And it's the *only* reason I'll help you." I paused. "I just don't think it was a *Tramposo* that killed Mary Quinn."

"*Sí.*"

At this, the man firmly holstered his pistol in the belt behind his back so he was sure I noticed.

"*Diez minutos.* Ten minutes. No less." The arrogant man turned slowly and didn't bother looking back at me before walking up the sandy path towards the freeway where a fresh set of headlights waited for him.

The Great Horned Owl swooped back down to its perch in a

scrubby cedar at the edge of the pond. When the bird hooted, I felt possessed.

I leaned down--no sandals, no undies, no slacks, only a miniskirt of a blouse--and scooped up a handful of pond to wet my forehead. It was the same water that had sucked away Mary's last breath. This same water was where we'd also honored her spirit. Conflicted by it all, my resolve stiffened. I looked up at the silhouette of this owl. I definitely needed to become more than a pawn in our spirit war where darkness and light were colliding.

Mary knew how stubborn and willful I could be. At this moment, I felt more determination than I ever believed possible.

I don't know how long I sat in my Loyale gripping the steering wheel and trying to make any sense of having been so pistol-whipped and violated. The *Tramposo* had left the driver's door of the Subaru open. My keys were in the ignition. Once I stopped and sat, the body heat I'd regained from walking back up to the car vaporized into the clear, crisp night. I found myself welcoming the cold, though, thinking it would make me reckon with the brute ugliness I'd narrowly escaped. With a wimpy flashlight from my glove compartment, I found a suit-case-sized brown box in the back seat.

Stepping outside, I stripped off my big-buttoned, large-pocketed blouse, and even unhooked my ample bra. Breathing deeply, I allowed the chill, springtime air to awaken every bare pore and shrivel each orifice on my body. The near freezing air cut through my numbness and shock. For this strange relief, I welcomed the frigid assault. For seven minutes, I withstood the cold until my strange, inner-clock of motivation ordered me to begin the dreaded follow-up that this night still demanded.

I remembered my gym clothes in the trunk, the ones that hadn't quite inspired the necessary first step to exercise--a spinning class at the Big Bend College gym. In the back of the Subaru, I also found my jogging sweats and latest Japanese tennis shoes that Kuma had gifted me when he came last winter from Tokyo to claim his and Mary's baby girl, Grace.

Still naked, I went over to the thick, locked gate near my car and grabbed my tan slacks still draped there. I flipped on my car flashlight to locate the silky undies a few feet away on the ground. None of these clothes were going to hang in my closet again. I stuffed the blouse with its wide, brown buttons in the bottom of a brown box, then shoved the slacks and undies on top before overlapping the top flaps and tossing it in the trunk. I slamming it shut. I knew it was impossible to bury such a fresh, raw memory, but I was going to give it a try by destroying the reminders. I shined the light across the dry, dormant bitterbrush not caring if I ever found those stupid Birkenstocks.

When the *Tramposo* had started raging at me, I'd been absolutely certain. Rape and death by drowning were to be my fate on this ugly night. I shivered uncontrollably from the cold spring air.

Before putting on my sweats, I leaned my front seat forward and threw the blanket that the *Tramposo* had contaminated onto the ground behind me, wanting it to decay into the high desert dirt like a fetid memorial to my abduction. My flashlight revealed what I needed. Wedged in a backseat crease was my undyed, lamb's-wool cap, the only mother-natural thing from Mom's hippie fashion décor that I totally adored. I pulled the thick, knit cap over my crown before donning anything else. I was probably only imagining that I was warmer, but the soft, perfect winter beanie slipped over my straight blonde hair and small freezing ears and started warming my brain.

A semi blasted past me on the interstate. My reflection appeared in the side windows of my car. For a fraction of a moment, the sight of my thick curves were revealed in their full fleshly glory. In all my nakedness, the contours told me I was still intact. My girlhood dignity had been threatened, but not violated.

I clasped the bra at my naval, and then wrestled it over my breasts before taking another heavy breath. I pulled the sweatpants over my panties and disappeared inside the sweatshirt to find the neck and arm openings. It had no hood or pockets, only *The Dalles High School* emblazoned on the front. I rubbed my upper arms vigorously and allowed the thick cotton to soothe my angry goose bumps. Lastly, I slipped on the tennis shoes which did nothing for warmth, but protected my newly abused soles. I looked again for my reflection in the driver's window, but the darkness captured only a black abyss.

I got into the driver's seat and engaged the clutch before starting the engine. The heater, even turned on full, blew frigid air off the car's manifold. My limbs shook anew, so I turned it off and drove slowly to the Chevron mini-mart. Its sign glowed blue neon like a beacon.

I didn't need gas, but forced the box with my undies, big-button blouse and matching tan slacks into a dumpster beside the taqueria. Then I headed inside the mart. At the counter, I asked the clerk if they had hot chocolate. "Sorry. No cocoa. The coffee ain't too fresh, but plenty warm."

"As long as its warm, then charge me for two 20-ouncers––black with no cream."

"It's fresh and piping hot," he promised.

In the car, I made sure the plastic covers were secured and placed one in the center console holder. I closed my eyes and sipped the other cup before driving. The dark, hot liquid flowed down my throat and soothed my nerves enough to drive. I crossed my fingers and, for the three blocks until arriving at the field office, deliberated how I should say what I needed to say.

At first sight of the state patrol parking lot, my numbness eased. At least I felt safer. Condran's unmarked Crown Vic was still in the small lot. I pulled my beanie farther down over my ears and again commanded my nerve-wracked wiring to calm.

I knew what had to be done and wanted it over with. You've got this, Biff, I told myself for the dozenth time.

I turned off the engine and rang the bell used after business hours and mostly to alert any graveyard and swing-shift troopers doing paperwork at one of the many desks in the open area of our back office. The captain looked exhausted and surprised to see me at the door. "Boss. I really need to share something with you."

"What's wrong, Biff?"

I fibbed big-time, but didn't hold back. "When I got to my doublewide, one of the *Tramposos* was wearing a mask. He greeted me in the driveway with a stone-cold message."

The captain jerked his head back in surprise. "How did they know you're renting Gunnar Larsson's old place?"

"This is *Tramposo* turf, Boss. I bet they also know you're holed up for the investigation in that extended-stay hotel."

Condran placed a forefinger to his lips. "Hold your thoughts," he said softly. "Let's go in back and sit at our table where it's warm."

"And once we're done, Boss, I'm definitely going to be taking Mrs. Larsson up on her backup offer."

"What did Darla offer you?" he asked and opened the field office door for me to enter first. It reminded me to hand him the coffee that my lips hadn't contaminated. He lifted his full cup high as though to toast me for reading his mind. After he locked the front door behind us, we both wrapped our hands around the warmish cups.

"Mrs. Larsson said that if ever the doublewide didn't work out, for whatever reason, then I could rent Gunnar's old bedroom, the one downstairs at their lakefront home. That's house you came up empty at when you searched it last December while looking for clues related to Gunnar."

"I hadn't forgotten. I've been coming up empty far too often lately," he responded. "And, I definitely feel a whole lot more comfortable if you're staying there than all alone at that doublewide," he said once we were inside.

In the big, open room of the field office, Condran sat and pivoted in his cushy desk chair. I set down my paper cup and lifted my four-legged, uncushioned, oak chair so I was facing him. Squeezing the ends of my oak arm-rests helped me focus. I had to tell myself to breathe deeply knowing how, for the discussion ahead, I was in the loathsome position of being an apologist for the repugnant *Tramposos*.

"First things first, Biff. Are you okay? Your knuckles are white. Did the *Tramposo* make physical contact with you in any way?"

"No." I relaxed my fingers. My fib needed to be as firm as possible to convince the State Patrol's highest ranking detective.

There was no way I was going to talk about an abduction that, 'for my own wellbeing,' would remove me from this case, whether because of WSP policy, or when my mother cut my short frame off at the knees if I insisted on continuing after being abducted. "It was nothing like that," I fibbed again. "But the *Tramposo* was firm and I did make a devil's bargain with him."

"What sort of bargain?" he asked, seemingly okay that I held fast on being okay.

"I agreed to be his messenger in exchange for him leaving me alone."

"He threatened you?"

"No. I chose to be his messenger before he needed to harm me." The actual harm part was true, but I was fully aware that I'd yet to begin processing his threats to my very life.

"What was the message?" he asked, seeming totally spent from his day orchestrating a S.W.A.T. operation that had gone nowhere.

Part of me wished he knew that his frustration with the failed bust scarcely compared to my evening of being abducted at gunpoint. Even in the lukewarm field office with hot coffee dripping through me, I couldn't stop shaking from the cold. "The *Tramposos* are dead serious about you knowing that none of them killed Mary, or that they were definitely *not* part of the heroin deal at the Bone Shrine that night."

"I've been beginning to believe that as well," said Condran, in a way that startled me. He slurped with such gusto from his cup that I figured his evening was young.

"What makes you believe?" I asked.

"For starters, I'm sure Sergeant Pack was right. The *Tramposos* were tipped off about today's bust by someone working at Wanapum County. That's the only reason we couldn't find one single roach or even a bong at their compound," Condran said.

"That makes a whole lot of sense, Boss," I said, wishing I hadn't had to face an abduction to tell him he'd already figured out what he needed in order to shift his focus away from the *Tramposos*. "My thinking only came from my gut," I said and adjusted my sweat pants to get more comfortable on the hard oak.

"A conclusion you reached after the *Tramposo* gave you the message?" he asked me.

"He seemed real serious about getting you that message," I said realizing how the captain seemed to genuinely appreciate my opinion on things, so long as I didn't forget who was the boss.

"Why did he choose to go through you to message me, Biff?"

"Because, even with the mask on, I knew he was the one who rolled down the window of his Hummer when Dr. Schloss and I waited outside Martha's Inn today," I said and reminded myself that nothing I said from the thug would be about honoring a promise made from the wrong end of a gun. This was about helping Mary's case. "He knew I couldn't arrest him like you would have, if given the chance."

"There is that," said the captain, also clutching his coffee tightly. "From this failed bust, I also came to a belated realization. This *Tramposo* gang was never in a position to totally corrupt the crime scene at the Bone Shrine. We have strong, repeated evident that they do move dime bags of heroin, but not kilos. They're hustling a hit or two at a time. Makes more sense that they would be the buyers of that China White than the sellers."

I shrugged. "Not to profile them ethnically," I said, "but they seem more like a Mexican Brown kind of gang than China White pushers. The Brown comes from Mexico, the White from Asia."

"Except we're convinced that the China White snorted by the young man who overdosed on the night before Joe's trial ended had been procured, uncut, from a young *Tramposo* dealer."

Since he was the boss and I was the lowly intern, I didn't dare tell him that I'd already been piecing together this same scenario. Even though he did pick my brain, I sensed it was better to let the captain think that the big revelations were his own. "What if that China White came from the uncut bundles that Roger Riggleman pilfered from the First Aid Kit on the night that Mary died?" I asked.

"It definitely did," said Condran. "Dr. Schloss confirmed my suspicions this morning. "I was actually hoping to find more China White out at the *Tramposo* compound today. No such luck."

"There's one thing I don't get, Boss. If the smack that killed the kid in the Wanapum Jail was uncut, why did it come from Roger Riggleman who had all the tools in his basement workshop to cut it down to street standards?"

Condran, for the first time today, grinned. "Perfect question, Biff. I have a theory."

"What's that, Boss?"

"Someone in Roger Riggleman's sphere worried that Joe might have a mistrial or hung jury. As a contingency for losing their fall guy, the actual culprits needed a different suspect to take the spotlight off them. The *Tramposo* gang was next in line."

I finished my last warm bit of stale coffee, "So the *Tramposos* were being set up with that far-too-potent heroin?"

Condran shifted uneasily in his seat. "Since I was the dupe who bought into the *Tramposos* as the prime movers of the China White to the point where our case is now in jeopardy of being shelved, I think that's the best explanation left."

I really liked how, even though the captain fully assumed the mantle of 'boss,' he also could be humble when things went south-- and tonight our case had gotten cold enough to crash-land in Antarctica. "Sounds like the right question to me, Captain. I mean, how would the *Tramposos* be in any position to mangle Mary's crime scene?"

"I'm pretty sure the *Tramposo* we nearly apprehended during the bust today was the same one we saw on the jail videotape trying to rough up Joe Gardner in jail the morning he was arrested."

"The thicker *Tramposo*, not the skinny one who got his skull cracked," I added. "I'm pretty sure that's the same burly one who told me to give you his message. He has distinctive eyes. Very thick brows."

The captain nodded. "The one that Escher bit."

"About thirty-years-old," I added.

"I'd estimate the same," he said, "but you say you trust him that the *Tramposos* weren't involved in the Bone Shrine murder or drug deal. Why trust a major drug player?"

"For one, not many guys as young as him are major drug lords."

"Actually, Biff, he might be a 'lieutenant' running the foot soldiers here in the Columbia Basin. Nothing in our intel has the local *Tramposos* delivering or buying high dollar product."

"Or selling a quarter million worth of smack giving them motive to murder my friend and, as you said, the ability to mess up a crime scene like what happened while Mary was being hauled off to the morgue." My voice rose and the back of my hand tried to stifle a wave of emotions. I lifted my cup for the warmth mainly, but it didn't stop my tears from landing on the lid.

"Are you okay to continue?" he asked.

I nodded and told myself to keep it together--for Mary. "What self-respecting, big-time, gang leader takes the lead in roughing up someone like Joe who's fresh in jail. Don't they typically delegate the rough stuff, especially to someone lower in the pecking order?" I asked.

"I suspect the whole *Tramposo* gang is at the street level," the boss said, "and sometimes hired to do the dirty work––"

"Like roughing up Joe so he'd beg to be kept in solitary confinement and under control as the culprit's fall guy."

"I was also hoping that arresting a few *Tramposos* today might help us piece together this puzzle," said Condran.

"Considering the suspicions you just shared, are you planning on backing off the *Tramposos*?" I asked, hoping I didn't sound to the captain like I was being a devil's advocate for the gang.

"We do need to change our focus, Biff. From my conversation with my boss in Olympia, this case has until the end of April to show strong new leads, or I'll be closing down the investigation. That doesn't mean I want the *Tramposos* thinking that I'm backing away from them."

"So we'll be focusing higher up the food chain?" I asked.

He nodded and slurped again.

"Boss, that *Tramposo* also gave me a strange hint, maybe even a lead."

"Solid enough for them to think I'd back off their dealings?" he asked.

"That's for you to decide, Captain." My mind raced when one thought crystalized on the lengths the burly *Tramposo* had gone with my life so he could offer Condran an olive branch. "The *Tramposo* also told me to tell you that you need to find *El Gringo Loco*."

"Who in the hell is that?" Condran asked.

"I'm not *La Gringa Loca,* but my limited high school Spanish says it's a white dude from the U.S.A. who's crazy." I smiled as best I could when the words came out. "Do you think Roger Riggleman could be *El Gringo Loco*?" I then asked.

"You've met Roger Riggleman and so have I," he said without hesitation. "This investigator may be despicable, but I wouldn't call him the least bit crazy," said the Captain. "Besides, he's locked up in the state pen. From reports there, he's not been communicating with anyone on the outside––no visitors, or even letters sent or received. Only sees his lawyer every other week or so. Very aloof."

"So you're saying Wanapum's chief detective isn't acting like he's running the show from behind bars?"

Condran nodded slowly. "He was definitely the key player to corrupt that whole crime scene, but I highly doubt he's been the ring leader, the drug lord we're looking for."

"Maybe what the *Tramposo* told me to tell you was only a crumb," I said. "They just want to steer you away from their Latino gang."

"Not only are the local *Tramposos* street smart," he said, "but I suspect they also figured out from the jail overdose on uncut heroin that their gang was being set up to connect them to the China White from the Bone Shrine. The goal behind the bust today was to exploit this betrayal, but without arrests or more evidence of any China White heroin, our efforts today were for naught."

"So they're hellbent on not taking Joe's place and becoming the new fall guys," I said.

"Exactly," said the captain and slapped our bulletin board with the back of his hand, nearly knocking it over. "Let's not assume this is a total falling out warranting the *Tramposos* going to war with *El Gringo Loco's* drug operation," he added. "They know they need to tread water, but don't intend to drown."

"Yes," I said. "And I wasn't exactly given the social security number and home address of the crazy white dude."

"But as long as our fresh thinking leads to fresh, compelling evidence, we can press forward" he said, seemingly pleased with our brainstorming.

I watched as he wrote something in big block letters. He thumb-tacked the paper on the cork in the very middle of all our criss-crossing yarn. "Let's wrap things up and I'll give you an undercover police escort to the Larsson's place," he said and moved away from our board of yarn and leads. That's when I first read what he'd written–– bigger than any other name on the board:

EL GRINGO LOCO.

At Darla's and Nil's lakefront home, Condran watched as I locked up my Loyale and walked to the rear of the home. Darla's Saab convertible was in the driveway, but not Nils' pickup. Probably on a business trip.

No need to disturb Darla. I'd tell her in the morning that I wouldn't be renting Gunnar's doublewide any longer. I'd always felt vulnerable out there.

In late November, Darla had invited Kuma and me to stay as houseguests in their lakefront home. Joe Gardner's trial was almost over then. Kuma had flown in from Japan to unite with his and Mary's baby and Darla showed us where she hid the key to the basement door.

Condran walked with me into the backyard and waited until I lifted a brick hidden beneath a dormant rose bush. I found the key still there and gave him a thumbs up. Once I opened the back door, I put it back where I'd found it. Only then did he leave.

Inside, I decided against flipping on the light of the recreation room with its pool table and dart board and TV–Stereo. Gunnar's bedroom took up the rest of the finished basement. Craving only to curl up and escape this horrible day, I closed my eyes. Except for the hoo-hooing of an owl calling across Moses Lake, I forgot the world. I kept my lamb's wool cap pulled over my ears and, along with help from the comforter, the chills lifted from my bones. I needed the surge of peace, as temporary as they were of late. Only then did the lucidity come. Only then was I dream-flying again:

Mary and I soar above the potholes. She drifts away.

I feel no joy. Not for what I see unfold.

Below, I see a fat, bloated, scaly carp. The fish rots atop the landing of stones.

My owl nature flies clear of carrion. The fish stinks so bad that the vultures will drop down to the pond at dawn. Bulrushes and cattails line the shore. A full moon rises. The surface of water is cut up into bits of jagged glass.

I land on a nest at the top of a thick cedar. Joe climbs the tree below us. He holds a box wrapped in a coyote hide. He rushes to my tree. It is not tall for a cedar. It's scrubby, two or three times taller than Joe.

The cedar sways. He climbs it and wedges his box through a tangle of branches. *He turns the white metal kit of a box so it fits. I see a red cross on the side. He pushes the kit upward, and pushes again. It finds the gap through the branches.*

Joe pokes his eye, grunts, scratches his neck, groans, and grunts again. He is close to me, close to the top. He twists sideways. The first-aid kit is under his trailing arm. Joe inches through more branches. He's one yard below the nest. I watch, but don't move. He doesn't see me. The fledgling and I peek over the edge. We have watched his clumsy climb. He breaks through two wrist-thick branches. Joe groans. He wedges the hide-wrapped box flat against the main trunk.

"What in the hell are you waiting for, Joe, our second child?" I hear Mary yell. I see her stand beside the car.

"I dropped something," Joe yells to Mary.

"Nothing like I'm about to drop," she bellows. "Don't be such an idiot. We really gotta get to the maternity ward."

Joe brushes off bits of cedar. Then he runs. He reaches the car. Mary lets him kiss her cheek. "Our fortune is turning," he tells her, full of strange energy.

"What's wrong with you?" Mary asks. She pushes Joe away. They stand beside the passenger door.

Joe knows that the box he was hiding didn't belong to nobody. "I'm sorry, Mary. I've been stumbling."

She holds both sides of her womb. Mary glares. "But what's wrong with you, Joe? You smell like the wood in a sauna."

I hoot loudly. Joe turns to see my silhouette. I fly up into the dim sky and circle the pond. I look for any small animals drinking in the twilight. The same chorus of frogs belch. I hear no other animals. I see no telltale movements. I spy Mary's car. It moves close to the Bone Shrine beside the dead carp and stops.

I circle and look for small animals to eat. Mary is soon in labor. She cries like I never hear from any human. Joe paces and scratches his hair and arms. He goes back to help Mary. He has little help to offer.

I land on a nearby rock outcropping and watch. Joe kicks the stinking carp into the pond. I ignore the cries of the owlet from the nest. I have my own growling stomach to feed.

Where were the fledgling's own parents? The stench from the carp forces me to fly to the other side of the SUV.

Mary edges out of her Pathfinder. She rips off the front buttons from her skirt. It drops to the ground. She kicks it to the stone landing. It falls on top of the stinking fish.

Joe helps her onto her back inside the rear of the car.

He looks to see me circling the pond again. The frog chorus goes quiet. The hot breeze dies down. The croaks are replaced by a buzz. The swarm of mosquitos block out most of the moonlight.

At long last. "She's here," I hear Mary cry. She is still inside the back of her old car.

I kicked off all my blankets. In Gunnar's cold basement room, I gasped for air.

CHAPTER 3

A REQUIEM FOR MARY

A resident wild raven croaked from the museum rooftop. My mother was the director there and wanted to catch up with me, so I'd tagged along until the local artist she was expecting to meet arrived. While they talked, I stepped outside on that Easter, late morning, two days after our failed bust.

"I was told you'd be out here," I said to Joe at the little raptor aviary between her museum and the edge of the bluff overlooking the Columbia River Gorge. I pulled my gray lamb's-wool cap from out of my windbreaker to dull the chill on this clear, blustery day.

Joe turned and smiled broadly, maybe even glad to see me. The Great Northern hooed several times when he turned. He sounded both surprised and almost excited. When the owl flapped its tawny feathered wings, Joe remembered his task and spoke low. "It's alright, Amber, it's only Biff."

Joe was inside the enclosure feeding the bird. "Is that a new owl?" I asked, ignoring his ever-so-slight slight. "The name matches those eyes. When did Amber arrive?"

"Last month." Joe wore his same worn handler's glove that he'd used when he'd worked here in high school. Inside the small aviary, talons clamped down on his fist and the spring sun radiated through marble-clear irises.

Joe's attentiveness to the owl's needs was great to see. "At least *you* get to fly free now," I said.

It was the first time he stared directly my way. "We keep this cage cleaner than my cell was. But I'm being descuzzified, you know, both clean and out of that slammer."

"What crime did this owl commit to be locked up?" I asked.

"Blind Amber was found stunned on Big Muddy Road near the old Rashneeshee Commune."

"With those beautiful eyes––blind? Nothing scuzzy about her," I said. "You'd never know by looking that she can't see."

In the bright noontime light Joe's blue eyes glowed, too, with a calmness that I hadn't seen in years. He always got this way when bird-handling. I'd worried he might have become jaded, but the traumas of the past year had mostly dignified him and definitely aged my friend. He now looked 19 going on 26. His demeanor with this raptor was purposeful, firm and kind, words I never would have used before to describe the former, cocky and impulsive version of himself, especially when he'd been all strung out. I could always tell when he was loaded or high, but seldom said anything to Mary. She kept a blind-eye towards her boyfriend's ugly habit. Seeing him free from jail was wonderful. So was his clear-thinking from being off the junk.

Joe reminded me that his baseball season––the Tri-City Dust Devil's grand opening game––was next Wednesday in the team's brand new ballpark. "They gave us Easter off, but I need to get back this evening for tomorrow's practice. There's a chance I'll be starting at third base."

"Good for you," I told him, trying to sound upbeat, but still too rattled from Friday evening's assault.

For some reason I connected with the big blind owl when she stared through me with those rich, amber eyes. It wasn't the blindness, though, but her attentive ears that captivated me. Amber was definitely paying rapt attention to the conversation that Joe and I were having, turning as though facing her handler when he spoke, and then towards me when I responded. "She's beautiful," I said, and the Great Horned Owl, still on Joe's glove, turned, closed her eyes and then nodded at me.

Before exiting the aviary, Joe placed Amber back on her perch and waited for the main handler to step into the cage with a mouse for her feeding. Joseph actually patted me on the shoulder when he came out. A greeting hug would have been too much to expect from my lifelong nemesis.

"Being a blind owl," said Joe, "is like hearing and knowing you're getting close on Mary's case, but you just can't spot the dirty little rodent."

I half expected to see a curl of sarcasm on his lips, but he was being serious. "My ears and brain haven't registered any helpful clues lately," I said. "The investigation is pretty frustrating."

"Don't worry," said Joe. "I won't call you 'Blind Biffy'."

He'd called me far worse over the years, mostly slams of the overly obvious 'vertically-challenged' ilk, like telling a ticket-taker that I wasn't quite four-foot-twelve when we were getting on a carnival ride at the county fair. Mary had tossed an icy cola in her boyfriend's face when I was actually denied access for being barely under sixty-inches tall.

"Oh, I almost forgot," he added. "Mom told me to tell you that you definitely needed to stop by the house before heading back to Moses Lake."

"Did she tell you why?" I asked, but I had planned to pay her a short visit anyway. Rochelle and I had gotten real close during Joe's trial.

"Nope, and I didn't ask," he said in his usual blunt style with me. "I'm about to walk to town and back home now if you'd care to join me."

I nodded and told him I needed to let my mother know first since she was expecting to be my ride.

"Grown kids with mommies," Joe said and we both laughed.

I hurried back inside the museum. The Gorge Discovery Center was designed to look like two huge, native longhouses, side-by-side. At the far end of the grand hall, I spotted my mother, her back towards me. She was still talking to the local artist, a man I recognized from his salt-and-pepper, beatnik hair and short freeform beard. This was the same spot where I sat stunned when our town had memorialized Mary. I'd never forget that huge, whole-town vigil here, a few days after my best friend drowned.

I walked towards the wall of windows that showcased tall fingers of golden hills dipping into the river's edge. The sculptor leaned over the tail end while Mom stood at the head of a monster fish––17-feet-long and glistening with enough lacquer to make the hardwood striations seem wet.

"Oh, hi there sweetheart. You remember Mr. Stewart. He'll be doing some touch-up on his gem here."

"A wild wedding reception," the sculptor said. "The groom tripped during the first dance. On the way down, my fish caught the diamond edge of his new ring before slapping him good with its tail."

"Let's hope their marriage goes more smoothly," Mom said.

"I've always loved this sturgeon of yours," I told the artist, before kneeling to rub my hand over the gouge. "What kind of wood is it, again?"

"Black Walnut. Took me eight years to coax this river monster out from inside the trunk."

"I almost forgot," said Mom to me when I told her I was taking off with Joe. "A little Easter present. It's our newest addition to the museum gift shop."

Mom wasn't much for hugging but I squeezed her tightly anyway letting her know that, despite my chronic independent streak, I appreciated and missed her. I stuffed the little gift-wrapped present in the pocket of my windbreaker.

"I always loved this wool beanie I got for you, too," she said and held me by my earlobes. Have you decided to like those Birks, too?" she asked.

"Joe's waiting. I really gotta run," I said, not wanting to think of the shoes being spun like frisbees into the Moses Lake scablands. I adjusted my winter cap. "So good to see you. Thank's again for the gift, Mom!"

∼

Joe stood by the Oregon Trail wagon near the museum entrance and tapped the wooden driver's bench to the rhythm of a song that played in his head only. I took a wild guess and imagined him hearing Mary singing. Spotting me, Joe jolted from his reverie and towards the river we walked.

The wide, frothy Columbia rolled in the distance. The frigid April breeze pushed us from behind. I pulled my beanie down over my earlobes and we headed upriver towards town. Away from the parking lot, we descended the riverfront trail that led into The Dalles. Lewis and Clark supposedly camped near here, but no one knew exactly where. Joe motioned for us to sit beneath a good-sized Oregon Ash that only partially blocked the wind. When I looked up at the branches, I recalled how significant this tree was for Joe and Mary. So why was he stopping here with me? Below the wool cap, my short, blonde ponytail whipped at my neck.

He sat while I stood shivering. "How's your whirling life with the Dust Devils?" I asked him.

He perked up. "The hot corner's cool. Beats a cold jail cell." He winced when a gust with dust blasted his sandy hair into a fluttering banner. "Mom got a box seat along the third base line. Wednesday at seven. You should drive down to my opener and sit with her."

"I'll definitely try."

"George Brett, best third baseman in major league history, owns the team," he said. "Oh, and by the way, thanks for giving me a ride to the Tri-Cities this afternoon?"

"A ride? I'll think about it."

"After all I've done for you?"

"Pretty long list, but only if we include what you've done 'to' me. Help me fill up my tank and I'll give you a lift, Mr. Rich Pro Baseball Stud."

"You have me mixed up with Kuma, top pitcher picked by the Chunichi Dragons."

I felt uneasy, but not because of the unrelenting wind, or due to our normal banter. That's what seemed strange. The spot beneath this tree held an energy, like I shouldn't be seated here. I stood and pulled my collar higher so the wind didn't hit my bare neck. I toyed with the wrapped gift first in one hand and then the other, and only then did I picture Mary seated here with Joe at age fifteen.

"What did you get?" He pointed up at the little gift bag I was tapping absently with my fingers. "Something for me?"

"From my mom." I took my time opening the present which, I knew, drove Joe crazy since he was not the sort to patiently save his wrapping paper. Still standing, I turned away just enough so that I was the only one who could see what the small box inside held. "Oh my word. It's perfect, Joe!"

All my emotions hit at the same time when I lifted up the silver medallion by its sterling chain. Same design as the large tattoo covering Mary's back. The engraving of a stylized bear was from a petroglyph on a cliff-face across the river from here. I dangled the medallion for him to see. The attentive, ovoid eyes resembled an owl's. I could feel Mary's presence.

"*She-Who-Watches,*" I said, not expecting my voice to quaver. Without warning, my shoulders started shaking.

"If you were so into Mary's big tattoo," said Joe, "then why didn't you get one of your own, a smaller one even?"

"Because I hate needles." I clasped the chain around my neck and saw how the sterling chain for the medallion made a 'V' down to my breasts.

With my eyes cast at my feet, I decided to confide in Joe. "You have to totally promise me that you won't tell anyone," I said, trying not to blubber. I'd thought I could maintain my resolve not to tell anyone. "Promise me, Joe."

"Jeez, Biff. I promise," said the guy who grew up trying to get one over on me at every turn. I doubt Joe had ever seen me this teary-eyed. After all, he was locked up both during Mary's vigil at the museum, and a hundred days later for her memorial at the Bone Shrine pond.

"After our bust on Friday, there was this guy. I thought he was going to rape and kill me."

"What the holy––I mean, who?!?"

I found myself holding a palm over the medallion when I continued.

"A *Tramposo,*" I said. "Pretty sure it was one of the two guys from jail that tried to kick the holy crap out of you."

"Big dude with a gravelly voice and a howling coyote tattoo on his cheek?" he asked.

I nodded.

"You're lucky that tough ass didn't--," he started to say.

I looked towards the river. "After firing off three bullets at my feet, he assured me that he wasn't there to harm me. He just wanted me to let Captain Condran know the *Tramposos* weren't the killers of Mary and they weren't the China White dealers he was looking to bust."

"Strange way to send a message."

"Except, if he'd approached the State Patrol directly, he'd have been arrested and left trying to make demands from inside some jail. That's why he abducted me. I'm sure of it."

"I don't think those punks murdered Mary," said Joe. "They're small potatoes, not the kind of dealers to be moving quarter-million dollar bundles of smack."

This was good to hear as one more confirmation of my own thinking, but I didn't feel relieved. I'd already told Condran as much. Beyond finding the Bone Shrine culprits, I was barely recovering from being violated and slimed. "The big bastard was hiding in the back of my Loyale and pressed a gun barrel at my temple to take me hostage. "It's just that--"

"--just that what?" he pressed me to answer.

"I just don't think the *Tramposos* killed Mary or were selling that big stash of China White, either, but maybe for a different reason."

"Like what reason?"

"When he told me to relay a message to my boss, his eyes changed. I think he wanted to make me think I was about to be raped and offed so I'd take being his messenger seriously."

"A man of honor? I don't think so," said Joe, almost snarling. His face turned a shade of red that bordered on purple.

I was wondering if I should have told Joe anything about the abduction. His nostrils flared and, with his strong, digging fingers, he unearthed a fist-sized stone. Joe stood and reared back. His throw landed all the way into the wide Columbia. "So you weren't that worried?"

"Like making me go down to the Bone Shrine pond at gunpoint? Nah, I wasn't the least bit rattled. The bullets landing by my feet were no big deal either. And what woman is afraid of being raped at gunpoint? That polite *Tramposo* asked me so sweetly that I couldn't resist telling him that I was all in about getting Captain Condran his precious message."

Joe took a deep breath before looking at me. "Sorry. Just let me know if that lowlife comes near you again," he said. "Trust me. I won't ever be caught, but I've got your back on this one, Biff. For real."

"The *Tramposo* had a gun, so if he'd wanted to rape me, then I would have been raped. If he'd wanted to drown me, then I would have ended up just like..." My voice faded and I rubbed fresh tears from blurry eyes. "I had to tell someone," I said, once I could speak. "Just don't let that foul temper of yours get in the way of your goal, Joe. Make something of your baseball talent. I believe that *Tramposo* bastard when he said that *El Gringo Loco* did it."

"Who's that?"

"Some crazy white guy. Your sparring buddy from jail wanted the State Patrol to know that there weren't any Mexicans involved in the Bone Shrine crimes." I inhaled slowly, deeply, and told him about our failed bust out at the gang's compound.

Joe's knuckles whitened around another throwing stone.

I felt a surge of energy as I talked faster. "No drugs found anywhere during the bust. The gang was tipped off somehow. The *Tramposo* scared the wits out of me, but I believed the bastard."

Joe tossed his new stone several feet directly above him and caught it a few times, like he was thinking.

I looked up at the wind-trembling, Oregon Ash that was just showing its first buds of spring leaves.

"Wasn't this where you and Mary first kissed?" I asked, deciding I needed to change the subject. I tapped my *She-Who-Watches* medallion again before dropping my hands to my side so the chain could hang free.

Joe ignored me by lobbing his rock onto the railroad track where it hit an iron rail and sounded off like a dull bell.

"What if Mary's love for you brought about your eventual justice?" I asked. "What if my love for her has me seeking justice on her behalf, even if avenging her brings risk to myself?"

"Shit happens like it's supposed to happen," Joe said in a very matter-of-fact tone. "For three months, I was locked up in the hole.

Life had sucker-punched me so hard that my head got clear for the first time in over a year."

"How do you mean?"

"Once my thinking got clean and the cravings were gone, then I knew."

"Knew what?"

"No way was I ever again going to be slave to that fake joy flowing through my veins."

"So, you're saying that no way would you have gotten and stayed clean, if you hadn't been set up and framed?" I asked.

"You always had my number," he told me in a low growl. "Yeah, I needed a baseball bat between the eyes to face-plant and then wake up." Joe patted the trunk of the tree we were leaning against and looked up at me. "Some bats are made from ash, and this is Mary's tree. So keep on swinging away as hard as you can, Biff. She still needs you to find her killer."

He stood up and we left Joe and Mary's tree. I followed him down the riverfront trail. We both turned back briefly towards the Discovery Center when we heard the singing. The music was drowned out, though, when a fast-moving freight train clanked past us. Joe walked faster. With shorter legs than his, it took two of my steps to keep up with each stride of his. I was out of breath when he stopped at a bench beside a pond that was a bit above the big river, just enough to overlook the enormous Northwest Aluminum plant. Rippling in the stiff breeze, the pond's layer of duckweed shimmered lime-green in the noon sun, the same color as my Loyale.

"Mary came to me last night," Joe sat and said.

"Tell me," I said, catching my breath and seating myself beside him. We looked towards the vacant smelter that shimmered in the sun much like my medallion was doing.

"Her ginger hair was full and flowing," he said of his dream. "She looked beyond pretty in a red, silk kimono. Even her lipstick matched."

"What did she say to you?"

"Mary never *says* anything when she comes to me.

"What do you think the Japanese robe means?" I asked him.

"I don't know, but Mary was all tender and rocking Gracie in her arms. Then--no mistaking it--the baby looked straight at me and smiled real big."

I looked at the medallion my hand held and saw Mary's owl eyes staring back and shimmering. "When Kuma flew in to claim his baby daughter last winter, he kept calling you 'Uncle Joe'."

Walking up the wind-protected cul-de-sac of old houses to Rochelle's Victorian felt strange, relaxed even, a nice change of pace. Four doors down, a new homeowner was gardening beside a re-roofed and re-sided Cape Cod, the rundown one Mary's mother had rented for years. The man was on his knees and his toddler would hand him a tool or clumps of pansies to plant. The flower beds were never tended when it was just Mary and her mom living there. And when Joe didn't treat mowing their yard as though it was an extension of his own family's lawn, then his girlfriend's place looked as disheveled as the captain's unruly hair.

Joe and I turned around and looked when we heard Rochelle's Dodge Minivan rolling towards us into her driveway.

Rochelle pushed open the driver's door with her elbow. "Joe, can you please grab some luggage? She turned and told the passenger that the bathroom was behind the stairwell.

When Joe walked around the rear of the van to get to the sliding door on the passenger side, the young woman in the driver's seat got out and eased around the front bumper before taking a few steps towards the front porch. I'd seen her in photos, but it took a second to register. "Welcome," I managed to say without telling her my name. She turned back and smiled, palms pressed at her chest.

"Yes. My brother speaks of Biff McCoy. You write him many letters." At this she bowed to me with Japanese gracefulness. "My name is Tomiko Kusumoto."

Instinctively, I returned the bow.

I expected Joe to razz me for bowing, but maybe jail time, or most likely Kuma's sister, was taming him, at least foe the moment of being such a smart-ass.

"Thank you for your help, Joe Gardner," Tomiko said before

pivoting and bowing toward him too. "So nice to meet you."

After a tongue-tied pause, Joe managed a shy, "likewise." I noticed how he hadn't taken his eyes off her until she acknowledged him. Then he'd immediately looked at his feet. I'd never seen him this shy before.

Tomiko hurried up the entry steps into the house. Again, Joe watched her every graceful step. The boy was full-on moonstruck. What would Mary be thinking? Maybe it had something to do with the red kimono that Mary was wearing in Joe's dream. Still, August to April had only been eight months.

I fetched Tomiko's smaller suitcase and a duffel bag and promptly carried them into the antique-adorned living room where I set them beside the upright piano. The last time I saw Rochelle, she'd let her hair go gray at the roots. Not today. She was obviously delighted to be meeting Kuma's slightly older sister and had restored full burgundy-in-a-bottle to her thick locks.

While we waited for Tomiko to freshen up, I went into the dining room that separated the kitchen and living room. I loved the small grotto recessed into an inside wall of the dining room. In the recess, Rochelle displayed the coolest small statue of Mother Mary holding the infant Jesus. Above the grotto, Rosary Beads hung from a cross that was same size as the statuette. This reminded me that I'd left my *juzu* beads, or Buddhist Rosary, in the Moses Lake doublewide and needed to retrieve them, but only if Gunnar's dad, Nils, accompanied me to their rental.

A lone, narrow window opened into Rochelle's backyard and the laced curtains over all the inside windows perfectly matched the Victorian feel of her well-appointed home. The walls were filled with color photos of Joe showing his progression from T-ball through Little League, and then Babe Ruth into American Legion baseball. A nicely framed one featured him and Kuma holding up two trophies for most valuable hitter and pitcher when their Columbia Gorge Hustlers won the State of Oregon's Legion championship in 1999. I definitely didn't blame Rochelle, but I noticed how she'd purged her home of any photos showing her ex-husband. He'd left her for Mary's hard-drinking, blues-singing mother a few months before Mary's drowning.

We assembled in the living room. Rochelle sat on her piano bench facing away from the keyboard and towards Tomiko and me. We occupied her couch while Joe sat upright in the recliner. His mom apologized for not having an Easter dinner for them, despite having just driven to and from the Portland International Airport, eighty miles away.

"My dad said he'd pick me up in a little bit," I told Rochelle, "but I'll do my best to snag some thick ham slices and mashed potato leftovers at home to bring back here so you guys can enjoy a bit of Easter feasting. Then Joe and I can hit the road before dark."

"I have a Chamber Luncheon tomorrow and am going to the Tri-Cities for Joe's opener on Wednesday, so it would be really awesome if you could take both Joe and Tomiko with you," she said in that lovely tone of hers that no one could refuse——not that I wouldn't help with this request. "And, no I don't want you driving back up there in the dark," she added.

The daylight driving bit sounded exactly like my own mother's style of worrying. "That's more than fine, but where exactly will I be taking Tomiko?" I asked.

"Of course. I almost forgot. We wanted this to be a surprise for you," said Rochelle. "Someone nice to keep you company in Moses Lake."

Tomiko looked at me squarely. "I am new student for JATP at Big Bend College where you study," she said. "My brother say that you do Nichiren chant."

"I do," I said, but not as much as I should." Maybe she and I could chant together sometime, I thought. Had Kuma sent her sister to befriend me?"

For some reason, I assumed she'd come to do an exchange by staying in The Dalles with Rochelle. It might be nice, actually, to have her in Moses Lake. It's not like I'd made any new girlfriends there.

"What's JATP?" Joe asked her.

"It is Japanese Agricultural Training Program," said Tomiko. "Two months of time I study American farming."

"Darla called about coming to Joe's home opener," Rochelle said. "My sister mentioned that you'd slept at their place in Gunnar's old bedroom on Friday night because you were getting worried about being alone in the doublewide. She didn't want to bother you over Easter with your family, but said to tell you, once again, that of course you can stay at her home if that makes you feel more comfortable."

"Perfect," I said.

"I am to stay at a Big Bend College dormitory," said Tomiko to me. "You please visit me there. And JATP have me work for Joe's uncle at Columbia Gorge Potato Grower Association. I learn to market spuds."

The idea of hawking boring potatoes made me laugh. "I thought your father sold Columbia Gorge cherries in Tokyo. "Bings taste so much sexier than spuds!"

"Yes, I help market fresh fruit in Tokyo. Our family import produce from all over world. "We buy Bing and Rainier Cherries from here when ripe and firm. They come on jet airplane inside vacuum-seal."

"Those vacuum-sealed cherries are what brought Kuma to The Dalles and our home," said Joe.

I also noticed how he Bing-blushed every time he spoke to her.

"That's how your Dad was introduced to my Mom and she found out Kuma was a pitcher looking to play in America," he added.

"Yes. This is good way my family join your family to be friends," said Tomiko.

"So cool he got to live here and pitch on my team." Joe said, his voice was definitely softer than usual. It sure showed that he'd really forgiven Tomiko's brother after Kuma visited Joe in jail when he'd come to America to accept responsibility for raising Gracie.

"We had no idea Kuma was so highly rated as a young Japanese pitcher when he came," Rochelle said to Tomiko and she nodded humbly.

We all looked at one another unsure of what to say. Finally, Joe, still so uncharacteristically on best behavior, spoke to Tomiko. "My mom plays some kick-ass piano."

Tomiko laughed. "She kick this piano in butt?"

"It's actually true. Rochelle's a really talented pianist," I said and smiled at Tomiko. "You should have heard her accompany Mary Quinn," I added. "This sofa we're sharing was the best spot for listening to Mary's voice and Mrs. Gardner's playing!"

"I like this necklace," Tomiko leaned in towards me and said. Even with a compliment as simple as this, Kuma's sister came off as downright classy.

"*She-Who-Watches*," I told her, but stopped short of saying anything about Mary having this as a tattoo nearly covering her back.

Joe explained how it came from a nearby petroglyph. "Rock art by Indians," he added, getting Tomiko to look at my medallion in a way that she finally understood.

Even up close, I couldn't get over how much Tomiko's face was a gracile, feminine version of Kuma's.

"So when is baby Gracie going to pay us a visit?" Joe asked.

"My mother and father bring baby for visit when I finish agriculture-exchange student program in Moses Lake," Tomiko told him. "They come in middle of June."

"That's the perfect Bing cherry time," said Joe, blushing again. He looked away when she turned her Japanese doll-face his way again. I recalled Kuma saying his sister was two years older than him. That made her twenty-one or thereabouts.

When I complimented Tomiko on how well she spoke English, she said that, as children, she and Kuma had the same English language tutor.

"How's the Bone Shrine investigation going?" Rochelle asked me.

"It's going," I said, "but we could sure use some fresh clues."

"Kuma and I chant every day for you to find killer of Mary Quinn," said Tomiko. Beneath the poise and her decisive manner of sitting and speaking, I sensed a strength in Tomiko that her slender frame and gracious refinements belied. This made her loveliness shine.

"I chant, too," I told her, not adding that I'd skipped too many days lately.

"Yes. Kuma tell me this," Tomiko said when she stood to go open her large suitcase parked at the base of the stairs. "I have new photos of Gracie," she added.

Rochelle shifted over to the couch so she and I could see the beautiful child of Mary's and Kuma's. Joe stood behind the sofa, so he could also see. He smiled at the sight in a way that told me he'd moved beyond his earlier animosity towards Kuma.

Rochelle went over to her piano keyboard and played Mary's

lullaby, my friend's signature Oregon Trail song.

The door knocker startled us. Joe got up to see my father standing in the threshold. I got up, excused myself, and promised to return in an hour or so with Easter leftovers and my Loyale gassed up to roll.

~

CHAPTER 4

NO STONE UNTURNED

Captain Condran had been strategizing all weekend. First thing after I showed up on Monday after lunch, he was speaking to the cork bulletin board. In my college notebook, I jotted down: *April, the 16th, riffing with the boss.*

When I sat in my usual oak chair, feet hooked around the front legs, the boss pivoted around on his swivel desk chair to face me, his elbows on our *Investigation Central* table.

Tapping the bulletin board with his pointer, the captain then singled out Linh Riggleman's name. It was connected by yellow yarn to her father-in-law, Roger, a gray one to her husband, Zach, and a pink one to baby Grace's and Mary's card. Roger's card had yarn connecting him to most everyone connected to this case. "Like I said in our helpful brainstorming session on Friday night, since Roger's locked up and awaiting trial, I think it's someone else running the show. Otherwise, why wouldn't the *Tramposos* simply finger the chief detective since they suspect he's already about to go down for many years?"

"Good point, Boss." I said, and stood before stabbing Roger's card with another thumb tack into the letter 'o'. That man laid our crime scene to waste."

Condran tapped my new, metallic tack with his pointer. "Never saw anything like it in my thirty years of detective work," he said and winced. "I'm still trying to figure out how I was suckered into thinking the *Tramposos* were our chief suspects in this case."

My eyes widened. "Simple, isn't it, Boss? Like I said before. They were close enough to all the action."

The boss pressed his lips together and nodded. "Yes, but it's more plausible that they caught on to being set-up as the new fall-guys. That's when threatened *Mr. Loco* with blowing his cover completely if he didn't show that he had their back."

"Like tipping them off that their compound was about to be busted," I added. "And then warning you, through me, to back off."

"Exactly, but by only giving you their internal nickname for their drug-dealing partner."

"As in, no one outside of the *Tramposo* ring knows he's called *El Gringo Loco*," I added.

"One more reason why we need to give our investigative effort one last, big push," he added. He patted my stack of index cards and pushed them across the table to me. "Start with all the banks in Wanapum County. Finding Gunnar Larsson's lockbox will likely confirm his role in our case."

Condran also handed me a life-sized photo of the safe-deposit box key. "I'll focus on our other key priority," he said and took off his tweed blazer, placing it on the back of a folding chair. "Help me pick a dozen or so people with a distinct connection to our case. For starters, I want to meet with Joe's lawyer, Angus MacIntosh."

Condran then plopped a small stack of his own WSP business cards in front of me. "In case you bump into anyone else connected to our case, please ask them to contact me directly, *comprende gringa?*"

I nodded, not wanting to show him I was psyched to take on most any task that wasn't office-bound. "We could definitely withstand an avalanche of newly turned over stones," I said.

The Moses Lake branch of the Columbia Basin Credit Union, a sterile, all-windowed financial institution featured barely audible Muzak playing in the background. The musical notes were so low they sounded like faucet drips more than a melodic tune. The head teller, jaw clenched and arms crossed, stood guarded. I think she thought I was out scouting for the branch's security vulnerabilities. "Our keys look nothing like that," she said tersely. "Is there anything else I can help you with?"

I thanked her and visited the next bank on my list situated a block away in the small city's open downtown area. The manager of the sparse Wanapum Bank was downright congenial, but no more help than the last lady. He took me into the vault where their lockboxes were and showed me their bank's master key. It wasn't as long as the one dredged up by the old fisherman. Its brass glistened like the bank's key, but was a different thickness of casting.

The assistant manager of Farmers Bank of the Northwest was polite, even though he kept clearing his throat like he was about to choke on a dry potato chip. An irate customer was berating a teller. I could tell the man I was speaking with needed to attend to the outburst. "Sorry, Miss, but our keys aren't even close to the one in your photo," he then rasped and, with a forced smile, he ushered me hastily out the front entrance.

The next bank displayed a sign in front bragging about being part of the largest and oldest financial institution in the Pacific Northwest. The stately building had a date of 1926 etched into the granite baluster welcoming customers up to the entrance. It also offered me someone helpful. A seasoned officer, old enough to be well past retirement age, came up and, before asking for details, gestured for me to follow his hunched-over gait to a desk in the farthest corner of the main lobby. He held my chair and pushed it forward before seating himself in his larger chair opposite me. The Cascade Mutual building had a much larger, more old-fashioned vault than the other banks, but the older man stayed and wobbled in his chair rather than hunt down the bank's master key. He introduced himself as Mr. Owen Schneider, manager emeritus, and took out a magnifying glass to look closely at the life-sized photo I showed him. "Young lady, have you looked at the four-digit number stamped into the top of the key here?"

"Yes, actually."

"Good. Then see this detail here," he said and turned my photo before letting me borrow his magnifying glass. "Look at the 'seven' imprinted on this key."

I hadn't noticed this detail before. "It has a horizontal slash in the vertical part of the number," I said, surprised.

"That's the European style of writing a 'seven'." He told me how he'd spent several years in Germany while in the service during the early 1950s."

"Are you thinking this lockbox key is from a German bank?"

He shrugged and smiled, as though he enjoyed the sleuthing. "I'm suggesting, simply, that it might not be for something used in an American financial institution, including our own here."

"Do you think the key might be from Sweden?" I asked, thinking of Nils and Gunnar Larsson.

"Might be," he said. "The Scandinavians use the same horizontal slash."

The older man started to describe the Hanseatic League of trading ports that controlled commerce across northern Europe from the 13th through the 15th centuries. I waited for him to pause before smiling broadly. "Sir, you've been a great help," I said, "but I do have a few more stops today."

He walked me to the door and stood there until I got into my car to leave. He reminded me of my own Grandpa McCoy. The mid-afternoon sun blazed overhead. I had to adjust the visor above my windshield in order to see. Everything about this case was blinding.

~

Dad had slipped me some cash before I left The Dalles the afternoon before, so I decided, on the spot, that I should show some appreciation to the Larssons for letting me stay in Gunnar's old bedroom. I was thinking I'd get some special goodies they might like. I found an empty Safeway cart at the entrance and meandered through the produce aisle deciding against veggies or fruits on my way to the cheese section in back. That's when I saw Big Max. He leaned into the case of frozen meats to load up his cart with burgers, pizza pockets, chicken strips, and hot dogs. He moved across the aisle to the frozen vegetable section for bags of succotash, green beans, and Asian stir-fry until it looked like he was stocking up for the next year.

Life always swept me this way or that with competing currents and whirlpools. Here I was, still unable to forget about the abduction, knowing I needed to focus even harder on the investigation, and also figure out how to harness my midterm paper. But this guy was so tall and big that he compelled me to check out if he was as handsome as I recalled from Joe's trial. He hadn't yet noticed me where I waited between a mid-day shopping housewife and a pokey grandpa studying labels without placing anything in his cart.

I remembered Joe saying how his jail guards treated him fine in solitary. Every day I'd watched the big guy escorting Joe in and out of the courtroom. Peeking around another elderly lady with poofed-up, blue hair, I studied Max, looked down, and then glanced again, hopefully without gawking. I had too much to do today, so why, when he turned away, did I instinctively follow after him––forty-feet behind?

Maybe it was just a primal, procreative urge where I projected that, one day, I'd have normal-sized kids with Big Max, this real tall, real big, real handsome young guy. Maybe my subconscious mind was calculating that my four foot, eleven-and-a-half-inch shortness mixed with his thick-chested, six-foot-five-or-more inch frame would grow perfectly normal, good-looking, six-foot-tall boys and five-foot-eight-inch, shapely girls?

I shook my head. Why was my mind fixating where I'd always landed on my duff?

Flushed with self-embarrassment, I stopped where he'd turned abruptly to face an grown man with the same oversized build and loading a stack of thick ribeye steaks into Max's basket. Bottles clanked when he lowered two cases of Henry's Private Reserve above the wheels that were beginning to wobble in protest. "Get this meat into your new freezer chest as soon as you get to the cove. You hear me, son?"

"Pretty sure I can handle that, Pops. Mom tells me I better not forget to vacuum up the mouse turds, too," he said with a wry smile. "Especially before you two come down and take your friends boating next week."

His father agreed. "We got us four other couples next weekend, so the cabin will be put to use when we're docked." When his flip phone rang, Max's old man opened it. "I need to take the call," he whispered to his son. "Serious business. I'll meet you at the car."

"Got some cash?" Max asked, before his dad could turn and leave.

His father pulled out a money clip and handed over some bills to Max. "Since you're moving to the cove, definitely follow your mama's shopping list down to the last item," he whispered. "Especially the cleaning supplies."

Joe's jail guard nodded to his father. The two didn't look much alike, except for their size. Of the two, Max was definitely the looker.

I trailed even farther behind when Max loaded his cart with tooth-paste, shampoo, deodorant, Ajax, Lysol, and Dove dishwashing soap and sponges, as well as a new mop and broom. He then added a few party-sized bags of chips.

To keep from being obvious, I read the label on a jar of pickled beets, the only vegetable I loathed. He pressed forward, but for no reason, pivoted back towards me at the far end of the magazine and greeting card row. I froze, except for picking up a day-after-he-had-risen-better-late-than-never Easter card. He stopped and wedged *Off-Roading Magazine* on top of his overfilled cart. He didn't seem to notice me.

The best test came when he rolled his groceries through the pharmacy section and bypassed the rack of condoms without so much as a sideways glance. Guessing that he wasn't a *playa* made me want to play with him right then and there.

Before he headed towards the bakery section, he seemed to look back at me, but kept moving. I stopped at the end of my aisle and watched him top off his cart with a few packs of sourdough buns.

He stopped again, turned his head, and stared straight through me. What if he didn't realize I was the same Goth chick in the gallery with black-dyed hair, the one there to watch Joe's trial most every day? I was pretty sure he'd been checking me out back then. So much for restoring my natural blonde locks.

"Aren't you Joe Gardner's friend from the trial?" he asked after rolling his cart up to mine.

He must have seen my face turning red. He actually did know who I was. "Yes. Hi. I'm Biff." I hoped my voice didn't reveal my nerves.

"I'm Max. My brother called me today. He's the groundskeeper at the new minor league ballpark in Pasco."

"Yes. You told us on the day Joe went free. He works for the Dust Devils," I said, squeezing the handle of my cart much too hard.

"Yeah. Talked to him today. Said that Joe was just named the starter at third base," Max said.

"Awesome!" I said, truly grinning with delight at the news. "Are you surprised Joe is as good a player as he told you he was?" I asked.

"MVP in Oregon's American Legion championship game is what he told me in his cell. Not the kind of thing a guy would lie about."

"When it comes to baseball, the skies the limit for Joe," I added.

"Well, I really gotta get rolling, Biff," he said. "Moving day."

I stood dumfounded, but then remembered to hand him a business card.

"What's this for?" he asked, looking surprised.

"A business card. For Captain Condran of the Washington State Patrol. I'm interning there."

Max looked at the spare official-looking card and jiggled it between his fingers.

"Maybe something will come to mind about the case."

"Why not call you instead?" he asked.

I froze, not sure what my expression was.

"Did your boss tell you that last Christmastime, he interviewed everyone from the Wanapum County Sheriff Department, including me when I was working my jail shift?"

"Maybe you'll recall an odd event or connection or something someone said in jail," I told him.

He shrugged. "Cool to see you again."

When Big Max turned his cart and left, I stopped at the section of fancy cheeses. He hurried up to a check-out register where no one was waiting. I remembered him promising Joe that he'd go to the opening game if my friend made the team, so why hadn't I said that I was definitely going, too? The day after tomorrow to be exact. Maybe I should have flirted with Max a bit more and he would have extended me an invite to sit with him. Or maybe not.

Before I checked out, I ended up buying a couple nice bricks of Scandinavian cheeses and a box of Aplets & Cotlets, a confection that was made not too far upriver from here. Darla and Nils would prob-ably approve.

I carried my single bag of groceries outside. When I reached my Loyale and opened the driver's door, I stopped to watch a shiny, black, brand new Lincoln Navigator with a temporary license plate parked behind me, three spots away. The SUV pulled out and rolled beside me. When the front passenger window lowered, Max flashed me an endearing smile and one thumb up. After a couple seconds, his father sped away.

My heart pounded. Big Max sure was hard to figure. It wasn't the sort of goodbye that fueled any hope of him liking me.

I checked the time and realized I needed to pick up Tomiko.

The Columbia Basin Potato Growers Association was located within easy earshot of the freeway. Tomiko was on her first day working as a marketing intern. I parked and entered a classy, glass building that looked like it was built in the late 1970s. The receptionist walked me down a longish hallway. Tomiko's face lit up when she saw me enter the front part of the executive director's office suite. She seemed so genuinely appreciative of me driving her to Moses Lake and getting her squared away in her Big Bend College dorm. I likewise appreci-ated her gas money and ever-polite company. Sure seemed like we were becoming friends.

"This young lady's refreshingly professional," said Nils when he came out of the big office behind Tomiko and smiled at me. He still possessed a hint of a Scandinavian accent. He was tall like Gunnar, with the same thin, light-blond hair and matching brows, but balding more on top. Nils was broader in the shoulders and he filled most of the doorway into his office. The thick, ornate, double doors opened inwards. Carved images of potato combines and bushels overflowing with spuds caught my eye. The relief images gave a depth to the wood and were 'quite convincing' as my mom would say when we'd visit art museums. Nils saw what I was examining and told me that the son of one of the biggest potato farmers in the area was a carver of wood, and the association had commissioned several works of his. "Oregon white oak," said Nils.

The way it was lacquered reminded me of Jeff Stewart's sturgeon carving. Nils had always been nice to me, especially since renting Gunnar's doublewide from him and Darla. She made Nil's come out to check on me every couple of days. He'd even taken me on a dirt bike riding adventure one afternoon along an obscure trail leading from Gunnar's doublewide to the Bone Shrine pond a few miles away. "Say Nils, could I have a couple minutes of your time before we leave?" I asked, trying to sound pleasant and relaxed since this was my first 'interview'––actually the second one if I counted Big Max.

"Let's do it now, but you'll have to ask Darla if it has anything to do with lowering your rent for Gunnar's bedroom," Nils told me with a wry smile.

I entered his large office that greeted us with a huge, matching oak wall mural and desk. The sectioned, two-inch thick carving, two feet high and in four sections across the wall behind Nils' head, featured a long row of farmers in coveralls holding spades. It reminded me a bit of "American Gothic" by Grant Wood. I ran my fingers over the lacquered surface of the desk before I sat in a padded, comfortable oak chair facing Nils. "What can I do for you, Biff?"

Even seated there, he loomed above me. "One of my intern duties is to re-contact anyone who might remember something new about what happened on August 17th and 18th, particularly in regards to Mary Quinn's drowning." Just asking the question caused a surge of emotion inside that I wasn't expecting. My eyes began to sting, but I held back my tears.

"This must be hard on you," said Nils. "I mean with Mary being your best friend and all."

I sat up straight and took a quick breath before speaking. "I just want to find who killed her," I said and pushed my blonde locks back over my shoulder, smiling in a way that was neither humored nor light-hearted.

I extended Condran's business card to him and he examined it front and back. "Anything you might recall from that night, or even after, such as something concerning the kidnapping of the infant––

Mary's baby. A small detail even, or forgotten until recently. If you think of anything whatsoever, then please call Captain Condran."

Nils Larsson examined my boss's business card, front and back, and remained very poised when he spoke. "So your leads are drying up?" he asked, in a matter-of-fact tone. "I've heard that some people think my son killed Mary Quinn. That is not true. If that's why the Captain sent you here, then please tell him—what is the expression? That he's clawing up the wrong tree."

The way Nils stood up abruptly and loomed over his huge desk kept me from correcting him. He seemed suddenly cold and impatient to send me on my way. "I will see you at home," was all he said once he ushered me back through his wide, reopened door.

He spoke to Tomiko at the small desk outside his office door and told her to do her best when reading the promotional materials for the association. "Consider it your first assignment starting tomorrow afternoon. You've done enough for today."

"Good history of potato association." She said and smiled at him with her lovely grace and a slight nod. A stack of brochures and booklets were already in a perfectly neat pile on a much smaller desk made of similar White Oak. She slipped the ones she'd read into a modest cloth satchel covered and set it beside the unread stack.

"Thank you for your help today, Mr. Larsson," she said after standing and bowing.

He smiled tensely and locked the big double doors into his office before ushering Tomiko and me politely into the hallway. Nils still held Condran's card when following us into the entryway. After we thanked him again and started across the vacant street to where I'd parked, I took a quick look over my shoulders. Nils was dropping the captain's business card into a tall trash receptacle. I didn't say anything about this to Tomiko. Nils had turned to talk to the receptionist.

Tomiko seemed quite delighted with her new opportunity to intern with Nils. She mentioned again that she never imagined the history of local potato farming to be so interesting.

"What was the single most fascinating thing you read today?" I asked her as we drove off to my last destination before taking her back to the dorm.

"Washington state potatoes from the Columbia Basin are same as most famous potatoes in the world."

"What makes you say that?"

"Idaho spuds. Most famous, but sandy soil and Idaho river is same as Columbia River land here."

I hadn't ever thought of it that way. She really was perceptive. "The Dalles is even a bit farther downstream, but we don't have much flat, arable soil."

"But you have Bing cherry trees."

"Yes. There are the orchards," I said and concentrated for the next address I needed, deciding it couldn't hurt to have Tomiko come inside with me.

"What is DSHS?" she asked as I drove past the sign.

"Department of Social and Health Services for the state of Washington."

It was already 4:00 pm so I hoped we weren't too late. The lady at the front office directed us to an adjoining building where Child Protective Services was housed. When we entered, it just so happened that Amanda Skerry was ushering a young Hispanic couple with their toddler from her office towards the entry.

"She looks like photo I see of Mary Quinn," Tomiko whispered in surprise.

"They do look alike," I answered just as quietly, "if Mary had lived to be thirty, that is."

"These two young ladies asked if they could have a minute of your time," the woman at the front desk said to Amanda.

She looked tired and ready to go home, so I expected I'd need to set up a formal appointment for another day. "Hi, I'm Biff McCoy, a close friend of Mary Quinn and now working as an intern on her investigation."

"Yes, hello," she said formally extending her hand. "I remember you from the day of the kidnapping."

"And this is Kuma Kusumoto's sister, Tomiko. She just arrived in Moses Lake as an agricultural exchange student. I came in today to touch bases with you. A minute or two is all I need."

She looked at her wrist watch. "I have another appointment now, but it looks as though they're running late."

"They just called and are ten minutes away," the front desk lady confirmed.

Amanda nodded my way and ushered us back to her office.

"I promise we'll make this very quick," I said again as we followed.

Amanda turned and looked at Tomiko.

"Your brother, Kuma. How is fatherhood for him?" she asked.

"He is good father. Our mother help much with the baby."

"From what Kuma wrote me, Aunt Tomiko also helps a great deal," I added.

"Good to hear. Send Kuma my best wishes. Such a darling baby."

I recalled that Amanda had cared for Grace in her own home until the temporary foster arrangement could be set.

After we sat, it only took me a couple minutes to tell Amanda why we'd stopped by and what we were hoping to accomplish by looking for fresh leads.

"I'll definitely give this some thought," she said. "And I'm glad the state patrol hasn't given up searching," she added.

I chose not to tell her how close we were to having our case shut down.

❧

SMOHALLA

I didn't have any classes so I spent Tuesday morning, the seventeenth, visiting the rest of the banks and credit unions in Moses Lake. The captain thought it best that I not wear my new Special Ops clothes, but hand out his card whenever it seemed appropriate, especially if I stumbled upon someone not on his target list that we'd overlooked for him to talk with about the case.

Even though my sage-colored, crepe blouse and pants suit seemed appropriately professional, what a total waste of an effort finishing up in Moses Lake.

It was the chance to make similar inquiries in Wanapum's county seat that I couldn't wait for--Big Max might just be in Smohalla. Wheatland Bank, Wanapum Credit Union and a few tiny branches of large chain banks like Washington Mutual offered no matches either.

I waited until 3:00 pm when I expected that Max might be coming off his day shift. Only then did I park my car across the street from the courthouse square in a spot adjoining the Methodist Church. I tried standing nonchalantly so I could watch the lot next to the Wanapum Sheriff building where the jail guards and deputies parked.

When he got out of an older, big box of a Bronco, I recognized Squat Sammy, Joe's nickname for him during the trial. Being vertically-challenged myself, I would never call Sammy that. He wasn't much older than I was and there weren't many men I could stare at eye-to-eye with, or even almost. I hustled over. "Can I talk to you?"

He looked over one shoulder and then the other with wide, mossy-green eyes that seemed too innocent for a jail guard. He wasn't sure if it was cool to chat with me, probably because quite a few of those working at the Wanapum County Sheriff Department knew I was interning at the State Patrol. "I remember you from the trial," he said, trying to smile. "What's up?"

"We're still trying to find Mary Quinn's real killer. You know she was my best friend, right?"

Sammy glanced over at the back side of the tall, rural courthouse probably deciding whether or not to talk any further with me. He motioned for us to walk across the street behind a church passenger van in the Smohalla Methodist parking lot. We stood out of sight of any prying eyes. This was the house of worship with steeple bells that rang with hymns every hour or so.

Sammy spoke just above a whisper. "We were told not to talk about the Bone Shrine busts to anyone. Strict orders. That includes both the murder of your friend and that screwed up heroin deal."

I wasn't going to let him off easy. "Did those marching orders come down last summer during the county's criminal investigation, or in December when the State Patrol's internal investigation of the Wanapum Sheriff Department began?"

"Since the troopers swept in," he answered right off which surprised me. "It's been about clearing with my boss whatever I say to anyone––chain-of-command stuff." Sammy also had a slight smile on one side of his mouth that made him seem happier than he probably was.

I handed him one of Captain Condran's WSP cards.

A late model Chevy Silverado pickup edged slowly up the alleyway behind the church until it got close to us. Sammy turned immediately and walked away in the opposite direction so he was out of sight of the truck driver. "I'll be right back," he said over his shoulder.

When the Silverado rolled slower, I recognized the lean man behind the wheel. He'd testified on the first day of Joe's trial. He braked and glared, so I held up a business card and walked directly towards him. Wouldn't it be grand if Deputy Sheriff Zach Riggleman was the one to help our investigation uncover Mary's actual murderer? I thought, except he rolled up his window, looked away from me, and accelerated across the empty street. This brave cop, the one so quick to point a Glock at Joe Gardner's temple on the night of the drowning, wanted nothing whatsoever to do with what I might be handing him. He most definitely knew where I was interning and what we were seeking.

Deputy Riggleman parked next to the civilian cars of his coworkers, including a cherried-out, red, Shelby Cobra Mustang from the early 1970s.

After watching the deputy step out of his pickup, Sammy returned with two cans of Diet Pepsi. "That is one killer, hot car," I told him and pointed. "I wonder who it belongs to."

"That's Sheriff Usk's ride," he said and politely popped open two cans. Sammy had us move half-hidden behind the church van again and handed me one of the sodas. "You looked like you could use a nice cold pop."

He wasn't wrong, but I don't know why he assumed I drank *diet* cola. "Thank you for the zero calories," I said making sure he saw me pat my ample hip with a free hand. "And you looked like you were running scared of that deputy. Why?"

Sammy shrugged and leaned in to talk softly. "Everybody's running scared of everybody inside the sheriff department these days, and since you're tied to the Washington State Patrol investigation, anyone who catches wind of that will run scared of you, too," he said looking over his shoulder.

"Why talk to me, then?"

"Because you don't look anything like a trooper, or some seasoned detective."

When his flip phone rang, Sammy extracted it from the thigh pocket of his black, jail work pants. "Yo Max, you won't believe who I'm talking to," Sammy said into the open receiver.

"Remember that short girl that always came to Joe Gardner's trial?"

I lifted my palms skyward and frowned to remind him that, sure I was short, but also standing right in front of him with perfectly functional ears. His one-sided smile grew bigger. My cheeks burned. Big Max might actually like me.

"No problem," said Sammy. "But I gotta get going, so make it fast." With his phone still flipped open, he handed it to me.

"Hello," I said, shyly. Max's tone was deep and I nodded before remembering that I needed to use my voice.

"Wasn't expecting to talk with you. It's Eliza-biff, right?"

"And you're Maxwell, aren't you?" I asked, trying, but unable not to giggle.

"It's Maximillian, believe it or not, but I go by Max."

"And you can call me 'Biff,' like everyone else does."

Sammy stood looking over his shoulder at the courthouse, his anxious eyes wanting us to hurry up with his precious phone.

"Should I call you Elizabeth if we go out for a formal steak dinner?" he asked.

Was he on the up and up? "If we're on a first date, you must call me, 'Ms. Elizabeth,'" I said, to which Sammy rolled his eyes before motioning me to hurry.

"How about tonight, Miss Lizzy Beth?" Max added. "Seven sharp. The Moses Lake Porterhouse Steakhouse."

"Sure. I'll see you at 7:00 pm, Sir Maximillian."

I stood stunned after handing the phone to Sammy. How had I managed to get a real live date tonight? There was something different than nervous joy churning inside me, though, no to mention that I still had work to do if I was to get anyone to share fresh lockbox key leads with my state patrol boss. So much confusion about my topsy-turvy life rumbled from guts to brain, including if I was ready to go on a date.

I wanted to ask Sammy if his distrust of other county workers included Max. Instead, he brought it up on his own.

"Just so you know, Big Max and me are buddies outside of work, too," he said. "Since before high school. Don't you dare say a word to him, but he was sure kicking himself for not asking you out yesterday when he saw you at Safeway."

"Thanks for letting Max talk to me on your phone. Oh, and the captain, the contact on the card I gave you, he's cool. He won't pass on anything you reveal to him," I said. "It's still all about finding Mary Quinn's killer. You want justice for her, don't you?"

Sammy nodded uneasily. "I gotta stay on my toes is all. And now I gotta get inside for a double shift--swing and graveyard." At this, he tucked his official evergreen jail-guard shirt into his pants and bolted across the street towards his Ford Bronco. I watched him reach into the glove compartment and grab some papers before disappearing inside the jail.

I still had my stack of the Captain's business cards left and crossed the empty Smohalla town street into the courtyard fronting the Wanapum County Courthouse. At the base of the steps, Jack Pack stood in civilian blue jeans and a snap-up Wrangler's rodeo shirt. As soon as I walked up and greeted him, he gave me the latest news. "I've been placed on indefinite administrative leave with a likely Loudermill next week. Also, tell your boss that Sheriff Usk is threatening to take Escher away from me."

"A dog isn't like a service pistol," I said. "This Wanapum sheriff election has turned some kind of serious." Escher rested on a blanket beside Pack who managed to smile at each prospective voter when handing out leaflets. There was only a light flow of people exiting down the courthouse steps and Jack seemed to know most of those that were county workers.

After asking him if it was okay, he nodded and I knelt down to pet Escher. From the lively tail, the Dutch Shepherd, still flat on the blanket, enjoyed my attention. "What's a Loudermill?" I asked.

"A legal hearing for unionized public employees to present their case against being terminated," came a voice from behind me. It was definitely higher than Pack's. Before I could turn around, Angus MacIntosh, the defense attorney for Joe's trial, was also on a knee and petting Escher. "How are you, Biff?"

I told him about my internship and the criminal justice program at Big Bend College.

"And I've hired Mr. MacIntosh to represent me at my hearing," said Jack Pack, handing another brochure to a passerby. "Sheriff Usk contends I shouldn't have participated in Friday's bust without his permission."

"With the probable intent that no one within the Wanapum

County Sheriff Department helps solve Mary Quinn's murder," said Angus when we both stood at the same time.

"Yesterday, the sheriff put me on administrative leave. I've taken charge of the K-9 unit for years and have always been available to assist other deputies and other area police forces, too, like on Friday. This is Usk's way of getting back at me for running against him."

"And another way to cover-up the heroin trafficking around here," I added.

Pack took off his worn cowboy hat and, standing stiffly, leaned closer to us. "For years, I heard no evil, saw no evil, and kept my mouth shut. No more. If this lowlife sheriff is going to go after me, then it's on."

"Election interference," I said, maybe a bit too loudly.

"You *should* go to law school," said Angus to me.

Sergeant Pack spoke more calmly than expected considering how his good job and pension were on the line. But, then again, Condran and Schloss probably had his back with an alternate job offer at the W.S.P.

"So, Biff. Are you out hitting the streets for Candidate Pack here?"

"Not enough time, unfortunately," I said to Angus and finished my last drops of Pepsi.

Sergeant Pack exchanged my empty pop can for one of his campaign stickers. "You can still slap this on that little, day-glo rice burner of yours," he told me.

"For sure," I responded and watched him drop the empty can on the cement sidewalk. Then, in one motion, he flattened it with the heel of his cowboy boot and used his pointed toe to tiddlywink the pancaked aluminum into the air. He caught it waist-high between his fingers and tossed it like a Frisbee towards the outdoor trash receptacle on the other side of Escher. The shepherd jumped up to bite the can, and nearly caught it in his fangs. When the can disappeared in with the trash, Pack ordered his dog to sit. Escher promptly obeyed.

"Impressive," said Angus and looked my way again after accepting his own campaign sticker from Pack.

"Could have just a tiny bit of your time, Biff?" Angus asked.

"Sure," I said, knowing that I'd visited all the financial institutions in this small community.

"How about walking with me to my office? There's a folder there that I need for my next meeting, but that's not why I want to talk with you." Before leaving, Angus turned back towards the aspiring sheriff. "Good luck with your campaigning, Sergeant Pack."

I hurried my pace to keep up with Angus. "Did Captain Condran call you yet?" I asked.

"He did, but I've been too busy. Let me try him right now."

I handed him one of the captain's business cards and Angus opened his flip phone once we were standing at the nearest cross walk. I could tell the moment the boss answered.

"I'm leaving for Seattle on a family matter late tomorrow morning, so the best I can do is meet you for breakfast. How about 9:00 am at the Wanapum Diner? I'm a regular there, so they let me use the booth in the very back. It's my *defacto* meeting spot with clients––very private."

I knew that Angus was high on Condran's investigation review list, so the boss wasted no time to agree on the time and place. Joe's lawyer slapped his flip phone shut and I followed him across the sidewalk. Angus tapped his temple as we walked, and without saying anything to me, he seemed to be riding the rails on some particular train-of-thought. The man had an odd way. He could be so formal and lawyerly in court, but came off as an absent-minded, yuppie professor when outside the courtroom. Once at his office entrance, I remembered waiting one day out front in Rochelle's van while she'd gone inside to pay Angus's legal bill.

We entered his narrow, long office. Once inside, I realized from the disarray why Angus preferred meeting with his clients at a private booth in the diner.

"I'm pleased that Captain Condran wants to meet with me. I can definitely see some fresh angles he'd should consider pursuing in this case."

I sat across from his seat at the desk. "Great! The boss will love to hear your thoughts, but it's best you save them for him. I'm trying to be careful not to step on his toes. That's not to tell you again how cool that whole 'arrested judgment' tactic was for saving Joe. Don't ever tell him I said so, but thanks so much for saving his butt."

Angus chuckled. Right above a *ZIPPY the PINHEAD for President*––

2000, he adhered his new *PACK for SHERIFF--The Honest Choice--2001* sticker. Both campaign decals would be visible to any traffic approaching his bicycle from behind.

"I only have ten minutes if I'm going to get back on time to my meeting at the prosecutor's office," he said.

Angus opened a desk drawer to find both the file folder he needed and a Max Headroom bobble-head that was affixed to what looked like an egg-boiling timer, except that there was no dial, and when he touched the digital screen, the greenish male surfer-dude face emitted a stuttering, stammering stream of computerized beeps. I couldn't quite make out what Max Headroom said, his skull bouncing up and down along with that animated, techno smile of his. "How cool is that?!!?" I said.

"I put the timer on so I don't forget the time if I get rambling with you." Angus flicked Max Headroom's plastic skull with his index finger until the computer cartoon character head bounced wildly and the digital screen let out a low electronic belch. He set the timer for ten minutes ahead. "A rare little contraption, but I'll tell you what, Biff. If you can arrange a dinner for me, then I'll give this to you."

"Are you talking about having me set you up on a blind date?" I asked, a bit confused.

"No. Not blind. With a woman I know." His voice sounded wobbly.

"Why use me to arrange this? I have enough trouble matchmaking for myself."

Angus rocked back in his oak, office chair, and placed a palm on his forehead. "Because it wasn't appropriate when I had the chance to ask her in person," he said, way too nervously for a man who was at least in his early forties. "Besides, you know her way better than I do."

"Who in the heck are you talking about?" I asked, more curious than ever.

He hesitated. The shyness was kind of cute, actually.

"Do you think that Rochelle Gardner might be interested in having dinner with me--in The Dalles, of course. I wouldn't expect her to drive all the way up here, and there must be some cool eating spots where you're from."

I leaned across the desk and patted his hand. "Take a deep breath, Angus. I mean it. You have no idea how much she appreciates you saving Joe from serious prison time. I'm sure she'd be flattered, delighted even, to go on a date with you."

I could totally relate to his date-o-phobia, so I suspected he'd been petrified to call Rochelle directly. I could see him picking up his phone time and time again, but never quite working up the nerve to make the call. And, to think how many times I seen him fully in the zone while lawyering and making impressive legal arguments. Then again, he was always a touch odd, definitely eccentric, so I could see how, when it came to laying his heart out there, he'd freeze––too petrified to call. That said, the lawyer was salt-and-pepper haired handsome, even if the lack of eye contact took some getting used to. "I've known Mrs. Gardner since I was in grade school. How about if I just tell Rochelle that she has no choice?" I asked.

"Absolutely not. I'm serious––," he said, "––about liking her. She's got to want to––"

The voice of Max Headroom filled the office: "C-c-c-catch the w-w-wave. C-c-c-catch the w-w-wave. Catch the w-w-wave," and on until Angus rapped the bobble-head with the rubber eraser on his pencil. Headroom's bobblehead jiggle suddenly stopped.

Once again, his strange ilk of shyness still had him not looking me in the eyes. "Thanks for offering to help," he said, standing.

"Say Mr. MacIntosh, I know I'm supposed to steer people with possible leads towards Captain Condran, but I feel so powerless to help in any meaningful way."

"Please call me 'Angus'," he said. "There is one unexplored avenue where you may have an advantage over anyone else."

I tilted my head back in surprise. "What might that be?"

"Why don't you ask Joe Gardner if he had an arrangement, or designs, to use his cousin's drug network to do business? I suspect my former client knows more than he's let on to anyone."

I'd never dared broach a come-clean encounter with Joseph, either leading up to, or during his trial––actually, not afterwards either. "Joe and I did connect better than we ever had over Easter weekend. I'll give this some thought. He might just shut me down since I know he really wants to move forward with his life."

"Worth a try don't you think?"

"Maybe. Any other suggestions of uncharted turf that might help us solve this migraine of a case?"

"Perhaps, but since I have to get back to the courthouse now, I think it's best if I save my suggestions for the morning when I'll be meeting with Captain Condran."

"Of course. I'll be happy to talk with Mrs. Gardner on your behalf. I'm pretty sure she likes you plenty enough to date you."

Angus picked up his briefcase and opened his door to the sidewalk. "Hope so," he said, and held it open for me to leave before closing up shop.

CHAPTER 6

HOLY, HOLY, HOLY

Outside, when I headed back towards my car, Jack was still handing out "Pack for Sheriff" brochures at the base of the courthouse steps. This time I didn't stop to chat when I reached the adjoining street. In front of the Wanapum County Sheriff's Department, I thought I recognized Sheriff Colton Usk, the incumbent, Pack's boss, the looming man he was looking to unseat. He was about to climb into his cherry, Shelby Mustang.

When I suspected he'd stopped instead and was glaring my way, I looked down and crossed the empty street away from the courthouse. This man had no love lost for my Washington State Patrol boss who had led the investigation into his county sheriff's department. I'd been there one time when the two went at it and the sheriff denied the captain access to his own files. The obstruction became department-wide. Condran's efforts yielded our case next to nothing.

On cue, it seemed, loud chimes filled the cool April afternoon like the melody was a message from Mary. In my head, her voice filled in the lyrics of *Holy, Holy, Holy,* the song she sang so well. I made an easy beeline to the front of the church near where I'd parked my car.

An elderly woman with blue hair and deep-set crow's feet happened to be exiting the front door into the church just as I arrived. She smiled broadly and even held the door for me with the rubber end of her walking cane. Unable to be heard beneath the loud chimes, I nodded with whatever smile I could muster. She left me inside and pushed the door shut. The latch clicked. On the inside of the big door I noticed a neat handwritten sign taped there: *Please Keep Shut & Locked.*

I turned and looked into the worship sanctuary. The chimes were more muted within the building, but still loud. I looked up at the exceedingly modest decor at the far end of this protestant house of worship. Behind an unadorned altar, a large brown cross filled the two-story wall. The sparse cross, and smaller silk crosses looking like candles with flames left me thinking that this house of worship was designed for parishioners to focus solely on Jesus Christ's resurrection.

I decided to still myself and calm my nerves. I sat halfway up the rows of pews. The blond-colored wood looked no different than the benches across the street where I'd sat so often during Joe's trial.

From within the melody of these chimes, my mind heard a rich, male voice chanting *nam myoho renge kyo.* Then I remembered how Rochelle, Joe's mom, had described her day in that big, ornate cathedral in Sweden where Gunnar Larsson had greeted his aunt and mom with our Nichiren Buddhist chant. Even the *Butsudan* shrines for our personal Buddhist chanting were more intricate than this Methodist altar, especially when we focused on the *Gohonzon,* the Buddhist mandala it held. I guessed that this was the point for the Methodists, to keep the focus of worship unadorned so their followers could go deep inside themselves and find their belief.

For me, my Nichiren chant replaced the *holy, holy, holy* that was enveloping my head. I don't know why--except it had nothing to do with religion--but I felt like I was in a fever. My pores opened and soaked my blouse. Mary used to tell me, "Hey girl, did you know that men sweat, women perspire, and ladies glow?"

I surprised myself by laughing inside this Methodist sanctuary. The chimes overhead swallowed the sound.

"So what am I?" I had asked her. "Since I'm not quite a woman or a lady?"

"You're on the crazy cusp. You're just starting to glow, girlfriend," she'd said, and with that, we'd shared one of our good, silly, best friend giggles. I wasn't sure if I was just laughing inside my mind, but thinking of Mary caused real tears to roll down my sweaty, glowing cheeks. The cool, cavernous room chilled my wet skin. I closed my eyes and could hear Mary's voice:

Holy, holy, holy
All the saints adore Thee
Casting down their golden crowns
around the glassy sea.

Somehow, on the other side, Mary was connected, purely, to the mystic truth of the universe. I never adored anyone more than her. If I had anything in my being like a golden crown, I'd cast it into the pond that took Mary away. Involuntarily, my shoulders heaved, my legs shook, and my throat closed.

Without speaking or even forming the words, I knew I was far from ready to go on the dinner date that was due to start in a couple hours in Moses Lake.

"I'm not ready!" I yelled, causing my eyes to open wide when the words echoed through the empty sanctuary. "Not tonight, Mary," I said without shouting. "Not after being abducted." Then I shook my head. "How about a gun to my head as the ultimate romantic buzzkill? Besides, I hardly know the guy."

Mary, if she had an opinion on the other side, wasn't conveying it to me. Big Max seemed nice and soft-spoken with his deep, poised voice. He even had a crush on me. The feeling was mutual. I'd been thinking I was so ready for a boyfriend, but even imagining a warm, wet kiss had me shudder, and not in the good way that I liked.

On the other hand, I'd sure felt Mary's presence when facing down the same fate that she'd suffered in that pond. I buried my face in my palms only to see the image of my body floating dead in that glassy water.

"I'm really trying to find your killer, Mary. Every day. So much of my attention. I might end up flunking out of this backwater community college because of your unsolved case." My words were swallowed by the chimes. Was she even listening? When the music stopped, I stood. Without any words inside, I thanked Mary anyway, even if her comfort was too far away. I couldn't be angry. Her after-life-being defied any comprehension I had of what really happens when people die.

I knew where I needed to go, though. "No, not to the Porterhouse Steakhouse," I said out loud. "No, not back to Gunnar's bedroom to spend the night alone again second guessing everything about my life." I knew where I needed to spend my evening, if possible.

Slowly, I left my pew and walked to the same church door I'd entered. When I reached down and pushed it open, someone yanked it wide to let in a barrage of afternoon light. The huge silhouette blocked most of the ray. Definitely a male body. I lifted hand to brow, but my eyes wouldn't adjust in the harshness.

"Why are you breaking and entering into the Methodist church?" the huge man asked me, harshly. He held the outside handle with one hand, his silver badge with the other. Squinting, I shuddered once I recognized Sheriff Usk. My short body went stiff. He towered above me, as big as Big Max. In his coat pocket, I could see a dozen or so "Usk for Sheriff" brochures. At the sight of the acne-pocked scars on his face, I found my backbone and refused to show any trace of fear. Not that I was all of the sudden being brave, but I realized that this man knew who had actually killed Mary. My instant loathing of him made me steely from toes to crown.

"You know I know who you are," I said. "What's this *BS* about breaking and entering?" I asked and scoffed. "You can't be serious."

The sheriff crossed his arms as one of his deputies stepped forward. "She most likely jimmied the church door to get in," said the man. I instantly recognized him as Deputy Zach Riggleman.

I felt my face redden with the two law enforcers working in tandem to put me on the defensive and maybe even in jail for the night. "When you buttheads force me to have that sweet 80-year-old church lady––the one who just let me in––speak on my behalf with the local news reporters, then you'll get plenty of exposure for the Sheriff's re-election campaign." My voice went from even-keeled and stern to angry. "And, while we're at it, which one of you two tipped off the *Tramposo* gang about Friday's bust? There wasn't so much as a single stinking roach clip at that compound."

Deputy Riggleman, sneering, lifted metal handcuffs from his

skinny waist belt. "Looks like we also have Elizabeth "Biff" McCoy slandering you, Sheriff."

I turned to run back into the church. "Resisting arrest, too?" the deputy yelled and edged his skinny butt between the church entrance and me. I held my hands high and started to yell back at him when he stepped up to me and reached down for my wrists. Sheriff Usk held up his hand for Riggleman to stop.

Behind me, the front door swung open. "Hello, Sheriff," came a man's high, pleasant voice.

"We caught this teen breaking and entering your church," Riggleman said to him.

I whipped around to see the portly church reverend stepping into the afternoon sun wearing a clergy collar and looking perplexed at both the sheriff and his deputy about to arrest me. "This young lady? No vandalizing. I saw her praying in our pews two minutes ago."

Sheriff Usk glanced fiercely at his deputy before turning forward again with a forced smile for the minister. "Just making sure, pastor. We know your church was broken into last month."

I almost thanked the Lord on high for his divine intervention, but that wasn't the internal, Buddhist way. Still, I made a calculated decision not to let slip away whatever this opportunity was. "Reverend, when do you hold your adult bible studies?" I asked as innocently as I could and surprising both Usk and Riggleman enough that they started mouth-breathing.

From a table in the entry, the minister handed me a sheet of paper. "I happen to have a list of when our adult study group meets each week. Please take it," he said, with a tone and benevolent smile that made me believe he believed I was about to become his congregation's next true believer.

"Thanks so much. I'll see what fits into my college schedule," I said and folded it into my pocket. At least I hadn't overtly promised that I'd attend. "You have a lovely church," I added and hurried away. After only a few feet, I twisted halfway around. "Reverend, my name is Biff, by the way." All three men were still watching my retreat.

The last thing I heard was the church pastor telling the two cops what I nice girl I was. I hurried towards my car in the alley. After starting the engine, I released my clutch and continued through the alley away from the courthouse and church. No cop was tailing me, so I gunned my wimpy engine up the hill and out of town.

~

The visit was quick, almost a blur from everything happening this day, but I decided to stop by unannounced and visit Tomiko at her dorm near the edge of Moses Lake on the Big Bend College campus. A few of the Japanese students in her Ag Exchange Student program were away as guests at farms too far from us. There was an impromptu party, all Japanese, of those placed closer to Moses Lake. Tomiko was her usual gracious self, acting very glad that I'd stopped in. I was getting too tired to handle much commotion, especially since I didn't understand a word anyone was saying, so when I ate some sushi, I told Tomiko that I had homework to do and would stop back and visit longer the next time.

In the din of laughter and Japanese conversations, she tugged my sleeve and guided me towards the dorm room she shared with another girl who had already departed to intern at a popular winery near the Tri-Cities where Joe was playing minor league baseball. She turned on the light of the small sleeping quarters. On her study desk were several photos laid out flat beside a postal envelope with both English and Japanese writing. My eyes were drawn to one in particular.

"Today I opened mail. My brother sends me many new photos," she said. I turned on the desk reading lamp and leaned over to see.

The close-up photo of Kuma and Grace was precious. Daddy's big grin brought out the same in his daughter, except there was no doubt that the eight-month old, even that young, had her mother Mary's wide beaming smile.

I noticed another photo he'd sent to Tomiko, an older one from the year before. I'm standing between Kuma and Mary, and, from the other side of her, Joe had his arm wrapped around Mary's shoulders. We all looked happy. I lifted the image for a closer look, definitely remembering this day of better times.

"Kuma ask me to give this photo and one of baby Grace to Uncle Joe after his game tomorrow. I take Greyhound Bus to Tri-City.

"I need to go now," I told her, not adding that the sight of the baby and Mary was one thing too much for me to handle right then. And, what was this crap about Uncle Joe? Joseph Gardner was Mary's boyfriend, not her brother. If anything, Gracie should be Joe's baby girl, not Kuma's. I decided to write off the 'uncle' thing to Japanese slang. "Hey, I'm driving to the game myself tomorrow. Why don't you join me?" It was the least I could do, my onslaught of emotions aside.

Tomiko, even by Japanese standards, was statuesque and gracious, and found herself bowing to me with a beautiful smile. "Yes. We spend good time together. I pay for gasoline."

"Then, I'll pick you up at noon," I told her and made my way down the dorm hall and through all the Japanese exchange students. I drove out of the college parking lot and looked across to the air traffic control tower near the airport lobby where Linh Riggleman had come so close to whisking Grace away to Vietnam––forever. The girl would have never known her real father, or 'Uncle' Joe, if she'd grown up in Ho Chi Minh City.

On the last highway mile into Moses Lake I checked my watch. Seeing the time, I realized I could still change my mind, rush to my guest bedroom at the Larsson's so I could change clothes quickly. I would add a touch of eyeliner and lipstick. I never wore foundation since Mary, when we were thirteen, told me I had such cute dimples. "Why mask them?" she said. I remember shaking my head at what I was seeing in the mirror. I never thought I was close to as pretty as she was.

I pulled into Moses Lake and passed the Porterhouse Steakhouse.

No way, I told myself shaking my head side-to-side. I wasn't ready for a serious date. Too much crap filled my mind. The pounding stress from this case was about to make me implode from overload.

I continued to the lake shore drive of nice homes and into the Larsson's driveway. They had me park on the gravel to the side of the concrete so I wouldn't block their garage access. I took my backpack with our investigation notes and a heavy criminal justice textbook that hadn't been cracked. At the front door, I fumbled for the door key that Darla had given me.

Inside the empty home, I hung my lightweight windbreaker in the entry hall closet and continued to the kitchen and opened a door into a thin, antique wall cabinet painted with Scandinavian *rosmaling* on the doors where Darla had asked me to leave their spare front door key. The cabinet was used for teacups up high, but the bottom row held an assortment of keys to the boat, dirt bikes and who-knows-what, where I added the house key. I admired a few tea cups on matching platters. I wondered if this stand-alone cabinet was one of the few family heirlooms that Nils Larsson had brought with him from Vikingsville, or wherever his parent's potato farm was in Sweden.

At closer look––my neck still craned upwards––I noticed the round edge of another key protruding ever so slightly over the lip of the very top teacup shelf. I had a funny feeling when I reached up for a closer look.

Yes! A wave of excitement rushed through me. It was the right shade of brass and same length and thickness. My body shook when I rummaged through my backpack to find the investigation folder that held the life-sized photo I'd shown every assistant bank manager in Wanapum County.

The same number, 1897, was etched in the top with the same European script. A hash-mark could be seen partway down the '7'. I wished I hadn't held the actual key with my fingertips, but how could it not have had one of the Larsson's prints on it, either his dad's or mom's I guessed.

In any event, the shape and number, 1897, matched, but the key pattern didn't. This told me that the lockbox we needed wasn't in some financial institution where the bank held the second, complementary key. The lockbox must have been hidden by the Larssons' somewhere since they possessed both keys needed to open it. Gunnar had possessed the one key the angler had landed. This second one I found in Darla's kitchen featured a different shoulder, tip and biting cuts. After Nils had acted so defensive at his office, I was thinking that all the Larssons were linked, somehow, to whatever their secret lockbox hid.

That was when my stomach fell. How would I be any safer sleeping in this place if his parents were in any way tied in with the local heroin trade. I needed to calm down and not get ahead of myself.

I didn't have a clue what the lockbox might hold for safekeeping—family lineage paperwork, property deeds, birth certificates, or citizenship documents——that kind of stuff, but I had to find out and find out soon what clues it might hold for our case. But where was this box? I'd have to really watch my tongue if I was going to stay in this home.

I needed to lie down and close my eyes, but just as I placed my fresh discovery into my blouse pocket that held the Methodist prayer group schedule, Darla walked in.

She hung up her light springtime coat in the front closet where mine was. "Just getting ready to go downstairs and study," I said to her.

"How's the investigation going?" she asked before patting my shoulder and continuing into the kitchen.

"Always hoping for more clues," I said, but then I heard the sound of a small cupboard slam shut with a harsh rattling of the keys dangling inside.

I'd never seen this look on Darla's face before, like she was biting her tongue and wincing at the same time. She grabbed the phone hanging on the wall near the tea cup cupboard and dialed. "Say, Nils, are you sure you don't have that key? It's not where we keep it."

I pressed my palm over the one I'd slipped in my blouse.

"No. I haven't touched it, Nils. And this is the first time I've gone to retrieve it." She held the phone away from her ear when her husband's frustration from wherever his business hotel was had him roaring with a dull anger on the other end.

"Of course I understand, dear. Now calm yourself."

When the coiled phone cord stretched thin, Darla stood in the dining room glaring at me, her face now red. "But Nils. I'm sure I told you that. Gunnar's key was hidden in his Buddhist stuff and lost in the muck of that pothole pond. You have the other copy of that one. It's not my fault this is the only copy of the second key we need."

I had a hard time breathing.

"Yes, I will. Right now," Darla said and placed her hand over the mouthpiece. "Nils wants me to ask you straight up, Biff. Did you take one of the keys from this cupboard?"

Her stern voice left me dumfounded. My tongue froze and my mind raced to figure out what to say or do. Somehow, I answered calmly. "I hung the front door key back inside on its cupboard hook. That's it."

"I know the matching one was there when Nils left on his business trip today. He assures me he doesn't have it with him."

"Matching to what?" I asked, to which she then ignored me and searched her teacups a second time.

She put the phone up to her ear again. "Yes. I know what to do," she said acridly. Darla gave no clue about what important things their box held, but from how upset she was, I figured it must have been something significant. There was something in the way she then glared at me, for only a moment.

Before she hung up with her husband, I jumped up, grabbed my backpack, and sprinted for the stairs. I told myself to forget my windbreaker or the stuff in the guest bathroom upstairs. Grab what I could. In the stairwell, I slammed shut the door and locked the flimsy knob figuring this might buy me twenty seconds at best. Fortunately, I was living out of my old suitcase that was opened wide on the wall near Gunnar's childhood bed that I'd slept in. I squeezed and latched it shut. Even though the sleeves of some garments stuck out, I made sure my backpack full of investigation notes and college books was strapped to my spine. When I ran from the bedroom, the flimsy door at the top of the steps slammed open with a loud kick.

"Thief!" Darla yelled, and pit-patted her middle-aged legs down the steep stairwell. "You give me back that key, right now!"

I found unexpected strength in my arms to carry that oversized behemoth of a suitcase towards the narrow basement door and into the backyard. I turned back and, once her frame entered the rec room, I yelled back. "I have a gun, Darla. Don't you dare follow me! I'll kill you like Gunnar killed Mary!"

I had no idea where that came from. I had no pistol and I wasn't at all sure if Gunnar had drowned my best friend. All I cared about was how Darla froze on the bottom steps.

"You're way in deeper than you know, girl," she yelled.

I glimpsed her flushed face that looked both scared and pissed, a strange mix.

My bluff held, but my heart pounded the inside of my ribcage. I hurried across the lawn hoping I wouldn't slip. The little wheels on the fat suitcase bounced wildly across the grass. Then, I had to drag the thing across the gravel where I'd parked my Subaru.

Nils and Darla were far bigger players in this Bone Shrine mess than I ever imagined. Nils came off as some understated and poised Swede. Darla was like her sister Rochelle, but more of the housewife type.

I tapped my blouse pocket and was relieved to find yet another key that mattered--the one to my ignition. I started the car and hurried down the empty streets far too fast. I wasn't sure where I should hide out for the night.

~

CHAPTER 7

AUNT TOMIKO

Tomiko's face beamed when she saw me walk into the dormitory common area. Someone offered me a slice of raw salmon sushi. Tomiko came over with a cup of warm green tea. It helped with my dread about what might happen when Nils Larsson returned from his business trip.

When I said I needed to find a motel room for the night, Tomiko insisted I stay in her room. "My roommate is making wine in Tri-Cities. You sleep in her bed."

Tomiko rolled my suitcase into her room where I left it next to the vacant bed. I was exhausted from my afternoon in Smohalla and the showdown with Darla. When I slipped out of my blouse, I wasn't expecting the precious matching lockbox key to clang on the hard floor of the small dorm room.

"I wish I could find the lockbox for this," I said. It might help us find Mary's killer."

"Where do you find this key?" Tomiko asked me.

"At Mr. and Mrs. Larsson's house."

"Is this why Mrs. Larsson say you must leave her home?"

"Pretty much," I said. "Mr. Larsson was on the phone and upset that the key went missing. Mrs. Larsson knew I was the only one who would have taken it from inside their home. I'm only borrowing it for our investigation," I said and lifted the key closer so she could better see. "Then they can have it back."

"How will key help find killer of Mary Quinn?"

"Depends on what's inside."

"Karma is cause-and-effect," Tomiko offered very quietly. "Finding the second key is our karma. I have been chanting to help find killer of Mary. This will be effect. You will see."

I nodded, thinking about how I'd been neglecting my own chanting during the hectic, last days.

"You are tired, Miss Biff. "You must sleep."

I took her advice. My stomach churned and tossed for a few minutes of worry, but my body needed to crash into as sound sleep until her voice stirred me awake again. "Biff. Biff McCoy. Biff. Biff McCoy," I heard her voice repeating.

I managed to pry open my eyelids, but my brain didn't know where I was, or what foreigner was speaking. The digital clock on the built-in desk of the small room read 4:44 am. I shook my head vigorously to focus on who was shaking me awake. Tomiko was on her knees on the floor beside my bed, looking too wide awake for this time of the morning.

When I sat up and rubbed my eyes, she spoke in a whisper. "I know lockbox of Mr. Larsson. It hides at his office.

"Really?" I ask, not comprehending.

"I am putting potato grower information in packet and need to ask question. When I stand at his door, Mr. Larsson doesn't like when I am watching. I turn and pretend I do not see. The lockbox is closing."

Her words woke me up. "Mr. Larsson is on a business trip," I said. "He's not coming home until later today. Do you think you can get into his office and check out the lockbox. I think we can get both of the keys we need."

I noticed she was already dressed with shoes on.

"Yes. When morning rises."

I sat up, slipped into my jeans, t-shirt, and zip-up hoodie. I made sure the front pocket of my Levis pocket had no hole when I inserted the Larssons' key inside.

There was also the matter of getting the complementing key of Gunnar's stored in Captain Condran's locked file cabinet at the field office. We absolutely needed the dredged-up key before driving to the potato grower's headquarters.

What if Tomiko was right and the lockbox held the clues we needed? She had already packed up her suitcase. The girl was prepared for this one-way gambit to snag whatever clues the Larsson's were hiding. There'd likely be no returning to innocent interning for either of us, no matter what we found inside the lockbox. Without saying anything to one another, we both knew the stakes of our actions.

Tomiko followed on my heels when each of us hauled a heavy suitcase into the entry lobby of her dorm. We both stopped cold when the community phone in the common area rang. Except for the resident insomniac busy studying who decided to answer before the second ring, we would have ignored it. He answered in Japanese, but quickly turned to English. "Yes, Tomiko is here," he said into the receiver. "May I offer to her your name?"

He held his hand over the receiver and spoke to Tomiko. The only word I understood was a rough version of the name Larsson where both the 'L' and 'R' were so difficult for Japanese speakers.

Tomiko whispered to him in Japanese and the young man returned to the phone. "I make mistake. This is different person. Miss Tomiko sleep now. Note on door say 'Do Not Disturb'."

He had to hold the phone away from his ear. "No. I so sorry, but I do not disturb if note say 'Do Not Disturb'."

The young man held his hand over the receiver and whisper. "She ask if American girl is here."

Tomiko told him something in Japanese. She sounded emphatic.

He turned his back away from me. "No. I do not see this girl at this moment."

Tomiko motioned to me for us to leave the dorm. We made our way out to my lime-green car parked two buildings away and hidden by some dumpsters. We rolled the bulky suitcases over the blacktop and I helped lift hers into the well in front of the backseat where the *Tramposo* had hidden before pulling his pistol on me.

In the car, predawn, I drove a bit too quickly to I-90. Only a few semis roared past in either direction. We crossed Moses Lake interstate bridge to the first exit. I told Tomiko to wait in the car and entered the Field Office.

"Morning, Biff," said the lone trooper seated inside at the front desk. I wondered if he was just finishing up paperwork from a night out on the highways.

"How was your shift?" I asked as casually as I could. He muttered something about the same old, same old when he went back to his paperwork and buzzed me into the back. I glanced at the big cork bulletin board with its cobweb of yarns and too many suspects and opened the drawer of Captain Condran's desk.

We desperately needed some overdue luck if we were ever to identify the perp. I located the desk key and unlocked the file cabinet as I'd done many times for the captain. In a tiny manila envelope, I found what we needed. Maybe we were finally onto something.

From what little I'd read in my criminal law course primer, any search warrant required a police request convincing a judge that there was probable cause of criminal activity. This one would involve Gunnar, who was never charged with anything, or his parents––both distinguished locals with no likely criminal records. This pursuit of the Larsson's might well come off to any self-respecting judge as a fishing expedition. Besides, due to suspicions about Gunnar, their home had already been searched last December and Condran's team had come up empty.

The challenge we faced made the veins in my heart tighten. Calling the captain for the go-ahead would have been a dice roll. He was a stickler for process, but I knew we didn't have time to delay before Nils returned to Moses Lake and emptied his lockbox of whatever was inside. Tomiko and I had to beat Darla to her husband's office and then go undercover. Otherwise, Nils would hunt us down once he got back to Moses Lake. I didn't mention the risks to Tomiko. She seemed to have a hunch. She also needed to be as calm as possible for her task ahead.

I kept reminding myself that this was our only window for finding out whatever was so important to the Larsson's. Besides, I would be returning Gunnar's fished out lockbox key to the Captain's desk before he came in. Only then did I notice the note from Condran taped on our worktable by my chair. He'd set up a last-minute breakfast meeting with Angus MacIntosh at the Wanapum Diner, 8:30 a.m. "Good work, Biff!" The compliment had me wondering how he might react to the work in store for Tomiko and me.

When leaving the field office, I asked the trooper to tell Captain Condran that I'd be driving my own car to meet him in Smohalla for breakfast. "If you're in touch with him, that is."

"I'll do that," he promised.

I tapped the pocket of my casual windbreaker that held both lockbox keys. My stomach dropped. The Captain would surely kill me if he knew what I was up to. I really had to get the key back inside his desk before he noticed it was missing.

Tomiko waited inside my Loyale and, when I took the wheel, she reached back and emptied her school satchel before placing it on her lap. Her paperwork and books remained on the backseat. She seemed as tense as I'd ever seen her when we retraced our way back on I-90 and got off at the first exit across the lake from the field office. "I will bring to you all things inside the lockbox," she promised.

"And be absolutely certain to bring back those two lockbox keys," I responded, knowing that no one would question her presence in Nils' office.

She slipped the two lockbox keys inside a zippered outer pocket of the empty satchel.

I parked and we sat in the silence waiting for the first employee at the Columbia Basin Potato Association to arrive. At 6:30 a.m. a woman appeared at the front door. She opened this early to serve its membership of farmers.

She was dressed in a professional suit and inserted her key in the glass front door. As she pulled it open, Tomiko stepped out of my mint-green Loyale and walked evenly across the street with her usual grace. The last I saw of her then was when she was nodding to the woman holding the door--the receptionist no doubt since she sat at the desk in the lobby. Tomiko had disappeared down the hallway towards Nils' office.

My mind raced with how this might play out. My breaths grew short.

I finally spotted her emerging from the hallway behind the receptionist. She was clutching a full satchel to her chest. Something the receptionist said caused Tomiko to spin around quickly and face the nicely dressed woman. The Japanese intern nodded, but didn't stick around to chat; she looked like Kuma did when he'd spin off the mound to snag a come-backer single.

Arms still full, she used her elbows to burst through the door. She tried to stay cool and walk, but ended up trotting towards my car. I started my car and opened the passenger door for her. The woman yelled. The coil of her phone receiver was pulled as close to the entry as it would allow: "Tomiko! Mr. Larsson says he needs to speak with you, *right now!*"

"Not now," she said and jumped inside the Subaru. Out of breath from nerves or running or both, she clutched her satchel tightly. When I tapped it, I felt something hard.

"Go, Biff, go!" she yelled as soon as her car door shut. I pushed in the clutch and jerked forward. I glanced over my shoulder. Watching us leave, the receptionist stood stunned . She held the phone receiver at her waist.

No one was chasing us, but I had no doubt that, one way or another, the Larssons' would be in pursuit, no matter what was in the satchel. Tomiko pointed straight ahead. "Drive car, please."

"You seem like you found body parts, like an ear or finger?" I said, half-seriously.

"Gold. Lots and lots of gold in lockbox," she said. "Wood art swings open to lockbox."

"Did you close it when you left?" I asked.

"Yes, but I have no time to lock when I hear my name. I close it only. So many coins of gold inside," said Tomiko. "I am scared." She grasped her satchel more tightly.

I patted her elbow. "You did real well, Tomiko. This is sure better than closing down Mary's investigation."

"I hope gold help to find killer of Mary," she added.

"Me, too, because you are right. Everything just got hot for us."

"Yes. Very dangerous," she said. "Finding killer will calm spirit of Mary." The brief smile on her perfectly round face turned to alarm. "But how do I stay in America?" she asked. "Mr. Larsson sponsor me."

I nodded. "That's what I mean by this getting too hot for us. We have no idea if Mr. Larsson will press charges before we find out whether his gold was part of his illegal drug deal."

"Will he come after us for his gold?" she asked.

I didn't have a clue. "We need to be very careful," I said. "Really cautious."

"We will be smarter than Mr. Larsson," said Tomiko, surprising me with her resolve. There was a toughness beneath her doll-like face.

I tried to think about the likely chain-of-events being initiated by the Larssons. If the receptionist described to Nils the car Tomiko fled in, then it was only a matter of minutes before Darla would have gotten a phone call from her husband. They both knew I had at least one of the two keys to the lockbox. How would I be able to go underground within Moses Lake, their turf?

I wondered if the receptionist had gone back down the hall to Nils' office to see if it had been disturbed. Maybe he wouldn't want anyone else to know about his secret lockbox and he definitely wouldn't be describing to anyone at his work what it had contained. I reached over and lifted the handles of the satchel Tomiko held. That thing was lead-belly heavy. With this much in gold coins, Tomiko and I were most definitely about to be on the Larsson payback list. I breathed in the cool spring air, doing my best to hide my fright.

Tomiko kept hugging the satchel tight to her chest. "I am in big trouble in America."

"Not necessarily, but Nils Larsson will no doubt contact JAEP and end your internship. He won't be giving our little heist as his reason, though."

"Then I have no host," she said. "If I am not in program, then I lose student visa for U.S.A."

Tomiko definitely needed protecting. I knew first-hand that those involved with the Bone Shrine were not to be trifled with. "Then let's keep the Larssons from finding you."

Who could I trust? I wondered to myself as we approached the modest Greyhound Station. Inside, she refused my money and bought a ticket on the next bus to the Tri-Cities. She would get a taxi and find her dorm-mate. "I'll meet you there before we go to Joe's game," I said.

Not wanting to leave all that gold in my Subaru, I gave her a light sisterly goodbye hug, uncertain if such a thing was appropriate for Japanese culture. She then bowed to me, her face looking nervous.

What about all this gold? I wondered. Now I got what Joe had been thinking when he unearthed that First Aid kit full of heroin.

CHAPTER 8

I found a parking spot on a Smohalla side street a few blocks from the Wanapum Diner, the one serving as the favored breakfast and lunch eatery for county workers. I lifted Tomiko's stash-filled satchel onto my shoulder, the weight of the contents reminding me why I had my fingers crossed. I needed Angus MacIntosh to show up for breakfast before Captain Condran arrived. I knew what I had to do, but what would the boss's reaction be towards this whole lockbox caper, not to mention me crashing his planned breakfast with Angus?

When I walked, the satchel strap dug into my shoulder. I adjusted my bra, forced my posture upright, and kept my eyes peeled on the end of the street. With more treasure than I'd ever dreamed of carrying, this was no time to be interrogated again by Colton Usk, that joke of a sheriff. The streets were largely empty like they usually were in this backwater town that was even smaller than The Dalles.

I sat on a sidewalk bench next to a bike rack near the front door of the Wanapum Diner. The gold I carried weighed on my conscience. A few county employees, finished with their breakfast, walked out the diner door towards the courthouse. The place definitely did a steady business. A few minutes before 9:00 a.m., Angus startled me by braking his fancy bicycle directly behind me.

"Maybe I should buy a million-dollar policy, in case my lucky stars burn out on me," I answered. "And to test what luck I still have, I really needed to talk to you before Captain Condran shows up."

"What's so urgent?" he asked, and pulled out an origami owl folded in the intricate Japanese tradition. "It's my latest hobby to keep the hands busy."

How did he know to give me an owl? "So cool!" I told him and shifted the heavy satchel off one shoulder and onto the other to examine the delicately created wings. "Kuma and his sister would be impressed," I said. "Awesome paper feathers. And, just so you know, Kuma's sister and I did find something of the Larssons that may help the Bone Shrine investigation." I spoke too rapidly, as usual. "I need you to represent me, just in case I handled things wrong. I'm going to hand what we found over to Captain Condran this morning."

"Haven't you been staying at the Larssons?" he asked, not looking remotely like a lawyer in his protective helmet with a small round dental mirror perfectly positioned for seeing the vehicles driving behind him when riding.

"Well, yes," I said and clutched the satchel tight to my ribs. "Except that now I'm looking for a new place to rent. Maybe a dorm room will open up soon."

Angus asked for a single buck from me. I found four quarters and, with a puzzled look, handed them over to him. "Now I'm your insta-attorney." He assured me that, with this dollar, then whatever I told him would be protected by our new lawyer-client privilege.

"Last night at the Larsson home, I stumbled upon the second key needed to open Gunnar's lockbox. I was chased out of the house once Darla Larsson discovered it was missing." My grip tightened on the satchel. "This morning we pulled this out of the Larssons' private little vault."

"Without a search warrant, I presume," he said.

"I doubt a judge would have issued a warrant, even though what we found justifies one." I held the satchel up for Angus to lift. "I sure wasn't expecting to find a treasure chest of gold coins," I told him.

His eyes widened once he felt the weight. "Have the Larsson's filed a stolen property report with the Moses Lake police?" Angus asked.

"Of course not," I said, "I'd be shocked if anything in the lockbox wasn't related to Gunnar's drug operation."

"Makes sense," Angus nodded and said.

"Let's go inside and claim my usual booth," he added and, after pointing toward the diner, he handed back the unopened satchel. I walked alongside and waited for him to lock his bike securely in the rack next to the front door of the diner. "If not for his parent's help, how did Gunnar Larsson access enough money that very morning after the drowning to bribe his way out of jail and then flee the USA?" he then asked.

I tapped the satchel three times hard to make sure Angus was looking at me. "The case has missing tubes of Krugerrands. These are the same exact type of gold coins found in the tubular framing of Linh Riggleman's baby stroller."

"Initially earmarked for the purchase of the Bone Shrine heroin before the deal went sideways?" he said. "I'm speculating, of course."

"That's sure what I'm guessing, too."

Angus opened the door leading into the diner and motioned me through. A waitress led us back to the lawyer's reserved booth, the most private one in the place, tucked in the far back. We both sat down in the high-backed booth with vinyl seats straight out of a 1950-era roadside eatery. When he held up three fingers, she immediately brought a pitcher of ice water and three place settings.

"All the coins in the satchel were found in Nils Larsson's potato association office," I told him.

"How did you manage to gain access there?"

"I didn't. It was Kuma Kusumoto's sister, Tomiko. She's an agricultural exchange student working short-term as a marketing intern for Nils." I explained how she'd happened to see him closing up a lockbox vault behind his work desk and how we hoped it would show who wanted to buy the China White that night. "It sure wasn't Gunnar acting alone," I added. I told Angus how Darla came to know I had one of the lockbox keys. "She came after me pretty hard once she got off the phone with Nils last night. That's why I need to be so careful now. The Larsson's will be after me."

Knowing that Condran was about to arrive, my fingers shook. I drank down a glass of water in one long, thirsty tilt before slipping the case of coins out of Tomiko's satchel and opening it for Angus to see.

"Some of the highly-desired, South African Krugerrands," he said after a close look. "These are 99.9% pure, 22-karat South African gold. I have some in my own portfolio," he added. "I certainly don't have this many tubes, not six rows by five columns," he said, multiplying under his breath. "Looks like ten of the tubes are missing their coins," he said.

We both looked up at the same time.

"There you are," said a cheery Captain Condran standing behind me.

I scooted tight to the window so my boss had room to sit beside me in the booth. Before he slid in, he stiffened and looked wide-eyed at the gold coins.

Angus glanced at me and jumped right in as my legal representative. "The Bone Shrine investigation has some key new evidence thanks to Biff McCoy and Tomiko Kusomoto," he said and tapped the edges of the case that resembled a poker playing set with columns of casino chips. "They were acquired inside Nils Larsson's office this morning by his Japanese intern."

Condran's complexion turned red and he spoke too loudly for this public setting. "By 'acquired' you mean pilfered, don't you?"

Angus cleared his throat. "Hold on, Captain. Due to all the complications that this new development might pose, Biff has asked me to represent her, legally, which I am. Before we leave the diner, Biff will turn over, as bonafide evidence for your case, all the gold found by Tomiko in the lockbox."

Angus was doing so well as my lawyer that I decided to keep mum. He pointed inside the case at the ten empty tubes. "I own a few Krugerrands. One-third of the coins look to be missing out of a case made to hold roughly $250,000 worth of gold in today's market." Angus closed up the case and slid it across the table to Condran. My boss set the case of coins inside the satchel and placed it on the bench between where he and I sat.

My boss glared at me, but spoke to my attorney. "Mr. MacIntosh, would you please tell this young woman that if she ever launches a search-and-seizure without a warrant then I'll personally charge her with a felony." From the tone alone, I could tell how much Condran was fuming inside.

"Yes," Angus agreed when Condran stared at him. "She *should* be running decisions of this magnitude past you, Captain."

My boss turned back at me and shook his head before Angus continued.

"I'll be surprised if any of the Larssons will be going to the police, though. You've just found evidence from the intended purchasers of the China White heroin last summer. Any Larsson fingerprints found on the coins in the baby stroller used to smuggle them to Asia will confirm that this was the same money used as a bribe to free their son, Gunnar, from jail. And maybe, before the Bone Shrine tragedy, the $250,000 worth of gold was intended to help buy the entire kit of displaced heroin."

"The U.S. Customs confiscated these Krugerrands during Linh Riggleman's act of currency smuggling, so their criminal customs case doesn't require any tests for prints," the captain said, his voice growing agitated. "So far Customs has not seen any need to check those coins for fingerprints."

"Don't you have contacts at the Drug Enforcement Agency?" Angus asked, not missing a beat.

"I'm working on that angle," said Condran.

That angle was no doubt working through Dr. Schloss. He had contacts with forensic labs worldwide. The forensic's expert had told me while we waited for the *Tramposo* bust to conclude.

Angus pressed the captain. "With suspicions that these coins are related to major drug operations, then perhaps the United States D.E.A. can convince the United States Customs to cooperate in examining this as evidence related to wider federal felonies." Angus suggested. "I've defended cases where we've been able to trace the direction of the fingerprints."

"Go on," said the captain.

"Well, if by chance there are any of the Larssons' prints on the smuggled Krugerrands that are all neatly bundled in columns like these are, and you don't find any of the Rigglemans' prints, then you have a very strong indication which direction the coins are going."

"Such as showing that the Krugerrand's were very likely utilized as the bribe money to free Gunnar Larsson from jail when he should have been a key witness for solving the Bone Shrine crimes?" the captain asked, almost like he was talking to himself.

"Exactly, Captain," Angus said, "and Gunnar's suspicious disappearance was my single greatest frustration during the trial when trying to establish reasonable doubt for Joe Gardner."

I realized that I'd just hired the finest attorney that a dollar can buy.

When the waitress arrived, Condran ordered only a coffee, black. Every day on this case, my boss drank his constant morning cups in tiny slurps the same way that hospital patients in a universe of hurt would press their bedside tube to release little drip-drops of morphine.

Angus looked up and ordered a country breakfast with orange juice. I asked for the same, eggs over easy.

We spoke in low voices when she left. Fortunately, the nearest booths were vacant. We had the rear of the diner to ourselves.

Condran turned to Angus. "Please tell your new client that, since she's stolen these coins, they won't be admissible as evidence in a future trial."

"Captain, these coins give you the focus your case has lacked," Angus said in an even tone. "They should show that the Larssons weren't the sellers of the heroin that night. It's a strong clue that, as the probable buyers, they didn't have the motive to drown Mary Quinn."

Condran had emphasized this very point often. It was why Tomiko and me did what we did this morning. I was relieved to hear Angus reemphasizing this.

"You still need to find your killer," Angus added. "Figuring out how to convict the murderer with admissible evidence will come later. Fingerprints on the baby stroller coins might help you exact the confessions you need from Mr. or Mrs. Larsson."

Sounded logical, but first Nils and Darla would expect their money returned. "Boss, I know I should have called you first, but after Darla chased me from their home last night, I knew that Nils or Darla would have snagged anything of any importance to us from the lockbox if Tomiko didn't get inside it first thing this morning." I spoke quickly, but quietly.

"Why not inquire with me whether a search warrant was possible?" Condran asked me with a scowl.

"It wouldn't have been," said Angus. "You didn't turn up anything after searching the Larsson home in December. They're too upstanding in the Columbia Basin to be harassed with multiple searches."

I turned and looked straight at the boss, but did my best not to talk to him with any trace of an attitude. "We had to act fast, but I was pretty shocked."

"Why? Did a wave of guilt overwhelm you?" the captain asked, not sounding the least bit convinced of any honor in our actions.

"Nothing of the sort, Boss. I was startled because Tomiko came out of the office carrying a treasure trove of gold."

Condran stared at Angus when he responded. "Please ask your client––the one who *borrowed* the matching lockbox key from my own office desk this morning––why I shouldn't terminate her as my intern?"

"Because nothing like this will happen again," I said. "I really promise, Boss."

"Excuse me," I heard a woman's voice say behind us. "Captain Condran, I was pretty sure I saw you come in. I'm Amanda Skerry with CPS," she said looking him. "After you called me yesterday, one odd thing came to mind about those days following the Bone Shrine drowning."

"Please sit," the captain said, motioning to the bench next to my lawyer. "This is Angus MacIntosh, the attorney that represented Joe Gardner last fall," he added when the lawyer scooted farther into the booth.

"It's probably nothing," Amanda said, nodding to Angus, but insisting she stay standing.

Short like me, Amanda looked very professional in a dark, wool-pleated skirt and suit jacket over a non-frilly blouse. Even though her resemblance to Mary Quinn was uncanny, I could see myself presenting myself the way she did––in ten or fifteen years that is.

Amanda mentioned how she needed to be in court for a custody hearing and only had a couple of minutes to spare. "I did remember one thing from a couple days after that ugly drowning," she said softly and looked around. "It's probably nothing."

"We'd appreciate anything you have to offer our case," said the captain.

"A few days after Mary Quinn's drowning, I was tasked with interviewing prospective, temporary foster homes for the surviving newborn. That took me inside the home of Zach and Linh Riggleman."

"Is this something confidential you wish to share?" Condran asked looking straight at Angus.

She waved off his concern. "Oh nothing like that, and I'm probably over-imagining what I noticed."

"What's that?" I asked.

She turned and looked at me. "Well, we were scurrying to place the newborn. The infant's stay in the hospital was running short. At Child Protective Services we have a shortlist of potential families for emergency placement. We were hoping for one suited to take on a newborn. Linh and Zach Riggleman had been hoping for a baby of their own for three or four years so I arranged for a home visit."

"How did that go?" the captain wondered.

"Fine, actually," she said. "The home was quite tidy, immaculate even, and there would be a nice bedroom space for the newborn right next to their master bedroom. Also, with him as a deputy sheriff and her doing well at her nail salon, I saw nothing wrong with awarding them temporary custody. But after you called me, Captain, there was one thing I remembered."

"What was that?" Condran asked.

"Well. On the closed door into the Riggleman's laundry room, I saw a sheriff's uniform hanging there. It was all washed and pressed."

"Zach Riggleman is a Wanapum Sheriff deputy. Why was that so odd to you?" Condran asked.

"Well, Zach Riggleman is rather lean," she said. "His father even more so. It was just strange."

"How so?" the boss asked a bit too impatiently.

"The shirt filled the width of the door. It was quite wide. And the cop-style cargo slacks on the hanger were far from lean. I'm talking at least XXXL big, with longish legs. The pants were black and the buttoned-up shirt green, was like they wear at the sheriff's department. I wish I'd looked closer for a name embroidered on the shirt, but I wasn't probing for evidence to help a murder investigation," she added.

"Maybe Linh Riggleman washes and presses clothes on the side," said the captain.

"Unlikely. I've had my nails done in Linh Riggleman's Lotus Nail Salon," said Amanda. "It's always busy there. Linh doesn't even have her own station for painting nails. Rents them all out to the other nail techs. She's too much in charge of the show for me to imagine her going home and doing laundry for anyone but her own family."

We looked up to see the waitress returning. She filled Condran's coffee cup and he asked if she could please leave the glass pot next to him on a wide coaster. Our server nodded and placed a glass of juice in front of Angus and another in front of me, although I was no longer in the mood to sip anything.

"Thank you for sharing this," said the captain to Amanda when the waitress said she'd be back with our food in a bit. "We won't rule out that this may have been a dirty, cover-up deed, not some regular laundry service."

Amanda smiled and tapped her Lady Hamilton wrist watch. "I really need to go now, but seeing the oversized uniform not put away in such an orderly home struck me as odd."

"This really could be something," I insisted. "You saw it right after the drowning. Even the forensic expert said how surprised he was that the investigation didn't uncover hardly any pond muck."

Condran held up his hand for me to stop. "One more quick question, Amanda. On your visit to their home, did either Zach or Linh Riggleman act nervous or suspicious to you?" Captain Condran asked.

"No. They aren't the most relaxed humans, but they were very polite to me and, one thing was certain. Mrs. Riggleman *really* wanted to foster this part-Asian infant. There was also no reason to deny them custody––at least not by the standards set by Child Protective Services."

"Except that the deputy was part of the same investigation related to why the newborn needed placement," Angus said, a bit too loudly.

"That night he arrested Joe Gardner, acted like he'd just found Mary's body, and then ever-so-heroically, saved the newborn."

"Just for the record," Amanda said, looking at Angus a bit defensively with furrowed brows. "My boss took a good amount of heat for approving placement of baby Grace in the home of someone so closely involved in the Bone Shrine drowning and drug deal. That was above my pay grade, sir. I was just conducting the home screening."

"Understood," said Condran. "Please let us know if you can think of anything else."

"Most definitely," she said and turned to leave. The easy way she pirouetted and left us, showed no wasteful movement. No more dead ends. That's what we desperately needed if we were to resuscitate this investigation——better focus and no more time-wasting moves.

Angus twisted his neck to watch her leave. "One thing is unmistakable, Captain. The whole Bone Shrine mess was pinned on the outsider, Joe Gardner, the convenient addict with a juvenile drug record."

"And, had he been there, Joe would have tried to protect Mary and the baby. That much I'm sure of," I said making my voice as adamant as I could.

Condran shot me a look. "Angus all but proved that in the trial. That hasn't led us to the actual killer, though, has it?"

Both the captain and I had lost our appetites, but watched Angus relishing his breakfast. He picked up a thick slice of bacon with his fingers and savored the smoky flavor. I nibbled at a corner of toast after slathering it in raspberry preserves. The captain sat with his arms crossed, and like me, not touching his utensils. We both let our meals grow cold.

Turning to address Condran, I almost upset his steaming mug. "I can totally see the Larsson's spending $70K or 80K to get their son out of harm's way. If Nils hadn't, maybe he thought Riggleman would have framed his son for the murder and drug deal——Gunnar as the fall guy and not Joe."

Angus leaned in. "Captain. Do you have some kind of police protection program planned for these two interns——Biff and Tomiko? The Larssons won't know that $160,000 of their gold coins are in your possession. They'll think these two still possess the gold and will come after them." Angus drank down his water. "Also, how you leverage this cache of coins needs to be carefully thought through."

"What are you proposing?" Condran asked before patting the satchel that leaned against his thigh.

I piped up. "I am admitting that I helped snag the Krugerrands. To make it up to you, why don't you let me be the one to put a sting on the Larssons so they'll admit to being part of the Bone Shrine deal?"

"Exactly how do you propose to pull this off?" the captain asked looking as though he'd had more than enough of me this morning.

"Put a wire on me this evening."

"What's this evening?" Condran asked, perplexed.

I told him how Joe Gardner would be the starting third baseman in the first ever home game for the Tri-City Dust Devils. "Rochelle Gardner reserved a box near third base. She invited me, Tomiko, along with her sister, Darla, and, possibly, Nils Larsson, too."

"Joe's aunt and uncle," Condran said softly as though reminding himself of the connection. He handed a credit card to the waitress when she came over to collect our dishes.

"That's actually not a bad idea as long as Joe's mother is there," said Angus with a firm tone. "Actually, Captain, your young intern here might be the only one breathing life into this moribund case."

"Consider yourself on probation as an intern," said Captain Condran to me and scribbled an address on a piece of paper. "I need you to drive to the Tri-Cities and get yourself to this parking lot at precisely 4:00 p.m.--no earlier or later."

I read the address.

The captain let me know again--firmly--that I had created a slew of unexpected work for him today. I wanted to tell him that this sort of chase was surely what we'd signed up for, but I snuffed the urge to speak out. "Once you're safely there, then we'll arrange for you to wear a wire at the game tonight," he said quietly.

"I'll be there, Boss," I responded, trying my best to sound confident. "Tomiko is already on her way. In order to keep her safe, I put her on an early Greyhound going to the Tri-Cities. She's been looking forward to seeing Joe's game."

"Since she's the one who actually took the coins, I'll have her seated next to me far away from the Larssons," the captain said. He stood and lifted the satchel of coins, not taking his eyes off me. "Say, Biff. Has anyone ever called you the *Chaos Kid?*" he asked.

Angus laughed, but I ignored him.

CHAPTER 9

SILENT FLIGHT

After nearly an hour behind the wheel of my lime-green beater, I stopped for a break at the desolate pull-off above the Columbia River to view what was left of the B-Reactor. The aging factory-of-doom glinted in the midday sun with just a hint of the glow that must have destroyed Nagasaki in 1945 when *Fat Man* exploded with atomic fury. My mind took me to the day, a year-and-a-half earlier, when I'd visited this very spot. Joe's mom, Rochelle, had driven her exchange student to this oddest of tourist attractions, but a place he'd ardently asked to see. Joe, Mary and me were along for the ride.

My friend, Kuma, had stood here teary-eyed. *Fat Man* had killed his grandfather that day, and only because his grandmother had only survived because she was staying with relatives near Tokyo with his infant father.

He'd told us how the founders of his sect of Nichiren Buddhism had been imprisoned in World War II for not joining the war effort. While in prison, one founder persevered during years of retched conditions by chanting, *nam myoho renge kyo*. By doing so, one thing came to him in a way that saved him. He realized throughout his same harsh, daily stillness that his faith embraced the essence of *life force*. Mary and I started chanting the next week.

Maybe all the addictive crap, like heroin or booze, were modern man's inner soul-leaching, a kind of personal nuclear poisoning. Maybe standing up for justice and truth against all the Bone Shrine injustice was my Buddhist path. I had to stop fibbing, though, and I really had to protect Kuma's wonderful sister, Tomiko.

Kuma was truly shaken when looking at the B-Reactor. This place had enriched the poison plutonium for the bomb dropped on Nagasaki. For our ride back to The Dalles he steeled himself into a polite coldness. Kuma didn't talk, but I kept reading his face and the deep sadness that connected him to his beliefs, his grandparents who'd been killed in one of the mushroom clouds, and those imprisoned spiritual teachers. That was when and why I started chanting––when Mary began chanting, too. Kuma embraced a resolve that I didn't understand then, but totally got now. *Nam myoho renge kyo.* A chill river wind blasted through my rolled down window when I continued on towards the Tri-Cities.

Once I was at the outskirts of Richland, I glanced at the business card that Tomiko had given me for *Silent Flight Winery* where she was visiting her friend, also an interning student from Japan. I found a real estate office figuring they would know where such places were located. Also, in my hurry to escape the Larssons' home, I'd left my flip phone on the nightstand beside the downstairs bed, so I borrowed a landline at the real estate office and called the vineyard to give Tomiko a heads-up that I'd be arriving soon. The Realtor gave me a map of the Tri-Cities after drawing a small arrow to my destination on a ridge to the west. "*Silent Flight* is famous for its classy pinot grigio, if you're old enough to drink."

"Not quite," I said and thanked her for the help.

I filled my tank with gas and prompted the Subaru up the ridge until I found a narrow, paved, private drive with one lane and pullouts on the hairpin curves for passing. Rows of trellised vines with barely budding green leaves tattooed the tan hillsides on both sides of a road that flattened near the top. There, a thick black iron gate awaited me. Half-opened, it welcomed visitors with thick oak carvings mounted to the black columns. The winery's emblem––a stylistic, Great Horned Owl in flight––was mirrored on both the closed and open half of the gate. I smiled and eased through the open half into a modestly large parking lot. One huge barn with open doors revealed huge stainless steel storage tanks and vats. I suspected the vineyard was far more chaotic during harvest season. About the time I was born in 1982, the winery industry had boomed along the dry ridges of the Columbia, a topography and climate similar to that in the wine country of the Mediterranean.

I knew Tomiko was relieved to see me by the way she waved and smiled while standing beside her Japanese friend. They stood at the entrance of the wine shop and its adjoining restaurant built to look as though the structure belonged in renaissance France. The parking lot was partially full of employee vehicles on the end nearest the barn. I pulled in front of the Silent Flight Bistro where the two Japanese exchange students welcomed my arrival.

"This is my friend, Sakura," Tomiko said then introduced me in English as her American sister. Tomiko insisted she buy me and her friend lunch, but Sakura bowed out. She needed to finish her work in the winery warehouse.

Tomiko was a good bit leaner than her brother, but both Kusumoto siblings shared a similar strong presence when engaging people. She and I sat at a small table in the corner of *Silent Flight Bistro* beside a large picture window. I pointed down out at the three small cities stretched out well below us. "The two on this side of the Columbia River are Kennewick and Richland. Across the river is Pasco," I said and pointed. "That's the brand new ballpark where Joe will be playing tonight," I said and pointed.

"I am excited to see baseball!" she said. Her eyes sparkled in this moment where we forgot the danger we'd created for ourselves. No way was Nils Larsson going to hurt my new friend. One way or another, I wouldn't allow it. I leaned in and whispered. "Listen, Tomiko, I'm not sure that you should stay at the winery tonight."

"Why?" she asked.

"Because this whole situation has gone totally crazy. Mr. Larsson will be looking to get back his gold coins. My boss, Captain Condran, is sure about this. But he also said maybe these coins could help us find out what the Larssons actually know about the night Mary died."

"I don't wish to hide here at winery," she said looking upset. "I wish to help you find killer. When I come for my exchange, Kuma tell me to help you find who murder Mary."

Tomiko may have looked too petite to be tough, but the more I watched her in action, the more impressed I'd become with her willpower. More poised and graceful than I'd ever be, we were lock-step with avenging Mary's death. Considering that she'd never met my best friend, this stubborn resolve was pretty incredible. Too bad Darla Larsson wasn't as loyal an aunt to Joe as Tomiko was being on Gracie's behalf. High time we found the dirt bag who drowned the baby's mother.

"I wish I'd thought of this before you came to the winery," I said, "but Mr. Larsson has probably talked to the boss of your ag program this morning. The director would have no reason not to tell him that you're visiting Sakura at *Silent Flight* here. He probably even told the head of your program that you stole valuable items from his office." I cleared my throat. "After lunch we need to get out of here and keep you safe," I added, assuring her that I knew of hideout options I actually didn't have.

I'd never seen Tomiko act the least bit scared––well maybe when she came out of Nils's office building with all that gold. I wasn't sure she realized the extent of my immediate concern. We stopped discussing our plans when the waitress arrived and told us about their special––a French Bouillabaisse accompanied with garlic buttered French bread made fresh here daily.

"I need to see some ID if you're going to order wine," the woman told us. I shrugged and smiled. "I'll have Perrier water to go with the special."

"I will drink the same," said Tomiko. I knew she was twenty-two, so I was pretty sure she drank bubbly water out of her politeness to me.

The waitress smiled and nodded and returned with a liter bottle of the effervescent French spring water, pouring it into glasses before leaving us to our conversation. My stomach growled.

"I may have made a mistake by having us go after the lockbox on our own, but this current problem is worse."

"What mistake? You must trust me and I must trust you," Tomiko replied. "Mr. Larsson is bad man."

She sat tall and proud, the same way that Kuma would.

"The real danger is that Mr. and Mrs. Larsson know it was you who took their gold. For that reason alone, you will need protection from them starting with Joe's baseball game tonight."

"Will Captain Condran keep me safe?" she asked.

"Yes," I said, hoping it would prove to be true. I glanced around for eavesdroppers, but we were the only two in the restaurant, and discussing our plight in low voices with soft jazz in the background masking our words.

Fortunately, Tomiko was pretty rational. "It is not easy to hide Japanese girl in American town," she said, "but I help find killer with chanting. We eat now and hide me soon."

"Silent flight," I said to her, not wanting to spell out the evening plan of having me wear a wire at Joe's game. Captain Condran probably preferred she wasn't at Joe's baseball game either, but I knew Kuma had insisted that his sister be there to watch his friend. She was definitely *not* going to miss this game.

Our server left a basket of thin, garlic-buttered, French bread, already sliced, in a basket. To clear my thoughts, I leaned in to first smell the mix of seafood in the soup and then the freshly baked loaf centered between us.

I avoided thinking about wearing a wire at the game by focusing on the meal. The soft, buttered French bread was perfect for sopping up the bouillabaisse broth. Tomiko's eyes widened after she followed my lead with the bread.

The jazz CD ended as we finished our meal. We both chose to skip dessert due to this antsy, looming vibe, no doubt. Tomiko found her money clip full of mostly twenties, and left a big tip for our expensive lunch. I would have protested and tried harder to pay, but I'd only been rich for a very short time this morning.

Sakura came in as we were leaving the restaurant and offered to give us a full tour of the wine making operation. "*Silent Flight* make many wines with many awards," she told us.

"Have you talked to your Ag sponsor today?" I asked her.

"No."

"Then please thank them, but say that Tomiko will not be able to stay here with you today or tomorrow."

Sakura looked puzzled--not happy at the news. Except for the words "Dust Devil" and "baseball" in English, I had no idea what

Tomiko's Japanese version of the change of plans was, but Sakura nodded and smiled at us when we got into my Loyale.

Before we rolled out the open gate of the winery, I looked in my rearview mirror. A middle-aged woman, stylishly dressed, hurried up to Sakura and pointed towards us. "We're leaving in the nick of time," I told Tomiko.

"What is 'nick of time'?" she asked.

"I'm thinking that the owner of Silent Flight Vineyard just got off the phone with either the director of your program, or maybe even Nils Larsson."

"Then I will not intern anymore," she said, folding her arms on her chest.

"Probably a wise choice," I said, wondering if a return to the ag program would even be an option any longer. I needed to concentrate on the hairpin gravel turns leading us down the dry ridge.

I sensed that Tomiko was starting to feel her life closing in on her, the same way it was on me. I pointed quickly and, when she looked, I made a comment about this crazy life winding and riffling like the Columbia and Snake Rivers as they converged far below us.

Shuddering and gluing my eyes to the road, I started chanting. The turns were tight on the steep, gravel road. My car rattled in protest. Tomiko joined in––*nam myoho renge kyo*––but soon had us chanting faster. I eased around corners, but at the bottom of the gnarly ridge I breathed deep when I could finally accelerate on the straightaway where gravel turned to blacktop.

At the edge of Richland proper, I slowed for a four-way stop and looked over at the same gas station where I'd just filled up a couple of hours before. I did a double-take.

The bright red Saab convertible faced away, its top closed on the cool, clear April afternoon. There was no doubt. The man stood near the driver's side gassing up while his wife got out of the passenger door to stretch. My lime-green Subaru would surely give us away to them. I didn't bother slowing at the stop sign, but turned sharply on a residential road away from the gas station.

"Was that Mr. Larsson?" Tomiko asked.

"Yes."

"Hurry, Biff!

I made three more street turns in the general direction of the Columbia River towards the state patrol office where we were supposed to meet up with the captain.

Tomiko placed her delicate hands on my dashboard. I expected them to be shaking, and was about to place my own palm over her outstretched fingers, but she clenched them into fists instead. "Do they come to get me?"

My throat had gone dry from chanting and nerves. "Or me, more likely. Darla and Nils will be afraid that their gold now connects them directly to the Bone Shrine drug deal. The Larssons will know that the authorities know they know who killed Mary."

Had we left Silent Flight Vineyard five minutes later than we did, then we probably would have been hood-to-hood with that red Saab convertible racing up the vineyard's single lane road.

"Hurry!" she said again. "We hide now. Soon we catch the killers!"

CHAPTER 10

THE HOT CORNER

At the new ballpark, the sun set over the bone-dry, Horse Heaven Hills. An outline of the ridge filled the distance where the *Silent Flight* vineyards hid within slurping distance of the Columbia River's irrigation waters.

Captain Condran pulled his undercover Crown Vic into the Dust Devil's parking lot. I followed. He pointed to a spot for my Subaru between a panel van and a large Dodge pick-up although my mint-green paint job still wouldn't provide camouflage. For the day's last briefing, he parked directly in front of me.

The boss motioned for me and Tomiko to get into his car. He wasn't keen on me driving my own vehicle here, but I insisted on having my own ride after the game. I needed to go to The Dalles the next day for my Mother's surprise 50th birthday party.

Most importantly, I needed to make sure that Tomiko was safe. I was hoping she would stay with Rochelle in Oregon until we figured out what was best for her.

"Act natural," the captain reminded me for the fourth time. "If you ask leading questions," he added, "then try to pick a moment in the conversation where what you're saying fits in––

"––naturally," I added. Jeez. I got accused of talking as much as anyone, but once in a while, like now when we would be luring the

Larssons into talking, my unfailing eloquence might actually come in handy. When I twisted my torso, I could feel the police-wire taped to my chest and hoped my 'glowing' skin wouldn't slip-and-slide it out of place.

The captain double-checked whether the one-way mic was picking up my voice. We were good to go, except he told me to wait until he and Tomiko went inside before taking my seat in the box that Joe's mom had purchased behind third base.

Tomiko would be sitting high above home plate next to Condran in the elevated announcer's booth. I went back and sat in my own car when Condran drove with Tomiko closer to the ballpark's personnel entrance.

I checked my watch and noticed how rapidly the parking lot was filling for this sell-out––the Tri-Cities' first ever Dust Devil home game. I kept my old Subaru running so I could stay warm. When the sun set, I worried I'd be chilled to the bone inside the brand new ballpark. On this windless, mid-April evening, a clear sky sucked the warmth from our little surface of earth.

The ballpark lights obliterated any view of the stars overhead. My walk from car to the Will Call window was casual by design. I waited for my ticket and decided it wouldn't be undercover-cool to twist back around and see who might be watching, but I was glad the wire was already live just in case Nils came up and yanked me out of line. Captain Condran had two troopers positioned in the parking lot if anything did happen. The time was overripe to the point of rotten for Darla and Nils to corner me and Tomiko. Rochelle had left us tickets. Tomiko's was going to be wasted.

When I edged my way inside the new stadium, it was nowhere near as big as the new major league baseball park I'd seen in Seattle for the Mariners, but way modern, too, and able to hold three or four thousand fans. The locals were filling the stadium to capacity. I felt safer doing this undercover surveillance in a good-sized crowd. Nils would be less likely to strong-arm me.

The box seats behind home plate were filled with well-dressed dignitaries, probably local politicians and Tri-City business leaders here to honor their new minor league franchise. Tall stadium lights obliterated my vision when I stared up at the sky's last traces of dusk.

A brand new scoreboard painted with Dusty, the team's mascot, shimmered in the glow.

When an usher in the left field seats of the ballpark pointed me in the direction of Rochelle's box, I spotted Trooper Elaine Fonk with her premature white hair. Undercover, she wore a lined REI parka that no-doubt hid her service pistol. Earlier this afternoon, the captain detailed how Trooper Fonk would be teaming up with a second undercover cop. Both would be stationed several rows in back of and to each side of Rochelle's box seats. I glanced, but couldn't pick out the second hidden trooper.

The boss had also assured me multiple times how these two were trained to converge on the Larssons if either Darla or Nils provided self-incriminating evidence or in any way endangered my physical wellbeing. I wished I could say I felt no fear. I checked out the modest announcers box balanced on high, vertical steel I-beams, but neither the captain nor Tomiko were leaning far enough forward for me to spot them.

I took slow steps down the stairs, but couldn't see Rochelle. When I edged past Trooper Fonk, I knew better than to nod or smile her way.

I looked at my ticket stub and then at Rochelle's box located near third base where Joe would play. Was anyone going to show up, other than me, the one with the best excuse to steer clear? I didn't want to be the first one seated so I took the last two steps to the railing beside the visitor's bullpen in foul territory along the left field wall. A few feet from me, the opposing pitcher tossed easy warm-up throws.

I wondered if the boss's earphones captured the warm-up grunts from the pitcher. An on-field announcer stood beside the main pitcher's mound thanking a parade of locals who'd made this new minor league franchise a reality after several years of diligent community effort. Someone representing the Kansas City Royal's Hall-of-Famer, George Brett, one of the Dust Devil owners, accepted a plaque-of-appreciation from the City of Pasco. Even I'd heard of this ball player.

After the customary "Star-Spangled Banner" and first pitch thrown by the mayor of Pasco, Joe sprinted out to third base. I was surprised and secretly delighted when he pointed directly at me. He sported a big smile and gave me a quick wave. I returned a thumbs up, but once I felt my raised arm tugging on the hidden wire, I lowered the elbow to my side.

Most of my baseball knowledge came from watching Joe play American Legion while I sat beside Mary. She'd help me with the rules of this odd, but cool, game with its bunting and balks, suicide squeezes and cans-of-corn. I'd learned why Joe positioned himself on the infield dirt only a few feet from third base. Crouched there, he'd face the batters up at home plate. Joe's glove at the 'hot corner' would prevent hard hit grounders from screaming past him to roll far down the left field line. When he was at the plate, Mary called her boyfriend a 'doubles machine,' but we all knew he'd already made it to home plate with her. Joe actually did have a knack for hitting pitches into the gaps between the outfielders for his many doubles.

I looked up the stairway. My paranoia had me expecting to see Darla and Nils, but it was Rochelle instead. Watching her draw closer, my nervous heart calmed. I waited for Joe's mom to find her box.

"Hello, Mrs. Gardner," I said before she sat.

When I walked up to sit beside her, I told her the game hadn't even started. She stood and gave me a half-hug while pressing her cheek tightly to mine.

"Sorry I'm late, but I got stuck behind an accident on the I-82 bridge by McNary Dam.

As soon as she sat, Rochelle reached into her huge purse that was more like a tote bag. She pulled out a nice photo with a gilded frame and glass. "Kuma's parents sent me this."

"What a great photo of Baby Gracie!" I told her. "Look at the personality in that precious face." The infant girl was holding herself up and smiling into the camera, looking delighted with life.

"So precious, and only eight months old," said Rochelle. "The Kusumoto's are flying to Oregon in June when Tomiko finishes her ag exchange program. Guess who they're bringing with them?"

I squeezed her forearm and said I was definitely going to be there to find out. I decided this wasn't quite the time to tell her that there was no way Tomiko would be returning to the ag program after all the commotion the confiscated gold coins was causing. Two months from April to June didn't seem too long a time to keep Tomiko occupied and hidden.

When I glanced at Rochelle, her face turned steely. She was looking behind and above me. I pivoted nervously and did my best not to register surprise. The two sisters looked uncannily similar down to the same burgundy shade of dyed, neatly-cropped, shoulder-length hair. They held their heads upright at the same slight tilt. Rochelle was thinner and maybe three-inches taller. She moved one seat over to open a seat between us for Darla whom she eyed icily. "Do try to make yourself comfortable," Rochelle told her. Maybe offering Darla a box seat was an olive branch of sorts, except it sure seemed that Gunnar's mom should have been the one making peaceful overtures to Joe's mom after all that had gone down.

Once Darla sat, she intentionally ignored the 5" X 7" framed photo facing upwards on my lap. I reached across Darla to hand Gracie's little portrait back to Rochelle so she could slip it deep inside her big purse.

I pointed to Joe on the field and Rochelle beamed. Her son was focused on the batter.

"You're just in time for the first pitch," I said.

"Where's Nils tonight?" Rochelle asked Darla when the umpire barked out his third *steeeeee-rike* and the Eugene Emerald's lead-off hitter slunk back to the dugout below us.

"Not sure where he is," said Darla, obviously lying.

The second hitter grounded out meekly to the first baseman standing on the bag for an easy force out.

Rochelle stared at a side profile of Joe still protecting the third base line. She spoke softly. "I'm so, so glad to see my son doing what he most loves!"

"Look at how healthy and happy he looks," I added.

Rochelle teared up when taking measure of her boy. She, no doubt, felt waves of relief seeing him living out his boyhood dream rather than spending decades in the state pen.

With two outs, the third batter in the lineup went deep in the count, fouling off pitch after pitch. Joe definitely looked healthy. We could hear it in the way he shouted out encouragement to his pitcher. The batter took a wild swing and missed a fast ball. I'd forgotten the reddish cheeks Joe had as a younger teen before he tumbled into addiction. His ruddy color and robust demeanor were back. Rochelle and I applauded when Joe ran across the diamond to the home team dugout. He even surprised us by turning back towards our box and waving.

"I'm actually surprised to see you here tonight," said Darla to me, turning so only I could see her glare.

"Why?" Rochelle asked from behind her sister. "I can't see Biff missing Joe's opening game. No way. Not for the world."

The lead-off batter for the Dust Devil's first-ever opening home game was greeted with a standing ovation. On the first pitch, he proceeded to hit a pathetic little bloop that barely made it to the pitcher's mound.

"Is Nils planning on coming to the game at all?" Rochelle asked.

"Don't worry," said Darla. "I'll reimburse you for his ticket."

Rochelle glared at Darla, but her sister refused to look away from the hitter.

"So, is Nils checking out the local wineries, instead?" I asked, surprising even myself with the snide probe, even though I would breathe much easier knowing Nils Larsson's actual whereabouts. Tomiko and I needed to steer clear of his revenge. Maybe Darla's, too.

After a quick glare my way, Darla ignored the question and turned back towards her sister. "Nils flew in today from a convention. Said he would drive separately to Joe's game if he's not too tired."

I bit my fat tongue. At least the Larsson's hadn't notice that I'd spotted them filling up their gas tank a few hours earlier. So where was the heroin pusher lurking? I loathed Gunnar Larsson, but I was now convinced that his scumbag father was leading their family's wheeling-and-dealing .

Darla kept on the offensive with me. "Why isn't Tomiko at the game?" she asked loudly, her stare trained on my face again. I could tell that this wasn't going to be some instant, public confession by Darla, although the way she spoke so bluntly, I suspected that our wired audio would be crystal clear for Condran to hear up in the announcer's booth. "Tomiko only showed up early this morning for a couple of minutes of work at Nils's office."

"Maybe that was her most important task of the day," I said.

Darla started to respond, but stopped herself. So much for luring a quick confession from those glossy, hypocritical lips.

"Well, I definitely expected Tomiko to be here, too," said Rochelle. "Funny, but when I called her dorm first thing this morning, the Japanese boy on the other line said she'd just left with her American friend. When I asked who, he told me she was short with blonde hair. Sounds like you, Biff."

"That does sound like you, Biff," said Darla, turning away from Rochelle again, allowing only me to see her vile expression.

"Yep. I took her to meet another exchange friend," I said, looking past Darla at Rochelle.

"Who would that be?" Darla asked, her eyes still fiercely staring my way. I was beginning to wonder whether it was Darla or me doing the better job of interrogating the other.

My coat stayed unbuttoned. The open flaps assured voice-activation for capturing any incriminating talk. The crowd showed many under-dressed fans shivering, but I was warm enough. The State Patrol had provided me with a cozy jacket today––Abercrombie & Fitch, no less––complete with hood, wide buttons, and a thick-quilted lining. My own shivers were from nerves, not the plummeting nighttime temperature.

"Who was Tomiko visiting?" Darla asked again.

'The friend? I'm not sure what her name was," I said, reminding myself to take Captain Condran's advice and stay cool no matter how peeved I got.

"Why not?" Darla asked, pressing me.

"Because I have trouble remembering Japanese names." I said looking past her to tell Rochelle that Tomiko wanted her to know how sorry she was that she couldn't make Joe's game.

A cotton blouse and the top of my bra hid the mic, but the tiny device started to itch. I didn't dare scratch with my fingers or so much as press my hand on the mic, so I took deep breaths and thought back a few hours. Captain Condran had been riffing about the improving size and quality of hidden police wires and something about it being solid state and digital with a tiny voice-activated, omnidirectional microphone. Best of all, the new wires were so much better than the bulky contraptions he used to use. Too bad they still itched so much, I wished I could tell him now.

The Dust Devils did no better than the Emeralds in the bottom of the first. Three up, three down, including a weak ground ball to the second baseman for an easy out. Joe would lead off in the bottom of the second inning.

"Too bad George Brett isn't here to see Joe Gardner's hot corner glove," said Rochelle. She'd been following her son's baseball career since signing him up for T-ball.

"Cute jacket," she then said to me. "Is that new?"

I smiled. "Got it today. Not too heavy, not too light. Perfect for these cool spring nights." Just saying it, though, brought the itching mic back into focus. And what if I needed to hear from Condran? I wished I had my flip phone, the one I'd left at Darla's home last evening. Oh well. When it came time to bolt from the Larssons' home, I'd bolted.

In the top of the second inning, the Dust Devil pitcher walked the first two batters. The next one hit a hot line drive just inside the bag at third. Joe dove and snagged the ball before it ended up in the left field corner where both base runners would have definitely scored. Instead, he jumped to his feet with ball in mitt, touched third base for force out number one and threw a rocket to the second baseman for out number two. Rochelle was on her feet and roaring with approval. When the second baseman threw the ball to first, it might have been one of those really rare triple plays, but the ball sailed over the first baseman's head winding up in the Dust Devil dugout.

"Way to go, Joey G," someone up the steps behind us yelled.

The umpire awarded the hitter second base. I turned to see who was yelling, surprised to see four of Joe's former teammates from the Columbia Gorge Hustlers. They moved quickly down the steps towards our box seats.

"Thanks for inviting us, Mrs. Gardner," said Lyle Murdock, a classmate who'd also graduated with me and Mary the spring before. "We got caught up behind that bad accident on the Columbia River bridge."

The sight of these four surprised me. Not one of them had shown up to visit Joe in jail or attended his trial.

Lyle played a decent first base, but like me, he waddled more than sprinted when he ran. "Heya Biff. I hear you're a detective these days," Murdock said to me.

"Not many 19-year-old police detectives," I answered, catching a glimpse of Darla Larsson squinting at me just enough to make me shudder.

"Why not tell these friends of yours how you're unearthing all sorts of treasures in your precious case?" Darla said without looking away.

"Just helping the investigation," I answered and, for some reason, I looked at her hands. "Those nails of yours are awesome, Darla." I said, probably failing to sound sincere. "Do you still go to the Lotus Salon?"

"No," she said, tersely.

"When did you stop going there?" Rochelle turned and asked her sister. "You've gone to the Lotus ever since Linh Riggleman, our kidnapper, opened it."

Darla fidgeted. "I go there, but Mrs. Riggleman doesn't do my nails anymore."

"Well, of course not," said Rochelle. "She's been languishing in jail for a few months."

I wanted to scratch the skin around my hidden mic nearly as much as I wanted to come out and ask Darla if Linh's connections in Southeast Asia were the source of the China White unearthed at the Bone Shrine. At least the nail salon question had thrown Darla off her high-and-mighty game. She seemed a bit rattled.

The Dust Devil's pitcher, on cosmic cue, threw too far inside and hit the next batter. This placed the hitter on first with the guy from the almost-triple-play still standing at second base.

I loved seeing Rochelle so genuinely happy over Joe's big opportunity on the Dust Devils. The oblique exchanges between Darla and me might have her a bit baffled, but there hadn't been a hint that she knew anything about the newly found lockbox key or captured gold coins, telling me that, since Joe's release from jail, these sisters weren't exactly confidantes.

The next Emerald's batter worked a full count and had all of us on the edge of our seats in this game with no runs yet scored. Except for Darla, we all leaned back and exhaled when the catcher held onto a foul tip for out number three.

"My son's off to a good start with this team," Rochelle said turning away from Darla and speaking to Joe's ex-teammates.

"Joe plays a sweet third base," said Lyle, motioning with his hand towards the hot corner. "Always has."

"And, he'll be the next Dust Devil up to bat," Rochelle said, sounding more excited than I'd heard her in a long time.

I looked across at the home team dugout where Joe stood in the on-deck circle taking practice swings with a heavy metal donut around the barrel of his bat.

Lyle Murdock addressed me from one row back on the far side of Rochelle's seat. "So, Biff, any leads in finding Mary's killer?"

"Not that I can disclose. We're still looking for some missing Bone Shrine clues."

"She's been mostly looking for trouble," said Darla.

"What's that supposed to mean?" Rochelle turned toward her sister and asked, furrowing her brows.

"Just joking," said Darla.

"Bullshit," said Rochelle. "Nothing related to finding Mary Quinn's murderer should be taken in jest."

"I'm not the one taking anything," said Darla, and jabbed her elbow into my arm so no one else noticed.

The sisters glared stiffly at one another. The uptightness seeped into our collective mood.

The Emerald's pitcher leaned down behind the mound and dried his palms with a rosin bag before positioning himself on the rubber. Joe stepped into the batter's box.

"Joey's demeanor is more serious than I remember when he played for the Hustlers," said Darla.

Rochelle rolled her eyes and crossed her arms. "Maybe that's because your nephew's life has grown a whole lot more serious." Her wool Pendleton blanket was the biggest 'tell' of their frostiness. She hadn't offered to share even a corner of it with Darla right beside her.

Joe fouled off four straight pitches––all long foul balls down the left field line. "He's too quick in getting around on those pitches," said Lyle from behind us.

"Relax, Joe!" Rochelle urged her son, knowing that she was just another voice within this good-sized crowd.

With this, Joe launched a high towering fly ball to dead center field, 400 feet from home plate. The centerfielder drifted back, back,

back and leaped up at the deepest part of the park. The outfielder plucked the baseball from where it was about to hit the top of the wall. He showed the umpire that he had the ball inside the webbing of his mitt.

"What a mammoth shot wasted!" said Lyle, groaning.

Joe's former teammates had shunned him following his stint in juvie. Two seasons ago he was the best position player on the Columbia Gorge Hustlers. Only Kuma, Tomiko's brother and a first round draft pick of the Chunichi Dragons in Japan, was a truly elite player, but Joe, who had loads of potential, wasn't far behind. Yet, he wasn't allowed back on the Hustlers--not after his heroin conviction.

Lyle and these same baseball buddies had spouted off during Mary's vigil on that evening at the Gorge Discovery Center. Most everyone from our newly graduated class at The Dalles High School came. I remembered too well Lyle's voice roaring through the grand and long center at the heart of the museum. Everyone heard him. "It's totally sick how *heroin* made Joe Gardner drown his own girlfriend."

I wasn't ready to forgive these knuckleheads, even if Rochelle had. But, what did it matter now? I needed to focus on Darla and getting her to tell us something useful about our case, something to get her arrested, and maybe Nils, too. How could I draw her out?

"How's Gunnar doing in Sweden?" I finally asked, trying to sound matter-of-fact. "When's he coming back home to Moses Lake?"

Rochelle's face soured.

"He's doing fine," Darla said, her back arching. "He's helping out his grandparents at the family potato farm where they're starting a distillery."

"A distillery, I asked. "For making vodka?"

"Absolutely," she said, "but *Vikingstad Vodka* tastes better than *Absolut.*

Rochelle turned her head to look at Darla as though this was news to her. She didn't inquire any deeper.

With one out, the Dust Devil batter popped up weakly into left centerfield, in that spot called the Bermuda Triangle where wimpy fly balls would fall for hits by mysteriously disappearing into some sort of mystical abyss. The outfielders sprinted in and the middle infielders ran out looking over their shoulders. In this case, though, the shortstop––a fast, skinny kid––managed to dive and stretch out. He caught the ball in the webbing of his mitt before it hit the grass. The centerfielder ran the opposite way and veered off before colliding with his shortstop. Two down.

The third Dust Devil hitter struck out looking. It only took three pitches and we were done with the second inning.

Top of the third inning and I watched Joe, his mitt ready, hustling out to his third base spot. He pounded his fist into the palm of his leather glove, a baseball player's way of both applauding good plays and appealing to the gods of hardball. I would have better appreciated how happy Joe was to be in his element and playing pro baseball, but my task at hand was getting Darla to talk. I probed the abyss of mystified brain for something clever to say that would trigger a revealing response.

"Do you think Gunnar will ever come back to America?" Rochelle asked, her voice on edge. "To sell his Viking State Vodka, perhaps?"

Darla glared at me again, but just as quickly turned to look sweetly at Rochelle. "It's *Vikingstad*. Nils and I are planning to visit Sweden in December for yule. Yule. That's the word they also use there for 'Christmas'."

"Like Yuletide," I said, but Darla ignored me.

"I'll let you know what your nephew's plans are once we return. And, say!" she added, jabbing her elbow hard into my tricep like a warning. "I hear there's a new French bistro at the *Silent Flight Winery* above Richland."

I couldn't believe the way Darla kept her voice even-keeled while landing the hard shot. This secret recording effort was going to be a crazy challenge. "We should really go to the new winery sometime," Darla whispered to her sister. "We could use a bit of heart-to-heart."

I knew that Rochelle had season tickets and would be in the Tri-Cities often this summer, but it rankled my unsettled brain to hear Darla––the two-faced heroin dealer––working so hard to make nice with her sister. I breathed more easily when Rochelle ignored Darla's hypocritical crap.

The first Emerald's batter struck out on three pitches, one looking and two swinging. Joe's expression while playing seemed focused. He was in his element. For the next three innings, it was three up and three down for both teams. This pitcher's duel kept the game moving along at a fast pace for baseball, but too fast for my mission. I hadn't gotten close to hearing anything from Darla warranting criminal charges of any sort.

This game was halfway over, but I did manage to see the bounding grounder hit right to Joe. He smothered a short hop and threw a bullet across the diamond to the first baseman. Two down.

Before this fast contest concluded, I really needed something from Darla that somewhat resembled a confession. Otherwise, what a golden opportunity wasted. Then I had an urge, not too revealing, I hoped. I leaned forward and turned towards Joe's mom. "Say Rochelle, did I tell you? It looks like we're past any danger of Mary's case going cold? At least for the time being."

"That's wonderful! Can you tell me more?" she asked, her eyes suddenly more tuned into me than the game.

I figured since Darla hadn't mentioned this part overtly, then I would, but only by keeping my eyes glued on Rochelle. "Can't divulge much, except it has to do with the lockbox key. We found the match for the one fished up by a local angler at the Bone Shrine pond."

"How?" Rochelle asked.

"I can't divulge that, but we have important new evidence now."

Darla squirmed. I could tell she was trying to keep her fresh anger in check, but what would she dare say? Darla crossed her arms, her face turned steely, and she clenched her jaw and set her sights on centerfield.

Finally, she was reacting in a way where she might lose her temper and say something she'd regret.

"Nice glove work, Joey G.," Lyle shouted from behind Rochelle.

"You go, Joe!" a deeper voice roared from the stairwell behind me. "Hey, Joe! It's me, Max! Remember me from jail!"

Before I turned around, I saw Joe's jaw clench, as though he couldn't believe that his former jail guard would shout such a thing for the world to hear.

"Time to shut your trap, Max?" another voice said a few steps above him.

"Don't be telling me what to do, Squatty," Max responded when I turned around. Sure enough, Max was on the steps in front of Sammy, the two guards charged with bringing Joseph in and out of the court-room throughout his trial. Lyle and the other boys from The Dalles also stared at Big Max, looking baffled by the inebriated young man who seemed about to join us.

Max was intent on getting Joe to respond, though, so he stepped right past my row until he was leaning over the bullpen railing where, totally sauced, he could yell at Joe again. "Hey, Joe. You ignorrrrring your jail guard?" Big Max's voice boomed.

"Down in front," Rochelle yelled at Max.

In the field, Joe somehow stayed focused on the next pitch.

"Go back to your seat, Max," Darla said firmly. I'd forgotten that she would have known him through Gunnar. Sammy had mentioned that the three of them graduated from Moses Lake High School together, nearly three years before.

Max spun around and looked straight at me, like he thought I'd just told him to be seated. "Me get seated?" he asked me. "You snobby little runt! You wouldn't even sit down to a steak dinner with me."

"Leave her alone," Sammy warned him.

He'd totally lost his patience with Max, but Max simply turned back around. "Answer me, Joe Gardner! You stuck-up, too? You're damn lucky not to be in the slammer."

"Shut up, Max! Put a sock in it!" Sammy yelled.

"Yeah, dumbass, let Joe play baseball," Lyle added.

Man, I was sure glad I never went out on a date with this lush, but once Max pivoted, it got worse. "What did you say, Squat boy?" Foam oozed over the lip of his tall beer cup like molten ash.

"You heard me," said Sammy. "It's time we get back to our seats."

"No! Don't you be telling me to put a sock in it," Max shouted. "Snort this up your snout," he added, then, from a yard away, tossed all of the beer in his nearly full cup at Sammy who tilted his head to one side.

I wasn't so quick. What didn't hit Sammy's face, which was most of the beer, landed on Darla and me. Darla stood instantly. "How rude! What do you think you're doing, Max," she scolded and wiped suds from her woolen jacket.

I might have screamed at him, too, but the beer had sopped

through my blouse. I peeked to see. The liquid exposed the wire like I was in some wet T-shirt contest for curvy, undercover cops.

Sammy wiped the foam from his cheek. His face turned red with rage, but he didn't yell.

I sat there drenched, trying my best to zip up my new Abercrombie & Fitch jacket. I feared that Darla would turned around. Once she did, she'd notice the recording device.

Quickly, I pulled the zipper all the way up just as Sammy dove off his step and all but flew towards the bullpen. Sammy wasn't tall, but thick and way stronger than I'd realized. Max looked too shocked to react. Sammy's flying tackle sent both of them over the rail and into the bullpen like being in a car crash when everything slows.

The visiting team's bullpen pitchers had already twisted around to watch the commotion. Full-force on top of Big Max right at the pitcher's feet, Sammy's stocky body landed. The thud and crack sent a dull pain into the pit of my own stomach.

Sammy rolled off Max who then rolled and reached for his hurt shoulder. Max lay limp. The fans nearest us let out a collective groan at Max's wailing.

When he opened his mouth, I expected him to yell at his fellow jail guard. He moaned like a bawling calf instead.

The third base umpire stopped play. Joe hustled over to the opposing team's bullpen. "What the hell are you two thinking?"

Max grunted and then spoke. "My shoulder! Can't move my arm!"

"Lay still," Joe ordered. A medic ran from the Dust Devil dugout towards the bullpen. The third baseline crowd stood, trying to figure out what was happening.

An ambulance had been parked near the ballpark entrance. Someone on the field crew opened the gate next to the left field wall in foul territory. With lights flashing, the EMT's drove towards the bullpen. Two Pasco City policemen descended the steps. Sammy looked at me. "I guess I make a rotten babysitter for drunks," he said, not seeming the least bit remorseful. In fact, Sammy walked so calmly up the steps towards the cops that only one ushered him from the stadium while the other interviewed witnesses, starting with Darla.

During the delay, Lyle and his friends walked the three rows down to where Joe was standing. Lyle asked him how the minor leagues were treating him, even though this was only the first home game of the season. I stayed put, not wanting to disturb my microphone. I really hoped the liquid hadn't damaged the audio. I so needed more incriminating conversation. I worried that Darla, in her sopping wet jacket, wouldn't leave the game.

When play resumed, the opposing team's batter ground out meekly right to the first baseman.

With two outs in the bottom of the sixth inning, the batter ahead of Joe in the line-up walked. Joe stepped into the batter's box and dug out a good grip for his cleats. On the first pitch––a slow curveball–– we heard the crack of his bat. Everyone was rooting for the Dust Devils, except for Darla. We all stood and cheered when Joe's line-drive hugged the right field line and barely stayed fair.

Darla showed no interest whatsoever when Joe sprinted out of the batter's box and rounded first base. Rochelle and I yelled.

The walked batter ahead of Joe sprinted around third base just as the throw from the right fielder was cut off by the second baseman. The infielder pivoted and threw a seed to the catcher at home just as the runner slid. He would have been called out at the plate except the ball popped up and out of the catcher's glove when the runner spiked the thick mitt. Joe's standup double was, not only the first Dust Devil hit of the game, but a run-batted-in as well.

I had to remind myself that I'd probably made Captain Condran go deaf from my screeching. I'd also felt the thin mic and wire in my bra tug at my skin when I'd lifted my arms in glee. When I felt the pull, I put my arms down immediately. I sure hoped my zipped-up jacket wasn't muffling our talking voices. Nothing to do about that problem, except to hope for the best, I decided. I really needed to focus my brain on getting Darla to talk more.

What was Darla getting out of staying here for this one-to-nothing game? Making nice with Rochelle wasn't working too well for her. Was Nils using Darla to help set a trap for me and Tomiko? Would he ambush us after the game?

I did my best to focus again on the game. There were two outs as the crowd stayed on their feet and kept cheering. I stayed seated next to Darla, her arms folded tight.

When the Emerald's starting pitcher walked the next batter, the team manager slowly strolled out to the mound. A visiting reliever had been warming up with loose pitches a few feet below us. The lanky kid nodded to his skipper that he was ready to enter the game.

A first-pitch pop-up got the Emeralds out of the inning. Joe was left stranded at second base. More than whether the one run would hold up for the rest of the game, I worried mostly that the game was nearly over.

The top of the seventh was quick too and had me freaking out. What could I say to Darla that wasn't so blunt it gave away my awkward fishing expedition?

There were only a handful of Dust Devil pitches in the top of the seventh inning. Three easy grounders resulted in the side being quickly retired. This game was rip-snorting fast. What to say? How would I say anything to get Darla to reveal something of substance for our case?

Everyone sat down when the two teams returned to their dugouts. Rochelle turned and looked harshly at Darla. "Why the pissy attitude at Joe's debut game?"

"What do you mean?" her sister snarled in response.

"Remember how sly you and Nils thought you were being when you invited me to Sunday dinner during Joe's trial? Nils asked me all sorts of questions about Joe's trial strategy. You both talked about your nephew, Joe, as the 'red herring' kept there to keep attention away from the actual Bone Shrine crime perps."

Darla turned to face Rochelle. "Joe was exactly that. So what? I suspect that the alternative for your son would have been a bullet between the eyes for stealing that stash," she said, folding her arms even more tightly and turning to stare out at the field.

"Sounds like Gunnar, and maybe you and Nils, know every hidden detail about Mary's murder and that heroin sale?" Rochelle wasn't backing off and I surely hoped my mic was working.

"Keep guessing," said Darla. "Gunnar swore in a church pulpit that he had nothing to do with Mary's murder. I believe my son." She shot me a glance that sent shivers down my spine just as Lyle and my other classmates jumped to their feet with the rest of the Dust Devil crowd.

I wasn't ready for the seventh inning stretch when the crowd broke out singing. When I heard the words––*Take me out to the ball-*

game–– my head turned to see what Darla was up to. I looked up the stairwell. With Sammy and Max gone, I expected to see Nils storming down the steps fully primed to do something violent. Even when the fans praised the peanuts and Crackerjack, all I could picture was Nils taking me out––here and now––at this ballgame.

I couldn't breathe. I definitely had trouble focusing. What if Nils really was waiting for me and Tomiko after the game, somewhere, someplace beyond the ballpark lights?

Lyle and my other former classmates were oblivious to the testy back-and-forth between the sisters. It only took three quick outs in the bottom of the seventh to retire the Dust Devils and three more 'K's' to set down the Emeralds in the top of the eighth.

Darla and Rochelle decided to sit like stone statuettes with arms crossed. I was the one never at a loss for words, but I sat dumbstruck. I feared the words that came to my mind would risk too much about the inner workings of our murder investigation. Darla may have been only indirectly involved in that heroin deal, but I knew that she, along with her husband and son, knew a whole lot more than she'd let on.

The bottom of the eighth inning featured three batters before Joe came to the plate again. A pop fly out to the shortstop, a strike out, and a screaming line drive snagged by the pitcher at his ear ended the frame. I could relate to this opposing pitcher's adrenaline when he sunk to his knees before leaving the mound. How had he reacted so quickly from the come-backer that nearly took off his head? A sure-fire double had been thwarted. Joe reacted from the on-deck circle by dropping his bat and lifting his arms in frustration. He wasn't going to get a chance to bat again, unless the Emeralds scored to tie the game or go ahead.

He also knew that three more outs without a score would seal the one-to-zip win for the Dust Devils. What a waste it would be if I couldn't get anything from Darla to help solve our case. What if she decided to leave early?

The tight game created a buzz in the stands, but this was my last chance. The first Emerald's batter, a left-handed hitter, struck out on three pitches from the Dust Devil's left-handed reliever. One out and only two to go if the Devils were going to win by keeping Eugene off the scoreboard. Joe's manager motioned to the Dust Devil's bullpen for his right-handed closer.

During this pause in the game, I leaned forward and turned so that Rochelle could see my face and Darla could hear when I spoke. "I'm not sure I'm supposed to tell you this, Mrs. Gardner, but remember when the U.S. Customs confiscated all the gold Krugerrand coins, the ones that Linh Riggleman was smuggling in her baby carriage on the day she tried to kidnap baby Grace?"

"Of course, I remember. About $80,000 worth. Gunnar's bribe money, no doubt," Rochelle added, glaring at her sister.

Darla's mouth seemed set with a return glare at Rochelle and she crossed her beer-sogged arms even more tightly across her chest. Not even this accusation could get a rise out of her. Time for me to ratchet up this probing ordeal.

The Dust Devil's right-handed closer finished with his last warm-up pitches in the bullpen along the opposite right field wall.

"Well, there wasn't only a lockbox key hidden in the incense box that the fisherman dredged up," I said to Rochelle. "There was also a gold coin hidden in a dry plastic sleeve within the carved-out space where we found the key. The back was protected by the wood. It has Darla's print on it."

I don't know why I fibbed, even partially, but I wanted it to sound like I was talking about a Krugerrand even though the Buddhist medallion had been imprinted with a crane lifting its wings into the air in a manner sacred to Nichiren Buddhism. No. I knew why I lied. I was growing desperate.

"I've got to go," said Darla and stood to leave.

She seemed like she was about to kick her way past my knees when Rochelle stood on the other side of me and spoke loudly. "So Darla, you used those Krugerrands to buy Gunnar's freedom, didn't you?" With a firm tap on Darla's shoulder, she demanded that her sister tell her.

"Gunnar didn't kill anyone!" Darla looked over her shoulder and said.

"Maybe not, but your fall guy, your nephew Joe, most definitely didn't murder Mary Quinn!" Rochelle said.

Instead of watching the close ballgame, Joe's old teammates turned to watch us. And this was with the Dust Devil's closer tossing a couple warm up pitches from the mound with one out in the top of the ninth.

"Answer me, Darla," her sister said. "Did you and Nils buy off the Riggleman's with those gold coins so that Gunnar could flee to Sweden?"

I tried to tone down the confrontational tone of the sisters by speaking softly, but firmly. Anything to keep their words flowing into my mic. "Mrs. Larsson, we have strong evidence that you reallocated a portion of your gold coin stash to pay for this bribe. We're aware that those were the Krugerrands you earmarked for buying all the China White at the Bone Shrine before the heroin was seized. Your fingerprints are all over them."

Maybe they were, and maybe they weren't but the captain hadn't gotten the forensic report back on the coins.

"One way or another, you and Tomiko *will* reimburse us for the gold coins you stole," Darla all but yelled. "Now get out of my way."

I wasn't much shorter than Darla, but pretty strong, so I stood and held my ground with outstretched arms to hold her back. Darla's face had turned the color of brick. "If you cooperate, I can get your lockbox key back to you," I told her. "And everything inside it, too."

She seemed like she wanted to kick me. "You and Tomiko will need to make us whole, or else."

"Or else what, Darla?" Rochelle demanded to know. "Did Gunnar and Nils have Mary murdered with an 'or else' threat when your heroin went missing?"

Darla's eyes flamed before she turned back at her sister. "For the record, that was never Gunnar's heroin. Whether Biff here needs her parents to mortgage their family home, or Tomiko needs her rich baseball pitching brother to bail her out, we expect to be fully reimbursed."

"So you definitely know who wanted to sell Gunnar that heroin. Otherwise, why the need for him to leave the country hours after Mary drowned?" Rochelle asked. "He could have pointed out the sellers, the ones with a motive to drown poor Mary."

I hoped, finally, we were starting to get somewhere with our covert taping.

From behind, Rochelle all but growled in her sister's ear. "You're not going anywhere, Darla. Just sit down and tell us right now. Darla wedged herself between Rochelle and me. "So why would you set up your own nephew to take the fall for a murder he didn't commit, for a drug deal that--unlike your son--Joe had no part in."

Darla glared at her sister. "Why not own up to the truth about Joey? Once a pathetic junkie, always a pathetic junkie."

"Screw you, Darla!" Rochelle said trying with all her might to keep her voice down. "Gunnar was the one who got Joe hooked on smack, and you know it."

The patient right-handed pitcher who took too much time between pitches to the plate, went deep in the count. The crowd paid much more attention to the game than I could. A third strike had the batter caught looking on a borderline pitch. The Emerald's manager ran from the dugout below us to bark at the home plate ump.

"And--their skipper gets booted!" Lyle yelled while waiting for the umpire to react.

I glared at Darla. "I, for one, don't believe that you and Nils and Gunnar were directly involved in murdering Mary," I said. A handful of fans close to us watched me rather than the game. "That said, we have evidence that your family obstructed justice in your nephew's trial. The chief crime investigator was bribed on the morning after Mary Quinn drowned. That much is beyond doubt."

"The gold you stole was given to us by Linh Riggleman to invest in Vikingstad Vodka," Darla said with a snarl. "The coins were mine to count. I keep the family books."

Even with the batter who just struck out still jawing at the plate ump, I noticed more and more fans in the left field stands nearest us turning towards our commotion instead.

"Except for one thing, Mrs. Larsson. "Your prints, and only your prints, are on the coins that Linh Riggleman was smuggling out of the United States when she was kidnapping Gracie."

I sure hoped that proved to be true. The captain hadn't yet gotten any fingerprint tests on those coins, either. "The matching Kruger-rands connect you directly to Roger and Linh Riggleman," I added, in a whisper.

"I don't believe you," she screamed at me and elbowed Rochelle in the ribs. "Now let me out of here before I slug you both."

"Your own prints prove it," I said again, crossing my fingers. From her expression of dread, I could tell that Darla did believe me.

"How could you sit through Joe's trial like you did?" Rochelle shouted back, not caring if anyone in the crowd heard her. "For my son's entire torturous ordeal you pretended to give a crap about your flesh-and-blood nephew. Tell me, Darla! Who killed Mary?"

I sure hoped my mic was working.

Darla stood more upright, veins popping out of her forehead. "I don't have a clue."

"Gunnar knows who killed her!" I yelled. "We know he knows. So where's Nils? I'll bet he knows, too. I saw him and you today in your Saab gassing up in Richland. Is your husband out in the parking lot ready to kidnap and extort me and Tomiko?"

Darla sat defiantly. "Why not? And what would you expect? You two stole the gold, our investment money. And, as for being the fall guy, Hot Corner Joe never should have ripped off that stash."

Hadn't she just admitted to a plan to extort Tomiko and me? Had the Captain heard my heart pounding against my ribs, or enough from Darla to indict her for planning to kidnap me and Tomiko and then extort us until we made them whole, plus some, on what we snagged from the lockbox?

My eyes stole a peek at Joe and the close game. Big mistake on my part.

Darla's wimpy fists pummeled my jacket where the mic hid until she unzipped my jacket from neck to naval. I lifted my arms to protect my face, but in a cat-like swipe of her fingernail blades, she tore open my blouse, drawing blood. The same swipe exposed the wire and dislodged the covert microphone. "You wired-up, bitch," she yelled. "You're not leaving my sight. Not until Nils and I get our money back!"

Rochelle grabbed the back collar of Darla's jacket and pulled hard. "Like hell!" she screamed at her sister.

I shuddered at the thought of this clandestine recording with all its risk ending as pure static in the boss's ear. I guarded my face and body from Darla's pathetic assault. Rochelle restrained her sister with a bear hug from behind. I looked up when I heard heavy steps behind our seats.

Trooper Fonk in civilian clothes surprised Darla by cuffing her wrists. Funk's undercover partner held a service pistol towards her head.

The noise was too crazy for either cop to read Darla her Miranda rights, but I took the cuffing as a chance to spot the reason why the crowd had erupted into a frenzy of noise.

Joe was waving his teammates away and stared up into the new stadium lights.

Darla landed a sharp kick to my shin as the undercover troopers pulled Joe's yelling and screaming aunt up the steps. I yelped, but no one seemed to hear. I rubbed my bruised leg, but kept an eye on the field where Joe was looking up. I managed a glance behind me where the cops disappeared into the standing crowd.

Somehow, I managed to locate the high floating baseball as it drifted towards us. Joe shut out everything in his world except for this task.

Joe edged closer and closer to us. Rochelle buried her face in her hands. Lyle and the boys sat on the edges of their seats. Joe drifted to the bullpen, his focus still fixed up into the stadium nightlights. He leaned over the fence as far as he could.

Joe fell into the bullpen much like Max had, except that no one had pushed him and landed on top of his clavicle.

He popped onto his feet almost as fast as he toppled into the bullpen. Snow-coned in the webbing of his mitt was the baseball.

Even if no recording survived, there were still plenty of witnesses in our box who might be willing to attest to what Darla admitted so openly about threatening to take me and Tomiko hostage.

The sell-out crowd was still whooping and clapping at Joe's great, game-ending catch.

～

CHAPTER 11

BIG RIVER INN

"Follow us," said Trooper Fonk to Tomiko and me. Condran and a uniformed state patrolman walked a good bit ahead of us while escorting Darla Larsson. She looked straight ahead as we made our way through the exiting lines of cars. Tomiko had told me that the captain was hauling Darla off to the Franklin County Jail in downtown Pasco.

"He get good tape of her," Tomiko added and pointed to Darla being lowered into the back seat of a marked Washington State Patrol car.

"Yes," said Trooper Fonk and looked at me. "The captain wanted me to thank you for your good work with the wire. He said he had enough to charge Mrs. Larsson with attempted extortion of you and Tomiko. He also said that he'll have a formal debriefing with you in the next day or two."

I wondered if he'd get Darla to make a thorough confession about the Bone Shrine crimes before he had her locked behind bars for the night. We watched Captain Condran, in his unmarked Crown Vic, follow the patrol car out of the stadium parking lot.

"Right now, the boss wants me to make sure you two get safely on your way," the state patrolwoman added when we continued through the emptying parking lot.

"Still no sign of Nils Larsson?" I asked Trooper Fonk.

The officer shook her head. "No, unfortunately."

"Isn't that another state patrol car?" I asked, pointing towards where I remembered leaving my Subaru before the game. No lights were flashing, but I could make out the cop car silhouette in the dim parking lot.

"I believe you're right," the trooper said. We hurried our steps, but I told myself to stay calm and not run towards my car.

"What's the matter?" I called out to the patrolman when I got near. He was bent over along the side of my Loyale that was shadowed by a streetlamp. The little hinged door had been opened wide and my gas cap unscrewed.

"We just pulled up here," said the cop, "but your car was definitely vandalized." He pointed the beam of his flashlight downwards. An empty, five-pound bag of granulated sugar was wedged between the pavement and my rear tire.

"Biff, if you turn over that engine, then you might as well get yourself a new car," the patrolman looked at me and said.

"Why the vandalism?" I wondered aloud. "Do you think Nils Larsson might have done this?"

"That's a fair guess," said Trooper Fonk. "I doubt he knows we've arrested his wife," she added," but he likely wanted to send you a harsh message."

"Once he knows the State Patrol has possession of his Krugerrands," I said, "then he'll work even harder to corner Tomiko and me so we pay him back."

I shook my head and stepped in for a closer look at my Loyale without disturbing anything. "He probably expected my $800 beater of a car to seize up and strand us. I don't even want to think of what he might have done then."

Fonk pointed towards a tow truck winching the Larsson's red Saab convertible onto the back and asked the second male patrolman if the tow company could also take my car to the nearest import auto repair shop in Pasco. "Maybe they can clean the sugary gunk out of your tank before it causes any damage to your engine," she turned and told me.

"Definitely worth a shot," I said. I dreaded the thought of calling my mom in the morning and explaining why I needed her help to pay for a replacement gas tank, or worse, a loan for a new used car. I started to seethe. I loved my loyal little beast.

Rochelle pulled up in her van and rolled down her window next to Trooper Fonk. "Feel free to join us at my suite in the Big River Inn. A little celebration for my son's new life as a professional baseball player. Tell Captain Condran, too. There'll be plenty of pizza and wings."

"Thank you, ma'am," Trooper Fonk said, "but I'm still on duty until midnight with tonight's report to file."

I walked over to the trunk of my car and asked the patrolman if he was okay with me opening it.

"It's your car," he said.

I popped it open and saw that my suitcase and Tomiko's were still there.

The muscular cop helped me lug both suitcases over to the van where Rochelle had slid open the sliding side door. We hoisted the baggage on top of The Dalles Area Chamber of Commerce boxes.

I turned back to see an oversized, 1970s, Pontiac GTO rolling up. The voices of Joe's old teammates filled the air. Joe sat smiling in the back of Lyle's prized *Goat*, not saying anything when--with the big engine gurgling--Lyle assaulted Trooper Fonk with questions. "Did they lock her up? Does this solve the case? Will Joe's aunt and uncle go to prison for this?" Before the patrolwoman could answer, he slapped the bucket seat beside him and twisted his neck to look in the back at the star of the game. "Wasn't Joey G. totally in the zone tonight?"

Joe was far more willing than I was to forgive these knuckleheads, especially Lyle, for the way he'd rushed to judgment at the vigil and accused Joe of drowning Mary.

I motioned for Tomiko to climb into the front seat of Rochelle's van while I found a full box of Chamber brochures behind her where I could rest my backside. Lyle promised Rochelle that he'd see us at the Big River Inn once they stopped at a grocery store. The State Patrol car in front of us was no doubt the only reason he didn't burn rubber when leaving.

"Keep a close eye on these two girls," Fonk said to Rochelle and handed her a card. "Call me or Captain Condran if there's any sign of Nils Larsson."

"Of course," said Rochelle and held up her cell before slapping it shut and chucking it into her mega-purse. The clock on her dashboard said 10:00 pm. The starry night was moonless and black. With an electric crackle, the lights of the baseball park suddenly shut off.

The cop beside my Subaru and Trooper Fonk whipped around in the darkness at the sound of a powerful dirt bike emerging from a grassy, undeveloped field behind the outfield wall of the ballpark. The motorcycle seemed to hit seventy miles-per-hour when screaming along the far edge of the parking lot and off on a trail through another empty commercial lot. The bouncing taillight of the dirt bike disappeared into the night. The whine melded into normal night traffic.

The two state patrolmen beside my car started to jump in their State Patrol SUV, but Trooper Fonk told them to hold up. "Slim chance of catching him," she said. "I suspect he checked out a few off-road escape routes before arriving tonight."

"Sure sounds like the Husqvarnas that Gunnar and Nils rode," I said before filling my lungs with the chill blackness surrounding us.

"Are you sure?" asked Fonk.

"I'm pretty certain, Ma'am," I said. "Nils let me ride one with him when I rented the doublewide that Gunnar abandoned."

"When was this?" she asked.

"A couple, three months ago, before––"

"––before?"

"Before I had a clue that the parents were in thick with the Bone Shrine crimes."

"In thick?" Fonk asked, sounding persistent.

"With the heroin deal that went sideways."

The other State Patrolman got off his radio. "Just sent out an all-points bulletin," he told Trooper Fonk.

"Don't hesitate to call us," she told me and Rochelle before joining the other officer in his patrol car.

I definitely needed a new cellphone to replace the one I abandoned at the Larssons'. At least I hadn't lost the second lockbox key when I fled.

~

Rochelle had us carry up the boxes of pizzas and wings she'd pre-ordered from Shakey's Pizza Parlor. A few minutes later, Joe and his former teammates also arrived at Room 222.

Before any of the boys dug in, Joe told them to wait. He held up a baseball for everyone to see. "First off, let's give Big Max some healing thoughts," he said. "Max was my jail guard and pretty cool to me when I was locked up."

Pretty cool to me, too, I thought with a cold shiver, but told myself not to grimace or shrug or react in any way. After Joe hesitated and everyone had his full attention, he turned to his mom and signed the ball he'd caught to close out the game.

"Mom, I can't ever tell you this enough, but when it looked like I was landing in the state pen, you never stopped believing in me." Joe got choked up and Tomiko leaned into my shoulder. Joe tried to speak again, but couldn't make any sound. He handed his mom the baseball and she pulled him in close for a giant hug. She cried, too, when she did her best to read the inscription:

I'm free because of you, Mom.

Love, Joe.

After passing the ball around the room for everyone to inspect, Rochelle wrapped it within an excess of napkins we got from the pizza place, and stuffed it deep inside her huge purse. "Don't be waiting for me to stop blubbering," she said to everyone in the room and pointed at the pizzas. "And make sure none of this good grub goes uneaten. Hear that, boys!"

I reached out to open a box of deluxe pizza, but Lyle tried to wedge in. I slapped him hard in the shoulder. "Girls first, butthead," I told him.

Lyle took a step back when Tomiko and I took two cans of 7-Up and deluxe slices before making our way to the other side of the room. Our exchange student scarcely took her eyes off Joseph when he moved around the room talking to everyone there.

Then came the knock on the hotel door which, for some reason, I decided to answer.

I walked quickly past the bed and then paused beside the bathroom, before grabbing the door handle. But what if it was Nils Larsson standing there? I pressed my pupil slowly up to the eye-hole. Exhaling, I turned the lock and opened the door.

"Mrs. Gardner left her credit card at the main desk," the young woman told me. "Is she here?"

Before I could turn around, Rochelle stepped up from behind and, with a big thanks, took the card from the front desk clerk.

"Come on in?" Lyle offered from behind me. "Help yourself to some food."

The girl blushed and, before she left, muttered something about it not being allowed.

I wondered how badly Big Max had hurt himself. I assumed he had broken his clavicle and would need to be set with screws inserted. He was such a sloppy drunk and out-of-control that I knew I never wanted to have anything to do with the jerk and was lucky I chose to stand-him-up. Sammy had tried his best, but his oversized buddy wasn't easy to corral.

I went back and filled my plate with chips and dip. My brain ping-ponged from thoughts of Darla's arrest and the fate of my Loyale. Think positive, I told myself. Maybe it wouldn't cost an elbow and a knee to fix. The patrolman standing beside the sugar sack had explained how it was the pistons that would gum up from an overdose of sticky gunk.

Rochelle stood nearby me and took a call on her cell phone from Captain Condran. They spoke in a business-like fashion for a few minutes. When she got off, she sat down close to Tomiko and me. "It came as no surprise to the captain, but Darla insisted on having a lawyer present before she would talk to him. Her family attorney won't be in Pasco until tomorrow at the earliest. Until he shows up for the arraignment, my sister will be locked-up down here in Pasco as a potential, violent threat to you two."

"What else did the captain say?" I asked. "I suspect he would have called me, if I hadn't lost my cell phone."

"Tomiko, how would you like to come to The Dalles and be my guest there until the dust clears?" Rochelle asked her.

Tomiko sipped on her *7-Up*, gave me a quick look, and then measured her words. "Yes. Thank you. I stay with you in Dalles until Biff find place for us to live in Moses Lake. Then I help Biff find killer of Mary," she said.

Her intentions were great, but I just didn't see how she could be of much help for our investigation. I turned towards Tomiko. "Until then, you can use Kuma's *Butsudan* upstairs at Rochelle's. Be sure to chant for Mary's murderer to show his face."

"It's settled then," said Rochelle to Tomiko. "We'll go back to my place in the morning."

"Hey, Joe," I said when he came into his mom's side of the suite, and before he helped himself to the pizza. "I need to ask you something. Can we go out on the balcony for a minute?" I hadn't spoken with him since the day we were at the Gorge Discovery Center when he insisted––after my abduction––that I needed to go back up to Moses Lake and not give up on finding Mary's killer.

He looked at Tomiko and then at his mom and shrugged. "Sure, but you're keeping me from those thick combo slices."

Normally, I wouldn't be so secretive, but I didn't know when I'd see him next to ask him what Captain Condran wanted to ask anyone remotely associated with the case. And no one was more involved that night than Joe Gardner.

"This is about Tomiko, isn't it?" he whispered when we walked over to the sliding glass balcony door.

"No, but I'm cool with you and her, so long as you think Mary would approve." Strangely, I sensed that she'd set up the two of them from the other side somehow.

We stepped into the chill April night air.

"So what is it you want to ask me?" he asked, definitely wanting to change the subject.

"Remember the CPS worker, Amanda Skerry, the one who was first involved with placing baby Grace?" I asked him.

He nodded. "Sure. The one who awarded emergency custody to the scuzzy Rigglemans."

"Amanda told Captain Condran and me that she remembered something from when she was doing a home inspection and foster placement interview at Zach and Linh Riggleman's home. She said the house was neat and clean. There was a nice bedroom for the infant. Then, when Amanda was about to leave their place, she told us she'd noticed a Wanapum Sheriff's uniform. It was all neatly pressed and hanging from the utility room door."

"Why would that be a surprise?" Joe asked. "Riggleman is a deputy sheriff."

"Except this uniform was really wide and tall and took up the width of the door. Zach Riggleman is pretty lean--not all that tall. Amanda said this was a triple 'X' sized uniform, at the very least."

"Hmmm."

Joe always hummed like this when thinking about something. "It struck Amanda as odd," I said. "So Joe, I know you must be dog tired from the game, but is there anything you recall from that night that didn't come up in your trial? I mean, like maybe you saw something odd at the crime scene when Deputy Riggleman found Gracie and Mary?"

Joe fidgeted, his feet shifting nervously. "Or what about that second black garbage bag in the back of the Sheriff Jeep on the night of the murder?"

"What about the bag?"

"The deputy had made me take off my gritty tennis shoes if I was going to catch a ride back to the pond inside his vacuumed, cop rig."

Joe leaned closer and whispered, not that anyone else was listening. "Come to think of it, I'd guess that the other black bag was full of wet, mucky clothes."

"What makes you say that?" I asked.

"I started to move the first bag to one side so my smaller bag would fit beside it. That's when the deputy told me not to touch the other garbage sack that was there. I already had, though. It made a squishy sound like whatever it was that was inside was sopping wet."

"Why didn't you share all this with Angus?"

Joe shot back at me, sounding defensive. "Oversight. I guess I didn't know it mattered--until now when you told me about the washed uniform and then took my mind back to a time and place I've been trying to bury."

"Did you see any sign of mud on the plastic bag?" I asked.

"No. The Jeep's dome light wasn't bright enough to see anything like that. The bag was thick black plastic and heavy. Soggy like I said." Joe paused and looked at me again. "What if Deputy Riggleman was ordered to take care of a mucked-up uniform? What if those were wet clothes that belonged to a fat, killer-cop, the one who actually climbed into the pond and drowned Mary?"

"And what if the killer didn't want to have those wet, incriminating clothes in his possession?" I asked.

Joe's voice was firm, bordering more on angry than upset. This case had been haunting him, too. "Maybe Zach's father ordered him to get rid of the evidence."

I patted Joe on the elbow. "It's making more sense why Linh or Zach Riggleman would wash and press the murderer's uniform since he was the first responder at the crime scene, and could have bee the first to clean up any evidence."

"But why not just bury the clothes?" Joe wondered.

"Because no matter when they were found, those clothes would provide direct evidence," I said. "Dried pond muck would still be stuck on the fabric that could bust the killer. But not if the uniform was washed and pressed."

"But why wasn't it washed by the owner of the uniform?" Joe asked.

"Maybe Zach was taking orders from *El Gringo Loco*," I said, almost to myself.

"Who?" Joe asked, sounding baffled.

"Never mind."

"Well, Deputy Zach sure didn't seem too surprised when we pulled up and found Mary floating face-down in the pond that night," said Joe, his face hardening. "The minute we pull up to the pond and get out, he points his Glock at my temple. The only part of his rescue that seemed like he wasn't acting was when he found Grace floating in the reeds. I'd better get back inside," Joe said and opened the sliding door. Of course, he intentionally locked me outside when he stepped in. Just his style.

"Where is Biff?" I could hear Tomiko ask through the door.

"I tossed her over the railing," said Joe who, in one motion, unlocked the door and slid it wide to allow me back in.

"Can I see that baseball, Mrs. Gardner?" I asked sweetly.

"Sure," she said, and pulled it from her ample purse and unpeeled the napkins protecting it. Only then did she hand it to me.

By rolling it slowly with my fingertips, I inspected the seams and inscription from Joe to his mom. "May I bean your son between the eyes with a fastball?" I asked, and kept it away from Joe when he reached to take it back. Joe's old teammates roared and even Rochelle laughed.

When, finally, I handed Joe the ball, Lyle and the boys were anchoring their butts below the television in the other room to watch a re-run of the Seattle Mariner's game played a few hours earlier. "Say, Tomiko," said Joe, gently, "that new Japanese outfielder is on TV—— Ichiro Suzuki. Would you like to watch the game with me?"

Tomiko smiled with delight. "Yes. Ichiro! I wish to watch!" She said and pronounced, *Ichiro*, like a rock fan would say *Cher*, or *Sting*, or *Prince*. To her, he was already a singular-name kind of star.

Joe placed his hand on the small of her back and escorted her into the other room to watch the game. I stood watching at the door that separated the two rooms.

"That little guy can slap hit anything pitched anywhere near the plate!" Joe said.

"Everyone in Japan love Ichiro!" Tomiko told him. They sat side-by-side on one queen-sized bed with a few inches separating them. "He is funny man," she added, and almost on demand, this small Japanese player hit a double in the gap, one that was farther into the outfield than Joe's game-winning hit tonight. It cleared the bases for three Mariner runs.

"This M's team is off to an incredible April start," said Lyle. "A 15-4 win-loss record in April already."

Rochelle stood beside me in the same doorway. She watched her son and beamed at the sight of him acting and looking like the old Joe——her pre-addiction son——relaxing and enjoying himself with his peers. She couldn't take her eyes off Tomiko, either. I'd picked up on the same chemistry that she noticed. Both Joe and Tomiko lit up when glancing at one another, like the moment they met in The Dalles on the day she arrived from Tokyo.

Joe acted almost shy around her, both then and now. I shook my head. Shyness was so alien for him.

The boys yelled at the TV after a Mariner drove in Ichiro to take the lead. Joe turned and looked at Tomiko with an excited face. "I think we're going to sweep the New York Yankees!" he exclaimed.

"What is 'sweep'?" she asked.

Very patiently--a whole lot more tolerant than he'd ever been with me--Joe set down his pizza slice and held up both fists. "Two nights ago, the Mariners beat the Yankees in the first game of their series." He held up one left finger. "Last night the Mariners beat the Yankees in the second game of their series." Joe held up a second left finger and kept his right fist clenched. "And, if the Mariners hold on and win tonight, then they will have won all three games in the series. The Yankees will have zero wins. Looks like Ichiro's hit just gave us a 'sweep' of the New York Yankees!" With these three fingers of his left hand, he leaned down to the hotel carpet and, with a back-and-forth motion, imitated a little whisk broom. "And that's how the mighty Yanks are swept away by the upstart M's," he said when, on TV, the last out of the game secured the win.

I needed air. I stepped through the sliding door on Rochelle's side of the suite and looked across a small city horizon of neon that was glowing above streams of vehicle lights.

Watching Joe and Tomiko, I felt the same envious emptiness as when I'd been the third wheel with Joe and Mary, especially when they got all amorous and forgot I was seated in the Pathfinder behind them. I wondered what Mary was thinking from the other side? Not sure whether conscious thought was part of our being in the afterlife, but I still had this powerful sense that Tomiko and Joe were not only 'Mary-approved,' but also had the blessing of Kumo who held a deep-seated blame and shame for being Grace's father. At a visceral level, he knew the baby's parentage should belong to Joe. It wasn't as though Tomiko was acting against her own will, though. She truly liked Joe. It showed.

Tomiko and Joe slipped through the sliding door of the adjoining balcony. I stepped back tight against the glass. They were only fifteen feet away, but hadn't seen me. Her eyes were on Joe who was still clutching his signed baseball. He leaned in and whispered something for only Tomiko to hear. Her face lit up and she smiled, perfect teeth gleaming in the night like fine pearls. He pushed her long, black hair off one shoulder and leaned down. Her long, thin arms were about to be wrapped around Joe's neck.

That is, until a whiny roar had the three of us turning our attention to the parking lot below. The motorcycle sped into an open parking space. Oh, crap. The way Joe jumped to the short balcony wall for a look, I knew he also recognized the kind of Husqvarna he'd also ridden through the Potholes. We watched the man lower his kick stand and hop off.

Joe had Tomiko press her back against their sliding glass door so Nils wouldn't see her.

I slid closer to Joe when Tomiko slipped back inside the hotel room.

"Pssst, Joe!" I said before he could follow her inside. I pointed to what he held and whispered firmly. "Bean your uncle *real hard!*"

Uncle or not, this man was no ally of Joe Gardner's. From the adjoining balcony, I moved far enough to see Nils' motorcycle down below, and then him next to Rochelle's van. He was unscrewing Rochelle's gas cap and lifting a full bag of granulated sugar. Joe took a big step forward. With a perfect baseball throwing motion, he hurled his newly-signed baseball as hard as he could.

I stepped forward to see it hit the side panel of the van like a mallet striking a bass drum. The baseball ricocheted hard. Nils dropped his bag of sugar beside Rochelle's wheel when the ball nailed his groin. The groan made me wince. Joe grimaced, too. Must have been Joe's own horrid recollection of that foul ball to his nads, but he collected himself enough to shout, "Yo Uncle. Don't screw with any of us again!"

I wondered if Joe would have aimed for his uncle's skull had Nils not been wearing his motorcycle helmet. Why would Nils want to disable both my old beater and Rochelle's work van if not to strand us, and if not to extort us for the gold we snagged?

The darkened mask on the helmet turned upwards to face us. The boys filed onto Joe's balcony and then back out. Lyle held a baseball bat and the boys stormed back through the hotel room. We could hear their feet stomping down the outside stairwell. "Get that mutha!" Lyle yelled when Nils jumped on his motorcycle. Nils tried to start the Husky. It spurted and spat as the boys ran towards him.

Just as Lyle rounded Rochelle's van, the 500cc engine roared to life. Nils wasn't quite quick enough. When the rear wheel burned rubber, Lyle threw the baseball bat like it was an ax.

The motorcycle finally moved away, the barrel of the bat came down on top of Nils' helmet before careening down and off his rear fender, cracking the hard plastic. Both bat and fender hit the moving tire and spit backwards. Lyle jumped sideways to keep from getting hit. The Husky raced away. We stood frozen until the powerful whine died down in the dark distance.

Rochelle appeared directly behind me. We looked out at the highway beyond the parking lot. She spoke to her son. "Your uncle is always out of town on 'business.' Yet he's always somehow in the thick of things too, isn't he?"

"Yep," said Joe.

Lyle Murdock's voice boomed from down below. "Hey Joey G. Catch." With one hand, Joe snagged the perfectly arching ball when he reached up high at the edge of the balcony wall. "Should I chase him in my Goat?" Lyle yelled.

"Good luck with that," Joe told him, his arm around Tomiko's shoulder, his free hand again holding the signed baseball. That man knows every farming backroad all the way up to Moses Lake."

Upstairs, after the buzz of commotion died down, Rochelle consolidated several pizza slices into a single box for the boys from The Dalles to devour on their drive home. They were antsy to leave, took some pop to go with the pizza, and said their goodbyes.

I heard a faint knocking. What had those knuckleheads forgotten? Rochelle was busy telling Joe and Tomiko about how Big Max doused me and her sister with beer. With no desire to relive that moment, I got up to open the hotel door.

I stood in shock. I wanted to smile, but I wasn't over the whole thing with Nils Larsson. "You just missed all the action," I told him with eyes wide.

"Worse than when I tilted my head and you and Joe's aunt got drenched in beer?" Sammy said.

I must have looked stunned since I didn't know how to respond.

"Nothing on purpose. Not on my part," he said, looking cuter than I remembered. Maybe that was because his green eyes sparkled from the light behind me maybe, or that I'd had no clue how strong he was until he tackled Max.

Sammy handing me a notecard. Even though he and Max scored box seats from Max's brother that were behind home plate, this was from Rochelle in her neat personal handwriting inviting Max and a guest to sit in her box along the third base line. *Pizza Party to follow, Room 222, Big River Inn. Come celebrate Joe's new career in professional baseball during and after the game!*

"You can be my guest," I told him, holding the door wide open for him to enter.

"I'd love to be your guest since Max has no clue how to treat anyone."

"Let him in, Biffy," Joe interrupted before motioning his former jail guard inside the hotel room.

"How's Big Max holding up?" Joe asked, leaving me to shut the door.

"The doctors think his collarbone is broken in three places," Sammy said. "He needs to wait until the swelling goes down before any surgery or screws. The day after tomorrow, maybe. He's pissed at me, but not pressing charges, so that's a relief.

"What about tonight?" Rochelle wanted to know."You're not driving back home now, are you?"

"No. I'm towing Max's boat. It's out in the parking lot. Me and Max were planning on going river fishing in the morning. I'm thinkin' I'll just crawl into the V-berth and zonk out there."

"Hardly," said Rochelle. "Both these hotel rooms have two queen-sized beds and you can sleep in the room with Joseph."

Joe walked onto the deck and looked down. "Is that the cherried-out Bronco you bragged about getting when I was in jail?"

"Sure is. My '79 Bronco II with a manual V8 and 400 cubic inch engine."

"That's a pretty sweet boat Max has, too. Why'd you tow it with your Bronco and not Max's diesel Dodge?" Joe wondered.

"His rig is in the shop."

"So all this boat hauling is going to waste?" I asked. "Why don't you take me fishing instead?" I asked, completely surprising myself.

Sammy looked at me and totally blushed.

The whole room went quiet with everyone looking at us. I expected him to say that it wasn't his cabin cruiser to use, but he managed a laugh instead. "Let's go bright and early, then" he said. "Me and Max are all set to go anyway––bait, poles, boat fuel, and all." His voice was reserved as though the words he was inventing on the spot came with too much uncertainty. "Max shouldn't have been such a drunken chump tonight."

"You shoulda seen my Uncle Nils when I nailed him in the nuts just now," Joe said, holding up his signed ball for Sammy to inspect. "He deserved it."

"The same way Big Max got what he deserved," said Sammy while reading the inscription on the ball.

Rochelle snatched it from Joe's hand and guided Sammy by the elbow to the remaining pizza and pop. "Help yourself to anything that's still left."

Sammy declined the few remnants not taken away by Lyle and the boys, but thanked her for the can of Pepsi she handed him. Rochelle wrapped the ball with the last unused napkins and returned it deep inside her purse.

I was exhausted from the long, demanding day, but a rush of delight coursed through my body. Joe and Tomiko went into the other hotel room and turned on a "Columbo" rerun loudly enough to mask whatever they were up to. Rochelle excused herself to get ice from the machine down the hallway.

I felt awkward sitting alone with Sammy until he leaned over and kissed me on the cheek, his wide, green eyes locked on mine.

"I was so glad how you stood Max up. He usually doesn't spring for a steak dinner with the girls he asks out."

"Why were you glad?" I asked.

Sammy hesitated. "Because I was jealous."

"Really?" I asked, my face turning red now, too.

"I was always sneaking a good look at you in the gallery during Joe's trial. You're even hotter as a blonde."

I laughed. "You didn't like my Goth-black hair?" I asked.

"I didn't *not* like it. I just like this better."

"I love your diplomacy," I told him, especially since I agreed. "Much more diplomatic than Max can ever hope to be," I added.

"Thanks for going fishing with me," he said.

"I didn't mean to put you on the spot."

His lips curled into the sweetest little smile. "I've been wanting to ask you out since––"

"––since when?"

"Since I was stupid enough to let you borrow my flip phone to talk with Max."

"No. I was a total idiot for ever having any interest in that big oaf."

Sammy took my hand and led me to the deck where we could stare down at the boat. "I'm really happy you'll be joining me. Hate to see those morning fishing plans go to waste."

"You don't think he'll mind?" I asked. "Pretty expensive looking cabin cruiser he's got there."

Sammy looked at his feet. "I'm thinking of it as my fee for towing the boat down here and back."

"I've only gone fishing a couple times," I warned him, worried that my burning cheeks were revealing too much about how I was feeling inside. "You'll have to give me some pointers."

"No worries," he said. "I've fished this river plenty of times with Max."

"I have to get back to Pasco by noon, though," I said, deciding not to go into how Nils potentially ruined my engine with sugar.

"And I'll be working graveyard at the jail," he said. "Need to be in Smohalla by mid-afternoon.

Sammy leaned in for a light, sweet kiss that turned deep and soulful. When we heard Rochelle come back into the hotel room and then open the door to our deck, Sammy pulled away shyly. She saw us and stepped back into the hotel room without saying a word.

My eyes scanned the sky for a silent flying owl. I thought I'd see Mary swooping down approvingly, but the black night of stars shimmered like too many shards of glass.

～

CHAPTER 12

FISHING

Sammy was one of those people you could ride along with in quiet, not feeling any need to fill the empty airwaves. It was Thursday, the nineteenth. I reminded myself to write down the date in my journal once I retrieved my car at the Pasco repair shop.

Sammy pointed off to the side of the Lewis & Clark Highway towards a bird flying above and alongside his Bronco. I squinted into the dawn traces of light and gasped. My eyes hadn't deceived me––an owl, for real.

Sammy slowed to a stop on the opposite side of the road when the night bird veered off and down an embankment. In seconds the owl reappeared and lifted into our headlights. Something was writhing in its talons. When the bird and prey came into focus, I placed the back of my hand on Sammy's shoulder. The owl flew off with a Pacific Rattler, about four feet long and writhing in its talons.

"Mary comes silently," I said, the first to break the lovely silence of our ride. "She flies in without words. It's her ghost spirit. Mary can't let go of our living world here––not until she's avenged."

Sammy patted the steering wheel gently with the palms of each hand. "Just so you know, when it comes to finding Mary's killer, I'll help you if I can, but I'm not gonna get you or me killed. Working for the Wanapum Sheriff Department, I've got to tread real careful."

We drove down to the Columbia where the big river began to separate the states of Oregon and Washington. Just before sunrise, only the lights from the interstate bridge and McNary Dam disturbed the wet, wide ribbon of blackness.

"Do you think that owl with its poisonous rattler is telling you something?" Sammy asked.

My answer came without thought or hesitation. "Mary's telling us that there's venom in the air, and we've got to beware."

"Max and me have been hanging out less and less together," he said as he slowed for our turn at the tiny village of Plymouth. "When I was setting you up with Big Max for that date, I almost bit off my tongue not saying anything."

"Thanks again for protecting me at the ballgame," I told him.

"These days, I mind my own business inside the jail. They have me working the solitary confinement wing and mostly by myself. I don't go snooping around or asking too many questions––that is, if I want to keep my job."

"Did you see Joe much last fall?"

"Sure. Every night I worked. During the Bone Shrine trial, while I was guarding Joe on the graveyard shift, I saw how much he suffered for Mary Quinn."

He waited until I teared up before continuing. "Then in court, everyday, I saw you sitting in the gallery. I didn't want to stare at Joe's friend, this pretty Oregon girl in Smohalla for the big trial. I could tell how you were also facing your grief for her." He paused, put his hand on my knee, and continued in a soft voice. "I didn't know how I'd do it, but that's when I knew I really needed to get up the nerve to talk to you."

If I'd only known Sammy was really into me. I could have snuffed out my stupid crush on Big Max before it took hold.

"Like with you seeing Mary in that owl, I have visions of my own, too."

"Really?" I asked.

"It's like the first time I took Joe from the jail into the courtroom. I had a really strong feeling I was going to see someone really important in my life. Then, out of all those people filing into the courtroom every single day, you were the one glowing. From top to toe, I totally knew."

When I heard the words, I felt my insides glow, too. "Don't mess with me, Sammy."

"Never," he said in the tone of a solemn promise.

I decided to avoid prying for too many details from Sammy about his work at the jail. The tradeoff was pretty clear. I might get some minor detail for the case and push him away from me. It wasn't like he wasn't freely sharing, but Sammy struck me as the kind of guy who considered stuff before he spoke. He definitely didn't seem like the type to be pressured for information.

I needed to change the subject. "A bit awkward for all of us last night," I said. "Hanging in Mrs. Gardner's suite, I mean."

"Must have been crazy for you to see Joe getting all into that Japanese girl, so soon after Mary dying and all," Sammy said.

"Tomiko is baby Grace's aunt, so I guess it makes sense."

He pulled off the pavement onto a dark gravel road and hopped out of the Bronco to turn his hubs for four-wheel-drive. He jumped back in and rolled slowly forward on the gravel surface to a primitive boat launch on the Columbia River shoreline.

I climbed out when he positioned the boat on the top of the crude launch. The name across the stern said *ThunderMaxx*. Perfect for Big Max's boat, I guessed.

Three other rigs with attached boat trailers were parked near the sandy boat ramp. None of their boats were visible on the main river. Sammy could see me through his side mirror. He hardly needed my help. The boy knew how to back up a boat trailer and didn't stop until the tandem tires were in the river. I heard him apply his parking brake before jumping out and showing me how to uncrank the winch while he pushed the extra-wide vessel off the trailer with the help of rollers. Mostly the river took the weight and the boat began to float. Sammy handed me the bowline and unhooked the winch.

After taking the truck back up the ramp and parking it, he walked back, squatted down. "Piggyback time," he said and patted his spine so I'd climb on his back.

I hesitated for just a second, not sure I wanted him to feel how stout I was, but then I thought back to the night before when we hugged and kissed and he probably had good measure of me. Sammy hooked his arms around my thighs and walked me to the starboard side where he sat my ample backside on the eight-inch wide gunnel. He motioned for me to pivot until my feet were inside the boat. Sammy let himself get wet up to his thighs and climbed onto the transom to get inside the impressive boat with top-of-the-line everything.

In the first light of dawn, Sammy lowered the small 15-horsepower kicker motor, pressed the start button, and held onto an extender arm for turning and accelerating. He placed it in reverse and backed farther into the river. I stayed out of his way when he lowered the tandem 400-hp Yamahas and shut off the kicker.

"Any lifejackets for us?" I asked right after reaching into the pocket of my Abercrombie & Fitch jacket to make sure I still had my one-day fishing license that Sammy had just bought for me at an all-night mini-mart. Also, I wasn't much of a swimmer and I couldn't tell if, by hesitating, whether Sammy never wore life preservers when boating, or maybe he was having trouble remembering where Max stowed them.

The boat started to drift into the main current when Sam started searching. There were compartments under the length of the deck and more on the port and starboard sides, too. For better footing, diamond treading was molded into the aluminum hatch covers and also on the other deck surfaces.

"Great boat for fishing, camping, or smuggling," I said, unable to hold my tongue.

"Smuggling? I honestly wouldn't know," said Sammy, with a tone telling me that, even if true, he really didn't wish to discuss this.

He had to open a half-dozen hatches before pulling out two orange preservers from inside a large waterproof hold near the door into the cabin.

He helped me on with mine and I helped him on with his, pressing my lower half against him while adjusting his straps. Sammy didn't seem to mind.

That's when I looked up to see that we were a good half-mile downriver from where we'd launched. I didn't see any other boat on the river to rescue us, but it didn't matter once the big twin Yamahas fired up.

I grabbed the nearest railing when Sammy showed me just how much power the boat had. I burst out laughing from the unexpected g-force. He laughed at my surprise. The morning was ultra-calm, except for our boat's roar cutting through the air. Sammy raced against the main stem current towards McNary Dam which I could see beyond the interstate bridge. The huge concrete river impediment must have produced plenty of electric zap.

"A thousand megawatts," Sammy shouted, and pointed towards the same thing I was studying with my eyes. "Enough to light 700,000 homes."

That boy could sure read this girl's mind, especially how much I really liked him.

I noticed the boat had two helms for steering. One on the outer deck that Sammy was now using, and the main wheelhouse that I could see through windows inside a tall cabin that took up over half of the boat's deck. Sammy eased back on the throttle until we were holding in one place. *ThunderMaxx* steadied in place against a modest river current. He motioned for me to take the helm and went to the transom where he lowered the anchor and chain with winch and drum. With how far down the anchor was dropping, we seemed to be settling over a fairly deep fishing hole.

"Is this the magic spot?" I asked when the anchor hit bottom and held.

"Magical as you are," he whispered. We both went silent with impish smiles.

"Stay focused, Mr. Fisherman," I told him.

Sammy laughed and clicked a button to raise the big Yamahas out of the water before going to the 15-horse kicker motor. Sammy went into the main wheelhouse and found the key for opening the long locker below the port railing. Several rods and reels were well stashed inside.

"They're labeled. One for Max, one each for his parents, and four more." He grabbed two of these thicker ones. "These aren't for salmon."

From the unlocked rod rack he also pulled out a seven-foot long gaff and something else. "Carbon fiber shaft for the gaff and this short hook-out is heavy-duty, stainless steel." Sammy tilted the gaff next to the cabin on the side of the boat opposite the helm and leaned the hook-out on the deck directly below it.

Sammy slipped inside the cabin again, opened a small refrigerator inside, and returned with a small jar. "Herring wrapped around a dill pickle," he said after pulling one out. On the transom, he cut it in half, guided a large single hook through the fishy part and tightened a hangman's noose over the whole piece of bait.

"Why not use a bigger bait to go for a really big fish?" I asked.

"Got to be sure they suck the hook in their mouth along with the bait." Sammy lifted the hooked herring and a big pyramid hunk of lead hanging at the end of his leader. "See this four-ounce weight. It stays on the bottom. The hook and bait are tied above the pyramid so you can feel when a fish is on the bite. Yank up firmly if you feel a strong tap, tap, tap."

I smiled. "How will I know if I've hooked a big one?"

"You might not when they take the bait, but once the fish figures out it's hooked, you'll find out right off how much heft it has."

After making sure I was on the bottom with my lead, and with the line feeling taut, Sammy took the firm, long pole he'd be using. His line and lead to also reach the bottom on the side of the boat opposite mine. He used the rod holder there and came over, wrapping his arms around me, snuggling his nose into my shoulder-length hair before helping me reel in, just a bit, to tighten the line. "When you have a fish on, don't allow any slack at all. Lift the pole high when you're able, but do it without reeling."

"No reeling. That sounds fishy if I'm going to pull anything in."

He chuckled. "When your pole is up high like this," he said, showing me, "then you slowly lower the rod tip down to the water, reeling as you drop down, but never giving the line any slack. That way, loose line won't give your fish any chance to spit out the hook."

I could feel his body, short and stout like my own, pressed tightly against me. "Hold the pole," I said. When he held the cork handle, I spun around with both of his arms still on either side of my ears. He was only a few inches taller than me so I could see over his shoulder. I don't know how he managed to concentrate on my fishing rod he was holding, especially when I kissed the side of his neck and nibbled his earlobe before lightly biting it. When I opened my eyes, I ducked under his arms and moved quickly to the other side of the boat where the tip of his own pole was doing a crazy, up-and-down dance. "Check it out!" I yelled and lifted his pole.

"Reel it in real slow," he said.

I did as Sammy directed and this fish with no heft came right up. In one motion, I lifted it onto the boat. "I know what this is," I said.

"A Squaw Fish," said Sammy.

"You can't call them that anymore," I told him.

"Sure I can. I'm native. My father's side."

"Ooooo. That explains your exotic good looks. Not to mention those dreamy olive-green eyes that mama must have added into your handsome mix." Even the oval shape of his face and nostrils made sense once he said he was part native.

Sammy blinked and looked away shyly. "Mom's blonde, blue-eyed, and on the short side like you. Real good at talking, too. Took one tough, single mom to keep me in line all these years."

Sammy knelt and removed the twelve-inch fish from the hook, but looked up at me when I asked him what tribe his father is from?

"Wanapum, except that my dad's dead. Died up elk hunting when I was seven."

"So sorry to hear that."

"I never saw him much, even when I was little. The tribe didn't want my mom around."

"Why?"

"She wasn't supposed to, but she sold some photos she took and recordings she made of a *Washat* drum-and-dance ceremony."

I rubbed the upper arms of my nylon jacket. "My mom runs the museum in The Dalles. She's curated plenty of cultural items from the Columbia River tribes. Takes me to Celilo Village every year for their First Roots celebration. I think that's part of the *Washat* tradition."

"My great, great, great uncle was Smohalla, the Dreamer. Or maybe it's four 'greats,' I'm not sure. He was the native prophet who spread the *Washat* faith.

"Are you enrolled in the tribe?"

"No. Thought about it, though. I mean, now that I'm twenty-one," Sammy said.

"What's in the half you got from your mom?" I asked.

"My grandparents on her side came to America from Poland."

"How was it growing up as an only kid with a single mom?"

"We do fine. She sets me straight when need be."

"Like how?"

Sammy laughed. "When I was fifteen she sat me down. Her eyes were fierce, so I was sure I'd done something bad, but I didn't know what."

"What did she say?"

"She said, 'Samuel Puck, you choose carefully, son. You'll know when you've found the right girl to give yourself to.'" Sammy rose up on his knees and looked at me. "That's you, Biff. I can feel it."

I blushed. "Just so you know. My mother told me the same thing, except that my name's not Samuel Puck."

I looked at my own pole that remained still, mostly because I was scared to see Sammy's expression. Already, I couldn't stand the thought of ever losing the crazy, heart-bopping feeling this boy was creating inside of me. I'd never felt this way about any boy before.

Sammy placed his pole back in its rod holder and knelt by his fish again. "Squaw Fish eat way too many salmon smolts," he said.

"So what do you call a male Squaw Fish?" I asked him.

"Say goodbye to Mr. Pikeminnow," he said, and tossed it back in the river.

I smiled warmly. "This really is quite a cabin cruiser," I told him and tapped at the aluminum hull. A quick peek inside the main cabin showed how it was decked out for cruising as well as for fishing. Mahogany paneling and matching cabinets above marble counters. Everything else was stainless it seemed, including the big wheel with all the accompanying dials, gages and toggles for navigation. Even the cup holders were stainless steel. This big boat was definitely stylin' with a Garmin radar tracker the size of a wedding cake. Seemed like the finest Columbia River cruising boat that money could buy. "Still surprises me that your friend is letting you use his family's boat," I said.

"To be honest, I never asked for permission, but after all that fun at the ballgame, I don't know if I'll ever be fishing with Big Max again," he said.

"Because of him dousing me with beer?" I asked.

"Truth be known," Sammy said in a low, almost sad voice, "I don't know if I want to be around him much anymore, but since he insisted I tow his family's boat down here, I figure I'd get one last use out of the thing before I haul it back to Rattlesnake Cove this afternoon."

"Where's Rattlesnake Cove?"

"Max lives in a cabin there. It's on the Columbia River just below the Gorge Amphitheater. That's where they keep this thing."

"Can you hear any cool concerts from his place?"

Sam winced, but I couldn't figure why. "The only way to hear any music at the Amphitheater is if you take a boat and anchor it in the river right below the stage."

"How's the sound quality from there?"

"Really fine, if it's not all windy."

"You should invite me along so we can party and get wild and I can throw a pitcher of icy beer in Max's face."

Sam nodded, but didn't smile. "Even I didn't get to go boating with him last summer. I've had it with that fathead, even though we've been friends since kindergarten."

"Sounds like the falling out with Max has more to it than just the ballgame last night."

Sam reeled in to check his bait and dropped it back down to the bottom before continuing. "When the nurse let me inside Max's hospital room, his OxyContin hadn't kicked in. Once we were alone, the first thing I did was apologize for tackling him too hard. He hardly looked at me until he decided to unleash his anger."

"Two broken shoulders. He couldn't have been too happy."

"Nope. Stone-cold stare, but there wasn't a shred of thought in his brain to admit he'd been wrong to dump his beer on you."

"So tell me what he told you."

"Nothing about you. Just that if I so much as touched him again, then he'd break my neck."

I shuddered. Max was a huge, strong man and I'd seen his stony-eyed stare--right before the jerk showered me with beer. Sammy really had put himself on the line standing up for me. "Since you two have been buddies for so long, has he been acting weird, like before yesterday, I mean."

"Sure. He keeps away from me at work. Come to think of it, I was surprised he asked me to go fishing, except I told him about this one hole I knew about near the Tri-Cities here."

"So you came to the game still being friends enough to fish together?" I asked.

"Why not? We go way back. That's not to say he's not a jerk to me, too."

"Like how?"

"Like last August. Max invited me to go with him to the Poison show with him. On the very last day before the concert, he called to say he had to take someone else."

"So who did he take? Every Rose who has her thorns?"

"Hardly," he said and chuckled, "Max went with Gunnar Larsson. Said they had some serious shit to discuss."

I shot a look at him. "August of last summer? Do you remember what date?"

"Middle of the month, a Sunday."

I counted backwards from Friday, the date Mary's body was found. "August 13th?"

"Sounds about right. Wait. I never thought of that being right before the whole Bone Shrine stuff went down. It was mostly that I'd taken time off that day so I could go. That's why being ditched pissed me off so much."

"So why did Gunnar Larsson go instead of you?" I asked.

He shrugged. "It's not like we haven't all known each other since grade school."

Then it came to me––the reason behind the Wanapum County cover-up guided by Roger Riggleman. "What if Max and Gunnar were the two advance men needing to arrange the Bone Shrine deal?"

He grimaced this time, like I'd made him uncomfortable. "Max can be a bully, but no way would he kill Mary Quinn. I've known him my whole life. He's mostly pretty cool."

"But you say he's changed."

"There was nothing weird that Gunnar and Max going to the

Poison concert together. It just wasn't cool how Max ditched me, last moment and all."

I kept thinking how this cabin cruiser was plenty big for a dozen people. *ThunderMaxx* was wide and 28-feet long. Plenty of space for Sammy, for a big party even. That's what made me suspect that this was all business with Gunnar as the only one invited onto Max's boat so he could sample the wares and then give Max a down payment--a few Krugerrands maybe.

I was jolted out of detective-in-training mode when Sammy told me, tenderly, how cool my loyalty to Mary was. "Tells me you got a big heart."

I kissed his cheek and let my lips linger there before whispering in his ear. "Thank you. And just so you know, Sammy. I am big hearted."

He pulled me tightly into his torso, like a bear hug, except more tenderly so he could reward my words with a loving, quiet response.

"Shattered my heart to bits when my best friend was killed," I said feeling like I could tell this kind man most anything. That's not to say I didn't keep wondering if Sammy's old school buddy also helped Gunnar get out of jail the morning after Mary Quinn drowned?

When I sucked in a lungful of the chill, sobering April air, I didn't want to be pushy with Sammy--not this soon. Instead, I wrapped my arms even more tightly around his thick, solid torso. That's when I saw the pole bend and I went bug-eyed.

"Look! Look!" I yelled out before rushing over to my pole. "What do I do?" My tip was bouncing a whole, whole lot more than it did with his squaw fish of unknown gender.

"I'll help you," Sammy said, and reached around me to also hold the pole. I didn't even mind his pikeminnowy hands.

"See. We just lift the rod a tiny bit. Once we feel another tug, then we'll pull up quick-like to set the hook," he said, "Just not so hard that we yank the hook from its mouth."

And just as he started to lift the pole the smallest amount, with my hands sharing a fine cork handle, an eighteen-wheeler crossed the freeway bridge a couple hundred yards upriver and laid on his Jake brakes.

Startled, we both felt the tug, not real strong, but unmistakable. Sammy pulled up hard and high and held the pole there for me to take. "Hold on, girl!" he yelled. I loved the sound of his words when he stepped away, or maybe how he was trusting me to play my own fish.

I didn't have any chance to reel in when the rod tip was yanked down to the surface of the river. "Don't reel! Not yet!" Line started to whine off the reel as the fish raced away from us. "Pull the tip up out of the water and let the big beast run."

"This isn't some bluegill," I yelled, remembering the palm-sized, pan-fish I'd once caught––now the second biggest fish I'd ever hooked. I was too excited to concentrate when this fish on my line took off towards the bridge. "Don't let me run out of line," I yelled. We looked down at both my shrinking spool and the steady and deep current of the big river slipping beneath us.

"Hold on!" Sammy told me and hurried to the kicker motor..

"What if it's taking us to Yellowstone Park?" I asked, but then saw huge McNary dam blocking the river.

For Sammy's part, he pulled up the newly dropped anchor, started the little motor which at full-throttle eased us towards the fish. "Now it's time to reel. No more yanking. No slack at all. None," he reminded me in a most excited, masculine way.

"This has got to be bigger than any big king salmon," I said, reeling in when I felt slack. When the line seemed to be directly below the boat again, my pole wouldn't budge. I couldn't lift the rod tip, and when I reeled, the end of the pole disappeared again under the river surface.

The little motor mostly kept us above the fish and in one place in the river. I tried to tug on my line. The third time was a charm, if you call waking up a monster, charming. This huge fish decided to let me know how pissed it was from the thrashing feel of its big tail down below. I reeled just a bit when I could, and yielded even more line when the fish dove deeper.

"You're doing great, Biff!" he told me as the down-and-up and down-again fight repeated itself. Ten minutes seemed like an hour so our fish fight had to have been several hours long by that reckoning.

"Way to keep the line snug!" he added.

My arms ached from trying to land this leviathan. Sammy positioned the trolling motor and throttle so he could come up behind me and squeeze my bicep. "You're some strong kind of girl," he told me.

"Well this girl is due for a break." Nothing in my life had ever prepared me for this kind of physical test. When the fish stopped, I pulled up one more time and reeled my tip down to the river before pulling up once more. "Perfect!" he told me. "Are you ready to switch places?"

"Yes!" I'd begun really hoping he'd ask to share my fish fight with me.

He placed his thick hands on my waist and eased me to one side for our exchange. "Once I take your pole, then go grab the kicker-motor handle."

The hand-off went smoothly and he shouted, "Yep, you're definitely one strong fisherwoman! And this is one seriously big fish!" Sammy's bugged-out eyes showed how surprised he was at the size of what we had on the line.

He reeled down firmly, never yanking on the fish to bring it closer to the boat. "Got to let them tire out on their own," he said. As soon as he said this, the fish dove to the bottom again. Sammy was breathing hard in no time. I did my best to keep our boat in one place facing upriver towards the dam. There was something sexy about this fisherman. He was no weakling and pulled up strongly at least every half-minute to coax the fish into moving. After a few minutes of this, it moved away from us in an upriver direction again. Sammy reeled fast whenever the well-hooked fish gave him a chance.

"Wanna take over again?" Sammy asked me.

My arms throbbed. I wasn't ready to take back the pole. Besides, as soon as he asked me, the fish decided to head to the surface. "Keep watching!" he told me, reeling in fast. "We might just catch a peek of this monster."

I did my best to look, but then I heard the reel whining. The fish peeled off more line to dive towards the bottom again. Sammy tightened the drag down pretty good, but said he still needed to let the fish run whenever it decided to. "One hundred pound, braided line," he told me. "It only dove part way down. Maybe it's tiring."

This time——and it felt we'd been fighting the gigantic fish for half a day——the sturgeon allowed itself to be pulled towards the surface of the Columbia River. "Hold this," Sammy said, but didn't wait for an answer. I took the pole and, just like he told me, I reeled in when the line slackened.

The early morning wind was calm and the deep current smooth and steady.

Then my eyes nearly popped out of their sockets. "Oh man! Oh man!" I screamed towards the stern.

The fish showed its pointy nose and creepy shark-like eyes. The suction-cup of a mouth was three times the size of a toilet plunger. The surfaced outline of the body looked almost as long as the boat. My grip tightened on the pole. My arms, hands and body froze.

Sammy turned, reached past the long gaff to grab the arms-length, stainless hook-remover.

"The sculpture came alive!" I yelled.

"The what?" Sammy asked, confused enough to stop and look at me.

With buggy eyeballs, I glared and pointed at the prehistoric swim-a-saur. "Jeff Stewart's sculpture," I yelled. Sammy turned back to the river, but too late.

"That's the biggest––" Sammy also yelled when he saw the sturgeon and dropped his hook-remover. The ugly head went under and the monstrous tail lifted out of the river. "Shit! Shit!" he shouted when the huge fish slapped him off the transom and into the rush of current.

"Jesus Christ Almighty!" I yelled, when Sammy disappeared below the murky runoff. The tail writhed and hit the surface drenching my hair and life preserver. The river beast had stolen Sammy and ripped the expensive rod and reel from my grip.

"Sammy!" I screamed. But there was no sign of my new boyfriend. I leaned over the stern to see the loooooong, pissed-off tail of the sturgeon thrash one last time before disappearing into the deep river hole.

I stood as tall as my short legs allowed and yelled out for Sammy again. When I looked over the railing to starboard, the boat started to turn in a big circle. I hurried to grab the extension handle again. The trolling motor was sweeping us with the current and away from where we'd been fishing. I turned the throttle to full and made a half-circle until I was pushing against the current and frantically looking for any sign of a head.

An orange blob drifted towards me fast––too fast. I wanted to cry, but didn't dare. Focus and don't miss, Biff! Was I destined to lose everyone whom ever drew close to me? I pointed the bow into the current and left the 15 horsepower throttle on full bore.

I hurried to the stern, grabbed the long gaff, and kneeled on the transom that was inches from the water and reached out as far as I could with the hook. He was still face down. Dead?

What if I hooked him in the eye socket? Or punctured a lung?

When the sharp-tipped gaff found the thick nylon collar of the life jacket, I pulled back as hard as my sore arms could. Sammy's face popped out of the water gasping for air, choking. With all my strength, I pulled his body close to the boat. He spewed river water from mouth and nose and flailed until the back of his head hit the transom.

Sammy started swearing at the collision of his skull into the stainless stern, a really good sign. I dropped the gaff and didn't care that it slipped away into the current because I had this boy's orange collar clutched so hard that I'd never let go. We stayed in that position until I could gather my wits.

"I'm going to turn you around now," I said, never thinking I'd ever use such an endearing term. "Take deep breaths!"

I didn't care that the river was sweeping us downstream. What mattered was keeping a firm grip on the nylon strap of his lifejacket until he faced me. I told him I could help save him if he'd let me slide him onto the transom. Sammy shivered in the spring runoff filling the Columbia, but with one hand he managed to grab a bar on the railing. His other hand held to a bracket for one of the big Yamaha outboards.

I think he knew that if he wanted to live, then he needed more than my crazy pulling. He required something from inside of himself now. He sputtered and choked. From somewhere deep within, he knew to kick like a freestyle swimmer. I kept pulling as hard as I could and he kept kicking until I felt my strength leaving me.

"You can do it, baby!" I yelled again, until I felt myself losing the last of my strength.

Then like a seal launching onto the rocks, Sammy slithered onto the transom until his elbows hooked onto the steel surface.

He writhed onto the main deck until he was sprawled and coughing. I took off my Abercrombie & Fitch jacket and blanketed his orange life preserver. We had to get him dried off.

First, I hugged his face tight to my chest. "Ouch," he said when I forgot I was wearing my knew *She-Who-Watches* medallion.

"I didn't mean to emboss your cheek," I told him. We both laughed when he pressed his cheek even harder into the medallion. Sammy looked happy to be alive. I hugged his drenched, shivering body before hugging him some more. The enormous fish was long gone, along with the gaff and expensive rod and reel, but Sammy had surfaced––thankfully!

From a cupboard near the helm, I found a wool Pendleton blanket to wrap around my jacket. "Stay here and stay warm," I insisted on the afterdeck and tried to remember what I'd seen Sammy do a bit earlier. After fiddling with Engine One and Engine Two buttons, I couldn't get them to lower, let alone start.

Sammy disobeyed me and stood holding my jacket for me to put back on. He'd removed his wet lifejacket and stood with the blanket draped over his shoulders. He scooted to the anchor and hit the winch button for it to lower. The spool was nearly emptied before the anchor found enough bottom to hold us in place.

Sammy's black hair was sopped and he continued to shiver. "There's no hurry now," he managed to tell me. "Let's get warm."

"In the V-berth," I all but ordered him when I shut off the kicker-motor. After he tilted it up, we edged our way through *ThunderMaxx*'s cabin and into the sleeping area of the bow.

He clung to the wool blanket while I searched to find a stash of dry towels in a cupboard near the head and shower. I spotted a large photo on the wall of Big Max standing with his brother and parents on the deck of this boat. I recognized his father from grocery shopping at Safeway on Monday. Each family member, all large, held good-sized salmon. "Too bad you didn't get a photo of me and my gargantuan fish to hang here." I spoke knowing how much Big Max would love seeing me and my prize catch decorating his precious cabin cruiser.

"And too bad I have no intention of replacing the fishing gear that went overboard either," said Sammy.

"Was it even a legal sized fish?" I asked.

"That white sturgeon was way too oversized to keep," he said. "That's why I didn't grab the gaff."

"You should be glad I gaffed your life jacket, though."

"Totally. I'm so glad you hooked my drowning ass." He said when he could see me still studying the photograph. "Those Chinooks are pretty big fish, too. Not ginormous like the sturgeon today, but they fight like crazy. Max used to take me along with his family when the runs hit the Hanford Reach in the fall."

"Max looks like his mother," I said.

"But acts like his horse-faced old man. Max would live on this boat full-time, if his mom would let him," he said, seated and shivering.

"Where are the towels, Baby?" There, I'd said it again.

"In the marine cabinet outside the head."

I looked and found a couple beach towels to bring to the bow. His teeth had stopped chattering, but he still shivered.

The cabin was tricked out like a yacht with teak flooring over aluminum. Black walnut paneling had been custom cut and contoured for the bow of this family's boat. The cupboards were stainless steel but trimmed with more black walnut.

I opened a cabinet and smelled Max's mom's light perfume. The closeted, top-half held boating apparel on hangers, the all-weather gear on one side, sweaters and sweats on the other half in front of hooks holding two or three silky, after-swim robes. Small black walnut drawers hid undies and bras, socks and outdoor shirts and pants. I tossed two terrycloth robes on the bed. The big, bottom drawer had what I needed. I grabbed a thick, soft, nice-smelling, bath towel.

When I turned around, Sammy stood with his skin and hair still drenched. I closed my eyes in thanks. At least he wasn't lost to the big river.

We didn't speak. Rays of morning light popped through the cabin window and shimmered on wetness still clinging to Sammy's torso. He may have been short like me, but his thick, young man muscles were nicely defined. His dense, black hair dried with my toweling.

Gently, I dabbed his skin until completely dry and even bit his tiny nipple, probably too hard, just to see if he'd stand still for me. He didn't step away but smiled back, a bit wickedly.

His belt slipped free along with his socks, but the metal buttons of his Levis were a challenge to liberate. The wet denim slipped down his legs, one tough inch at a time. Sammy's eyes stayed shut until I dried his strong, thick thighs and calves. I piled his sopped clothes at the foot of the bed and admired his boxers.

Well, not his boxers exactly, but him. He leaned in and whispered, "You're my first. Honest."

He took my hand and sat us on the wider edge of the V-shaped mattress. I kissed the side of his neck before kneeling on my towel. Gently, I lowering his silky boxers. "We'll deflower one another," I whispered when he took my wrist and we eased onto the bed.

Tenderly, I made sure his skin, every bit of him, was dabbed dry. Slowly, above his fineness, I hovered.

Sammy took his turn and disrobed me, button by button. His eyes glistened when he unclasped the last of my clothes to see my all. I loved the kind, sexy way he took in the whole of me and kissed the backs of my nervous hands to instantly calm us. He whispered how he loved my strong, firm thighs. I started to protest the length of my legs, but decided that Sammy could enjoy me anyway he'd like.

In slow motion, I turned onto my back and pulled him to me. I hugged him firmly with enough strength to show him I was ready to give myself over. My arms and shoulders throbbed from earlier, and I bit his other earlobe to muffle my own cry. With the bite, Sammy winced when I did. We shared the pain and joy of this moment——the beginning of us.

Him so patient and masculine with our boat rocking slow, we floated on a mighty current. Waves lapped the bow lightly. A morning breeze ruffled the great river. Together, Sammy and I rolled on, giving my disheartened spirit a grand quenching of hope.

~

CHAPTER 13

PASCO

Sammy pulled up beside Import Repair of Pasco and found a spot along the main road for his Bronco and *ThunderMaxx*. He was dropping me off before towing the boat back up to Rattlesnake Cove. Captain Condran sat in his unmarked Crown Vic and awaited my arrival. When I got out and he looked up, he was sipping on a mug of coffee. No surprise there.

The slight morning breeze stiffened when we'd pulled the boat from the river, but had died off into a calmness that gave the cloudless, spring day an eerie moment of noontime heat. I went to the driver's side of the Bronco with my lone travel bag and kissed Sammy goodbye––nothing too lingering or public––yet still soulful.

When the captain opened his door, I walked away, but turned to blow a follow-up kiss to my new boyfriend.

"Don't forget to call me!" he said out the window, and pointed to his flip phone.

"I'll call you––I promise––just as soon as mine's replaced," I replied.

Condran was checking the two of us out and flashed an impish smile when I walked up next to him. He told me that my car would be ready to go any time now. We stood beside his open driver's door unable not to enjoy this bit of warm spring sun.

"Any luck fishing with the new boyfriend?" he asked, his teasing look still planted on his face.

"Sure," I told him as my unprocessed thoughts drifted back to Sammy and our strange, but precious morning.

"Rochelle told me you'd gone out first thing with Joe's old jail guard."

"Just one fish and a nice morning date," I told him, trying with little success not to blush, and forgetting to count the pikeminnow we caught before hooking our sturgeon.

"Just one fish? How big?" he asked.

"Seventeen feet long. A thousand pounds of catch-and-release."

The boss snorted hot coffee.

"And then my chivalrous knight dove into the moat to wrestle the monster fish," I added. "That's how he won over his fair maiden."

Still recovering from his snorted brew, the boss motioned for me to stop telling him what I'm certain he was sure was a fish tale. "Seriously, though, I remember interviewing your new friend at the turn of the year. Seemed like a nice kid, but since he works for Wanapum County, please don't be sharing details about our case with him."

"Not even if he can help us crack Sheriff Usk's wall of secrecy at the county?" I asked. The captain has no clue how unsettling it was to have a brand new, first boyfriend where one part of me wanted to share the depth of my soul with him and the other was afraid I might say the wrong thing that would scared him away. "But I do hear you, Captain. I'll be clear-headed when it comes to separating our case from my involvement with Sammy."

"Are you suggesting he has information that can help us?" the boss asked.

"Maybe. The cabin cruiser he's towing belongs to Big Max's family." I pointed towards the I-182 freeway where Sammy had just found the onramp. "I'm no expert on yachts, Boss, but everything about that 28-foot cabin cruiser was top of the line, down to the fancy fishing poles. Don't the people running a lucrative drug operation need somewhere to spend all their dirty loot?"

"That's often the telltale sign," said the captain.

"We should search Big Max's cabin at Rattlesnake Cove."

"Not without a warrant, and I'm not seeing any judge granting one on a whim, and definitely not so long after the murder."

I winced, expecting his answer. "I also learned that Sammy and Big Max have been close friends since they were little kids. Sammy was pretty pissed, though."

"How so?"

"Last summer, after he was invited, Max decided not to take him along to hear the rock group Poison at the Gorge Amphitheater. Rattlesnake Cove is where Max's family keeps their cabin cruiser. It's on the river a mile or two below the outdoor concert venue. A few days before Mary drowned, he took Gunnar with him, instead of Sammy. They anchored in the Columbia, right below the live show."

"Gunnar Larsson?"

"That's the only Gunnar I know," I said and told Condran that all three boys were the same year at Moses Lake High School. "Plenty of room on that boat for more than two people. The secrecy is telling me that Gunnar and Max were doing advance work arranging for the China White deal a few days later."

The captain's eyebrows furrowed. "That really could be a big lead," he said, without hesitation. "Ever since Joe's trial, I've suspected that Wanapum County Jail has been serving as a conduit for moving hard drugs throughout the Columbia Basin."

When the boss said this, I couldn't help but think back to the evil I saw in Max's eyes when he threw cold beer over my head. I could see him as Mary's murderer and the seller of the heroin they didn't expect to be stolen by Joe. The thought made me wince. "The Poison show was four days before the Bone Shrine crimes. Sammy says that Big Max told him he couldn't come along to hear the concert because he and Gunnar had some 'important business' to discuss."

"I can see where them boating alone on the river with such a noisy distraction wouldn't draw any attention to them," the captain said, seemingly agreeing with my larger suspicion.

I also wanted to know whether Max believed that Joe and Mary were in cahoots with cousin Gunnar. Had Max been convinced that the three designed the heroin heist to flat out steal a quarter million dollars of contraband? As much as I doubted it, I could see how the sellers of the China White would think this.

With these thoughts and a late morning April gust, a shiver coursed down my spine. I also bet that Max, on the night of the murder, had been wearing a triple extra-large corrections officer uniform when he forced her into the pond. I stretched my sore fisherwoman's arms. The boss could see I was aching, but didn't comment. He had more pressing things to share with me.

"I spoke with Dr. Schloss yesterday after you gave me the Krugerrands that you and Tomiko took from the Larsson lockbox. Schloss received the gold coins late last night so he can compare any prints to those of the Larssons."

I appreciated how Condran would bring me up to speed and respected me as a sounding board.

"Our forensic pro also told me that the federal Drug Enforcement Agency has finally convinced the U.S. Customs to allow our State Patrol lab to inspect the smuggled coins from inside the baby stroller. That allows us to compare them for prints, as well."

"What will this prove if, say, Darla's prints are on the coins in Nils's lockbox?" I asked.

"The better question at this juncture is what if Darla and Nils have prints on the coins in the U.S. Custom's cache, or if Linh Riggleman's prints are on the Krugerrands that were in Nils Larsson's lock box."

"Why do you say that?" I asked.

"Because, this morning, when I went to Franklin County Jail, I interviewed Darla to see if there was any possibility of her entering a plea bargain. Her lawyer––who also represents Linh and Roger–– insisted that Mrs. Riggleman was investing a sizable amount of money into *Vikingstad Vodka*, the Larssons' planned new distillery in Nils's home town of Sweden. The attorney will insist in court that the coins confiscated from Linh at the airport were not bribery gold from the Larssons to free Gunnar, but what was left over from those investment funds. I'm hoping the prints will help indicate the direction that the gold coins were flowing."

"And you don't want Mrs. Riggleman's lawyer claiming that the Krugerrands were hidden in the baby stroller to protect them from robbers and it was an oversight by her not to declare the money to U.S. Customs," I said feeling the boss's frustration. "Those coins were definitely bribe money to free Gunnar from jail on the morning after Mary was killed."

"Most likely," said the captain, "but let's see what Dr. Schloss finds with the evidence."

I cleared my throat. "But if the prints point in the right direction--Larsson to Riggleman--then we seek a warrant to search Zach and Linh's home." After a surprise wind gust, I pulled my Abercrombie & Fitch hood over my head.

Condran smiled. "Precisely."

"Boss, there's one more thing I learned-- from Joe Gardner. Last night." Condran gave me a perplexed look. "When I talked with him at his mother's hotel suite after the game, I told him about the oversized and washed sheriff uniform that Amanda Skerry described for us in the Café, the one she saw at the Riggleman's."

"What did Joe say to this?"

"He thought for a bit, then his face lit up. Joe described for me a heavy black garbage bag he saw at the mini-mart in the back of Deputy Riggleman's Sheriff Jeep. He said it was heavy and seemed squishy-wet inside when he tried shifting the bag over to make room for his own bag with gritty tennis shoes."

"Just to be clear. That was on the night of the murder, right?" Condran asked.

"Yes. Remember how Mary's Pathfinder ran out of fuel when the baby was born and he walked all that way to fill the gas can. He definitely thought that the other black bag held wet clothing or towels."

"Adding this to what the CPS officer said, are you suggesting that Deputy Riggleman had been tasked with cleaning a wet, oversized uniform to hide it as evidence?"

"That's the way I figure it."

"Why wouldn't that uniform have been destroyed or given back to the owner late last summer?" he asked.

"The uniform isn't likely to be at Zach and Linh Riggleman's. And, I agree. It would have been returned--washed and cleaned--to its owner," I said. "But maybe it's another way to get a judge to issue a warrant so we can get inside that home for a thorough search. And, then, who knows what we might find related to that night."

"I don't disagree with your thinking, Biff, but no judge will grant a search warrant into the home of a deputy sheriff to see if we get lucky and find more gold coins, more China White, or even the cooked books," he said and looked away from me. "We're too far past the date of Mary's drowning."

I didn't care for the captain's pessimism as we stood shivering in the jolt of chill air. I spoke fast and firmly. "There's got to be a way, Boss. The Riggleman home is the biggest unturned stone in our case. Why did you bother having me go around asking anyone and everyone remotely associated with Mary Quinn's murder if they remember anything at all from last August? Are we just going to ignore our fresh leads like the one from Amanda at CPS?" The captain had kicked my frustrated mind into *hyper-blast mode* as Mom would call it whenever I was set off like this. "Other than Zach Riggleman, we don't know of anyone else––other than Joe, Mary and her baby–– who was in the vicinity of the Bone Shrine pond at the time of the drowning. And we don't know of anyone other than Linh Riggleman who, through her father-in-law, has plausible cause to possess the bribe money paid by Nils and Darla Larsson to spring Gunnar from the slammer."

The captain pursed his lips and scattered gravel with his black shoe. He spoke quietly, but sternly, probably losing patience with my rant. "Matching fingerprints from Schloss's lab analysis will be our best chance for securing a judicial warrant."

The sun lifted higher in the sky, but the air stayed calm and cool. Some springtime buds were beginning to pop open. My stomach churned. The captain answered his flip phone, so I left to check on the status of my Subaru. As I entered the front door into the tiny office of the repair shop, the last thing I heard Condran say was something about a boat. The mechanic came behind the counter and told me my car was ready to go. "You dodged a bullet with this one," he said.

"What a relief!"

"We were able to rinse all the sugary gunk from the gas tank with solvent. No new parts necessary," the mechanic told me.

I pulled out my wallet, but the repairman waved me off. "That man you were just talking to out there. He paid the bill. Said you'd been doing work for him when it happened."

When he handed me the keys to my Loyale, I thanked him and

stepped out to thank the captain, except he was already behind the steering wheel of his unmarked Crown Vic and driving away, fairly fast. It wasn't like him to ditch me, but I watched him speed onto the I-182 onramp, the same direction I'd seem Sammy leaving with *ThunderMaxx.*

My heart raced and nausea filled my guts with panic. Was my new lover tied in with Max much more than he'd let on? Why else wouldn't the boss let me ride along in pursuit? Maybe Captain Condran wanted me nowhere nearby when Sammy was apprehended. My heart dropped into my bowels.

I opened the door into my Subaru and turned over the engine.

My Loyale was far from a race car, but after merging onto the interstate, I kept the old car's speedometer above seventy. My heart raced when I took the northbound clover leaf onto State Highway 395 towards Moses Lake.

The loving morning was morphing towards something like being slapped and nearly drowned by a monster fish. This case was monstrous. All this time, had there been nothing but huge lies from Sammy? Had he really been in thick with Big Max this whole time? If so, then why had my new jail guard boyfriend tackled his co-worker hard enough to break his collarbone?

Why couldn't my little import go any faster? The highway paralleled a ribbon of railroad track before climbing away from the Columbia River. I really needed to be going west to The Dalles, Oregon to pay Mom her birthday visit, but I really, really needed to know if Sammy was being chased down and the captain hadn't wanted to break this news to me.

The arid, tan slopes above the Columbia shifted into big crop circles of potatoes. When the landscape leveled, my car maxed out at 80 miles-per-hour on the straightaway. Where were they? Maybe Sammy had taken a different route north. Other than a few slow moving farm trucks headed the opposite way on the separated, four-lane highway, I saw no other vehicles. I passed a sign for the Northwest RC Speedway and some egg farm where the highway turned a bit to the right. I'd driven 15 miles already. Where were they? Why would Condran leave without telling me what he needed next or not even to say a polite goodbye? He just wanted my lovesick butt out of the way. I could feel it.

When Highway 395 bent back to the left, I hit my brakes hard. On the shoulder was a Washington State Patrol car with lights flashing. It was wedged between Captain Condran's unmarked Crown Vic and *ThunderMaxx.* Sammy's red Bronco was still hooked up to the cabin cruiser. When I jolted to a stop behind Condran, Trooper Elaine Fonk was escorting Sammy--hands on top of his head--over to where the captain stood next to his Crown Vic. My heart raced. Why wouldn't Sammy look at me? What had he done? How was he involved? Why was he looking at the boss, but not wearing cuffs? I turned off my gunk-free motor and hopped out of the car.

Condran whipped around, unsurprised to see me. "Please stay away from the boat, Biff, unless I tell you otherwise."

I had so many questions for Sammy when he walked towards me. Captain Condran went over to help Trooper Fonk climb onto the big boat.

"Hey there," Sammy said to me, quietly.

I lifted my palms upwards in the air and shook my head, not knowing where to start.

Sammy came closer and held up Captain Condran's business card for me to see. "After Captain Condran interviewed me at the jail in December, he gave me this. Said to call him if I ever had anything else to share. As soon as I got onto Highway 395, I realized that I had a boatload of stuff belonging to Big Max that might warrant being searched.

"So, the captain doesn't suspect that you're in thick with Max?" There. I'd said it.

Sammy lifted his own palms upwards and shook his head, more confused than angry. "This whole thing we're doing right now has to look like a routine traffic stop." He spoke real quietly, as though he didn't want what he confided to be recorded somehow. "Don't you get it, Biff? I was the one who called your boss to set up this State Patrol search."

"What made you decide to call Condran?"

"Holy crap, Biff. To help you find Mary's killer. Also, for the same reason I tackled Max on those steps. To protect you."

His voice sounded both agitated and passionate.

"I told your boss that if he wanted plenty of fingerprints on Max, then he should pull me over. That way the investigators could gather up samples on Max without any search warrant. Then they could compare this evidence to any other stuff they have."

I squeezed his arm tightly.

He hesitated, then continued. "I didn't want to say anything to you before," he added, "but Max has really been keeping me at arm's-length for the last year or more."

"Why's that?" I asked softly.

"He has a pretty good suspicion that I know he's running a drug racket through the jail. That's why those two *Tramposos* had such easy access to beat up Joe last summer, and why that other *Tramposo* was released before that deadly China White overdose could be pinned on him."

I blushed big time. "I'm really, really sorry, Sammy. I never should have assumed the worst."

When he leaned in and kissed my forehead, I could breathe again. I squeezed his forearm, looked at the nearest squad car, and whispered that we'd better not get too lovey-dovey on the trooper's surveillance video. "You set up your traffic stop pretty darn well, though," I added.

"So long as no one knows it was staged. I'm this 21-year-old who's pulled over while pulling a friggin' yacht." He pressed his nose through my hair and kept whispering, this time into my ear. "I told the State Patrol trooper on the surveillance tape that I was towing the cabin cruiser for a friend. They wanted to see for themselves if the registration was up to date and that this fancy boat wasn't ripped off by me."

"A whole lot easier for the troopers to pull off this than gathering evidence on a stale case through a formal search warrant," I said. I felt myself frustrated at this dilemma for our overripe investigation, swiping away my ping-ponging thoughts. "I'm such a dummy to doubt you."

"But your boss split from the repair shop without telling you why," he said. "You're no dummy. I get why you needed to drive up here to find out for yourself." He chuckled. "Besides, I already started to miss you."

I kissed his cheek, but shoved him away when Captain Condran turned from Trooper Fonk who was at the stern. He looked at me and held up a full, plastic evidence bag, like it was a prized fishing catch. The boss walked quickly our way. He placed the fresh evidence samples inside the trunk of his Crown Vic before turning to talk with us.

"These are clothing samples and a few cups, too," he explained with no more elaboration. "Biff, I'd like to show you something on the boat that Trooper Fonk noticed," the captain said. "Best if you stay here," he told Sammy whose butt was already pressed against my fender.

I followed the boss to where he could help me onto the transom and into the boat where the State Patrol officer waited for us.

"Use these," the boss ordered from the afterdeck while handing me a pair of latex gloves and slipping on his own. When the Captain opened the door to the cabin, I shuddered. I sure hoped that Condran wasn't about to pry for the intimate details of the morning deflowering.

I had no real choice but to follow him inside. I took a quick look into the bow and was relieved to see that I'd smoothed over the big blanket we'd used for sex.

"Trooper Fonk has only been taking a few things for prints and hair samples," Captain Condran said and took a seat on the tall, inside skipper's chair. He turned and looked at me before twisting back and pointing at the wide window shield that looked forward and over the back of Sammy's Bronco. I stood behind him and tried to see what he wanted me to see. Beyond the Bronco, all I noticed was an asphalt ribbon of this state highway leading well to the north.

"Not outside the boat, Biff," said Condran. "Inside and dangling from the compass."

My eyes took a bit to adjust to the black dome with its arrow also pointing to the north. Then I saw. "How on this wobbly earth could I have missed that?"

I started to reach out and touch, but the boss, rather gently, held me back.

"Sorry," I told him and stepped away. My voice cracked. "Definitely one of Mary's." I choked up. "That's her braided--wildflower."

I placed palms over my face so I could thank my best friend. It felt like a breakthrough. My fingers soaked with tears. She was really here and helping.

"That's what I was wondering when I spotted it," said Condran, patting my back. "When I took over the investigation, there was no sign of any braided flower dangling from her impounded Pathfinder's rearview mirror. When we found the Japanese dragon souvenir in the skull of the owl, you were the one who told me to be on the lookout for Mary's wildflower braid, the one that she always had in her car. However, it wasn't anywhere to be found."

'The killer hung it here." I lowered my hands and forced in a full breath or two. "And don't try to tell me this is a different one, somehow. That little wild flower is really, really rare, and the braiding is definitely Mary's."

"How uncommon is it?" he asked.

"The Poet's Shooting Star grows only on the hillsides of the Columbia Gorge near The Dalles," I told him. *"Dodecatheon poeticum* is found nowhere else in the world."

"It's not DNA, nor a fingerprint, but this is a solid piece of evidence linking our suspected new perp to Mary Quinn," said the boss. "I've seen the one you have in your Subaru," the boss said. "I even saw it there this morning. That's why I showed you this."

"Mary only made a half-dozen. This one has to be from her Pathfinder." I said.

"Why do you say that with such certainty?"

"She gave one to Joe, a second one to Rochelle, a third to Joe's dad who helped her wire the six into lasting pieces. The fourth one went to her own mother before she split for Memphis; the fifth one is mine, still dangling in my Loyale. This sixth and last one here, she kept dangling in her own car. I'll bet Big Max stole this at the same time he cut off Mary's thin braid of reddish hair dangling from her Chunichi Dragon souvenir baseball pin. Remember how he stuffed those inside the owl skull at the Bone Shrine. Max must have decided to keep the wildflower braid dangling in his boat as some sort of demented souvenir."

I looked back at Sammy propped patiently against my Subaru. "We can't let Max go free from the hospital before arresting him," I told the boss.

"As one of several items, this dried wildflower will afford us good circumstantial evidence linking the victim to Big Max," said the captain. "We need more, though."

"Why didn't I see Mary's braided wildflower swinging in this boat this morning?" I asked.

Condran chuckled. "I suspect you two were preoccupied—fishing, of course—and not thinking you'd uncover crime evidence," he said.

I pretended not to hear, still thinking of Mary leading us here. "Max took this wildflower braid from her Pathfinder's rearview mirror that night. Max is our killer. This proves it."

The captain started taking photos to show the wildflower braid from all directions where it hung inside *ThunderMaxx's* cabin. Carefully, he lifted the string over the compass with large tweezers and placed Mary's braided flower in an already labelled, clear plastic evidence bag. "He's definitively our most likely perp."

I sat on the captain's chair, but had to lower it all the way so my heels could rest on the bar encircling the chair above the floor. I imagined steering the boat through the kind of standstill waves we often had in The Dalles. The river current headed west and was blown wavy by strong winds pushing through the Cascade Mountain Range from the Pacific. It was the sort of standstill we'd been facing in this case since the drowning.

"To make sure I'm on the same page with you, the owner of the Bronco told us who owned the boat," said the captain. "When I saw the braided wildflower, I suspected it belonged to Mary Quinn. This justified our confiscation of this evidence on Max's boat. Do you have anything to add to this sequence of events?"

"No, Boss," I said when Trooper Fonk stepped onto the transom. "That sums it up here." He directed the policewoman to wait a few more minutes before allowing Sammy Puck to leave without a citation.

When she walked away, Condran's ringing cellphone startled both of us. "Dr. Schloss. I'm hoping you have some solid news for us." I could only hear the boss's end of the conversation, but the captain's eyes widened after the forensic scientist was done sharing his information.

"What days do you have open, in the event we secure the warrant?" Condran asked and waited for a response. "Today and tomorrow. Better than expected, my friend! Thanks so much for prioritizing this case."

I didn't want to appear too overeager when the captain slapped his phone shut, but I wanted to slap him when he climbed off the boat before sharing any of Schloss's news with me.

On the shoulder of the highway beside the transom, he whipped around. "Schloss is driving over tomorrow to help up secure a warrant for Zach Riggleman's home."

"What's the new development for that?" I asked, worn out by all the excuses I'd been hearing for not being granted one.

"There were no prints found of Linh Riggleman on the Krugerrands found in Nils Larsson's office lockbox. Only those of Darla Larsson. As for the gold coins hidden in the baby stroller, there were also only prints from Darla's fingertips. No others." The captain tried, unsuccessfully, to stifle a smile.

My eyes widened. "Wow!" I said. "The bribery gold flowed from Larsson to Riggleman so they could spring Gunnar from jail. That surely tells us that there was never an investment by Linh Riggleman in a new Swedish vodka distillery."

"Circumstantially strong evidence of a payoff," said the captain. "I just hope it's enough to warrant a warrant. With fresh charges against her, we can hope this will prompt Darla Larsson to enter a plea."

When I hopped down from the transom, Trooper Fonk accompanied Sammy as they walked towards us. I didn't really care what she or the boss thought when I pulled Sammy under the bow where the boat was hitched to the Bronco. When I hugged him, he wrapped his arms around me. His embrace was as tight as mine.

"This will all work out the way it's supposed to," he whispered.

"And thank you so much for helping," I told him with a big kiss to the cute Native dimple on his cheek. I could feel Mary smiling down. "Time for me to get to The Dalles for Mom's birthday," I whispered, but not wanting to let go.

CHAPTER 14

The old Victorian had no garage, so it was pretty obvious when someone was home. Rochelle's van, the one she also used for The Dalles Chamber of Commerce business, was parked in her driveway. I'd just arrived in The Dalles from my crazy morning in Pasco and stopped on the quiet street next to the Gardners' lawn. Just a quick visit to make sure Tomiko was going to be okay staying with Rochelle for a bit. The late afternoon sun cut through the brisk spring air, so I didn't bother putting on my jacket.

I knocked and tried the front door, never remembering it being locked before. After last night's baseball game chaos, she and Tomiko may have been catching up with sleep or out for a walk. I slipped in the backdoor, the same way Mary and I did in high school so we could hang with Joe. The gate latch along one side of her home had a thin rope that we had always pulled to make our way between houses. I pushed lightly on the back door and watched it swing open into the mudroom. I had a couple hours before needing to show up at the Baldwin Saloon for Mom's surprise 50th birthday party, a bit of a gala certain to be well attended by her Gorge Discovery Center board members, several friends, and my father, of course.

Rochelle's dim kitchen looked pristine without a single pan or dish on the counters or in the sink. I stepped towards the adjoining dining room, but needed a bit of light so I reached around the open arch into the dining room. Something was off-kilter, nothing that I saw or smelled, just another blind owl vibe. I found the light switch and flicked it on. A bright chandelier startled me, but nothing like the glint of the pistol barrel.

From a yard away, Nils Larsson pointed his gun at my nose. I all but swallowed my tongue.

"Just the one I'm looking to see," he said, too softly for comfort. My knees buckled. I reached out and grabbed the edge of the dining room table. It had none of the usual chairs around it and only a cut flower vase with no bouquet in the middle. I collapsed to my knees, palms straight out on the table for stability, but more as though he was arresting me.

Why hadn't I expected this? So dumb. Of course he'd know he could come to Rochelle's and intercept Tomiko or me.

"Where's your sister-in-law?" I asked, trying not to sound snide to this vile man with a gun aimed at my face.

With a mock-polite bow and rolling motion of his revolver he ordered me to get up and move. "Come in and join Rochelle for our special fireworks." With the end of his pistol, he pointed me into the living room.

My eyes widened. Through the arched dining room doorway, light from the dining room chandelier revealed Tomiko tied up next to Joe's mother. Both were at the side of her living room where her piano had always been. The two were fully gagged with duct tape that was wrapped all the way around their heads, hair and mouths. They sat wide-eyed, glaring at Nils. Nylon rope pressed deep into the flesh of their bare arms and around the stiff backs of two dining room chairs. A third, stiff-backed chair sat empty beside Tomiko as though it had my name etched on it.

Nils motioned for me to step through the arched opening between the dining and living room. He let the lights speak for his intent when, with one smooth motion of his fingers on the wall there, he turned off the dining room chandelier and flicked on the matching fixture in the living room. This time, my jaw dropped. I commanded my lungs to breathe.

What had been a dark shadow in the middle of the living room floor was every cherished, flammable item he could find in Rochelle home. The valued possessions were heaped and broken into a tall cone-shaped pile, filling the middle of the good-sized Victorian living room.

The largest possession was Rochelle's solid maple, stand-up piano that she had loved to play when accompanying Mary Quinn's magical singing voice. Nils was big and strong and able to scoot and tipped it keys-to-floor to start the heap that was covered next by the leather sofa followed by Joe's most memorable baseball bats. The remaining dining room chairs teetered precariously. There were broken wooden frames for her photos and art. The piano bench somehow made it to the top where it balanced upside down. Rochelle's wooden Rosary beads swayed from a broken leg of the bench. Kuma's small Buddhist shrine, with its door hanging open, lay across the bench.

"Sit down," Nils commanded me, the voice matching his six-foot, five-inch frame.

The three of us women seemed like we were being prepped to meet our horrific deaths on the top of a funeral pyre, and here I was wigging out over spiritual artifacts. He squeezed the handle of his pistol and stood to address me.

"Religion is the opiate of the masses," he said, once again too softly for my liking. "Rochelle raised her boy right here in this home. Joe's religion became heroin."

"Not to mention being your favorite contraband, too," I yelled, telling myself that I really did need to shut up. He knew Rochelle a whole lot more than I did, and his own sister-in-law was fully gagged.

"Mine is just business," he said coldly this time and, in one motion, pressed the barrel of the gun into my forehead. With a single hard yank of his free hand, he broke the chain holding my new *She-Who-Watches* medallion and grabbed it as it fell. He watched my reaction when tossing it over his shoulder and onto the pile. My expression went stone cold. I wasn't going to give this monster the pleasure of getting a rise out of me. When it disappeared within Rochelle's ravaged belongings, I folded my arms over the open 'V' of my sweater.

"Where are my gold coins?" Nils yelled in my face.

I started to say that the business of money was his religion, but he was overly intent on showing us who was in control. "Sit. Right now!" he commanded me.

I lifted my hands up, as though they could stop his bullets. "Okay, okay," I said, and moved quickly to the empty chair beside Tomiko. She sat between me and Rochelle, bound with a rope thick enough to hold a horse to its hitching post.

The barrel of Nils's pistol still trained at my head. I cringed when I noticed a serrated butcher knife under the roll of gray duct tape beneath the empty chair. My stomach soured when he wrapped the duct tape around each ankle and calf to the two front chair legs. He started to run out of tape after binding my shoulders to the tall, stiff chair and resorted to using what little was left to secure my wrists together behind my butt and the chair back. The tightness hurt my shoulder joints and made it hard to wiggle my fingers.

Nils got nose-to-nose with Tomiko. She winced when he screamed at her, "How about you? Where are my coins?"

He shifted over to glare into my eyes. "You two have them with you, don't you? Where's my gold?"

"Your Krugerrands were turned over by us to my boss at the Washington State Patrol," I told him without hesitating. My pounding heart had me believing Nils was serious about burning up his sister-in-law's home.

"Bullshit. You two stole them from me," he yelled again. "Where did you hide them?"

He turned back to Tomiko. "Should I cut off her big toe or her thumb?" he asked, turning back toward me. "Show her brother how serious I am about him wiring a quarter million to buy his sister's freedom? And that's in American dollars, not yen."

Rochelle shook her head side-to-side and moaned beneath the tape. Tears rolled down Tomiko's cheeks as she also shook her head frantically.

Nils lowered his gun and went to the wall behind us. He came and stood so we could see him thrust a music stand towards the tall ceiling like it was a javelin. It landed with a crash onto the pile and caused candles and saucers and the incense box from the broken shrine of Kuma's to tumble to the hardwood floor. My stomach rumbled when I realized the stand was what Mary had used for holding her sheet music while Rochelle accompanied her on piano. I decided not to say a word, but Rochelle grunted as though to tell him with her fierce eyes that enough was enough.

He ignored her and turned towards me again. "Or, little motormouth. Instead of gagging you, I'll just cut off your tongue with a dull knife. That way your mama will receive a bloody little discovery. Then she'll be sure to pay what you two thieves owe me."

I took in a deep breath and slowly exhaled. "If you didn't do anything illegal, then you can get the money back. Captain Condran knows those Krugerrands came from your lockbox."

"Shut up! I want my money in the next two hours or this house and you three in it will get torched."

Why hadn't I just gone to my parent's house instead of stopping here? "We'll get you your money, but it's too late in the afternoon to happen today." I tried to speak calmly to him, but I could hear my voice quavering.

His pocket started ringing before he responded. Nils slipped the pistol in between his belt and spine before pulling out the flip phone. Before opening it, he stormed through the emptied dining room and into the kitchen.

Tomiko shook with fear and, with Nils in the kitchen, she started turning and twisting any part of her body and limbs that her rope-wrangled muscles allowed. She even hopped up an inch or two. Luckily, her chair didn't topple over backwards.

I tried to work my tape so it wouldn't cut off any more blood circulation. My legs felt fused to the chair legs and my wrists gained just enough wiggle to stop my fingers from tingling.

In the kitchen, Nils answered his call, thinking we couldn't hear him.

"You're not just my wife's banker, Cochran. I'm on the account, too. Move the money overseas as directed. Do it now!"

Nils sounded like he was trying to gather up all his liquid assets, including the Krugerrands from us. But would he really kill Tomiko and me over this? And why Rochelle? She hadn't stolen anything from him.

"Yes, sir. Like I told you. Transfer it today." This time his voice verged on irate.

After slapping the cell phone shut and stuffing it back into his front jeans pocket, he stormed into the dining room and grabbed the last thing left in the middle of the dining room table––a thick-cut, glass vase. We watch him hold it tightly. Nils pounded the five-pound crystal over and over against the door of Rochelle's tall, china cabinet. She winced when he slammed the antique door with more and more angry force until every last bit of beveled, clear, stained-glass landed in bits on the floor.

It was anyone's guess why he was taking his anger out on his sister-in-law's home, but hammering the cabinet door into crumbs of glass seemed more on purpose than cathartic. Before returning to the living room, Nils startled us by grabbing Rochelle's prized Roman Catholic statuette from her small, dining room grotto. His eyes glowed demonically.

Tomiko and I stopped resisting against our binding rope and tape. Rochelle, though, grunted and her eyes grew livid when she watched Nils white-knuckling her Mother Mary and infant treasure. He looked first at his sister-in-law before pivoting and throwing it as hard as he could.

The statuette hit a leg of her piano bench wedged on its side near the top of the living room pile. The foot-tall icon broke into chunks of ceramic. The face and body of Jesus's mother popped up and landed inside Kuma's *Butsudan* shrine. The impact of the thrown icon also rocked the upside-down bench enough so that the sheet music inside began oozing like lava to the floor.

When Rochelle's statuette was thrown, the infant had broken off and ricocheted out of the pile. Baby Jesus landed at her feet. Rochelle jerked back as much as her bound up body allowed. Every flammable thing deemed precious in her home had been toppled, broken, or defiled by him. She locked onto Nils's eyes with a glare of fury. Her muffled scream raged through the room.

What next? I wondered with a shudder.

There was no waiting. Nils placed his hands on his knees so he could stare down Rochelle's muzzled face with equally angry eyes. "You don't get it, do you, Rochelle?" he said, sternly.

Of course she didn't fathom any of this. Rochelle's eyes widened even more. She had no clue why he was acting so horrific.

"You, not Darla, was supposed to be with me," Nils said with a forced evenness. "Then you never would have given birth to your junky son."

It didn't seem possible, but her eyes grew even wider and wilder with rage.

Nils seemed to like antagonizing her, knowing she couldn't respond. "Ever wonder why I let Junky Joe take the fall?" he all but growled. "C'mon, Rochelle. You know."

Tears welled up in her eyes and her shoulders started heaving. He sneered when he saw how he was upsetting her even more than the tight bondage had. He stared, never shifting his harsh eyes away from her.

I wondered what he was driving at. Whatever had gone down between him and Rochelle, including the framing of Joe, hardly justified him destroying her home. Maybe he blamed Rochelle because the walls of justice were closing in on him. Maybe Joe was the one who ruined his flourishing heroin empire by stealing the China White at the Bone Shrine. I told myself to take a long, slow stream of air into my lungs.

His flip phone rang again. This time he stood and continued staring down at Rochelle, but didn't leave the living room. "Don't worry about getting cash, Abe. Just put a bond on our house if you need to make bail for her. I don't really care if she stays in jail or not."

"Wouldn't that be Abe Steinke, the Larsson's family lawyer?" I whispered to Rochelle.

She nodded, her eyes still wide with fear. I wanted to tell her what the captain had shared about Abe wanting to treat Gunnar's bribe money like it was actually an investment in the Larsson's Swedish vodka distillery.

Nils was listening to what he was being told through the phone, but when he turned to look at us, his eyes rolled impatiently. We had no clue what his lawyer was telling him on the other end. "This is too soon!" Nils yelled, "Too damned soon! Yes. I will go to my backup plan, but you're my lawyer. You need to stall, Abe. Find a way to delay my arrest."

What did that mean? What arrest? I got the part about him moving their money and the part about bailing out Darla, but why burn down

Rochelle's home—–with us in it? I told my heart to stop pounding. No lawyer would be part of any delay that encouraged his client to complete a plan of arson and murder.

"Damn!" Nils said again when he slipped his phone back in his jeans.

Maybe his cushy, two-faced world was disintegrating. Maybe an ugly, heroin side-hustle was taking down this prominent director of a statewide marketing association for potato farmers. Nils pivoted and left quickly through the dining room and kitchen. We heard the outside screen door of the mudroom slam shut.

Tomiko groaned, grunted, bounced and battled with every ounce of her lean, small frame to free herself. How had I managed to get this sweet Japanese girl so wrapped up in solving Mary's murder? Why had I asked her to plunder Nils Larsson's lockbox? For this, we were all going to die?

The last thought had me testing what strength I had left in my fished-out arms—–side-to-side, up-and-down, clenching and pulling them together and apart with all my might. Nothing could make the wrap of duct tape budge. My shoulders ached almost as much as my wounded pride. Together, the fog of our collective doom filled the air.

Rochelle looked at me, at the living room pile, and then back at me, all with her eyes still raging. I had no idea what she was trying to say, so I tried to offer up a glimmer of hope. "If I don't show up at the Baldwin Saloon for Mom's surprise birthday dinner, then my parents will come here looking for me."

Rochelle simply closed her eyes. I had no idea what she wanted or was thinking or trying to tell me with lids shut. Had Tomiko's and my theft of Nils's gold stash caused him to totally lose it? We hardly deserved to burn atop this drug dealer's funeral pyre. Would any of us survive this madness?

"Oh crap. Here he is again," I whispered.

Nils appeared through the dining room window holding a can of gasoline in one hand and sticks of long matches in the other. We heard him stomping up the back steps and slamming open the screen door into the mudroom. He wasted no time to appear in the dining room under the arched threshold into the living room.

Through the long spigot, he sprinkled droplets of gasoline up and over most of Rochelle's precious belongings. "I didn't kill Mary Quinn," he said in a low voice that made him seem even crazier than he was. He unscrewed the cap of the gas can and, with an upward thrust, a thick stream of fuel sloshed onto the top of the pile. We watched it land on Kuma's *Butsudan* and dribble down.

He turned back towards me and spoke frostily. "Tell your boss that Gunnar didn't murder her either."

"He knows you two didn't drown her," I said, but when my words came out, he was beyond appeasing. The odor of liquid gas filled the living room when he poured a moat of gasoline in a full circle around the chairs of us three women. Maybe I had it all wrong. His fiery eyes and icy actions made me ask why he needed to murder us. "If you're not now facing any murder charges, that is."

He flipped gasoline at my feet.

"The gold Krugerrands, or cash somehow, we'll get you your stupid money." Why couldn't I shut my ever-busy lips? If I only knew what Rochelle and Tomiko wanted me to say. Why hadn't he figured out how to gag me, too? It would be easier that way if we were going to die. "Why Rochelle? What in the hell did she ever do to you?"

At this, he poured what was left of his gas over Rochelle's footwear, too. She tried to kick off the canvas slip-ons, but her ankles were still tightly bound to the legs of the chair. He pulled a dining room chair from out of the bottom of the pile and a few more flammable belongings cascaded to the floor. He straddled backwards ignoring the tumble. "You know what you did to me, don't you, Rochelle?"

Nils knew she couldn't answer so he leaned down inches from her nose and, for some wild reason, looked down at the tote bag between Tomiko's and Rochelle's chairs. When he lifted it in front of Tomiko's face, I could see the Japanese characters printed on both sides of the canvas.

"Are you hiding my gold coins in here, you little thief?"

Tomiko tried to rear back, but Nils grabbed his pistol from where he'd wedged it behind his back in his belt. He pressed the barrel against her nose. She grunted until, finally, he stood up with her bag. How had I gotten that poor girl into this?

The smell of gasoline filling the living room started to make me gag. Maybe my obsession to save Mary was fueling the karma of my own early death. My flesh would be consumed by flames; water had stolen her last breath.

Nils tipped the bag upside down and slung its contents onto the floor at Tomiko's feet. An open cellophane bag of Oreo Cookies sent black crumbs over her white tennis shoes and next to my feet. A glass frame fell and broke into three triangular pieces. The knife-like point of one fragment of glass had punctured through a photo of Gracie held in place by the frame. Another fell at Rochelle's feet next to the baby Jesus. When my eyes could focus, I made out the stabbed image of Grace Kusumoto, a gift that Tomiko, I suspected, had been planning to give to Rochelle. The last chunk of glass somehow landed between Tomiko's Japanese tennis shoes, below where her ankles were taped tightly together. The balls of her feet squeezed the big shard.

Nils didn't find any Krugerrands, so he ignored everything else from Tomiko's bag and, without looking, tossed it empty and over his shoulder onto the pile. He positioned himself in front of Rochelle again and kicked the ceramic of baby Jesus off towards the dining room so there was nothing between him and her. "You really don't remember, do you?"

How is she supposed to answer you? I started to ask, but didn't. How had I quick-sanded my way into this man's quagmire? Wacked-out crazy. Marbles lost. Devil possessed. That's what Nils had become.

And, like on cue, he yelled at Rochelle, "You were hoping I'd never find out that you aborted my baby! Didn't even tell me you were pregnant!"

Rochelle shook her head wildly like she needed to clarify. Her reaction made me think his accusation on the abortion was true, but it was still a sick reason for burning down her home, decades later, with her inside.

I'd seen enough to sense he was serious about taking everyone down who had caused his ass any grief––ever. "If Rochelle didn't tell you, then how do you know that you were the father?" I yelled.

"Her sister," he screamed back at me. "Darla told me years later. She'd driven Rochelle to the abortion clinic." Nils glared at Joe's mom.

"This bitch wouldn't tell Darla who the father was, but the timing told me all I needed to know."

"So you married Darla instead?" I asked. "Gunnar is no-doubt real glad to be alive."

"And Joe came in handy, too-- last year," he added, sneering. "My son didn't kill Mary Quinn," he said.

But, you know who did it? I wanted so badly to shout the words, but decided to hold my tongue for a change when he leaned down so his face was inches from Rochelle's. "So what was your reason for killing our baby?"

Nils didn't take off her gag. He really wasn't wanting an answer from her. He stared at me. "I always wished that Mary would have taken up with Gunnar, and not with my loser of a nephew." Nils glared some more into Rochelle's eyes. "That's right. It's almost like you framed me to marry your sister."

Rochelle groaned as loud as she could in protest.

"Now I'm leaving her for good," Nils added.

I couldn't help myself. "You're saying that you were *forced* to marry Darla? Christ! What twisted, loser's logic!"

Without looking at me, Nils lurched forward and backhanded his knuckles into my cheek bone. It stung and started to throb.

Rochelle moaned through the duct tape. Nils stared at her and waited. Once she calmed, Nils got close to Rochelle's nose and whispered. "That guy you decided to marry instead of me. What an ape-man." He struck one of his long matches and held it high before getting ready to really torch us. "Why did you have his baby--and not mine?" he shouted, glowering.

"Wait!" I cried and sucked in as much air as I could, but decided not to promise, once again, that Tomiko and me would get him his money. Nils was in too deep with this mess if his arrest was pending. He was crazed, but not stupid enough to think that our stolen gold would save him.

He blew out his match and looked at me like we were having a stare down. Who was he going to take down with him when he fled this scene?

"Wait? Why wait? I was forced to send Gunnar away last summer.

For this, Joey had to pay," he said to me. "He got in the way for one reason. One reason alone. Joseph Gardner is a junky."

He lifted another long matchstick from the box and leaned in closer to Rochelle. "We should have raised that child," he said and rolled the matchstick between his palms like he was holding Rosary beads. "Then none of this would have ever happened."

Rochelle grunted angrily.

Was Nils's brain stuck in some alternative mind warp? "Nothing that happened between you and Rochelle was Joe's fault," I said, my bruised cheek throbbing.

He looked at me and tapped the unlit, long match to its box as though he was deciding his next move. "But Joe stole the whole Bone Shrine stash. It didn't belong to him, did it, Biff?" Nils struck the second match, held it up towards my face. "Here's a flame as gold as the coins you two ripped off."

I didn't know how to react when Nils let it burn halfway down the long stick. "You and your girlfriend took what wasn't yours, Biff. Joey snagged all that smack. And Rochelle took away my child. Thieves every one of you." The long matchstick was three-fourths of the way to his thumb and fingers. His odd and wicked smile framed steely blue eyes. "So, I'll burn you three now. A fair punishment. Joe will get his later."

Tears rolled from Rochelle's eyes. The match burned closer to his finger. The man was a sicko. What a way for us to die.

What could my churning thoughts distill that that might free us from this madman? I hoped Sammy would remember me forever. The thought had my tears rolling. The tape and rope bound me so tightly.

His phone rang again. "Already? Good work delaying it," he yelled with angry sarcasm. "Screw the D.E.A!"

Nils wasn't watching his match when flames lapped at his fingers. He swore in Swedish and threw the last of the lit matchstick to his feet. In between us and him, a drop of gas burst into flame. The fire whipped around the three of us into an instant moat of flames. Rochelle reacted by tipped back. Her chair crashed into the old hardwood floor along with the back of her skull. When she landed, the thin line of fire behind us was snuffed out with her fall. In front, the gassy flame ignited the living room's big oval throw rug.

I closed my eyes tight waiting for the flammable pile to erupt in a big explosion. I wasn't ready to die. Too soon. Where were you, Mary? Where?

"I hope you cracked your skull wide open!" Nils yelled, pushing his chair aside and leaning over Rochelle.

When he jumped away from the flaming throw rug and hurried out of the living room, I started breathing until flaming gasoline fumes had me coughing. We could hear him run through the dining room and kitchen and kick-slam the mud door to escape this horror of his own doing.

We had no idea where the bigger dousing of gasoline was soaking into the rug, just that the flammable liquid was only a few feet from the big pile. Slowly, I sucked air into my lungs.

The mud door screen slapped open and shut in the late afternoon breeze. I yelled over the loud whine of his dirt bike that he'd stashed on the side of the house opposite the living room wall and the side gate I'd used. "I think he's gone for good."

Nils quick escape shifted my focus onto the living room throw rug. A whiff of the acrid smoldering woke up something practical inside my freaked-out brain. I looked at Tomiko. With an up-and-down, twisting motion, I managed to shift my chair to an angle where I faced away from where she sat bound. In one side-to-side motion, I tilted as far as I could away from her and then back.

Nothing.

I took a breath and tried again. The chair was old and heavy and too damn stable. I concentrated harder. "Yow!" I yelled, thrusting my hips together with shoulders and knees. Once I got my body parts in sync, the chair rocked in one motion. The legs on one side of the chair raised off the floor. My heart dropped once I started the sideways fall. Somehow, someway I tensed my neck at the right moment to keep my head from slamming on the hardwood floor like Rochelle's had. My chair landed on its side behind the line of flame. I knew Tomiko's tennis shoes were a few inches away from my bound hands.

"Hold your feet together, Tomiko, as tight as you can."

I couldn't see it, but my hands had a bit of give from having already pulled and pushed and lifted against the tape that bound me. Maybe the universe had made sure that Nils hadn't had quite enough duct tape left to wrap my arms to the chair back. I was able to move my arms just enough so the shard between Tomiko's feet created first a small rip, then allowed me to start sawing through the tape holding my wrists together.

"Tighter," I told Tomiko and edged an inch closer to her toes for more pressure against the cutting edge. Gasoline fumes and the smoldering wool rug made me want to gag. The highest remaining flame looked like it was taking hold and beginning to light the underlying maple floor on fire.

Had she been seated upright, Rochelle would have burned her shoes, feet and lower legs. The flames were only two yards from reaching the fuel-soaked pile. I told myself to ignore what I couldn't control, to keep my erratic brain focused. Concentrate on what I could feel behind me. The continuing flame, so close to Rochelle, kept diverting my attention.

The one good slit I'd managed to start in the tough tape finally began to rip apart without cutting into my wrists. And, at least I could hear Rochelle letting out a groan now and then, telling me she was still alive.

"Mmmm," said Tomiko from beneath her gag.

I slid the chair again to get even closer to her.

"Mmmmm!" she managed a bit louder.

I was afraid of dislodging the glass from between her feet when pressing into the tape.

"Mmm! Mmmm! Mmmmm!" She was trying to tell me something. It was our only chance, I thought, hoping what I felt was the tip of the glass.

"Hold it steady and as tight as you can!"

"Mmmmm!"

"Owww!" I yelled out when I felt the outside of my wrist being punctured, gouging through my skin and drawing blood. At least the bruise Nils left on my cheek wasn't bleeding, too.

As hard as I tried, I couldn't get the tape to budge.

I shifted slightly and pressed against the sharp point and kept puncturing through the glass tip again. After about six of these pokes, I stopped, closed my eyes, and gathered my strength. With every awkward muscle I had, I strained until I thought I heard another slight rip.

"Mmmmmm!" Tomiko managed through her gag, followed by a high pitched grunt to alert me to see where the floor of the house had now opened with its own gash. The burning hole in the floor fueled the flame nearest us with fresh air. Were we all about to fry from the whole home burning without the heaping pile even being lit into a house-leveling bonfire? It wasn't likely an either-or, I told myself as I poked more holes in the stubborn duct tape. After every few thrusts, I tried again to get the tape to tear apart and separate.

"Mmm! Mmmm! Mmmmm!" I heard Tomiko as she tried to warn me.

Of course my wrist was still bleeding from puncturing myself, but who cared now. I needed to be freed.

Finally, at long last, blood and all, I ripped through the duct tape.

"Grrrr!" came Tomiko's voice. Her eyes were as wide as Rochelle's had been. I remembered the serrated knife under my chair and––with suddenly freed arms and hands––I had enough flexibility to cut open the rest of the tape restricting me.

I looked at the flame, now waist high and edging closer to the pile of flammable belongings. It had consumed half of Rochelle's living room throw rug. I got up and ran to the pile. This flame needed a quick snuffing. I managed to fold some of the throw rug over the flames.

Halfway up Rochelle's belongings, I noticed the middle leaf from the dining room table. I pulled as hard as I could on the end that was visible, and stepped back when everything above it began cascading to my feet. Lordy, it was exactly what we didn't need to get the flammables even closer to the flames.

No time. No time for anything.

I freed the section of tabletop and turned to see the flame obscuring my view of Rochelle. She was still on her back.

"Mmm! Mmmmm!" Tomiko grunted out again.

I lifted the hardwood table section and slammed it onto the spot where the fire opened the hole in the flooring. This closed the space where the crawl space air fueled the flame. The board snuffed out the thickest remaining part of the flame, but by no means all of the fire. Tomiko all but squealed. My wrist still bled.

I took a quick glance at the edge of flame closest to the fallen items from the pile and figured there was only one chance. I sprinted through the dining room and kitchen and mud room and into the back yard where I found the spigot and was thankful Rochelle had her hose hooked up for the springtime. The nozzle was even attached. I turned the faucet spigot on high and didn't care that the leaky hose nozzle soaked me like a cold shower. I unwound the hose as I hurried back inside the house, grateful that it didn't kink. I hosed off my wrist blood as I pulled the green water snake through the mud room and kitchen and past the dining room.

In the threshold, I tumbled backwards. Like a huge rubber band, the hose had yanked me back onto my butt. I sat up stunned and flat on the floor at the arched opening. I managed to turn the nozzle to a hard jet spray and aimed it towards the worst of the fire.

Tomiko's latest, "Mmmmmmmmmm!" was masked by the sizzle of doused flames. I soaked the rug where Nils's gasoline might still be awaiting ignition. I couldn't tell, but from the muffles of Rochelle's grunts and Tomiko's squealing, I suspected I was drenching both of them. The room sizzled and turned cooler, almost immediately. I breathed deeply. Still no sign of bonfire.

I looked at her landline phone hanging by the kitchen door. I shut down my nozzle and dropped it, ignoring its steady leak on the dining room floor. I needed to call 9-1-1. "Seufert Street, The Gardner residence. Rochelle Gardner." I yelled. "Fire. We need cops and ambulance here, too. Stat! Emergency. Gotta go!" As soon as I heard the dispatcher say, "Ma'am," I hung up. They could trace the call to this address. No time for detail after detail. Too much still to do.

I went back over and managed to prop the nozzle up so the spray of water was constant. I could see how I'd punctured my lower thumb into the meat below my left thumb with the tip of that glass. I let the hose spray clean the cut of any glass bits.

"Mmmmmmmmm!!!!" Tomiko reminded me. I hurried over to Rochelle since she was worse off. Her eyes were closed tight.

"Mrs. Gardner! Joe's mom! Rochelle! Wake up!" I yelled out again and again.

She opened her eyes and groaned back at me, annoyed, like I was aggravating a migraine. Gingerly, in case she had a neck injury, I made short light tugs on the tape to uncover her mouth. I pulled out the gauze that Nils had wedged inside to gag her.

"I think I heard my neck crack when I hit the floor," Rochelle said, oddly calm, except for her eyes that couldn't conceal her pain. "No concussion. Not knocked out. I'm just afraid to shift my neck."

"Don't move then! And I mean that Mrs. Gardner!" I told her when I shifted over to cut Tomiko free with the serrated knife.

"Thank you for saving our lives, Biff," Rochelle added.

"Yes. I thank you also," said Tomiko, her eyes swollen from smoke and tears.

Both were soaked from nozzle spray and, when I stepped back, I nearly crushed baby Gracie's impaled photo. I bent over to pull the glass from beside the baby and threw the shard onto the soaking pile. The doused fire still sizzled at a few hot spots.

Tomiko was up and standing. "Fire is finished. I go turn water to off."

She left for the backyard before I could respond.

"I thought we were dead," Rochelle managed to say with a raspy, but grateful voice.

"Don't move your neck, Mrs. Gardner, "not even a quarter inch," I told her as sternly as I could.

"I won't budge," she promised in a whisper.

"You heard me call for the paramedics and firefighters, too," I added.

"I just hope I can lift Gracie when she visits us." She said meekly.

"The baby will love you."

Rochelle moaned again. "But my house--this home is ruined. How will I ever clean up this shit storm in time?"

"And, as for fixing this mess, you have so many solid friends in The Dalles."

She started to weep. I shuddered and shivered. None of us had been prepared to die, especially like this.

∾

CHAPTER 15

SEARCH WARRANT

Mrs. Kantadillo welcomed me and the captain warmly while standing on a quiet Smohalla street at the front door of her lovely Tudor home. "My husband will be right out."

Stately and white-haired like Judge Kantadillo, she held herself upright with similar bearing. "And I trust you'll be joining us for coffee and dessert," she insisted in a sweet, formal tone. She looked over my shoulder at an approaching vehicle.

"Perfect timing," said the boss, also looking back to see Dr. Henry Schloss parallel parking the Washington State Patrol forensic van two doors down and tight to the street curb. I hoped that unlike after our bust of bust at the *Tramposo* compound, Schloss's trip over the Cascades would be worth it.

The judge from Joe's high profile trial appeared in the living room behind his wife. He wore a Scottish tweed blazer, loose slacks, comfy slippers and reading glasses dangling from a lanyard. "When it comes to her desserts, my better half refuses to take no for an answer," said the judge. "Much like predisposition from you that I not reject your request for a warrant." He then focused on the slightly-built forensic scientist hustling across Smohalla's residential street of old, classy homes. "Welcome, Doctor," he told Schloss, his voice cheery and booming.

The scientist apologized in his reedy tone. "Sorry I'm running late, Your Honor."

"Right on time, I'd say," said Mrs. Kantadillo in a manner that let us know she was up to serving as our hostess.

Condran thanked the judge for meeting with us on such short notice. I was hoping to see Sammy, but when or where might depend on what happened here.

When Mrs. Kantadillo took my Abercrombie & Fitch jacket, she accidentally bumped my jaw and saw me wince at the throbbing bruise where Nils had backhanded me. "My husband said you had quite the horrible ordeal yesterday."

I placed my hand gently to my jaw and nodded.

She patted my wrist and held it there until the throbbing stopped and I pulled my hand from my face. She motioned for us to be seated. I also made sure my wrist bandage was secure when we took our seats around a long maple table in their open dining room. The judge and his wife sat at each end with Condran and me facing Dr. Schloss. His windowed silhouette helped showcase a tall, dry, golden ridge at the edge of Smohalla.

Our hosts looked to be about seventy. They probably grew up in the Great Depression, but had become affluent enough to own fine, sturdy furniture in a lovely, well-aged home with balustrades, wainscoting and old framed photos hanging from the walls, not unlike how Rochelle's Victorian was adorned before the ransacking. The comparison sent a chill through me, top-to-toe. A Grandfather clock down the hall chimed three-o'clock. An enlarged family picture in the dining room featured multiple generations in their Sunday best holding a baby in front of a shiny, black Model-A Ford.

"Hard to tell if it's a boy or girl, but which one of you is the infant there?" I asked, figuring the photo was from the early 1930's.

The judge pointed to his wife. "Bernice is from a well-to-do, New England family. Mine were hardscrabble Pacific Northwesterners—fishermen, mostly."

I sat and reached into a notebook for our investigation. It also harbored a new photo. At least this baby picture didn't get impaled during Nils's berserk outburst. "Kuma sent me this of Gracie."

"She's darling!" said Mrs. Kantadillo. "How old?"

"Eight-months." I handed the photo to the judge. "It's been eight months," I repeated, feeling my throat tighten.

The judge lifted his reading glasses over his prominent nose. "As in, we still don't know who drowned her mother," he said in a soft, quiet tone that I'd never heard in his courtroom. "Which is why we're here," He sighed before handing Grace's picture back to me. Despite the sympathetic words, his stiff posture made me wonder just how primed he was to grant us a warrant.

His wife set a homemade cheesecake near her own place-setting closest to the kitchen. We watched her cut the pie-shaped dessert into ample wedges. She placed three on small plates, handing them to me one at a time to pass on to the men. When I set down my slice, she stood and held up a modest, crystal serving dish filled with her own special raspberry sauce, asking each of us if we'd like for her to ladle topping on our dessert. None of us refused when she made her way around the table. Condran, the coffee hound, lit up when she then poured him and her husband fresh-brewed cups.

When I said I didn't often drink coffee, she offered me a bottle of Perrier water instead. Caffeine made me more hyper than my normal amped-up self. She twisted off the cap and filled a tall drinking glass for me and another for Dr. Schloss.

Man, oh man, I could never see myself being so subservient, not with a mother like mine who ran her classy museum with the same firm hand she'd used in raising me, my parents' only child. I'd carry my own water bucket like Mom does, thank you, I thought, but smiled with a nod at our polite hostess.

"Amazing!" I said after my first bite of the dessert. This woman's cheesecake was an otherworldly mix of tart and sweet.

"Yes, my usual compliments, Mrs. Kantadillo," said Dr. Schloss, indicating he already knew the couple, as well as her cooking talent.

"And we want to thank you again for the search warrant you granted for us this morning," the captain told the judge after setting his hot cup on its matching saucer.

"But you wouldn't be back now with such urgency, unless you found something major."

"That's correct, Your Honor," said Schloss. "I'm a touch late due to a call I received from my counterpart at the regional U.S. Customs office. He told me that our latest Krugerrand prints matched the recent arrest fingerprints from Darla Larsson, mother of Gunnar. This applies to the Krugerrands from Nils Larsson's own lockbox, too."

"So you suspect that she was the money handler for all the Krugerrands you located?" the Judge asked.

"By all appearances," said Condran. "We also verified that the handle on the confiscated baby buggy––which was wide enough to hide the columns of coins being smuggled––was the one switched from the original Strollers-R-Us model that was found in Roger Riggleman's basement this morning. The bolts and nuts attaching both handles matched perfectly."

"And from what I can see, so do the fingerprints of those," said Schloss. "We expected to see prints on the baby buggy from Linh Riggleman, but I used the prints we had from the day the chief detective was arrested. The ones from Roger Riggleman on the day of the kidnapping attempt indicate a preliminary, visual match to those on the stroller near the securement holes for the bolts."

The judge nodded ever so slightly as he processed the new information.

"Our lab showed no evidence of Linh Riggleman touching the gold coins or the rolls that held them," Schloss added. "A thorough analysis is scheduled for these new findings."

"Both the detective and his daughter-in-law went straight to jail on the day of the kidnapping," I said, trying to keep my voice from getting too amped. "Neither of them had a chance to tamper with potential evidence after that day."

Schloss propped his elbows on his side of the table. "As for this morning's search," he said, glancing over at Condran before continuing, "we were hoping to find more Krugerrands at Roger Riggleman's home, but they may have been trying to smuggle all the gold coins that they possessed."

The captain jumped in. "That seems likely. What we found strengthens our suspicions that Darla and Nils Larsson gave their bribe money directly to the chief investigator. Roger Riggleman then hid all the coins taken from Nils Larsson's lockbox for his daughter-in-law to smuggle to Asia," said the captain.

"Why weren't his prints on any of the coins?" the judge asked.

"We suspect that only Darla was inserting the gold coins into their investor rolls," Schloss told him, "but I will be inspecting the outside of the coin sleeves for Roger Riggleman's prints from when he slid the rolls inside the hollow, tubular handle. The friction from pushing those rolls inside the metal tube may have erased any prints."

"However, Darla's prints further suggest that the Larssons were involved in the high-end China White heroin deal at the Bone Shrine," Condran said.

The judge finished a generous bite of his wife's cheesecake. When I spoke up, he looked my way again. "That way the Larssons were able to spring their son out of jail on the morning after the drowning." I'd suddenly felt the need to clarify this for the judge. "These definitely weren't part of Linh Riggleman's supposed stash of gold coins being used to invest in the Larsson's new vodka distillery in Sweden. If there ever was such an intention, then Linh's prints would be all over those coins we found in his office lockbox."

Once the judge looked at me, a bit perplexed, the captain banged me firmly with his knee so that no one else at the table would notice. I guess I shouldn't have revealed this last bit of info. I fidgeted, but didn't care if it meant that Nils, Darla, *and* Gunnar might go down—falling real hard when they all landed in prison.

"Your Honor, there's a troublesome development with the Larsson's family lawyer, Abe Steinke," the boss said.

"I know this lawyer well. He's presented many cases before my court."

"Then you likely know that, in addition to Darla Larsson, Mr. Steinke also represents Linh and Roger Riggleman, both of them facing different charges in different jurisdictions. Steinke, in my brief conversation with him yesterday morning, tried to sow serious doubt for our basic premise that the Larssons were bribing the Rigglemans."

"How so?" Judge K asked.

The captain sat tall in his chair. "Steinke is planning to argue in court that Linh Riggleman had simply failed to declare what was left of her Krugerrand stash after providing Nils Larsson with a $160,000 investment in the vodka enterprise that Biff just mentioned. Conveniently for Linh Riggleman—— also his client——this is the total value of the Krugerrands remaining in Nils Larsson's coin case, one which only fit $240,000 worth of gold coins--$80K for the bribe plus the $160K remaining in Larsson's lockbox."

"So, if I understand this correctly, then, according to Steinke," the judge asked, pulling at his earlobe, "the Larssons' were going to launch a vodka business in Sweden with the help of Linh Riggleman's supposed investment?"

"Yes, Your Honor," said Schloss, "except these prints indicate that the coins were moving in the opposite direction. Darla touched them earlier, sometime before Linh tried smuggling the gold onto her flight out of the United States."

Condran leaned back. "Steinke also intends to argue in court that Mrs. Riggleman was simply hiding her coins from thieves and merely forgot to declare the funds to US Customs."

"And, in her federal case, he'll likely insist that the overseas trip to Vietnam was a short-term vacation with no kidnapping intended whatsoever," the judge said.

Before we could take any comfort in his words, Kantadillo turned to the boss. "What judge issued you a warrant to search the lockbox in Nils Larsson's office?"

I gulped. I really had said too much. Condran kept his eyes off me and on the judge's before speaking without any hesitation. "One of Larsson's assistants at the potato association had found the coins on his work office desk and brought them to us."

I noticed a light layer of sweat forming on the Boss's forehead, but was impressed with how well he kept his response vague enough not to implicate Tomiko. Our case didn't need that complication--not right now.

"It's a pity the DEA's warrant for Nils Larsson's arrest on felony drug charges wasn't issued last week, rather than this morning," Dr. Schloss said. "The Feds claim he's been running a boutique heroin distribution ring in cities all across the United States. And, now, after intending to torch the Gardner home in The Dalles, he's fled back to Sweden."

Judge Kantadillo turned and startled me by asking how I was holding up. Before we arrived this afternoon, he'd obviously been given the lowdown on what happened at Rochelle's.

I hesitated to gather my words. "I'm alive, and more determined than ever on seeing this case to its close, sir." I pushed my plate forward. "I saw Rochelle Gardner at the hospital in The Dalles, first thing this morning. She'll be in a neck brace for at least the next month."

"Looks like that man roughed you up, too," said Mrs. Kantadillo, not quite touching my face bruise before lightly patting my wrist above its bandage.

I touched my jaw with one hand and patted the seat I sat on with the other. "I was tied up to a chair like this one in an old home much like yours here," I said, and twisted to point into the living room embellished with antiques. "Imagine everything you treasure in your home heaped in a tall pile there, ready to be ignited." I turned away and stared out the dining room window to the tops of the dry, flammable ridge at the edge of Smohalla, thinking it was just a single lit match away from burning down this whole neighborhood.

The captain leaned into the table, both hands squeezing his coffee cup. "After Mr. Larsson fled the Gardner home, he rode his motorcycle through the night going north on backroads. At dawn, he slipped into British Columbia at a lightly used border crossing. I suspect that his Vancouver flight has landed in Sweden by now so he can meet up with the money he cleared out of his American bank accounts." The captain clenched his jaw. "This is all to say that, unfortunately, somehow, Nils caught wind of the impending Drug Enforcement Agency warrant."

"But, I'm sure glad he took off when he did," I said firmly. "If Nils Larsson hadn't fled right then, then that bonfire would have fried Rochelle, Tomiko and me into crispy long-pork."

The large-boned judge leaned back against his chair and laughed when he looked at me. "Long-pork. I haven't heard that expression for a while."

"Your Honor," the captain interjected, "we have one major unturned stone in this case. That's why we had a pressing need to meet with you so soon. The home of Linh and Zach Riggleman has never been searched, and certainly not by Roger Riggleman during the corrupt investigation he led. We now have a link strongly suggesting that his wife was an accomplice in this botched criminal investigation with all of its obstructed justice. We'd like the opportunity to search for anything there that would link them to the Bone Shrine crimes."

Judge Kantadillo folded his arms. "After eight full months since the drowning and related drug deal, not to mention four months since the aborted kidnapping and money smuggling attempts, I worry that this may be too much of a long-shot."

"I respectfully disagree, sir," I said. "Zach Riggleman was a hero on the night of the murder when he rescued baby Grace from the marsh. With his dad running the criminal investigation, he knew his home wasn't about to be searched. Then, after his wife was arrested at the airport and deemed a flight risk, she'd never had any chance to return home and cover up anything more. People like Zach Riggleman think they're above the law. They're likely to be careless."

"Why didn't US Customs search Linh Riggleman's home?" the judge asked.

The captain spoke before Schloss could. "Because the federal agency had no need for fresh evidence. She was caught in the act with both the gold and the baby."

Dr. Schloss jumped in. "Your Honor, it took my own personal contacts and the most delicate pressure to convince key U.S. Customs officials that they should allow the Washington State Patrol an opportunity to test their confiscated evidence for fingerprints," Schloss took off his horn-rimmed glasses and wiped the lenses clean. "My findings offer us a direct link between the Larssons and Rigglemans. This ties the parties to the Bone Shrine case through bribery. Any search of Linh and Zach Riggleman's home would be focused on further substantiating and expanding on this new evidentiary connection."

The judge cleared his throat. "Isn't Darla Larsson still in Franklin County Jail awaiting arraignment?" he asked.

"Yes, delayed until next Tuesday, since her lawyer insisted that he be present. It should be noted," Condran clarified, "these charges only relate to her recorded threats of violence at the Dust Devil baseball game against her sister and Biff. This has nothing to do with today's fingerprints showing that Darla was involved in this bribery and obstruction of justice matter that kept her son from forced testimony in Joe Gardner's trial."

"Why aren't these findings that you possess now evidence enough to force a plea bargain from her?" the judge asked Condran.

"Because, Your Honor, if any of the Larssons were present at the Bone Shrine that night and we can show this, then we can convince Darla Larsson that we know, beyond reasonable doubt, that she knows who it was that drowned Mary Quinn. This would be the sort of leverage to help us exact a plea that could fully solve our case.

I really needed to clarify. "It helps that Nils, by escaping to Sweden, just abandoned her to face this legal mess. It gives that scorned lady plenty of motive to finger her husband——and I'm pretty sure which finger she'd be using."

Mrs. Kantadillo was actually the only one who chuckled.

"It's her lawyer we need to convince of her legal jeopardy here," said the captain looking first at me and then at the judge. "Again, that will require unassailable evidence."

"If I may, Captain," Dr. Schloss said, his high voice animated as he tapped his fork on his empty dessert plate. "The level of cover-up and evidence destruction suffered in this case still leads the state patrol to believe that the murder involved those connected to the county itself. It's hard to imagine the county investigators and even the prosecution perhaps, to cover up for outsiders like the Larssons, or even for the *Tramposo* gang."

"If the Larsson's were the prospective buyers of the heroin, then they surely know who their sellers were," Condran added.

"Let me stop you, Captain," said Judge K. "This morning's search yielded confirmation on a kidnapping and smuggling case. Your search that I granted for the ostensible drug compound of the *Tramposos* yielded nothing, not even a single ounce of marijuana. Where are you going with this? These gold coins with Mrs. Larsson's prints were nowhere near the Bone Shrine crime site. Why are they now the key to solving the young mother's drowning or that actual heroin deal?"

The captain rinsed down his last bite of cheesecake by chugging the last of his brew. "Sir, I will be seeking additional charges and a plea bargain from Darla Larsson irrespective of any additional evidence we procure at Zach and Linh Rigglemans' home. However, this search warrant allows us due diligence. Currently, we can show that Mrs. Riggleman is complicit with both the Larssons' bribe and her father-in-law's obstruction of justice. This is new discovery."

I really couldn't help myself this time. "We need more ammo to convict her," I said, looking at the judge with my hands waving, but not too wildly, I hoped. "Darla needs to know that we know that she knows who killed Mary Quinn."

From the way he rammed his knee into mine again, the boss didn't appreciate my added input.

"You do realize that you're asking me to issue a search warrant for the home of an active sheriff deputy?" Kantadillo looked at the captain and asked. "Thus far, he hasn't been implicated in any way."

"He's the son of the man who corrupted the entire criminal investigation, but it's his wife's home, too," Schloss said firmly, but calmly.

"We also haven't ruled out that Linh Riggleman used her nail polishing business to smuggle into the U.S. the China White that was being sold that night," said Condran. "Also, Zach Riggleman may well have been an accessory to the crimes committed at the Bone Shrine that night."

I looked at Mrs. Kantadillo who was finishing her own piece of cheesecake and listening intently to our conversation. I decided to speak forcefully. "The Larsson family is now directly tied to Linh Riggleman's smuggling activities. Not to be too sexist, but I'll bet Linh, not Zach, would have been the one tasked with washing away the evidence on any oversized uniform brought home by Zach from the Bone Shrine pond that night."

"Okay. I'll stop all of you there," the judge said scratching his shaved chin beneath wavy-thick, white hair.

I'm not sure he heard what I just said, but from the captain's stern look at me, I figured I'd just overstepped my bounds again by bringing up the lead Amanda gave us at the diner. I wondered if Condran had only invited me to come to meet with the judge as visual evidence of Nils Larsson's violent escape from justice.

The boss also told me that I was supposed to assist Schloss, if we got our warrant. Now I worried that if Judge K rebuffed us and the boss blamed my comments, then I'd be dropped-kicked off Mary's case for good. I sucked in as much air as I could.

"Dr. Schloss has appeared before me numerous times as an expert witness," the judge said. "As long as he takes the lead and proceeds thoroughly--and I mean before the Wanapum County Sheriff Department catches wind of this warrant--then I will grant a one-day search for tomorrow morning. As far as I'm concerned, any corroborating evidence linking Linh or Zach Riggleman to the Bone Shrine crimes will justify your search," he added.

"In the morning? So soon?" Schloss asked. "I'll have to rearrange my schedule."

"If we can't find you a hotel room of your own, Doctor, then I have double queen beds in my extended-stay room," Condran jumped in and said, not about to let his stellar forensic expert weasel out of this investigative opportunity of ours. "You're the key for us solving this case."

Absently, the judge took a handkerchief from his pocket, lifted the glasses on his lanyard and wiped the lenses until clear. "Again, as long as Dr. Schloss is onboard, then let's get this warrant signed and sealed." Once the scientist nodded slowly, the judge motioned for the captain to join him inside his private office down the hall.

Late afternoon sunlight through the window illuminated the dining room. Mrs. Kantadillo stood and lowered the blinds half-way, but we could still see the base of the town's dry, rolling hills. The grandfather clock struck 4:00 pm.

I was pleasantly surprised when Dr. Schloss joined me and Mrs. Kantadillo in clearing the table. In the kitchen, she began washing them the old fashioned way, in one side of her kitchen sink. I stood next to her after pulling on rubber dishwashing gloves. The left one covered my wrist bandage. I followed her lead by rinsing soapy dishes with the hottest water my gloved hands could withstand.

Schloss grabbed a towel and dried the plates and cups just as I stacked them in the counter dish rack. He focused on each water spot and showed the same fastidiousness that made him a fine forensic scientist.

"Young lady," said the judge's wife when placing her china back in the cupboards, "this world needs smart women like you to provide justice in this world."

"Maybe I'll be a judge one day," I told her.

With his high, soft voice, Schloss chimed in, too. "You're right, Mrs. Kantadillo. The sky's the limit for this young lady."

This climb-for-the-black-robe ambition of mine had made both of them smile. I blushed, and when we returned to the dining room, Condran entered in front of the judge. The captain held the warrant while Mrs. Kantadillo spoke to her husband. "Sweetheart, I'm not sure when this investigation will end, but once it does, you'd be wise to scoop up Biff McCoy here as your intern."

The judge spoke up in his authoritative courtroom voice after he turned to face me. "Once Captain Condran rides off into the sunset, you come see me. I may be able use your help."

His voice sounded sincere and kept my cheeks burning. "We *are* going to solve this case, and, yes, I promise to pay you a visit afterwards, sir." I took a deep breath. "And thank you for recommending me, Mrs. Kantadillo."

"I like your investigatory resolve, Biff," said the judge. "Let's hope the warrant helps shed more light on this mess."

I smiled and slipped on my coat even though it wasn't needed on this fine spring afternoon.

Interning for a judge. What an opportunity that would be! I nearly stumbled on the outside step when Dr. Schloss and the captain followed me out the door and I told the captain that I'd figured out the focus of my midterm paper.

"What's the title?" Condran asked.

"'Navigating a Mangled Crime Scene.'"

"That theme will certainly work well with this case of ours," said Dr. Schloss. The captain merely nodded, barely.

Not that it would bring back Mary, I wanted to say. Instead, I listened as Condran told Schloss that, this evening, they should talk and discuss the logistics of tomorrow's search.

The boss and I watched Schloss climb into the forensic van and ease down the street.

"Did you know you'd be able to secure this warrant?" I asked Condran gingerly once the Kantadillos retreated into their classy old home.

"I was guardedly optimistic."

"Why?" I asked.

"Dr. Schloss is held in very high regard in this state. That and motivation."

"What motive?"

"The thing that moves anyone to act. Judge Kantadillo is still bitterly ashamed of what this county's Sheriff department did to his high profile trial."

"When corruption demolishes any semblance of justice," I added almost to myself, thinking how this might work as the opening words of my paper.

Condran glanced my way. "Just so you know, I had a heated conversation with your mother last night."

"Mom told me she gave you quite an earful."

"With good reason," Condran said. "After what Nils did, she was totally against you continuing as my intern. I told her that I understood."

"If so, then why am I standing here?" Without thinking about how defiant I must have looked, I placed both fists on my hips.

"Because I need all the help I can get on this investigation. You come cheap, and you're relatively helpful."

"That line of crapola wouldn't come close to persuading my mom. She wanted to scalp you after psycho-dealer Nils nearly torched her semi-precious jewel of a daughter.

Condran looked down at his feet. "You're right. I promised her, from the heart, that moving forward on the case, I'd do my utmost to keep you out of harm's way."

I was afraid to ask him what he meant by––'from the heart'––but it seemed to have worked with Mom since I was still cemented on the shifting sands of this case.

I reached into the pocket of my jacket.

When the boss climbed into his unmarked Crown Vic, I reached through the window he rolled down and set Rochelle's sealed message on his dash.

"When you meet with Darla and her lawyer, could you be real sure this letter gets to Darla? Please don't read it though. I promised Rochelle that no one would see it but her sister."

"What if the note makes matter's worse?" he asked.

"Well, Rochelle asked me if you'd please read it first. Then, only, give it to Darla if you think it will help convince her to tell the truth.

Condran held the note for a minute before unsealing the flap. I could see where the envelope featured a Poet's Shooting Star printed in purple and green along one side. The stationery had been folded to fit perfectly inside. Very slowly, the captain pulled out the letter. Read it silently, Biff, but along with me. Take your time.

April 26, 2001

Dear Darla,

So many crimes, and in the last years, he stole your son, too. He's gone. There's more you need to know.
I'm not your judge, but other than my son, you're the only family I have. I've thought hard about abandoning you, but here I am praying for our peace.
Today, Nils tried burning my house down. He bound me, Biff, and Tomiko beside all my piled up, precious belongings. He lit a fire that failed to rage. He broke my neck, but not my hope.
I've never told you, but before you met him, I chose not to bear his child. For this, he wanted me burned and gone today.
No one planned for Mary to die, though. No one imagined that Joe would become the fall guy, but this was the hell you, Nils, and Gunnar helped create. Today, only you can begin the healing.
Your own heart is your only refuge. My heart knows you were always the kinder, more loving sister.
Darla, you need to right this wrong. You know who was there that night Mary died. Please take a plea and bargain with your hard truth.

Love,
Your sister, Rochelle

"It's actually pretty convincing," Condran said once he saw that I'd also finished.

"Please use it, Boss," I said. "I can't see where it will hurt our chances of getting her to talk. Also, be sure Darla knows what Nils said to us."

"What's that?"

"It's just that--in taking off for Sweden with all their liquid assets--he made it clear that he'd also be abandoning her--for good."

Condran placed the letter back in its envelope. He nodded solemnly, tapped the note, and placed it into the inside of his jacket pocket. "I'll deliver it," he said and settled into his driver's seat. "Also, six a.m. at the field office. Be there, Biff. You'll be *assisting*, Schloss." He added with a cold tone. "This time work harder at keeping yourself in the background."

He was definitely upset with how much I'd butted in to help us get the warrant. "Sorry. I guess I'm not over all that went down at Rochelle's house."

"If you're not up to--"

"--of course I'm up to being at the search. I'd still be in my own bed in The Dalles, head buried beneath the pillows if I wasn't going to see this investigation through with you." I couldn't help but sound testy.

"Very well, Biff. I'll see you bright and early."

DRUMS

When my Loyale's smooth little engine turned over, Sammy, a whole lot more than upsetting Condran, posed the bigger frustration in my mind. Calling him again might come off as desperate, but while driving the twenty miles back to Moses Lake, I'd tried to call Sammy four more times. He still wasn't picking up. I knew his graveyard shift didn't start until late this evening. Had he moved on from me? Was he blowing me off? My stomach rumbled hollowly with every unanswered ring.

"We've been hoping you'd show up soon," said Mrs. Pack with a welcoming smile when she opened the front door and ushered me inside their newer Moses Lake rambler. She and Jack were just finishing dinner and, after telling me she was dishing up bowls of ice cream, offered me some.

I explained that I'd just finished my dessert. Just the thought of Mrs. Kantadillo's cheesecake had me wishing for more of her homemade raspberry sauce.

My true sweet tooth had me trying to call Sammy's cell again just before I got here. Why was I getting the cold shoulder from him? In three hours he'd be starting his graveyard shift and I wouldn't be able to talk with him until morning. That's if, at sunrise, he'd even answer my call.

Escher ambled over to nuzzle my hand when I sat on the family couch. "That's his favorite sleeping perch," said Mrs. Pack from their kitchen that opened into the living room.

"Escher likes you. Otherwise he'd be sulking in the corner ignoring all of us," K-9 Sergeant Pack added.

The biggest photo on the wood paneled walls, even bigger than a framed wedding shot of the couple, was the one of Jack Pack, decked out in his finest Wanapum Sheriff uniform, accepting a training certificate from a professional police dog trainer. Escher was photographed staring at the camera while heeling at the sergeant's side.

"There aren't many people that Escher cozies up to," Mrs. Pack added.

"With that nose of his, he remembers everyone, including you," said Jack of his Dutch Shepherd. "Tomorrow we'll be helping with the search. Condran just called and confirmed my availability––all as a private citizen doing contract work for the State Patrol, of course, since Sheriff Usk placed me on administrative leave at Wanapum County."

I looked at Escher's deep brown eyes before running my hands down the length of the shepherd's white and black coat. "We gotta put that nose of yours to good work in the morning," I said and looked at Jack. "The boss will be really glad that you and Escher, on such short notice, are joining our morning search. I'll be there assisting Dr. Schloss," I added.

Mrs. Pack handed her husband his dessert bowl. She sat beside him on the couch across from me. They dug into the ice cream, almost like they were in a hurry.

"Careful you don't give yourself headaches. I hate ice-freezing my brain!" I said, but they didn't slow down, except when Sergeant Pack stopped to respond.

"Since I'm on administrative leave, I've intentionally ignored any calls from the Sheriff Department."

"We know what they want," Mrs. Pack added.

"What's that?"

Jack sat tall and rocked his dessert spoon between two fingers. "They want me to hand over Escher this evening. One of my K-9 coworkers stopped by just before you came. He let me know that a deputy will be coming here in an hour or two."

Sgt. Pack called his dog. Escher hopped up and ambled away from me to his master. "The captain obviously has a great deal of confidence in you, being a young intern and all."

Earlier, at the judge's home, after stepping on Condran's 'sales pitch' for the search warrant a time or two too many, I wondered how highly he really thought of me.

Jack, after swallowing another big spoonful of vanilla ice cream, looked closely at me. "I think the captain sees his own daughter in you."

"Captain Condran has a daughter?" I asked, looking up from the dog at his feet.

Mrs. Pack patted her husband's knee. "He *had* a daughter," she said, looking straight at me, too. "His eighteen-year-old girl died of a heroin overdose two years ago. Jack and I met her when she was only sixteen at the statewide law enforcement conference. Seemed like such a bright teen."

Jack looked down at his dog, his wide mustache quivering. "Too many kids falling down that dark hole."

Mrs. Pack teared up. "Jack and I can't have kids, so news like this always hits us hard."

This time Jack set down his bowl and spoon and, with his fingertips, rolled the whiskers growing out beyond one side of his upper lip. "Actually, you kind of—never mind."

"I kind of what?" I asked firmly, really wanting to know.

Jack placed his hand on the head of Escher. "When I first met you on the morning of the *Tramposo* bust, there was a moment there where I was sure you were Elizabeth Condran. Then—just as the notion came to me—I remembered what had happened to Lizzy."

I nodded without speaking, a rarity for me. Here I'd thought I was the only one on our case with huge, uncured grief. I looked down at the dog. "Elizabeth is also my given name," I told them.

Mrs. Pack, distracted by the coincidence, stood with a scoop still left in the bowl. "It's probably time," she said. Jack handed her his bowl and spoon. She went to the kitchen sink and rinsed the dishes before turning back towards the living room. "We're really sorry, Biff."

"Well, I really didn't need any dessert," I said.

Sergeant Pack stood. "Unfortunately, we need to go to her mother's place for a while if we don't want to lose Escher to Sheriff Usk's shenanigans."

That's when I first noticed the three packed suitcases lining the hallway to their bedroom.

"But tell Captain Condran that I'll be at the search with Escher first thing in the morning," said the sergeant. Escher lay at his feet, eyes shut and letting out a noise stuck somewhere between a snore and a snort.

"I thought each K-9 was assigned to one officer," I said. "How can they take him away from you?"

"Escher may be our dog in actuality, but, legally, he's the property of the Wanapum County Sheriff Department," Pack explained. "And, as I've said, I'm on administrative leave—"

"—for having the bravery to run against the current, crooked sheriff," I'd added, thinking about how Sheriff Usk and Deputy Riggleman had shaken me down at the Methodist Church in order to scare me off the Bone Shrine case.

"We feel so bad after promising to accommodate you," said Mrs. Pack.

The sergeant pulled out his wallet and tried to hand me a three twenties. "Please let us pay for your hotel room tonight," he insisted.

"No. No. Use that for more campaign signs. Besides, Mom told me she'd help with lodging, if I ever need it," I said, firmly refusing his cash. The offer from my mother wasn't true today, though, not after both Mom and Dad opposed my return to Moses Lake following the near-torching of Rochelle's Victorian. Besides, I really didn't want to call my parents.

"You really need to safeguard Escher for our case," I added.

I slipped into my Loyale and drove off aimlessly only to find myself at the edge of Moses Lake parking beside the Wanapum County Fairground. Once again, Sammy refused to answer his cell. I willed myself not to cry. I couldn't believe he'd go so stone cold on me like this. Here I was in my car, darkness all around.

I opened and closed the new flip phone in my pocket, the one Mom had just purchased for me this morning. Once Captain Condran had set up this lodging for me at the Packs, there had been one less worry, but there'd be no call to my parents——not yet. I just wanted to hear Sammy's voice again.

My mind churned for options on a place to crash. Why would I think that Sammy might know of some crash-pad in his own home town? He wasn't even answering his flippin' phone.

In the chill, with my engine off, I traced my *She-Who-Watches* medallion. "Help me, Mary," I muttered. I needed to get my rattled brain to focus, except my body was commanding me to sleep.

It was too cold tonight with the clear sky sucking any hint of the day's warmth into outer space. Too bad, after my abduction, I'd chucked my car blanket into the bitterbrush. But I wasn't depressed enough to run the engine, crank up the heater, and die of carbon monoxide poisoning. I was not about to sleep in my car, I told myself.

What I really wanted was soft bedding, silence, and some place where Wanapum County's enemy sheriff deputies wouldn't cite me in the middle of the night for illegal car-camping. I really needed a morning shower before the search.

I turned on the engine and moved steadily forward, not knowing where I was headed. My Loyale, or Mary maybe, seemed to be showing me the way. Maybe it was sub-conscious steering, but the smoothness seemed more like dream-driving.

I pulled over at a neighborhood park along the dammed Moses Lake proper, the section made deep enough for water ski boats. This was no seep pond like at the Bone Shrine and I was hardly lost. I knew exactly where I'd parked. I got out in the dim evening and did my best to act nonchalant while locking my car.

I relented and called Sammy one last time for the night. Of course there was no frickin' answer. Nothing but voicemail. I decided to speak. "Looks like I'll be holing up at the Larsson's place since Darla's in the slammer and Nil's has flown off to join Gunnar in Vikingsville." I hoped I didn't sound desperate, especially when I ended with,

"Please call me, Sammy." I'd done my utmost to sound cheery and not pathetic, I hoped.

Walking with my overnight bag, I kept a steady pace to show any neighbor watching the street that I knew my destination. Stay chill. No need to rush. I eased along the side of the street with the neighborhood's waterfront homes. The elbow-shivering, night breeze was probably keeping the residents inside their warm homes. I walked alone down the eerily quiet sidewalk.

At the rear basement entrance, I found the same entry-key I'd used many times before. An intruder in my mind spoke clearly:

Darla was in jail.

Nils split, following Gunnar to Sweden.

Why not sleep here?

I was never evicted by the Larssons. Not formally.

Technically, I was still this family's renter.

Tonight, who cared if I crashed here.

I flicked on the switch in Gunnar's old bedroom. The mess I'd left when escaping Darla's wrath had been tidied away. My nightgown and slippers were gone. No sign of the flip phone I'd abandoned on the nightstand.

It wasn't that I was opposed to sleeping in Gunnar's bed, but I wondered if my inner Goldilocks might find cozier sleeping upstairs.

Even though my jaw throbbed, I wanted to disappear into sleep. I ascended the steps to the master bedroom. Part of me wanted to tear the home apart looking for the kind of evidence we hoped to find tomorrow morning, but I knew this home had been thoroughly searched last December by the State Patrol. Mostly, I was too tired to play the sleuth. I'd save all that focus until morning.

At the moment, I stepped inside Darla's and Nils's bedroom and found myself not the least bit cozy. I shuddered causing goose bumps to pimple up my arms and spine. I smelled the weird energy of this couple probably broken into an ocean of estrangement. Unless, the plan was for Darla to join Nils later in Vikingstad. As crazed as that man was, maybe he thought Rochelle would be his gal. I winced and rubbed one upper arm since my wrist was still too bandaged.

The thought of sleeping in their bed gave me the creeps. Mostly, Nils still haunted the bedroom. In their wedding photo, I stared at his eyes. There was too much white showing around the irises. I'd once heard how this was a sure sign of craziness. Looked like Nils had been all nutsoid from before Gunnar was born. The Swede hid it pretty well under all his formal airs.

I slammed their door and went into the living room finally allowing myself to seethe. The Quonset hut, filled with grown boy toys—the two Husqvarna dirt bikes, a Saab Sonnet sports car, and the family waterski boat—all needed a good dousing of gasoline and a single match. Same with everything I could locate in this lakefront home they'd owned for a couple decades or so. Cool Swedish landscapes were nicely framed on the wall. Stylish Scandinavian furniture. Their huge television.

I'd send them a message. I shoved the chairs and coffee table out of the way and rolled up the expensive throw rug so I could throw Nils's belongings onto the maple floor slats below.

I rushed over and started to pull the receiver from its cords, but right in front of his prized *Primare 30* stereo system, I saw a simple home-recorded cassette. The handwriting on the paper cover inside the plastic case was labeled with bold lettering:

COPY FOR: "To the End of the Trail"
English translation of original Swedish lullaby:
Carl Michael Bellman, den 18 augusti, 1787

August 18th was that date when Mary drowned. I didn't understand the lyrics when the Swedish lady sang them so softly and full of sorrow, but Nils or Gunnar had written out a translation. I turned up the song.

The melody, same as Mary's "To the End of the Trail" cut through me. I dropped to the rolled up rug and sat, face in palms. Wetness covered my hands. My shoulders heaved. Would I ever find my precious friend's murderer? I sobbed and listened. I listened harder than I ever had. There was no way I could *not* hear Mary's singing voice.

I got up and rewound the tape once I recalled what Mary had told me. The Swedish song was written by a troubadour when, during the same week that his toddler died, a new son was born. No wonder the lullaby was so sorrowful. I plowed away enough tears to read the English translation:

Little babe, sleep peaceful sweet,
time soon brings its war cries.
In time, the wounds of time he'll meet,
on battlefields of man's demise.
This world is an isle of woe,
best we breathe before we go——
Buried in the earth's replies.

I had to turn it off. I had to breathe and stop crying. I had to realized that Nils and Gunnar Larsson had abandoned this American home of theirs. Let them escape to their fatherland. Let them feel a lifetime of sorrows.

There was only one thing that torching these many belongings would do for me. It wouldn't be vindicating anything if I was charged with arson, especially when the whole house burnt to the ground. In a way, the place was already torched by them abandoning their home. I'd like to say I felt sorry for what was happening to Darla, but I couldn't forgive her karma, not for the involvement she surely had in covering up my best friend's death and setting up her own nephew for a life in prison.

I decided to take the only thing in this place that I coveted, the only thing that connected me to Mary. I popped the cassette from its player, put it in its case and found the lullaby a side pocket on the outside of my overnight bag. I carried this gently through the hallway, and opened the guest bedroom door that was next to the upstair's bathroom.

I set my overnight bag on the bed, found my toiletry kit, and went to brush my teeth. First, I tended to the wounds on jaw and wrist. Mom had sent me off with wide Band-Aids and Neosporin. The nerve-endings on my skin stung when pulling off the old gauze. The glass cut on my wrist had left a throbbing gouge. My backhanded jaw was still a mottled mess of yellow, blue, brown, and red.

Was this what Elizabeth Condran looked like once she was all strung out on dope? I felt myself tear up. If I did look anything like her, then it made sense why the boss had patience for me and my run amok tongue.

Only my mother called me *Elizabeth.* Once in a rare while she said it tenderly. Far more often, I became *Elizabeth* when I pissed her off.

In bed on the soft mattress, a thick down comforter floated atop my shoulders. I was too tired to be mad at anyone or about anything. My eyes disengaged when each lid insisted on closing.

～

Into my dream, I circled through the night of Mary's death.

I pound my owl wings. I drift through moonlight. Below me, a movement catches my eye. I dive towards earth like a rocket. I'm sure of a strike on prey, but my talons miss.

The black-tailed jack rabbit zigzags like my dreams and disappears into a burrow.

The crying owlet is still abandoned. It's not my own. I haven't hatched any eggs. Not yet. But the fledgling triggers a strong instinct. I hunt and wish to share my catch. No luck.

I lift and fly farther away from the pond. The soil of the wildlife refuge is thicker there. I scan for colonies of ground squirrels. But this is the prairie dog days of summer. Months of hunting success gone dormant. Hot August sunshine dries the landscape. The chipmunk-like ground squirrels don't surface to the top, to the parched earth.

I lift again and fly back to the hungry owlet. I circle over the cedar. I think twice. I decide not to bring the young bird a ripping of carp. I leave the fish floating and bloated in the seep pond. I tilt clear of the stench and land again. On the upwind edge of the pond, I perch on an outcropping. My night eyes see well. My offset ears hear better. I picked up on distant drumming.

With quiet wings, I circle in rhythm with a deep, distant pulse of drums. Talon bells ring at each closing and opening of my claws. I barrel-roll low to the ground. The pounding grows deep and clear.

Aaiii––pum, pum/ Pum, pum, pum/ wanna pum.
Wanna pum/ wanna pum.
Aaiii––pum, pum/ Pum, pum, pum/ wanna pum.

I don't see him. I feather along the surface of water. The qualal, qualal of my bells are my dreamer's truth, kin to the lure of his rhythm. Close to the pulse, I circle the pond.

Do I fly to Sammy? He doesn't answer the call of my bells? He must hear what I think. To be worthy, he must drum up my attentions. Drum for me, Sammy. Drum for me right here, right where I'm circling.

I have no urge to fly to the source of the pounding. There will be no winging across the scablands to Big River. Come to me now, Sammy. I shake off my talon bells and watch them drop, splashing lightly into Mary's pond. They land near her blouse. A baseball jersey drapes over cattails.

My head swivels to the rear. Two big dirt bikes roar up a rough trail. Father and son shut off the engines and take off their helmets. I circle higher to better see the landscape. A dozen yards from where I am, the dirt bikers kneel and hide. They keep watch over the pond where Mary sleeps with her newborn. The new mother is spent from birthing. She doesn't hear the dirt-bikers' arrival. Gunnar Larsson and his father, Nils, are dressed in leathers. Strapped to the back of Nils's motorcycle is a hard-clasped, shiny silver case.

Nils turns and whispers to Gunnar. My ears are fine tuned. They barely hear, "If Mary's here, then where's your cousin? Where the hell is Joey?"

Gunnar shrugs. Both he and Nils start up the motorcycles. Gunnar rolls down to Mary. Nils takes their dirt trail to a hidden spot. It's just beyond the Bone Shrine at the pond. I land on the same outcropping they vacate.

"Congratulations on the baby, Mary," Gunnar says. He stirs her awake. The newborn is cradled beneath fleece. The blanket covers her. "So, where's Joey?" he asks. He commands an answer.

"He went to get gas," she tells him. Mary looks groggy. "We ran dry before he could get me to the maternity ward." She sits up and unfolds the top edge of the blanket to show off her newborn. "Isn't she gorgeous?"

Gunnar leans in for a closer look. "Definitely pretty, but doesn't look much like Joey's kid. Let me get you squared away here."

He opens a four-inch pocket knife. The sharpness of his blade shows when he cuts off a single, long leather fringe from his biker leggings. "No need for you to be dragging this bloody mess everywhere you go," he tells her.

He lifts his knife to the baby. She holds onto Grace's umbilical. Mary holds her daughter steady. She never acts like he might harm them. In one swift slice, Gunnar severs the flesh. The cord falls free. He leaves a few inches hanging from the infant. He scoots the bloody afterbirth to one side at the very rear of the Pathfinder. This triggers my raptor's instinct. It's something to share with the hungry fledgling. Not now, though, while I circle above, dream-flying.

Next to the baby's naval, Gunnar ties his fringe of leather tightly around the infant's cord close to the naval. "This helps the umbilical fall off the belly button quicker," he tells Mary.

"I just hope Joe comes back soon," she tells him. "Were you planning to meet him? Is that the real reason why we drove all the way up to Moses Lake?"

Gunnar doesn't answer.

Something stirred in the bed. Over my shoulder, I saw Sammy. He covered my legs and shoulder with the down comforter and lay underneath with me. "You're shuddering, Biff. Let's get you warm." Sammy edged close, spooning the nakedness of my skin with his warm, bare flesh.

"How did you find me?" I asked.

"You rang."

"With my talon bells?"

"No. You left me a message," he said.

"What message?"

"'Meet me,' you said. '444 Lakeside Drive. Basement door. Under the flower pot.'"

"Then, I'm not dreaming this?" I asked, still not believing he was really behind me in this borrowed bed. "I was just flying through the most lucid dream I've ever had. I was an owl ringing for you at the Bone Shrine pond."

I reached back and cooed when he pressed his arms, chest, thighs and hardness against me.

"They're trying to get me to quit my job for hurting Big Max."

"How so?"

"I couldn't take those phone calls from you because they had me working the day shift today. Day, swing and then graveyard shifts scrambled all through the same week. And all to mess with my sanity, just so I will quit."

"Do you have bigger dreams, Sammy?" I asked, without yet seeing his face in the dark room.

"To dance with you, Biff. *Qualal, qualal.* You're the bell waking up my drum."

I blushed, but stayed faced away, not wanting to unspoon myself from his body.

"I mean more like becoming an honest sheriff or something."

His strong hands gently turned me at the hips until the front of my body pressed into him. He positioned my head so my ears would hear the pounding inside his chest. Loud, ancient, and steady we flew within his sacred rhythm, my night bell signaling our skyward flight.

CHAPTER 17

ESCHER

I'd slept crazy-safe in Sammy's embrace and was fresh for the search when arriving at the Field Office just before dawn. This was definitely a uniform day and my bag was where I left it in the same cubby-hole of the ladies room. I wasn't too worried about my cargo pants or even the Oxford, button-up shirt. The shoes still fit perfectly, too, but the jacket was a bit wrinkled for my taste. *Elizabeth M./Special Ops Intern* reporting for duty.

Stepping into the big field office room exactly on time at 6:00 a.m., the boss stood up front talking to the troopers preparing for the search. He hid his emotions well, but I sensed a general anxiety from him as he and Schloss corralled the search team into the needed tasks.

"I'd like to thank Dr. Schloss for being so responsive with our case. His help has been immeasurable." Condran said and nodded graciously to him before telling our assembled search party that I would be helping Schloss collect any forensic evidence inside the home. "His regular forensic assistant had a family emergency this weekend."

I knew most everyone in the room, so I don't know why I felt the spotlight shining too brightly on my sleepy eyes. He added that Jack Pack, who was dressed in civilian blue jeans and jacket, would be handling the K-9 search dog. "The rest of you will take perimeter positions in the manner we outlined. We need to seal off the ends of the residential street leading in and out of Deputy Sheriff Riggleman's home."

Once all the troopers had stepped out of the field office, the captain warned Schloss and me not to step out of the forensic van until he had Deputy Riggleman in temporary detainment. I guessed that getting the deputy out of harm's way made the boss comfortable enough to allow me to participate in the search.

I climbed into the same forensic van we planned to use at the *Tramposo* estate during that failed search. Dr. Schloss took the wheel. "Please just do as any assistant would during a search," Schloss said and pointed behind us. "Carefully follow my directions, such as always having those evidence bags on you at all times. I'll tell you how I want them labeled when the time comes. And remember that both of us will be following the lead of Sheriff Sergeant Pack when he directs his dog through the home."

"Escher has the most incredible nose," I said.

"Indeed," said Schloss. "I was there at that Wanapum County Sheriff's office when the dog sniffed out the heroin where it hid all but completely sealed inside a camera case deep within the chief detective's locker. Unfortunately, we're now headed into a stale search scene from an eight-month-old crime. We must be exceedingly systematic in our search."

"We're going to find something! Escher will guide us there," I said, not sure if my optimism annoyed or pleased him.

The boss had both Jack Pack and Dr. Schloss park several houses away from the deputy's home while several Washington State Patrol vehicles blocked the ingress and egress behind and in front of us. The main driveway was filled with the deputy's own Chevy Silverado pickup, Linh's late model Acura Legend, and an older Chevy Impala. It wasn't quite dawn, but light enough to see to the front door. There was no way of knowing how Zach, an armed county deputy, might react upon opening the door. His wife, the busted kidnapper and smuggler, was still being held by the Feds as a flight risk without bail. Her trial would commence in a month. Zach Riggleman would be alone this morning.

Trooper Elaine Fonk had been called up by the boss from Pasco to assist the morning search. She took a position on one side of the front door. Captain Condran had his service pistol out and his back against the side opposite of Fonk where the door to the Riggleman house would open. There were troopers on all four sides of the one-story ranch-style home when Captain Condran rang the doorbell and followed it with a loud knock. After twenty seconds, he rang and knocked again, followed by, "Washington State Patrol. Open the door."

Just as the boss rang the bell a third time, the deputy answered the door dressed in civilian jeans and t-shirt. Only Condran was visible to Riggleman since Fonk was pressed up with her back against the outer wall of the house, beside the entry door hinges. She grasped her revolver in both hands with the barrel pointed down.

I rolled down the window to listen when the captain showed the deputy the search warrant with Judge Kantadillo's signature. "Okay," was all Zach said before turning back and speaking to someone inside. I couldn't hear what he said.

Riggleman heeded the captain by walking outside with hands clasped on his head--no cuffs, since he wasn't being arrested. Trooper Fonk pointed and he lowered himself into the back of her patrol car that was parked right in front of Schloss and me.

Meanwhile, Captain Condran, his service pistol in both hands of his extended arms, opened the door wide and told whomever was inside to step out slowly, with hands where he could see them.

Zach Riggleman, through the open rear door of the patrol car, looked towards his house. "Come out!" he yelled to the silhouette inside the open front door. "This isn't an arrest."

A petite South Asian gal, not much older than me, showed herself in the doorway. When she stepped out of the front door, I wondered if she had worked for his wife, Linh, at her nail salon. Captain Condran ushered her to the same squad car where Riggleman was seated. When the woman walked, her bulging, pregnant belly had me look twice. I rolled my window down all the way so I could focus more clearly on her.

"Simply wait in the back of the squad car while we finish conducting our duly authorized search, after which you'll be free to continue with your day," Condran told them.

"Captain, are you sure you want them both in the same car?" Trooper Fonk asked.

It was a good question since our planning for this search hadn't predicted a pregnant girlfriend in the mix.

"That's fine," the boss told her. "Just keep them both inside your patrol car so we can conduct our business unimpeded." It seemed like the boss was saying this more for Riggleman's benefit than for Fonk who frowned at the advice.

The young woman placed her hands on either side of her womb and grimaced when Fonk helped lower her head inside the backseat opposite Riggleman. I saw the sheriff deputy place an index finger over his lips so she wouldn't say anything. Trooper Fonk was still discussing the situation with the boss so neither of them noticed when Riggleman leaned over to kiss the woman's cheek.

"She's got to be at least seven months along," I told Dr. Schloss. "I'll bet Linh Riggleman––who we now know is the one in the married couple that couldn't get pregnant––found out about these two about four or five months ago. I'm thinking that's a big reason why she freaked out and tried to leave the U.S. with the kidnapped baby in tow."

"And why she tried smuggling all that gold with her to Vietnam, too?" he asked.

"Maybe she extorted the gold since she knew about the bribe by the Larssons to her father-in-law, and who knows what else about the perps of Bone Shrine crimes," I said.

"As in a hard demand to her husband that 'I'm taking the baby and all the gold, if you don't want me to blow your cover'."

I nodded rapidly. "It was China White, not Mexican Brown at the Bone Shine, as you know, so I'm guessing she's connected to the Asian smack."

"The captain also suspects as much," said Schloss.

Schloss scratched his chin. "How convinced are you that Linh Riggleman was the source of this high-end heroin?

"After the botched kidnapping, I said that I thought Mrs. Riggleman might be using her Lotus Nail Salon as a family front for moving Asian heroin. Maybe that's where the captain made this possible connection."

"We did bust Roger Riggleman, in part, for having the equipment to cut and repackage the China White that killed the kid in jail on the night before Joe Gardner was set free," said Schloss.

We watched Captain Condran tap on the window of Jack Pack's SUV parked in front of Trooper Fonk's car. When Pack rolled down his window, he motioned for him to bring his dog to the front door.

The captain came over to the forensic van. "China White heroin is on the list of items we'll search for this morning. I have a tiny sample vial for the search dog to smell."

"Excellent," said Schloss and listened to his next instructions.

Condran hurried back to the front door and stood next to Jack Pack. Schloss parked, as directed, on the side of the level front lawn opposite the deputy's main driveway by backing onto an empty gravel pad, the kind usually reserved for boats or travel trailers. One of the uniformed patrolmen directed the forensic van until it stopped close to the gate leading into the backyard. In my side mirror, I watched a large barking, fenced-in dog jumping high enough so its black head was visible, again and again and again.

When Schloss stepped out, he ignored Riggleman's dog and opened the back door of the van to retrieve a large, leather case that resembled the satchels doctors once took with them for home visits. "Like we talked about at the field office," Schloss said to Pack while we all stood on the front porch. "Ms. McCoy and I will follow you and your shepherd through the home in case the dog finds any olfactory prizes, so to speak."

"Escher has been antsy to work this week," said Pack.

"Let's start with the gold coins," Dr. Schloss said and put on his gloves, handing other pairs to Pack, me, and Captain Condran. We all pulled the latex over our fingers while Schloss unlatched his big, black satchel. He pulled out a tiny box with a single Krugerrand sealed in plastic inside. "This is from the batch that was confiscated in Nils Larsson's lockbox," he added when he handed the plastic packet to Pack. We all watched as he introduced the coin to Escher.

The dog sat as commanded, ears pointed upright, eyes not wavering from his handler, and muscles tensed. He was ready to "play." When Sergeant Pack released his shepherd to enter the front door, Schloss told me that he and I would wait in the inside entryway while the handler made sure the dog inspected every nook inside the Riggleman home.

A single-level, ranch-style rambler, it wasn't large, so room-by-room, Pack directed the dog, starting with the good-sized living room. Nothing. Sergeant Pack then opened each of the three bedroom doors. The dog sniffed thoroughly, but again, nothing.

In the dining room, Zach Riggleman's own dog spotted Escher and started barking and pounding his paws against a mud-soiled, sliding glass door leading into the backyard. The thick, black Chow lunged at the slider again and again, its mouth flinging saliva. Fangs were bared between barks.

Escher stopped searching and turned toward the Chow. Fur on end, as though the Shepherd was sporting a Mohawk, Escher faced down the other dog through the thick glass. Pack stomped hard on the linoleum floor and clapped for his K-9's attention. "Tschhh!"

Instantly, Escher ignored the other dog. He gave full attention to his handler. I shut the drapes over the sliding door windows which silenced the Chow, at least for the time being. Then I turned on the kitchen and dining room lights. Pack again directed his K-9 to continue working his nose.

Escher checked out the main bathroom, hallway closets, and then the kitchen. Nothing, nothing, and nothing. Inside the double garage, the K-9 hesitated by a bucket of assorted screws, bolts and washers, but smelled no signs of gold coins.

"We can save the attic and crawl spaces for a later round of searching, if necessary," Dr. Schloss said after Jack commanded Escher to heel again.

I couldn't envision stuffing that medium-sized dog through crawl spaces with who knew what kind of fiberglass insulation or rat droppings were hiding there.

Jack Pack rewarded his shepherd with a small jerky treat.

Captain Condran opened his buzzing flip phone and listened.

"There's nothing we can do about that, Officer Fonk. Just keep the deputy and the young woman away from the house. Same goes for Sheriff Usk when he arrives."

"Usk is coming *here?*" Pack asked when the captain put his cell-phone away.

"Sounds like it," said the boss. "The county sheriff just left me a phone message asking whether our search had commenced yet."

"Escher may not have picked up on any scent yet, but this smells like big trouble," Pack said.

"That's only if he brings along a battalion of deputies to storm the place," Condran said.

"He's too shrewd to step on the state patrol's toes like that, especially with all the media attention our election is bringing," Pack said. "Hard to tell what he's up to, but maybe you should call the Moses Lake Police to have a neutral police entity outside the house."

"No need to escalate this search into some cop department vs. cop department standoff," Condran said. "Let's work steadily to finish our work here before he arrives." Despite his firm directive, I could hear aggravation in the captain's tone.

From his satchel of sniffing items, Dr. Schloss produced a garment packed in its own plastic evidence bag. Pack removed the item––an XXXL t-shirt––from inside its labelled bag for Escher to sniff. Once again, the dog went room-to-room in the main house, but nothing matched the shirt's odor. I followed Pack, Escher and Schloss after the dog was done with the kitchen and adjoining laundry room. Despite having closed the window blinds, the Chow went bonkers again in the back yard.

We all continued to wear latex gloves when Pack opened the door for Escher to re-enter the garage. Unlike the driveway, the garage was vehicle-free, except for one of those banned, three-wheeler ATV's parked near the windowless, backyard door. Pack ordered Escher to halt when his K-9 took interest in the empty food bowl between the back door and ATV. The Chow growled outside its swinging doggie door. Captain Condran yelled at Riggleman's dog to get back, but the Chow pressed a snarling muzzled through the swinging plastic. Before the Chow's shoulders pressed through and into the garage, the boss managed to wedge a partial sheet of plywood over the opening. He secured the wood with cinderblocks to keep the doggie-door from swinging open.

A wide selection of garden, woodworking and power tools covered a stout workbench against one wall. With all the hobby items, I could see why Deputy Zach didn't park any of his vehicles inside the garage. Pack had the dog search clockwise while Schloss and I stayed in the open middle. Again, Escher seemed bored with each of the plastic buckets of screws and paid no heed to the Round-Up and potting soil, nor the car washing bucket and off-road toys.

"Since we're here, let's start with the next garment in the garage here," said Schloss and gave Pack a Pendleton wool shirt, also very big, which he pulled from its clear plastic bag for Escher to sniff. The dog ignored the rakes and shovels and lawnmower. He hobbled directly to the step leading back into the laundry room. He held his nose high in the air, but had trouble getting high enough to reach what was hanging from a stout wall-hook off to the side of the garage light switches.

"It's the full, black plastic trash bag hanging by a yellow draw-string," I said, pointing. The bag could be easily reached by anyone standing on the single step leading in and out of the laundry room.

"Yes. That's what Escher wants us to see," Pack said and told his dog to heel.

Dr. Schloss then told me to pull the large garbage bag off its hook. I brought the bag to where he stood on the open concrete floor.

"It's so light," I said. In order to peek inside, I widened the opening it with my latex-covered fingers. "Full of lots of smaller sacks from Safeway."

"For picking up all the dog poop," said Captain Condran still monitoring the doggie door being rammed by the Chow.

When his phone rang, the boss answered and rolled his eyes. "I understand, Elaine. Let Wanapum County Sheriff Usk know that Captain Condran of the Washington State Patrol will be out there shortly to see what he wants. Don't engage with him and, by no means allow him inside this house unless he welcomes full censure from Judge Kantadillo."

When the boss excused himself and left through the laundry room, I went over to the garage door. Standing my short frame on a portable work-step, I peered through a narrow, rectangular window. "There's two Wanapum Sheriff vehicles pulling up right in front of Riggle-man's driveway," I said to Schloss and Pack. "One's a Ford Explorer with a bold "K-9" and sheriff decal on the rear quarter panel. And that's definitely Sheriff Usk getting out of a different Wanapum squad car. Captain Condran is approaching him for, what looks like, a private discussion."

"Then let's assume that time is of the essence," Dr. Schloss said, firmly. "Biff––one at a time––use this tong to spread the contents of the trash bag on the plastic tarp I laid out for us." He handed me the tong after continuing to smooth the tarp over a couple square yards of concrete garage floor. Pack stood several feet away still holding the same oversized Pendleton shirt. Escher heeled by his side.

I squeezed tongs to give him one ultra-thin grocery bag at a time from inside the large thick black garbage bag. He took each one with his own tongs and spread them over the tarp so they didn't touch one another.

At the very bottom of the trash bag, I reached in for one last item. It was the same kind of black bag as the large one holding all the ultra-thin bags, except that this one was wadded up. Dry grit fell off the outside. Foss placed it more carefully than the others on the last open area of the tarp, the farthest spot away from Escher and Pack.

Schloss motioned for Pack to allow his dog to sniff the Pendleton––one more time––before releasing him to work.

Without hesitation, the dog hobbled directly to the last bag I'd pulled out. "Please call the dog back to you now," Schloss said.

Pack called Escher over to heel beside him and rewarded him with another small piece of jerky.

At Schloss's direction, I used my tongs to reach inside and turn this latest bag inside-out. More dried grit fell to the concrete floor. Stuck to the sealed seam at the bottom of the bag was a blue latex glove made for an extra-large hand.

Schloss nodded to Pack who let Escher smell the Pendleton one last time and stepped back. The dog was in no way being directed where to go or even what to do. The shepherd ignored me and directed his nose down to the latex glove next to me. Pack immediately called Escher back and rewarded him doubly with jerky.

Schloss was on his knees with a powerfully small flashlight and large magnifying glass to closely inspect the glove. The harsh garage light was no help, so I turned it off leaving the garage door windows to light the garage. The scientist looked back at Pack and up at me before speaking. "We won't disturb anything at this juncture, but I see traces of dried blood and jet black hair in the small slits and puncture where the glove has been ripped. He then closed the glove up inside the second black trash bag.

"What do you mean by 'ripped,' Dr. Schoss?" Pack asked. "As in clawed through by human fingernails?"

"Perhaps. We'll be looking for that very thing, trust me."

"Mary Quinn had a Goth look on the night she drowned," I said, trying not to sound as stunned as I was. "Black-dyed hair."

I didn't dare say more when Schloss paused to consider my words. I wondered if this was the same garbage bag that Joe shifted over inside the back of Deputy Riggleman's Sheriff Jeep to make room for his own bag of gritty tennis shoes. If so, then this Pendleton-to-glove match might well be the crime scene clue we desperately needed.

I couldn't dwell on a connection so speculative, though. Schloss needed to work his magic in the testing lab.

I looked over at Jack and Escher and thought that the candidate for Wanapum Sheriff, was about to have so much statewide, even national press, that Colton Usk wouldn't have a prayer on election day.

Why hadn't Zach destroyed the evidence? Maybe Linh was only directed by him to wash and dry the uniform, nothing more. Linh Riggleman––a nail salon owner who wasn't anyone's servant––might have been miffed at being treated like a laundry maid, not something to encourage the painstaking disposal of evidence.

I could see her stuffing the black bag that held the uniform into this similar garbage bag used to recycle all their other thin, grocery sacks. This bag blended into the bottom of the other. And, especially since her husband was an accomplice to the crime, would he have risked telling her that the uniform came from the site of a homicide? Once Zach returned a cleaned uniform to its big-sized owner, I guessed that the black bag from the pond was forgotten, assumed to have been discarded properly.

This morning I was struck by the cocky way that Deputy Riggleman had all but welcomed our search. The bag inside the bag of recycled bags was only still there by chance––first in, last out (a removal that hadn't yet happened, until now).

Schloss carefully placed the promising new evidence inside his satchel. "I wish we'd found more clues on the victim's body during her autopsy."

"But think of it this way, Dr. Schoss," I said. "Imagine Mary in the pond with a big man wearing those gloves and then subduing her against her will. No matter what was being said back-and-forth, her resistance would have been at its greatest when he started pressing her head into the water."

"Go on," Schloss said, looking intrigued.

Pack listened to me, too, when I leaned over and lifted my hands through my hair to the top of my head so my fingers caught on a bit of my own hair. "This is what probably happened when Mary reached up to claw at the big man's hands that were pushing her under. My best friend was no weakling." I refused to allow my roiling emotions get in the way of this little demonstration. "Her black sharp nails gouged through the latex leaving matching strands of her hair in the small rips through the glove. They lodged there when the stronger assailant drowned her."

"I was suggesting to Captain Condran how unfortunate it was that Mary Quinn floated in the pond water for hours following her drowning," said Schloss. "That may be why no corresponding particulates of flesh or blood were found under her fingernails during the autopsy."

"But even if the strands of hair in this bag here match Mary's hair, won't that be enough?" I asked Schloss.

"Perhaps," was all he said in response. "If there is sweat residue inside the glove matching that of the perpetrator, and if the grit matches what we have from the Bone Shrine pond, then the forensic connections grow exponentially stronger."

"The smell residue indicates a match," said Pack tapping a shoulder of his obedient shepherd. "What's next for Escher? How can the dog and I disappear from here––like right now." He pointed towards the garage door and what was unfolding on the driveway outside.

"I have a tiny sample of China White," said Schloss just as Captain Condran burst through the laundry door looking animated.

"Sorry Dr. Schloss, but our planned heroin and gold coin searches in the house here will likely need to wait. But, Sergeant Pack, didn't you tell me that the Sheriff had decommissioned Escher as a County Sheriff search dog?" Condran asked Pack.

"That's what Usk said he was going to do when he put me on administrative leave."

"I just told the Sheriff that under no circumstances was he or any of his other deputies permitted to step inside this house during this duly authorized search."

"What did he say to that?" asked Pack.

"He said that, not only is this the second time in a week-and-a-half that his K-9 sheriff has participated in an unauthorized search. He also insisted that the dog was the property of the Wanapum County Sheriff Department, and definitely not of the handler." The captain took a quick glance at how well his plywood barricade was holding up against the pawing of the indignant Chow lurking outside. "I couldn't argue the logic of his point, except that I'm seeing a gray area here. Escher was allowed to be on administrative leave along with you, his handler. This is the first time Sheriff Usk has asked for you to turn Escher back to his department."

Dr. Schloss was busy securing the gritty bag and its latex glove inside his evidence satchel. "Captain, it's likely we just found some pertinent evidence," he said.

"So, you agreed to give away my dog?" Pack asked Condran in a low voice, looking alarmed and pissed, and before the captain could respond to Schloss.

"No. I'm just buying time to set our trap for him," Condran said rather urgently. "Bear with me on this, Jack. I have an escape plan," Condran then insisted that Pack give the keys of his personal X-Terra to me so I'd drive it back to the WSP field office. Pack looked confused, but complied.

"It's a shame we won't have time to search for any drugs or coins hidden here," said Dr. Schloss when he'd finished gathering up the evidence we'd found.

"I agree," said Condran, his voice tense. "Right now we need to bust butt, so to speak. I asked one of my troopers to stand next to the gate by rear of the forensic van so you can get the K-9 inside without being sidelined by the Wanapum Sheriff Department. Schloss and Pack will take the van. Biff takes the X-Terra and Trooper Fairhaven will follow both vehicles back to the field office. Right now, I need all three of you and Escher to wait inside the kitchen until you can leave through the sliding glass door and through the backyard."

"With that crazy Chow guarding his yard?" I asked.

"No. That dog won't be there," the boss said firmly. "Do not exit the house until after I tell you the coast is clear." Condran opened the door into the adjoining laundry room. "Keep the door open just a bit so you can hear my order to flee the house. Once I yell 'go!' Then you all move fast with Escher through the dining room and into the backyard. Then you need to take your direction from Trooper Fairhaven at the gate beside the house. Once you're in the van and X-Terra, then I'll instruct the trooper to escort all of you to safety. His patrol car will follow your two vehicles back to the field office."

Before I followed Jack and the Shepherd into the house, I worked quickly to help Schloss place all the ultra-thin bags back in the big, clean black bag that had held them. Captain Condran had opened a can of wet dog food into the Chow's bowl and placed the stinky mess onto the concrete right next to the inside of the main garage door. He then motioned for me to go into the house through the laundry room. From there, I watched through the open door crack when he tapped the empty dog food can. The Chow burst through the big doggie door.

Condran waited until the Chow got to his food before pressing the garage door opener next to the laundry room entrance. He pressed it until the garage door lifted two feet off the ground. I let the captain into the house and watched the Chow, after one bite of food, squeeze under the garage door and onto the outside driveway.

"Time to bolt," Condran told us, pointing to the backyard. Schloss was at the dining room slider and fully prepared to open it and flee. I followed Sergeant Pack and Escher out the door.

I glanced back to see the captain stepping back into the garage. "Here's the dog!" he yelled toward the driveway.

In the backyard, we stepped careful to avoid the many Chow droppings. On the side of Zach Riggleman's house that was opposite the garage, Trooper Fairhaven held the side gate open. Schloss opened the backdoor of the van. Pack ushered Escher inside and closed the same door.

Pack got in the front passenger seat as Schloss turned over the engine, but he waited to put it into gear. The Chow seemed to be occupying the attention of the County Sheriff and his deputies.

Trooper Fairhaven escorted me across the street. We could hear and see Condran in a heated discussion on the driveway with Sergeant Usk. Deputy Riggleman was beside Trooper Fonk and squatting behind the sheriff to calm his Chow.

"I wanted the Sheriff search dog!" Usk yelled at Condran.

"I misunderstood," said the captain. "You asked for the officer's dog." he added, and pointed at the Chow.

The last thing I heard when I was climbing into Sergeant Pack's vehicle was Zach Riggleman telling Condran that he was sure the search of his home "found nothing!"

I released the clutch of the X-Terra and drove forward once the forensic van and Fairhaven's state patrol car were ready to roll behind me.

As for Escher being returned to the Wanapum County Sheriff Department, I surely hoped the election of Jack Pack would make it all moot.

~

CHAPTER 18

TWO BULLETS

"Mornin' Sammy," I answered on my flip phone, opening sleepy, Monday morning eyes and no doubt sounding more tired than I'd have liked, except that well into the night I'd been working on a solid second draft of my criminal justice paper. Hadn't dared to tell my boss that I was staying at the Larssons' home again, and as far as I could tell, Jack hadn't let anyone else know that I wasn't staying with him and Mrs. Pack. "How was your graveyard shift?"

"No jail breaks. Pretty low-down boring," he said. "With this all-over-the-map work schedule, I could really use some shut-eye." His voice was definitely groggy.

"I'm done drafting my paper," I told him. I'd had all of Sunday, the 23rd of April, to myself. "Later today I'm going to proofread once more before feeding it to my professor."

"Make it delicious, girl!" he said.

"You're off a bit early, aren't you?" I asked, looking at my radio-alarm clock–– 8:11 am.

I could hear him yawn. "I'm supposed to stick around on Monday mornings so that I can go to our meeting for the jail-guards, except it was cancelled today."

"Called off?" I asked.

"Postponed. The jail boss couldn't make it. Word has it that he and his wife are going down to the hospital in Pasco. Their big bad boy, Max, is being discharged."

"This morning? Really?" I asked, my eyes growing wider.

"I wouldn't mess with that kind of news."

My brain shifted into overdrive.

Maybe Dr. Schloss had worked on Sunday and found a match for the bloody, latex glove. I was definitely being sidelined––I could feel it. "I really need to be in Pasco, just in case," I said.

"In case of what, Baby?"

"In case Mary's case is finally solved."

"You still think Max did it?"

"That's my hunch, but if the boss respected all I've done for this case, then he'd be sharing the latest discoveries with me, wouldn't he?" I spoke more quickly. "When I spoke with him yesterday afternoon, he didn't bring me up-to-date on anything. Simply told me to focus on my course paper."

I took a deep breath. It was time to get rolling if the avenging of Mary was to be witnessed by me. So what if the completion of my midterm paper would be delayed yet again?

"I'm going to head over to the field office, see if anything's going down. You get some sleep, sweet man," I told Sammy.

"I will. How about we get an early dinner before my shift tonight? The Porterhouse. My treat," Sammy said.

"Sounds delicious," I said, since I'd be back by mid-afternoon. "I'll call you when I get back in town," I managed to say before stepping into the bathroom.

My tired eyes stared back at me in the mirror. The rings said it all. This case was taking its toll. I took a quick shower, then full-tilt, I dried off and gathered my wet hair into a short ponytail.

My *She Who Watches* medallion, the last thing I noticed and recovered from the fire pile at Rochelle's, rested nicely over my whitest, laciest blouse. I pulled up my well-worn Levis and tightened the high laces of my cherry-red Doc Marten grunge boots. Before leaving, I filled my Loyale with fuel, and headed over to the Moses Lake Field Office.

The place was a mausoleum with only the office manager out

front. She wouldn't tell me what was happening this morning. I tried to call the boss, but he wouldn't pick up his phone.

Screw this place. I stormed out and lowered my beet-red face into my mint-green car and made my way on I-90 through Moses Lake to State Highway 395. Pedal to the actual worn metal of my floorboard, I rolled quickly southbound towards the Tri-Cities.

I hadn't gotten far when, irony of sick ironies, a State Bull turned on his lights and pulled me over. Did the captain arrange this intercept just to keep me away from the big arrest in Pasco?

My mind stewed.

Smile Biff, I told myself, remembering to be charming when the trooper approached the car. I rolled down my window and clenched both fists on the steering wheel.

"Hello, officer," I said, a bit quietly and remembering to loosen my grip.

"Are we in a hurry to get to the big arrest, Biff?" the man said from beneath his broad-rim hat that looked like the ones worn by the Royal Canadian Mounted Police.

Totally surprised to hear my name, I looked up to see Trooper Fairhaven, the same patrolman who'd escorted me to Jack Pack's X-Terra two mornings before so we could get Escher and our evidence safely away from Zach Riggleman's home.

"How did you know it was me?" I asked.

"This old Subaru isn't the snazziest car we have parked at the field office most afternoons, but the bright green paint job is pretty distinctive," he told me. "I do need you to slow down, though," he added.

"Yes, officer. Oh, and thank you for helping on Saturday, especially after Sheriff Usk showed up."

"My pleasure. I'm pleased that Captain Condran has what he needs for today," he said and closed his citation book. "On that note, good luck. Eleven a.m. for the actual hospital discharge and arrest, isn't it?"

"That's what I have, too," I said, nodding with a grateful grin. My car clock, one of the accessories that still worked, said 10:10 am. I took a deep breath. "And, yes. That's the only reason I was in too big of a hurry," I decided to confess.

"Please drive slower."

"I definitely will," I promised. Trooper Fairhaven tipped his hat to me and I eased into the sparse highway traffic.

Pasco couldn't arrive soon enough, especially since I was only going the speed limit and had no idea if I'd be there in time to witness Big Max being rolled out of the hospital, his fat wrists cuffed to a wheelchair.

I recognized the grain silo next to the railroad tracks and looked across Hwy 395 to the spot where Sammy had arranged to be pulled over while towing Max's boat. I wondered if Mary's missing flower braid––the *Poet's Shooting Star* found dangling in the *ThunderMaxx's* wheelhouse––was serving as helpful evidence.

I recalled the trial when Angus MacIntosh made a compelling closing argument that there was not nearly enough time that night for Joe to have 1) drowned Mary, 2) stuffed her Chunichi Dragon souvenir pin in the skull of an owl, 3) pushed Gracie into the reeds on an air mattress, and then 4) puked and 5) puked some more cold turkey during his 6) agonizing five mile walk to the closest minimart so he could 7) hitch a 28-mile ride to Rattlesnake Ridge where 8) he had time to hang up the last of the wildflower braids, the only one Mary had kept for herself, before 9) returning another 28 miles to the Mini-mart to 10) fill up the empty gas can and 11) bum a ride back to the Bone Shrine with Zach Riggleman.

Gosh, maybe Joe Gardner––freed on some obscure ruling called 'arrested judgment'––also *hadn't* actually murdered Mary Quinn.

With a badly broken clavicle, Max would be too wimpy to withstand having his arms zip-tied behind his back, but I found myself wishing I could cinch them up unbearably tight.

This whole investigation seemed like it had finally turned. That gashed glove was like finding a black rose on the darkest of nights where all rose bushes had far more year-round thorns than seasonal petals. Why wouldn't Condran let me in on what the lab work revealed?

My brain kicked into hyper-mode. The only thing the confiscated Krugerrands actually showed––with Darla's prints––was that the Larsson family had been involved in exchanging money with the Bone Shrine criminals. Not a strong enough clue to place any of them at the Bone Shrine or, what would have been even better yet for our case, in the pond where Mary was drowned. Too bad the Larssons' Kruger-rands didn't come with timestamps every time a coin was exchanged.

More than the braided Shooting Stars, those samples of clothes hanging in the cabin of Max's aluminum yacht were probably proving to be the best evidence taken from the *ThunderMaxx*. And it was all because Sammy arranged to have himself pulled over.

With Colton Usk controlling the Wanapum Sheriff Department, who knew when or if we'd have been allowed to find samples of clothes from his employees there? Maybe those boat clothes––and Escher's nose during the search––helped Dr. Schloss fast-track the lab work this weekend. Maybe the forensic evidence justified this morning's arrest of Max. I could only hope, even though I was no longer trusted to hear the key discoveries.

Still rolling along at the speed limit, I glanced up at a pair of Red Tail hawks hunting high above the natural grasslands alongside large crop circles. My brief look into the sky forced me to hit my brakes hard. I nearly crashed into a big pickup that decided to stop in front of me. A few cars in front of the truck also stood still while a farm combine, a lane-and-a-half wide, had merged onto the highway. Sitting there, I slapped my steering wheel which hardly helped my frustration. Seemed like forever before the stopped vehicles could creep around the oversized farm implement. My car clock read 10:27 am.

Ten minutes later––it seemed like thirty––had passed before Hwy 395 joined I-182 . I entered the outskirts of Pasco and soon exited into the modest downtown and did my best to find Lourdes Medical Center.

By sheer driving luck, I noticed quite a few Washington State Patrol vehicles assembled on a side street parking lot behind the hospital. I slowed to nearly a stop. There, between a couple of fully copped-out patrol cars, I spotted the boss's unmarked Crown Vic.

With his broken shoulder bones, what made these troopers think that Big Max would be so dangerous to arrest? Seemed pretty simple to me. At discharge time, get the killer into a wheelchair, cuff his wrists to the wheelchair arms, read him his rights, and roll him off to jail–– pure solitary confinement––until his trial.

Gosh, there was no way I would ever dream of intruding on the captain's big day, the one that wouldn't have happened without my hard work. My jaws clenched. The bum was using my supposed safety to take full, freaking credit.

I took a deep breath and drove around to the front of the hospital to park. When I saw a Washington State Patrol van parked in front of an ambulance by the main hospital entrance with its lift already all the way down for scooters and wheelchairs, I knew this would be the paddy wagon to haul Max away.

I felt a tinge of actual good luck when I located a 30-minute parking spot with a direct view of the front entry. I backed in, doubting I'd need to be here any longer than a half-hour. Since I was blatantly not invited to be a part of the arrest team, I figured that Captain Condran would be tempted to cuff me, too––especially if I barged my way up to Max's hospital room. Was stealing the boss's thunder a felony?

I decided to accept my lone reward. My obsession would be vindicated if I could see with my own eyes, the moment when Max was rolled out of Lourdes Medical Center and into the W.S.P. van to be whisked off to the Franklin County Jail, most likely, the same place where Darla was being held. The Washington State Patrol sure as hell wasn't going to take him up to the Wanapum County Jail where his upstanding co-workers would be sure to mollycoddle their favorite murderer.

The moment I reminded myself not to stew, I did a double-take.

Condran, on foot, rounded the side corner of the hospital wearing all-black, bullet-proof gear with a big white WSP patch sewn on the back. He didn't notice my presence, even though my distinctive, mint-green Loyale, while wedged beside another small sedan, was hardly camouflaged. I was sitting in plain sight a street width away, but wasn't about to greet him with a light honk. The boss hightailed with laser -focus towards the main entrance. My ever-strange luck this morning told me I'd arrived just in time. My car clock read 10:57 am.

Right after Captain Condran disappeared inside the hospital, a big, black Lincoln SUV arrived. The brand new *Navigator* pulled into a loading space adjoining the hospital building––one reserved for picking-up or admitting patients. The huge SUV was shiny, just like the luxury vehicle I'd seen parked beside a red Shelby Mustang outside the Wanapum sheriff's office when I was in Smohalla last week. My chest pounded out scared beats when Max's dad got out, his head held haughty and high. From the back seat, he found a stylish, Stetson cowboy hat that made his elbow of a chin look like Brutus's in the Popeye cartoons.

Al Weaver was very large, like Max. I recognized him mostly from watching the jail video that Captain Condran had acquired when the state patrol investigated the Wanapum Sheriff Department after Joe's trial revealed so many county improprieties. On the tape, Max's father appeared right after the two *Tramposos,* including the one who abducted me, had failed to beat Joe senseless.

Al Weaver leaned against the driver's door and waited for his wife to step out of the passenger side. The Lincoln had a natural tan leather interior and matching steering wheel cover. Not only did this car look as expensive as SUV's got, but the couple was stylishly well-dressed, too. To go with his Stetson, Max's dad wore Lucchese crocodile cowboy boots, fitted jeans and a chambray, long-sleeved Western shirt with too many pearl, snap-on buttons.

His tall, dolled-up wife––also about fifty––stepped back to open the back door on the passenger side opposite me. She moved a cardboard box from the rear seat to the very back of the Navigator, probably for herself since they no doubt expected their huge son to be riding home with them in the more-spacious, front passenger seat. I figured out where I'd seen her before. I remembered how I'd carefully examined Max's family photo where it hung inside their cabin cruiser.

She stopped and looked directly at me, twenty yards away. For some reason, I couldn't disengage my eyes from hers, and she didn't let her gaze stray from me. It was then that I recalled one other time. She'd been seated in the courtroom gallery next to her husband and Sheriff Usk on the day that Joe was granted his freedom. She'd remained in the gallery while we all congratulated Joe. That was when Max had invited everyone to be sure and go to Joe's opening day game with the Tri-City Dust Devils. This was a couple months before Joe had made the minor league roster.

I remembered her mostly because I'd had that stupid crush on Big Max. This woman's face looked uncannily like her son's. The two of them shared the same shaped eyes, nice roundish nose, and a cheek dimple that didn't disappear. I could see Max's good looks in his mother's face, including how neither of them looked the least bit content with life.

I expected she'd heard that a short, young, blonde state patrol intern was at the center of her son being so badly injured at the ballpark. Max's mom definitely had the look of someone putting it all together. I knew the instant she figured out exactly who I was––and I wasn't an ally of her family.

"Time to go get our boy, Maxxine," Al Weaver told his wife, loudly enough to be heard by me across the parking lot. My discomfort eased when she finally looked away from me and closed the back passenger door of the SUV. Then, after placing her hand in the crook of her husband's elbow, they followed the sidewalk under the drive-through awning in front of the hospital entrance.

It didn't take much more than an actual minute, not for the arrest of Big Max, but for both of his parents to come scurrying back out the main entrance door. Their eyes were wide when the cowboy-booted husband pulled his stumbling, high-heeled wife too quickly to their Lincoln. She nearly face-planted. The couple looked totally spooked. "Get in, Maxine!" the man yelled as soon as he clicked his car's remote to unlock both front doors. She jumped inside the mobster-black Lincoln looking worse than discontented. Her wide eyes were totally mortified.

Their Navigator backed out with a rubber-burning screech. The SUV was only a dozen yards away from me and slowed when the man's window lowered. The wife sat higher than where my driver's seat was in the Loyale. She reached across her husband, tapped his arm, and pointed.

Only a half-dozen yards away, he turned and aimed his handgun at me.

I tried to tilt away, but my shoulder belt held me upright.

A single bullet shattered my windshield.

I also heard the crack of a lone rifle shot behind me.

Max's dad dropped his gun onto the pavement when his head jolted backwards.

The terror in his eyes must have mimicked my own. All so fast, so fast.

He suffered one bullet-hole where his third-eye would have been.

I clutched my side and pressed. Ribs and lung pounded.

Chaos all at once. My favorite white blouse soaked up the blood. The circle of bright red widened.

My eyes grew wide, too. The shock was surreal. This hadn't really happened to me.

Max's mom screamed hysterically.

Numb, I slumped against my driver's door.

Through the spider web of a hole in my windshield, I saw the husband tilt back onto her lap. Their Navigator roared forward and crashed into a parked hospital ambulance. The boxy vehicle was sandwiched when the Lincoln pushed it into the rear corner of the Washington State Patrol paddy wagon.

Captain Condran saw me, hurried from inside the hospital, and ran towards my car. His jaw dropped the moment the Lincoln had crashed.

Even though the wheelchair lift was lowered, the state patrol van crashed into the brick wall of the stately hospital.

The boss looked back while rushing towards my Loyale. The Lincoln's radiator hissed like the red-spackled air spewing from every breath I exhaled.

"Medics!" Condran yelled. His voice stayed loud but quavering. "Bullet wound! I need a paramedic over here!"

I could barely breathe. *She-Who-Watches* glinted in the daylight. Why couldn't the bullet have hit me right in the medallion?

Except that shrapnel would have exploded like a grenade all through my heart. Mary loved me too much for that.

Mary. Please. My mind faded in and out.

Maxine jumped out of the Navigator, her make-up all blood-splattered. She screamed for help.

Blood dripped off my own fingers pressed tightly against the open hole in my chest. The buttons of my blouse turned pink from the flow of more red. All so fast.

A black-vested S.W.A.T. officer ran up to the shiny Lincoln. He cradled his rifle with care, the way a sniper would. Another S.W.A.T. cop came up to check for the shot man's pulse. He gave way to an arriving medic. A trooper hopped unhurt from the crunched WSP van and straddled the warm pistol of Max's father so that no one would touch what was now the evidence of my undoing.

I breathed. More blood gurgled from my single bullet hole.

Too woozy.

I barely heard the boss yelling again and again for a medic. Somehow, I pushed the button to release my shoulder belt.

Captain Condran had stepped in. Pulling the door handle, my car door opened. The parking spot on this side was empty.

We fell to the pavement.

He caught me as I landed.

His hand covered my hand until blood covered us both. He kissed the top of my head. His chest heaved.

"Don't leave me, Elizabeth! Please stay awake."

I tried to nod.

"I pressed to shut the elevator door," he told me in a whisper.

"Then, just before it closed, I saw them. Over and over I hit the open button. Too late."

I grew weaker, but heard him tell me that the jail boss knew why all the cops were there. He'd yanked on his wife to turn and run. "I pushed and pushed the open button, but the elevator stayed closed forever. "

He was Mary's killer, I tried to tell him. I'd just seen all the murder in his eyes. Blood garbled my voice.

The boss cried, but pointed towards the jail boss laid out beside the Lincoln and tried to update me with a ragged list of too disjointed details. "He's dead on arrival, but his Pendleton, grit from the same pond, Mary's goth-black strands. The elevator wouldn't open. I'm sorry. I could have *prevented*--"

A medic and trooper shifted me from the boss's lap onto a blanket.

"Stay awake, Elizabeth. Don't drift off," the boss leaned over me and whispered. "Not you, too."

"I'm about to give her fluid resuscitation on site, but she needs the Operating Room, stat!" I heard the paramedic radioing someone inside the hospital. "Acute bleeding. Yes! The O.R. That's what I said!

My eyes closed. Random thoughts fogged my brain.

I saw the lone sniper's bullet etched with the killer's initials.

My initials were scratched on the single bullet fired into me.

"Who can *prevent* karma?" I wanted to ask the boss.

Wherever I was, the killer drifted towards me. Our eyes locked, but he had no hate for me in his stone-cold irises. His long, thick arms and legs spread wide. His eyes widened, too. He wasn't expecting to be leaving––too soon, too suddenly––to the other side.

I felt too weak to loathe anyone, but, unlike him, I refused to let myself lift away for good.

~

When I woke up, my groggy eyes focused on the calendar. Mom and Dad were at the side of my bed. My father confirmed that it was Tuesday morning, April 24th. I hadn't managed to drop off my paper.

A sharp pang punched through my rib. I winced and recoiled. I was alive, not bullet-proof, but the pain proved this wasn't a dream. I couldn't speak. A large tube coiled down my throat. In the I.C.U, a half-dozen bouquets of flowers brighten my room.

"You're one lucky girl," Mom told me. "If that bullet had hit an inch higher, then it would have severed the main artery in your shoulder." Mom's eyes watered, a rarity for her. "We'd be visiting your graveside, not your bedside."

She slipped the surgeon's Operation Note on my hospital night-stand after reading a line from it first. "*300 cc blood in right thorax. Right Upper Lobectomy/Gunshot Wound with active bleeding and significant tissue damage.* You can read all the gory, clinical details of your brush with death when you're more alert, sweetheart."

"Imagine that," said my father, leaning in to touch my ventilator. "I didn't expect to see the day when my wonderful Biff was unable to speak."

I wanted to tell him how incredibly funny he *wasn't* since I so wanted off of this annoying breathing apparatus. Everything in my throat and chest ached, throbbed and rattled. I wanted to be a healthy kid again and breathing easy.

"Your bed in The Dalles has fresh sheets and is waiting for you," Mom told me and pointed to a pen and small writing pad on the nightstand.

'There's a young man in the waiting room," my father told me. "He slept out there all night."

I couldn't smile physically, but gave my dad a thumbs-up.

"He was very polite to us," said Mom, squeezing my thigh at the knee. "Your new boyfriend is handsome, too."

I tried my best to write something down, but had to use my awkward left hand. My regular right one was immobilized, strapped over that side of my chest.

"That's where they cut you open to repair your lung," said my father when he saw me unable to take my eye away from the stitches that showed at the edges of my hospital gown.

I tried to write again, but couldn't keep the pad steadied until Mom held it in place. My letters looked stupid, like I was in first grade all over again with one of those fat black pencils. I kept at it, but the brain-fog didn't help.

Mom leaned close to decipher my sloppy, block letters:

I am intern. Still.

"We can talk about that later," she told me in a tone that said she'd do everything in her power for it not to happen.

"An article went out through the Associated Press about how the suspected killer of Mary Quinn was killed," said Dad. "Captain Condran is quoted as saying, 'My Washington State Patrol intern, Elizabeth 'Biff' McCoy, is in serious condition from a gunshot wound, but is on the path to a full recovery. These last months she's been invaluable in helping us finding Mary Quinn's alleged killers.' Dad set that section of newspaper on top of the Operation Notes for me to also read later.

I wrote on my pad again:

K needs intern.

I thought Condran was spelled with a 'C.'

Judge K.

This time the 'K' was real big and sloppy.

"He offered you the opportunity?" Mom asked, looking relieved. "I remember how he presided over Joe's trial. And you definitely need bullet-free work."

I managed one more note, tore the page free, handed it to my father, and pointed towards where I thought the waiting room might be. *PLZz__I will C_______SAM meeee*

"What?" my father asked my mother.

"Let's go get her new boyfriend," said Mom. "You and I can grab something to eat while the two of them visit."

My father followed Mom out of the room, but turned back to wink at me. I was fading fast from too many morphine drips.

I dozed off, seeing Sammy pounding a drum. I dreamed I pressed the buzzer by my bed so he would come to me.

I woke to the proud face of an ancient, but young native. He stood above me looking strong, fierce even, a warrior to protect me. Sammy then sat, pressing against my leg and patting my thigh before squeezing at the knee in a way that told me--without words--how very glad he was that I'd survived. His earnest olive-green eyes never left mine.

With Sammy here, I tried my best to dance free from this nap-trap of morphine.

He clutched a clear, heavy vase holding a bouquet of the most beautiful roses--white ones with red tips that smelled divine. I closed my eyes and lingered with the scent before pointing him to where he could set the vase on the bigger table near my feet so I could enjoy his flowers more than the others.

I wanted off my ventilator. Practiced being off the thing, but the breathing tube was still jammed clear down my throat. So tired. I could only handle the limit. One hour visits. Then I had to--couldn't help but sleep. So rude, but too tired for them. Only 48-hours since being shot. Seemed like forever ago, then only an eye-blink away. Both were true.

Thank Mary," I wrote for Sammy.

"Why Mary?" he asked and took his hand off my knee.

She won't let me die.

"And all in spite of me," Sammy said, like something was weighing on him. "I called Captain Condran on Sunday during my break at jail when I heard that Big Max was being released from the hospital on Monday. I told your boss that Max's parents would be going to Pasco to pick him up, so I may have helped a bit," said Sammy.

Thx! For being here, 2 ...

"You've been in a spirit war," Sammy leaned in and spoke quietly. "Max, his boss-dog dad and that high-maintenance mom of his, have got some devil *skookum* heating up their veins, but they met their match going up against you and the angry ghost of Mary. Your Mary spared you from a different path of that bullet."

Yes. Mary is my sister. All ways.

For years afterwards, I would see that glare in the jail boss's eyes. He was seriously out to kill me for snuffing out his power as a drug king. We were at war and Mary was my spirit strength. Max's old man knew I was the one ending his long run through the Wanapum dark side.

Universe unfolds. I wrote for Sammy.

"How so?"

U pound Max. U pound drum. U Pound me 2 U.

"Bells and drumming," Sammy told me, sounding neither happy nor sad and looking fierce again as he scanned my hospital room.

I.C.U. and me.

He took my pencil and wrote clean letters.

I.C.U.2.

Sammy locked eyes with me. "We keep dancing," he said.

I couldn't bring myself to share with Sammy that I'd been guided by a blind owl to find Mary's killer. Those amber eyes, without sight, relied on sounds of truth. Sammy's rhythm with me was so true. Sammy and I would keep flying, silent and sure.

Sammy leaned in and kissed my cheek just as another rush of morphine coursed through my veins. "I wish I could hear your voice," he said.

U hear me.

"Big Max is in the Franklin County Jail," he said. "Deputy Riggleman is being held in the Chelan slammer. I guess they're looking for Sheriff Usk, too, but he disappeared."

R.U. safe at your jail?

He nodded. "Al Weaver's dead," said Sammy. "Max won't ever be allowed back. And assuming Jack Pack gets elected in a couple of weeks, then the Wanapum County Sheriff Department will be scrubbed of musky Usk and those scuzzy Rigglemen."

Sammy had helped me, but maybe I was doing a small part to help him restore the good names of *Smohalla,* the seer, and *Wanapum,* the tribe.

Sammy told me he'd taken some days off and slept in Joe Gardner's studio apartment. Joseph had visited his mom last night. Later today, Joe would be heading out on the road to play the Eugene Emeralds for his next few games. Tomiko was taking a separate Greyhound there to scout Joe for the Chunichi Dragons––and for life, too, it seemed.

My floor nurse popped in to tell us that there was someone else who'd been waiting outside my room. "You're not ready for the removal of your ET tube yet," she said with her hand covering my untethered wrist. "You've come down with a mild case of pneumonia. This will need to improve first. We'll be taking it one day at a time." Her prognosis washed over me. When I thought of locking eyes with Al Weaver and how close I'd been to joining him on the other side, I couldn't bring myself to worry about a slight case of pneumonia, or the tracheal plumbing descending through my throat. I was too tired to flip out.

Even Sammy could see I needed to sleep some more. He didn't protest being told by the nurse that in a couple of minutes he'd need to leave. I must have looked pretty messed up to be kissing, but this boy sure made me happy. Just him showing up spoke plenty, especially when he leaned in and kissed me on the lips. Then, very smoothly, he slipped outside just before the nurse returned.

I didn't have a moment for romantic reverie before Captain Condran came into my hospital room. On reflex, I gave him a left-handed, middle-fingered salute.

"Wow," he said. "My intractable intern. Most bosses would be firing you on the spot for your friendly wave."

I pointed to the bullet hole in my chest and then fired an imaginary gun. I took up pencil and pad:

Why no invite 2 arrest of Max?

"With your mom pitching me threats, how many times did I go to bat just to keep you on as my intern? Wasn't safe, Biff. I had a strong inkling that Al Weaver was *El Gringo Loco.*"

And I was a target. Why no kevlar?

The captain was having none of my blame game. "Don't we all

make ourselves targets in one way or another. Besides, you've already been fired from the investigation."

??? Why? So U get all the credit?

He read my words and burst out laughing. "Hardly." He pulled out the newspaper under his arm and tapped the article where he told me how he'd praised my work on the case.

"Oh, and Judge Kantadillo told me to let you know. Your internship with him will start once you're healed up."

!!!!!!!

I forced my weary face to smile. That was awesome news! I shut my eyes when the floor nurse hung a new bag of liquid painkiller. For the first time since my operation, I knew I was on track to survive. Then there was Sammy's visit which made me feel so loved, that is until the pangs of pain hit.

I needed more winged truth from Mary and pressed the button for more drips, more Morpheus, more enlightening from the God of Dreams.

"*El Loco Gringo* sure reared his ugly head," the captain added once he saw me wince and then relax. "Thanks to our sniper, he suffered his instant justice. I don't know why we didn't focus more on the head of Wanapum County Corrections considering how much contraband has been flowing through Al Weaver's jail."

My left-handed letters grew light and sloppy.

My term paper?

"Done. Your criminal justice professor called me this morning. Said to tell you to get out of the hospital and then come see her. Wished you a speedy recovery. In the world of criminal justice, you're big news around here."

I smiled.

Condran dangled my *She-Who-Watches* medallion from his fingers. "With all the close-call chaos, I almost forgot that the paramedic handed me this," he said.

My finger pointed for him to set it on top of the newspaper article. I jotted down my most important question.

Did Darla spill beans?

Captain Condran looked to see if any nurses or orderlies were listening before scooting his chair closer. He leaned in so I could hear his low voice. "She sure did. Darla was brief and to the point. Her lawyer was by her side." The boss told me how Darla claimed her son had told her the details of everything that happened that night. He cleared his throat. "I've been doing these pleas for many years. She was telling me the truth. I'm virtually certain."

~

CHAPTER 19

LUCIDITY

I couldn't tell when Condran stopped talking, or if the words he spoke in my hospital room were breaking through my stupor and giving life to this lucid dream. With every bit of focus that my eyes and brain permitted, I tried, but failed to stay awake for the boss. Behind closed lids, morphine swept me away, swooped me close to the seep pond.

Vividly, I watch the night in question unfold.

The big black car skids to a stop. I fly over the Pathfinder to find the outcropping. I watch. I see the whole tragedy unfold.

Big Max jumps out, in XXXL, cop-like uniform. The black SUV fishtails forward to the Bone Shrine.

Mary is not alarmed. She shows off new Grace to Gunnar and Max.

Max stays with Mary. Gunnar dirt bikes to the Bone Shrine.

I fly to the cedar and watch. The fledgling has flown the nest.

Al Weaver is also in XXXL Wanapum County correction's uniform. Waits by the shrine. Gunnar rolls up on motorcycle.

"Let's see what you have, Mr. Weaver," I hear Gunnar. The voice roars over his idling engine.

Hidden behind berm is XXXL Nils.

Circle of stones. Al crossing over the bones. Brittle, crushing, crunching. He kneels at altar. Like a gigantic ground squirrel——he digs and digs. Shards and shards fly out behind him.

"Where is the First Aid kit." Swear words fly behind Al like more shards. "The China White. Where the hell is it?"

"That's the big question for you," Gunnar answers. He crosses arms over head in an 'X'.

No deal. *Nils races off into the night. Strapped onto his dirt bike's seat is shiny-gray, stainless case. Gold coins inside. No doubt. Roars away through darkness. Through the high desert.*

Gunnar drives off, too. Hides behind a rock outcropping. Undetected. Able to see the pond.

Black SUV. Rolls up to pond. Too fast and too close. Al jumps from the moonlit Lincoln, shiny black.

He's in Mary's face, but asks Big Max. "Who's this chick? Why's she near our deal?"

"The girlfriend of Joe. Cousin of Gunnar Larsson."

Crazy, mad finger in Mary's face. Her Goth hair as shiny and black as his Lincoln. "Then where is Cousin Joe now?"

"Getting gas. We ran out."

"Why'd you junkies steal my stash?" asks Max's father.

Holds Grace protectively to her chest. Polar fleece blanket covers her bare body. Eyes widen. "What stash?" she asks Al.

He asks her and then she asks him. It's the same thing over and over for him not to believe her.

"You addicts lie your way through life."

Except she isn't addicted.

Circling above, even I feel the man's anger, over and over. The same question she can't answer. I stir in my hospital bed. Open my eyes for a moment. No one is visiting, no nurses in sight. I press for more juice from Morpheus, my god of dreams. I fly higher.

Below, Al yells more questions at Mary.

"So they're cousins?

"Yes. Like I said."

"So Cousin Gunnar and his old man, Nils, put you and Cousin Joe up to this heist, didn't they? They wanted to snag my goods without paying me."

"What goods?" Mary asks again.

I watch through the dark. Mary clutches her baby tightly.

Al stands. Hands on hips. Legs wide. Barrel chest puffed out. Pulls Grace from Mary's arms without warning.

I lift into air. Wish to dive-bomb him, to take out his eyeballs. Too slow. He hands the baby over to Max.

Mary screams in shock.

Al pulls his Glock from the holster on his calf. Points it an inch from Mary's nose.

"Max. Get in the water with the baby," he commands.

Max hesitates.

"Right now!" the father yells.

Max does as told. Keeps his shoes and uniform on. Climbs in pond with baby.

Mary shakes uncontrollably. Cries out, "Give me my baby! How would I know about your cop-hustled drugs!"

"Maybe we'll see if your addicted, junky baby can swim," says Al with a growl."Where did you hide the kit?"

Max dips the newborn's feet into the cool pond water.

"Give me my baby," Mary bawls. "You have to!"

Diabolical laugh from Max's crazed father. "I don't have to do nothing," he says. "But you have to stop lying."

Mary isn't lying. Calls him crazy. "There is no kit of heroin."

"Now I know you're lying," says Al and motions for Max to place Grace on air mattress.

"I'm not lying. I don't know about any stash of heroin."

Max trudges with newborn to the nearest cattails. Chunichi Dragon warm-up jacket is draped over the top--dry--not touching pond.

"Max. Drop that baby into the pond. See if the druggie's infant sinks or swims."

Max's eyes grow wide. "It stinks here."

What stinks? Your lies? The Corruption? Ugly drug deals? *I want to yell across the scablands.* More than just the rotten fish.

The insults fly. I circle the pond and blend into the night. A big barrage of words. Max holds Grace away from his body.

"Get in the pond!" Al's voice booms.

Mary looks at Max. He walks backwards. Takes him farther away with her newborn.

Will not drop the polar fleece blanket, the only thing covering her naked, new-mother body. She trembles. On the verge of hysteria. Nearly paralyzed with fear.

Al stands on Mary's discarded skirt that's still on the landing; still partly covered with slimy scales. Fires a round into the upside-down, bloated fish. The carp pops. The air turns putrid. There's no breeze. The odor sticks to scent glands like glue. "How's that for some stench," Al yells to Max.

Mary freezes. She clutches her blanket even tighter.

"Get in that pond." Al fires a second bullet.

Mary drops the blanket to the river stones. Her elbows cover her breasts. Steps gingerly into the pond. "Pleeeez!"

"Where's Gunnar's cousin?" Al yells from the edge of the pond. "Getting gas."

"Max, hold that stupid baby over the water again."

"Joe walked to the gas station. I'm telling the truth."

"Lower that baby into the pond," the crazy man tells his son.

The infant's frog-like legs and umbilical cord submerge.

"Believe me!" Mary bawls.

From above, I dive and take a swipe at Max. My talons gouge his skull. Tuft of dirty blond hair rips free. Blood oozes down his forehead.

He almost drops Grace. Catches her.

"Save your baby, says Al, "or lie for your junky boyfriend?"

"I Can't tell you what I don't know!"

"Where did you move my stash?"

"Your stash? See it's not mine," she screams. "You idiot. Guess what? I was having my baby tonight."

I circle back and dive-bomb the father. He stands on the stone landing. Squeezes his Glock handle. I claw his eyes out––except he swats me away before I can.

Hard blow. Pistol barrel slams me sideways. Dull jolt feels like lead lodged in my joint where back meets wing.

I manage to fly and land next to Gunnar. He hides. We watch. Stench from carp is much worse. We are too close to the pond.

Mary turns and mucks her way towards Max and the newborn. Walks right into the decomposing fish. It's no longer bloated. It's half- hidden beneath the surface.

*Her bare torso is slimed by the rot. **Arrrrrrrgh!** Mary lets out long, disgusted, irate and most desperate noise.*

I hear her gag––about to barf.

The bullet hits just in front of where she stops. Mary turns her head.

Al sets the service pistol and holster on the stone landing. On top of

Mary's fouled skirt.

He wears his uniform and boots. Pulls on XXXL latex gloves. Climbs into the pond.

Why is Gunnar not looking? His face is in palms. Al wades until he's only a couple of feet behind Mary. "No one screws with me. Not for a quarter million. Where's my shit, girl?"

I try to stir Gunnar, but he doesn't pay me any notice. It's like I'm not even there. But this is his chance to grab the gun.

He looks back at his dirt bike. Does he wish to flee, instead? Instead, he covers his face in his hands––again.

Mary dives beneath the surface. Tries swimming to her baby. A wake of turbulence rises to the surface.

Cuts off Mary's path. Mary is only a couple of yards from Crazy Al's grasp.

"Junkie bitch," he yells. She's not close to reaching Grace on the floating mattress.

Al reaches into the water. Yanks from her skull a braid from one side of head.

Mary reaches up in desperation. Face kept underwater. Only her hand emerges. The fingers clutch her own shimmering, Goth-black strands. From the air, I see fingernails through hair. They puncture Al's latex glove. Talon-like wound draws blood.

Al steps back. Mary rises up, gasps for air. She screams her last, death-piercing scream. Max by the reeds with Grace; Gunnar behind the boulder near me. He's numb and checked out.

I recoil. My high screech pierces the air. My wing gives off jags of pain.

Al pushes her back under. A full minute. She rises up again. Pulled out of pond by hair. He yells one last time. "Where's my China White?"

Mary chokes up pond water. Can't answer––not even if she has an answer for the raging man.

Crazy Al forces her underwater. Keeps her there. Forces out Mary's last air of life.

The final exhale erupts. From drowning spirit, through water, up into clear, night sky.

Gunnar turns toward dirt bike.

Max stands dumbfounded. Al laughs like a demon. "Toughen up, Maxxy," he says.

Al neatly slices thin ginger braid from the other side of her head. It holds a Dragon pin.

Mary's body floats next to the carp. Her foot touches the fish tail.

Max wraps Grace in the dry blanket. Pushes the raft and newborn towards reeds. Towards the farthest shore.

Crazy Al at the altar. Hides the souvenir pin--his murderer's trophy. Stuffs pin and braid deep inside owl skull.

It all drifts into the past.

How much did I see? How much was I told? How much resided in the vaults of horribly I'd been missing her?

I managed to fly to the top of the cedar. The nest was still empty. Gunnar had fled on his Husqvarna. Max and his father--their pond-soaked uniforms in a black garbage bag and them wearing dry, black sweat suits--tore away in the Lincoln Navigator. My own owl bones wouldn't stop aching and I had no more flying left inside me--

--until Mary touched down and preened my injured wing.

Then, I felt no pain.

We flew. Mary had shown me it all that night. All through our flight, we drifted in the in-between. She told me I needed to live, said there wasn't enough room on the other side for me--a girl with all my good mojo.

I looked at her wondering why I'd been put through such tribulation to avenge all that had wronged her that night.

Then I understood. My impulse to dive bomb the two jail guards was to avenge Mary. Only by vanquishing their wickedness could she and I rise above their darkness.

I so wanted to tell her all about me and Sammy, but I couldn't speak. This bird with the best hearing of all birds heard me, though.

"You and Sammy better name your kids Quinn and Gardner," she said.

I actually liked the sound of those two surnames as given ones, even though I was many years away from doing the mothering thing.

"You're always my best friend, Biff. Don't you forget."

How could I forget you? I wanted to say.

"You're safe now," she assured me with her softest owl call. "*Nam myoho renge kyo,*" she added before lifting away.

~

"Wake up, Biffy!" came the next thing I heard, loud enough to quake my whole bed. My eyes popped open. My heart sprinted from the blocks. Everything had changed! How or when, I didn't remember. The awful ET tube was gone, but when I tried to make a sound, I couldn't. My throat was too sore.

Strangely, I could first feel something not quite so annoying as the tube. On the right side of my chest, way in the back--in the scapula--I think it's called--there was a lump. Then I realized. It had to be that bullet. This must have been where the single round decided to lodge forever, the surgical report had said. To serve as a forever reminder, I thought.

Joe Gardner was looking around at all the medical contraptions in my room inside the Lourdes' Intensive Care Unit.

The oxygen prongs in my nose were annoying, but not nearly as bad as the tube. I rediscovered my right, writing hand. Newly liberated, from where it had been strapped to that side of my chest. I grabbed my writing pad with the left hand, and told my right one to pick up the pencil.

Before I could jot anything down, Joe loomed over me to tap my morphine line. "Careful you all drip crazy, Biff." he said.

Joe hadn't seen my surgeon, on his rounds, entering behind him. "The young man's right, actually," my physician said. "We'll be weaning you off your IV painkiller today, in fact."

If I could have talked, oh the story I'd be tempted to share with my doctor about Joe Gardner and those very risks that I knew all too vividly to avoid.

I nodded at my surgeon before smiling blissfully at Tomiko. She hung back shyly in the threshold of my hospital room, but returned the smile with a slight bow.

Lightly, I patted my entry wound with my left hand and gave the surgeon a right-handed thumb up. My right hand! I realized again, and grinned at my doctor.

"Your extubation went fine," said the surgeon. "Once you've finish up with your friends here, be sure to let yourself nap some more."

As best I could tell, it was pushing noon. I couldn't get myself from feeling tired—not on this morphine. Sleep was my mini-vacation from pain. The doctor finished jotting something on his chart and slipped out of the hospital room as stealthily as he'd entered.

The antibiotics were clearing up my infected lungs. Still, when I tried to take a deep breath, the air seared through my throat and lungs. Tomiko and Joe stood like bookends at either side of my hospital bed. Joe didn't ask me, but found the controller and tilted my whole upper bed forward.

"I heard that Aunt Darla came clean with what went down that night," he said, but hesitated before he finished, "Sounds like Mary didn't go under too easily."

I reached for the pad and scrawled very neatly. *And all the while trying to save Gracie.* My right-handed words fit neatly on the page.

Joe's jaw clenched. "The jail boss ran the county slammer with an iron fist," he said. "After that first-day, jail-fight with the *Tramposos*, I begged for him to lock me up in solitary. At the time, I had no idea he wanted me to be hidden away out of sight and away from the jail gossip so he could set my sorry ass up to take the hit for his whole friggin' night of crimes."

He paused to look out my hospital window and back at Tomiko. Then, with his most serious expression, he turned towards me again. "If I'd known the Weavers were her killers, I would have bided my time. Given the chance, I would have choked out Max or his old man. I think about how much they deserved to have their last breath stolen like they stole Mary's."

Mary sent a sniper bullet through Al Weaver's heart.

Joe looked through the hospital window and then at Tomiko before responding. "You told me on Easter Day how my life was resurrected.

Yes it was, Joe. You're a free man, clean and sober.

"You also told me not to screw up my dream of playing ball."

My eyes widened and I nodded. I couldn't believe how my old nemesis had actually listened to what I'd said on that blustery Easter day.

"Can you believe how lucky I am?" He motioned towards Tomiko. "Especially finding this one."

Losing Mary and then tiptoeing on the brink of serious prison time. That was So lucky!

"My night guard Sammy is cool," said Joe, changing the subject. "He even believed me when I told him that Mary was visiting my cell."

Sammy has the blood of a Native prophet in his veins.

"Smohalla himself."

When Joe told me this, I knew he was closer with Sammy than I realized. I suspected that he also approved of the two of us.

How's your mom? I wrote.

"We just came back from The Dalles," he said. "She's stuck in the hospital for more days of neck traction." He looked at Tomiko and smiled. "So weird, though, when we went into Mom's hospital room, guess who was there visiting her?"

I shrugged, doubtful that it was his father, J.J.

"My lawyer, Angus. He was there. Even brought her a big bouquet of roses and blushed once he saw me.

I gave Joe two thumbs up and tried my best to smile.

"Yeah, I guess that's cool," said Joe. "He did keep my backside out of the pen for a couple of decades. Oh, and Mom said to tell you that the two of you can race to see who's released first. She sends her love. Oh, and this bouquet she asked me to buy."

He bent over to lift the vase at his feet. I sniffed the twelve pink roses before he set them on the bouquet-packed, window sill.

Please thank her!

"Yes. We tell her," said Tomiko.

"Al and Max Weaver," Joe said, mostly to himself. "What I saw in that crooked jail makes sense now. The *Tramposos* were Al Weaver's foot soldiers, in and out of that jail whenever there were jobs to do. Max was his Master Sergeant inside those jail walls. The gang kept the drugs flowing inside the slammer and all over the area."

Al Weaver's a psycho-sicko.

"What do you mean?" Joe asked.

Took a trophy from his kill.

Joe still didn't get it.

The Chunichi Dragon souvenir pin you pinned through Mary's ginger braid. He stuffed it in the owl skull.

When Joe read that, he suddenly nodded, understanding what I'd meant. To think how close I'd come to seriously dating Big Max. What a stupid, dumb, idiotic crush I had on him.

Mary's own wildflower braid was hanging in ThunderMaxx, the Weaver's boat.

"Joe will play baseball with Chunichi Dragons," said Tomiko. "Start new, good life."

With you, Tomiko, I wrote and smiled at her again before writing some more. *You two will be Gracie's Uncle Joe and Auntie T.*

She blushed with her own sweet, classy smile. Tomiko knew I knew they were both smitten with one another. But who in this room wasn't madly in love these days?

Tomiko stepped forward with a loosely wrapped present and handed it to me so I held it with one specific end upright. I unwrapped it slowly. A small, *bonsai* tree. I smiled and gave it a close look.

I pointed for her to set it next to Sammy's bouquet on the table at my feet. *Teach me the art of the bonsai,* I scrawled.

"Yes, I show you when you visit us in Japan. It is ancient art," she said, and bowed, slightly. I really liked Kuma's sister.

I scribbled something else and showed Joe. *She was visiting me when you came to visit just now.*

"Who?" Joe asked.

Mary.

"I believe you," he said, tears welling in his eyes. I patted his wrist when the nurse came in the room. She looked the way she always did when my visiting hour was over.

I motioned for Joe to lean his ear close to my lips. Whispering my first words since the shooting, I winced. The sound rasped through my raw throat. With every bit of voice inside me, I shared what my soaring heart knew.

"Mary saved us both."

The End

~

• "To the End of the Trail" lyrics by the author ©2021. Inspiration from the traditional Swedish lullaby: "Vaggvisa för min son, Carl," by Carl Michael Bellman (Stockholm, August 18, 1787). First verse translation, also by the author.

• "Holy, Holy, Holy! Lord God Almighty" lyrics, Reginald Heber, 1826. The music, 1861, by John Bacchus Dyke.

• *Drummers & Dreamers,* (The Story of Smowhalla the Prophet and His Nephew Puck Hyah Toot, the Last Prophet of the Nearly Extinct River People, the Last Wanapums), by Click Relander, ©1986, Caxton Printers.

To my beta readers :

Brenda Mattson, *my ever supportive wife*
Cate Perry, *outstanding critique partner/editor*
Bob Abrams, *Oregon-raised cartographer*
Brittany Fedenuik, *Biff McCoy's inspiration*
Leo Genest, *English lit teacher extraordinaire*
Susan Grzadzlelrwski, *artist to the core*
Dr. Steve, *best brother/great surgeon*
Nick Mattson, *amazing stepson*
Jo Pemmant, *the best line editor––no baloney*
Nicholas Tanner, *composer on the upswing*
Dr. Carolyn, *awesome daughter-in-law*

Thanks so much for the extra eyes!

❦

∾

ABOUT the AUTHOR: Resides in Skagit River Valley with his ever-supportive wife, Brenda, also an artist.

Key mentors include the outstanding novelists Steve Heller, Ron Carlson, and Tom Legendre.

The Bone Shrine and this sequel benefited greatly from Cate Perry, an exceptional critique partner.

Personal Threads of Inspiration:

• Transit operator for 12+ years. A sundry flow of on-the-bus surprises often sparks the muse.

• Founding executive director of the Columbia Gorge Discovery Center in The Dalles, Oregon.

• "An Officer and a Gentleman," Paramount Pictures, 1982. Portrayed a U.S. Naval Air Officer candidate in Sgt. Foley's (Lou Gosset, Jr.) platoon.

• Univ. of Washington, 1979; Antioch Univ., Los Angeles, MFA in Creative Writing, 2005.

• Worked on the Basin Produce potato line in the summer of 1975 near Moses Lake, WA.

• *Katedralskolan* in Linköping, Sweden, Rotary International Exchange Student 1973-74.

∾

WHO? by Scott MacFarlane is the well-worth-the-wait sequel to *The Bone Shrine.* This novel takes off just a few months after the ending of the first book left us with that exact question––'Who?'––and carries us on a thrilling ride-along with Biff McCoy as she fumbles, mouthy and head-strong, on her quest to figure out who killed her best friend.

MacFarlane paints a beautiful picture of the eastern Washington landscape then splashes it with the corruption that drugs and greed have on friendships and family ties. As Biff's investigation starts to uncover truths and interactions between the people in her circle, she finds herself fighting not just for truth, but for her life.

"WHO?" starts slowly, then gains full speed as MacFarlane brings each character to life and establishes their ties to each other or the murder, then slams it all together in a tension-filled finale. Biff, as the main character, is so relatable, and her tendency to jabber when she knows she needs to shut up (*"Why couldn't I shut my ever-busy lips?*) makes for amusing situations.

I completely enjoyed this book for the robust characters and the unseen twists in their histories. As I got further and further into it, my opinion on who the killer was kept changing and I couldn't wait to find out at the end.

––Jo Pemmant, January 2025

Scott was totally on point with his 'Biff' character. I could totally see his main, 19-year-old character as a combination of Scott's and my outgoing personalities. I loved Biff's youthful determination. Even though she keeps putting herself in harm's way, will nothing stop her from finding the murderer of her best friend?

––*Brittany Fedenuik,* Skagit Transit Coach Operator, 2019 to Present

From Bookview Review Interview with author, 1/2/2025:

After the writing's finished, how do you judge the quality of your work?

This depends on how much I respect the person or entity providing me feedback on my prose.

For example, I was honored when a bus rider, one I'd carefully selected to be a beta-reader for the Bone Shrine Crimes series, told me that these were the best books he'd read in a year or more. He said, on the way to the methadone clinic, that he kept looking up and shaking his head in disbelief when he remembered that his bus driver was the one who had written what he was reading.

There were strong reasons I'd asked him to be a beta reader for the two novels. He was a constant and avid reader of quality books. I knew from conversations that he was well-educated. He was also in recovery, so I wanted to know if he thought that this aspect of my story rang true. Finally, he was eager to be a beta reader, so I sensed he would actually read the two books I gave him.

Nicholas Tanner also told me that he was a composer of music. One day when deep into reading *WHO?*, he looked up, suddenly. "Hey, Scotty, if your books get turned into a movie or mini-series, then I'd love to do the score," he said. "That is, of course, if you have any say in the scoring."

This sort of feedback made me believe that he sincerely believed in the promise of this novel.

–*regarding Nicholas Tanner, Composer*

My father was a circuit court judge and, before that, a county prosecuting attorney where I grew up east of the Cascades. The novel rings so true. I stayed up most of the night reading *The Bone Shrine* where young Joe Gardner faces an excruciating murder trial. Readers will be well served to acquaint themselves with the cast in *Book One* since most of these well-drawn, unpredictable, characters grace the pages of *WHO?*, the gripping mystery thriller.

    ––Bob Abrams

MacFarlane's second installment in The Bone Shrine Crimes series is **a taut, gripping sequel steeped in corruption, murder, and a relentless quest for justice.** Biff McCoy, a spirited college intern with the State Patrol, is determined to uncover her best friend's killer. But when a corrupted investigation turns cold, Biff faces mounting doubts —including whether she can trust her first lover to help solve the case.

Biff's journey anchors the story, her intuitive yet haunted nature adding depth and urgency. Joe is a tense mix of resilience, loyalty, and determination. Once defined by addiction and its toll on his life, Joe's return to vitality reflects his fight for recovery and redemption. The supporting cast, from the steadfast Captain Condran to the shadowy Tramposo gang, is richly drawn, their motives steeped in ambiguity and tension. MacFarlane expertly blends the personal with the procedural, crafting a high-stakes narrative that keeps the danger immediate and visceral. His evocative prose captures both the stark beauty of Washington and the suffocating tension of crime scenes, drawing readers into a world where **trust is a luxury and every clue teeters between revelation and disaster.** Building on the suspense of the first book, this installment examines the precariousness of justice and the unyielding resilience of humanity. Biff's personal stakes further elevate the story, making her quest as much about self-discovery as it is about vengeance.

A taut, clever sequel that's impossible to put down.

–Bookview Review

A lean, intelligent thriller that pulses with suspense and heart... MacFarlane returns to *The Bone Shrine Crimes* series with this sharp, compelling story where justice and corruption collide against a dark, haunting mystery. The story follows Biff McCoy, a college intern with the State Patrol, on an urgent quest to uncover the truth behind her best friend Mary's murder. As she digs deeper into the investigation, she faces mounting obstacles, including interference from powerful forces determined to protect their secrets. Biff's unwavering drive propels the plot, and her emotional bond with Mary imbues her actions with raw humanity. As she navigates the treacherous layers of corruption and deceit, **Biff evolves from a naive intern into a tenacious seeker of truth. MacFarlane masterfully portrays her inner turmoil and growth, pulling readers into her struggle with authenticity and intensity.** The prose is vivid and immersive, while the sharp, authentic dialogue heightens the stakes.The Bone Shrine site feels oppressively real. Throughout it all, the novel raises thought-provoking questions about friendship, ethical dilemmas, and the quest for justice in a morally compromised world. **A heart-pounding thriller that keeps readers hooked until the end.** *–Prairies Book Review*